Heir To The Sun

Jennifer Allis Provost

©2015 Jennifer Allis Provost
Sale of the paperback edition of this book without its cover is unauthorized.

Bellatrix Press, an imprint of Prince & Pauper Press

This book is a work of fiction. Names, characters, places, and incidents are products of the author's imagination or are used fictitiously. Any resemblance to actual events, locales, or persons, living or dead, is entirely coincidental.
All rights reserved, including the right to reproduce this book or portions thereof in any form whatsoever.

First Edition: June 2015

Jennifer Allis Provost
Heir to the Sun: a novel/by Jennifer Allis Provost
-1st ed. p. cm.

Summary: After learning that the king has sold her kind into slavery, Asherah vows to stop him.

Cover Design by Veronica V. Jones http://vvjones.com/

Interior layout by Jennifer Carson (print edition) http://www.thedragoncharmer.com/

978-1622510-20-7 (paperback)

Other books by Jennifer Allis Provost:

The Copper Legacy, a four book urban fantasy:

Copper Girl

Copper Ravens

Copper Veins--*forthcoming*

Copper Princess--*forthcoming*

A duology based in the Copper world:

Redepmtion

Salvation

The Chronicles of Parthalan, a six volume epic fantasy:

Heir to the Sun

The Virgin Queen

Rise of the Deva'shi

Golem

Elfsong

Blood Prince

Heir To The Sun

Prologue

From the beginning, there was the sky god, Olluhm, who ruled the land during the daylight hours and Cydia, goddess of the moon, who held sway over the night. Olluhm heard many tales of Cydia's beauty, and while he desired to look upon her they were forever separate, for the sun may never share the sky with the moon.

Once, during the moon's dark time, Cydia grew bored in her celestial palace and left it to walk upon the land. She took the form of a doe and leapt across the green land she guarded. After a time, she became weary and curled up in the soft grass to rest; the goddess slept overmuch and was still earthbound when the sun rose.

Thus Olluhm beheld Cydia for the first time, and as she was bathed in his golden light she reverted to her true form. Her beauty overcame Olluhm, so much so that he left his journey across the sky incomplete as he took the form of a stag and sought to know her.

Cydia did return to her dance in the sky, and all the land watched her swell with Olluhm's child. During the next dark time, she birthed a son called Solon, who followed his father's fiery path from dawn to dusk. The birth of their son did not slake the lovers' thirst for one another. Such was their passion that each joining resulted in a child, all with the long limbed, ethereal beauty of their parents and the pointed ears and large eyes of a deer.

In time, there were enough of the gods' children to form a separate people. Olluhm named them the fair folk for their beauty; in time, they were called the fae. With a mother's love, Cydia gifted her children the land where she and Olluhm had roamed as doe and stag and called it Parthalan. Olluhm crafted the fae's first home, Teg'urnan, as a replica of Cydia's home in the sky. The sun god placed it upon the meadow where he first lay with Cydia to remind his mate, and his children, of his eternal love.

Chapter 1

Hillel's head bounced off the dirt floor as the guards tossed her into her cell like garbage. Her lip split and she tasted blood; she savored the taste, willing it to overpower the rank stench of her captors that clung to her skin. She lay still as death until the door clanged shut behind her.

Once the guards had gone, Hillel rolled to her back and felt Torim draw her head onto her lap, her soft touch as she smoothed back her hair. Since they had no water Torim wiped Hillel's bloody lip with her thumb; they weren't due their next ration for some days yet. Hillel's eyes fluttered open, and she gazed up at her dearest, only friend.

"You must stop taking my place," Torim whispered, lest the guards hear her and beat them. "You can't endure this abuse alone. Next time, I will go."

Hillel smiled, flinching as she stretched her bruised lip. She didn't know how she'd endure the constant torture without Torim, yet Hillel couldn't say how she knew her. She often wondered if Torim was her sister, or perhaps her child. The rational, whole part of Hillel's mind, the portion the demons hadn't yet destroyed, remembered the sky, and the stars, and small flashes of her childhood. Yet, whenever she reached too far back in her memory she was confronted with the image of the *mordeth* dragging her away.

"They almost killed you last time," Hillel whispered. "I can't let them take you again."

"And what good would come of them killing you?" Torim asked. She cradled Hillel against her chest and rocked her like a baby. "Remember, the Asherah will come for us." Torim often told the story of Asherah, The Deliverer, who would someday come to free the fae from slavery and drive back the demons.

"Yes," Hillel murmured as she drifted from consciousness, "the Asherah will come for us, and we will all be free."

Hillel was asleep, curled up on her side in the filthy straw. Torim sat beside her, shielding her from the door, as she stared out the tiny window toward the stars. In the low light, Hillel looked almost peaceful, her white-blonde hair and pale skin glowing, but Torim knew better. Under Hillel's meager shift she was torn and bloody. No matter how badly they brutalized her, Hillel never cried out, never gave their captors a glimpse of the agony they caused her; that was why they preferred Torim, for she had never been able to muffle her screams. Torim wondered if Hillel's pride would ultimately mean her death.

Torim remembered the last time the last time they'd made her scream and cry until her throat was raw. She had been chained face-down to the table, as she always was. Usually only one demon set upon her, which was awful enough, however, on that day she had the misfortune of being favored by three. Once the victor had destroyed his opponents, he wasted no time in claiming his prize.

When they had finally returned Torim to her cell she bled and bled, so much so that Hillel ripped out handfuls of her own hair to pack the wounds, and shouted until a guard brought them bandages. That was why they had no water now; each slave received a single pail of water at the dark moon, not a drop more, and Hillel had used both of their rations for Torim's care. The moon would not be dark again for some days yet.

Torim noted the positions of the stars and knew that a certain guard would soon make his rounds. The guards were male slaves, enthralled to their demonic overlords to handle the females, keep them fed and quiet, and dispose of their bodies once they were no longer useful. Most of the guards were long since numb from witnessing the females' torture and the squealing, ruined babies they bore, but one was strong, and Torim considered him one of her few comforts.

There was a scratching at the cell door, and Torim saw the guard waiting. She didn't know his name, but that was just as well. Slaves never shared their names. He unbolted the cell door and opened it just wide enough to pass Torim a cup and a fabric-wrapped bundle.

"Here," he grunted. "That's all the water I could get, and there's a pot of salve under the bandages." He looked past Torim at Hillel's ravaged form. "I didn't think she'd last this time." He met Torim's eyes, and added, "They're starting to wonder why the two of you never get with child."

Torim knew exactly why. Whenever she or Hillel had the slightest fear that one of them was with child, they beat each other in the belly until they couldn't stand. Torim and Hillel had made a pact long ago that they would sooner die than bear a demon's whelp.

"I suppose it's our only fortune," was all Torim said as she held the water and bundle in the crook of her elbow. "You shouldn't risk so much. If they caught you, they'd kill you."

He snorted, and Torim saw a touch of arrogance in his brown eyes. "I have their rotation memorized, as well as the location of every entrance and exit. There is no way these vermin could catch me."

"If you have such knowledge, why not free yourself?" she asked.

"The thrall," he replied, and Torim asked nothing further. She had seen the magic handler many times, always with a collar and chain about his neck, led about by the *mordeth* and enthralling the guards to neither act against the demons nor attempt escape. In many ways, the thrall was more of a torment than anything Torim need endure; while it kept the guards' minds intact, it rendered their bodies captive to the *mordeth*, unable to help the women or themselves.

"If I can break the thrall, we will be free," he said fervently. "We will all be free."

"Do you think you can?" Torim asked. The guard began a reply, then he abruptly shut the cell door and left. Torim heard more of the demons approaching from further down the corridor. She held her breath and kept herself still, hoping the demons wouldn't notice her.

As soon as the footsteps faded, Torim returned to Hillel's side and took a sip of water, grateful beyond measure for that small hint of coolness. Once Torim's throat had gone from dry and cracked to merely parched, she propped up Hillel's head and roused her.

"Here," Torim said. "Drink."

"Where did you get water?" Hillel asked.

"The guard. He brought the water for you. And salve." Hillel glanced in the cup, then pushed it toward Torim. "I've already had some. The rest is for you." Hillel nodded and sipped the water as Torim unwrapped the bundle and set down the salve and bandages.

"Where would he have gotten these?" Hillel traced the metalwork on the pot of salve, then she fingered the soft bandages. "These items are fit for a king. What do you know of him?"

"Very little, other than he is kind and strong," Torim admitted. "He told me he was a soldier before his capture. He claims to have the guards' shifts memorized and knows every exit." Torim dropped her gaze. "He mentioned that we may someday be free," she murmured.

"We will," Hillel promised, "we will."

When the guard next made his rounds, he found Hillel waiting instead of Torim.

"I wish to thank you," Hillel whispered. "But I must know how you came by those items. Surely these demons have no desire to see us cared for."

"My brother is the one who keeps us in thrall," he replied. "On occasion, he will relax the hold and allow me to act on my own."

"If he is your brother, why not relax the hold enough to let you escape?" Hillel asked.

"I won't let him," he replied. "The *mordeth* has made it clear that if I escape, my brother will be killed. I cannot allow that."

"How does the thrall work?" Hillel pressed. "Why can you talk with us now, and bring us water when you shouldn't?"

"It keeps my body from disobeying the *mordeth's* orders," he explained. "I've never been ordered to not bring you bandages, so I may. I've also been ordered not to bring you your bucket of water until the next dark moon, but I was able to bring you that small cupful."

"Have you also been ordered not to send a message to Teg'urnan for aid?" Hillel asked.

The guard's eyes darkened. "I thought you knew."

"Knew what?" Hillel demanded.

"It is the king who ordered us here," he replied. Torim gasped so loudly that the guard motioned for them to be silent. He quickly checked the corridor, only returning to their door once he was certain that her outburst went unheard.

"What you say is treason," Hillel whispered. "Our king would not let us be enslaved by this vermin. How can you claim such things?"

"My brother says the king seeks to extend Parthalan's borders," the guard replied. "So he struck a deal with the *mordeth-gall*, Ehkron himself, to raise an army of demons loyal only to the king." The guard fell silent for a moment, dark memories skating across his face. "First, the magic handlers were given over to the *mordeths*, then they put the legion under thrall, one contingent at a time. We were then ordered to capture women and bring them here."

In the space of a few heartbeats Hillel went from shocked to angry to despairing. No one was coming for them, not the legion, and not mythical warrior women. One emotion, curiosity, overrode the rest, for Hillel was desperate to know something of her past.

"Did you bring me here?" Hillel asked.

"No," he replied. "I remember when you arrived, but I was not the one who brought you."

Hillel nodded. "Bring me a weapon."

"I cannot," he protested.

"You can, and you will," she hissed. "Bring me anything heavy or sharp, anything that could break or bruise their hides. Bring them in pieces if you have to. Enlist the other guards to help you, and keep away from those who would stop us." The guard protested again, but Hillel raised her voice to a dangerous level. "I want you to learn how many slaves have enough wits to leave with us and how many we will need to silence," she ordered, then continued in a quieter tone: "For those that wish to help us, get them weapons as well."

"I am in thrall—"

"Have you been ordered to not bring slaves sharp or heavy things?" Hillel demanded.

"No."

"Then I say again, bring me a weapon!"

Hillel stared at the guard until he nodded and withdrew. Torim dragged Hillel away from the door and to the far corner of their cell.

"What are you doing?" Torim whispered. "If we're caught with weapons, we'll be killed!"

"If they catch me with a weapon, they won't live long enough to speak of it," Hillel declared. She turned Torim's face to hers and softened her words. "You heard what he said; this is the king's doing. No one is coming for us, not even the Asherah. We can't wait for rescue any longer. We need to rescue ourselves."

Hillel stared into Torim's brown eyes, and despite the cold knot of terror that had formed in her belly, she knew she was right. If the king had engineered their enslavement, they would be used until they were dead. Escape was their only hope. Torim nodded, and laced her fingers with Hillel's. "Then rescue each other we shall."

Chapter 2

Caol'nir entered the Great Temple through the northern door, holding a small bundle close to his body. He waited for his eyes to adjust to the dim interior, and smiled when he saw her.

Alluria was seated atop a bench in the rear of the central chamber, her face serene in quiet meditation. A single shaft of sunlight enveloped her, reflecting off her long chestnut hair. Although closed, Caol'nir knew Alluria's eyes were a deep, stunning blue, so rich they made sapphires look like coals. As Alluria sat motionless in the morning light, she was more beautiful to him than any goddess.

Not wanting to disturb her morning ritual, Caol'nir sat on the floor before the priestess, his thoughts racing as he watched her contemplate the gods. He was hopelessly infatuated with this kind, witty, impossibly beautiful, and utterly unattainable woman. When a priestess took her vows, she became Olluhm's mate in the hopes he would visit her and beget a child. This meant that no priestess was to be touched by any man, for any reason, and the *con'dehr* protected the sisters' virtue with their lives. Caol'nir was achingly aware that he couldn't be with the one he loved, but still sought ways to be part of her life. While he pondered their situation, Alluria opened her eyes and smiled.

"My most attentive guard," Alluria said. "What brings you to temple so early?" He rose and offered his hand, as custom dictated he should, which Alluria waved away, also per custom. Caol'nir knew she wouldn't accept his help, but remained ever hopeful.

"I have the herbs you requested, my lady." Caol'nir held out the bundle, bowing his head as he did so.

"Such speed in your errands, warrior." Alluria smiled.

He returned a wide grin of his own, then quickly tried to regain his composure. Caol'nir knew he must look like a fool, always staring and grinning at her.

As Alluria accepted the bundle her fingers lightly brushed his, sending a jolt through his body as if he'd been struck by lightning. She let her hand linger upon Caol'nir's for the barest moment, the smile now gone from her face and replaced by…longing? He shook his head, for Alluria would not feel any sort of emotion toward him, surely not longing. If she wanted anything, it was a better supply of herbs, not to touch him in any way. Caol'nir realized she was thanking him and again bowed his head.

"I am here to serve," he replied, then turned to exit the temple.

"Warrior?" Alluria called after him.

"Yes, my lady?" He turned back to the priestess, assuming that she must need something else for her work within the temple.

"If you care to, you may kiss me farewell. My hand!" she added, then she straightened her back as she extended a graceful arm toward him. "You may kiss my hand farewell."

Caol'nir bowed low, his thick braid of sandy hair falling over his shoulder as he pressed Alluria's fingers to his lips; he noticed that she smelled of wildflowers. "Farewell, my lady."

The priestess watched Caol'nir walk away from her, admiring his tall form and broad shoulders as she held her hand against her breast. It was a dangerous game Alluria was playing, inviting one of the *con'dehr* to not only touch her, but kiss her. While it was perfectly acceptable for a man to show respect to a priestess by kissing her hand, it was not acceptable for a priestess to invite such contact.

But Caol'nir was so kind to her, and she knew that he would never hurt her or breathe a word of this little indiscretion. As he'd grasped her hand and had looked up at her with his pale green eyes, Alluria had felt as if she were falling into his soul. She knew he loved her, it was written all over his face; little did he know that she loved him as well. Soon after her arrival in Teg'urnan Alluria met the hotheaded young warrior, and it wasn't long before she looked forward to Caol'nir's morning visits to temple. In time, their awkward greetings had become a genuine friendship.

I am a priestess, friends are forbidden, she thought bitterly. He was also quite young—Alluria had taken her vows well before Caol'nir had been born—and she suspected that a good deal of his infatuation was due to his youth. Yet she could not deny the way she felt when he was near, the way her heart pounded when she caught his eye and he smiled. Alluria sighed, and returned to her cell. Of one thing she was certain: if she had known there was a man like Caol'nir in the world, she would not have taken her vows.

Alluria unfolded the bundle and spread the contents across her table, only to have her smile become a frown. The herbs Caol'nir brought were not what she requested. She wasn't angry, for many herbs had similar names and appearances, but she was frustrated. Before she and her sister priestesses, Alyon and Atreynha, had been forcibly relocated to Teg'urnan, she had always gathered her own herbs and was certain she had the correct ingredients for her pastes and poultices.

Those days were now in the past, for good King Sahlgren had decreed that it was unsafe for priestesses to roam the land. He had brought them all to the Great Temple in Teg'urnan on the pretense of protection; the king had gone so far as to make it a law of the realm. When Alluria first learned of the new law she scoffed. What sort of roaming did the king think went on in the outlying temples? To add further insult, priests were allowed to remain at their temples. The obvious inequity only added to Alluria's anger. Atreynha had barely managed to calm her before Tor, Caol'nir's father, arrived at their little temple and bore them away. She wondered if she would ever see her home again.

She picked through the plants and verified that none were of any use to her. Alluria contemplated asking one of the other priestesses if they had what she required, but changed her mind as Caol'nir's face returned to her thoughts. If she explained, very carefully, what she needed she was sure he would obtain them for her. With that, she rolled up the bundle and set out to find her favorite guard.

After leaving the temple, Caol'nir joined his twin brother, Caol'non, and their eldest brother, Fiornacht, who also served as their father's second, in the lesser hall for their morning meal. The three had just gotten their plates when Alluria entered the hall, unescorted and in direct violation of the king's most recent edict: any priestess who ventured forth from the Great Temple was to be accompanied by a *con'dehr* at all times. Caol'nir's gaze instantly went to the priestess, much to his brother's annoyance.

"Stop staring," growled Fiornacht. "Others are noticing your obsession."

"I'm not obsessed," he retorted. "I'm a guard, and I guard her. That's the end of it." Caol'nir would have said more but, much to the surprise of the brothers, Alluria approached their table. The three of them stood and bowed their heads in greeting.

"You may sit," she said, her voice like chimes on the wind. They sat, and Alluria turned her attention to Caol'nir. "Warrior, may I speak with you about these wretched herbs?" she asked, indicating the bundle he had given her in the temple.

"Of course, my lady," he replied. As he stood Fiornacht grabbed his arm, his eyes silently reminding his younger brother of the penalties for associating with the god's women. Caol'nir glared at him in return, and muttered, "I know my place."

"See that you keep it," Fiornacht hissed. Caol'nir scowled at his brother, then he followed Alluria into the corridor.

"These are all wrong," she declared once they were alone. Alluria tried explaining the differences between what he had brought her and what she actually wanted, but each word confused Caol'nir more than the last.

"My lady, I wish I understood you, but my skill lies in swordplay, not with sticks and leaves," he said. "Let me speak to one of the healers, or maybe the *saffira*; perhaps they will be able to help you." She nodded, and pursed her lips. "You don't like that solution?"

"What? Oh, no, it is fine," Alluria replied, not wanting Caol'nir to think that he was the cause of her exasperation. He was the only person helping her keep her sanity. "It's just frustrating to have to send someone else, and a warrior at that, when I once obtained my supplies on my own."

"I cannot picture you frequenting the apothecary," Caol'nir said, recalling the dark, stinking hovel he had visited.

"I frequented no such place," Alluria huffed. "I gathered them myself. It takes many years of study to become as adept as I." She went on, detailing the minute differences of each petal she had committed to memory, when Caol'nir formed a plan.

"Do these plants you require grow near the palace?"

"Why, yes," she said. "I believe they do."

"What if I could help you gather them yourself?" Caol'nir asked quietly.

"I...I would appreciate that," Alluria replied. Caol'nir smiled, and beckoned her to follow him. They made their way far from the hall and deep into the living quarters of the palace where Caol'nir opened an unmarked door and led Alluria into a small chamber.

"Wait here," Caol'nir said.

"What is this room?" she asked as she stepped across the threshold.

"It's my chamber," he replied. "Now be silent, and I'll return in a moment."

With that, Caol'nir shut the door and left Alluria alone. She stared at the door, unsure how she had managed to get herself into such an improper situation. First, she invited a man to kiss her, now she was standing in his bedchamber, and all of it before noon. She covered her face with her hands, knowing that she would have to beg for her life, and Caol'nir's, if word of this spread through the palace.

She decided that what was done was done, and looked around Caol'nir's room. As inappropriate as it might be, she was curious about how her guard lived. Several swords leaned against a corner, and daggers and knives were spread upon a nearby table. He was, after all, a warrior, and only the best gained admittance to the *con'dehr*. The fact that he, his father, and his brothers were all members of the guard was a testament to their strong bloodline, rumored to reach back to Solon himself. Alluria traced the hilt of a sword with her slender fingers as she imagined Caol'nir wielding the weapon, only to feel her cheeks flush when she realized that, in her mind's eye, he was shirtless.

Alluria dropped her hand as her gaze moved about the room. Much to her surprise, she saw that it was an orderly, well-kept space. Colorful tapestries hung on two of the walls, and tall windows let in vast amounts of sunlight. A set of chairs was arranged before the hearth, and the bed was piled high with furs and cushions. She approached his bed and tentatively stroked furs, noting that they were easily as fine as her own. She'd always imagined the guards sleeping on heaps of raw hides, nothing like this sumptuous pile of softness and comfort. Alluria sat on the edge of Caol'nir's bed, at once excited and ashamed by the small thrill that coursed through her.

Caol'nir reentered his chamber, halting at the sight of Alluria on his bed. His voice caught in his throat, which was for the best. He couldn't be sure that the words would have been appropriate for a priestess's ears.

"I never imagined a warrior would recline in such comfort," Alluria said as she rose. Caol'nir regained some semblance of himself and approached Alluria, holding out a roughly woven dress. "What's this for?"

"It's a scullion's dress," he replied. "If you're dressed as one of the *saffira*, I can bring you outside the walls, and you may gather your own herbs."

Alluria stared from the dress to his face, her offense that he expected her to don such a common garment quickly giving way to amazement. "It's forbidden for me to leave the palace," she said. "You can be put to death for the mere suggestion."

"It's not forbidden for the *saffira* to leave the palace," he corrected, "and I assure you, I'm well aware of the penalties for my actions. I only thought that it would be easier for you to pick the herbs yourself, rather than send me back and forth."

Alluria regarded him as her brows knit together, then dropped her gaze and fingered the edge of the dress. "I cannot ask this of you," she murmured. "The danger is too great."

"You didn't ask me," he reminded her. "I give you my word that no one but you or I will ever know of this. However, if you would prefer not to go, I understand. I will escort you to the temple and never mention it again."

Alluria stole a glance at his face, handsome and guileless, and considered his offer. She knew that Caol'nir was trustworthy; moreover, she knew he was only trying to help. Alluria sighed again, and placed herself in her guard's hands. "I do miss being outside." She ran her hands over the coarse fabric before holding it at arm's length to assess the fit. "Where did you get this?"

"The laundry, where else?" he replied with an innocent smile. He indicated an alcove, and said, "I'll wait in the corridor while you change."

"You don't need to leave," she stated matter-of-factly, "just turn your back."

Caol'nir turned to face the door, the rustling of her robes nearly drive him mad. In one day, he had kissed a priestess, seen her on his bed, and now she was naked in his chamber. If he was not put to death for his actions, surely his heart would beat a hole his chest and kill him regardless.

"Um...I don't think it fits."

He turned back to Alluria and marveled that she would be beautiful no matter what she wore. The dress consisted of a dark green blouse and skirt, cinched at the waist with a brown belt. It was cut close to her body, unlike the loose blue robes of a priestess she typically wore.

"That's how it's supposed to fit," Caol'nir affirmed, watching her tug at the tight bodice. He handed Alluria the soft leather shoes he remembered to snatch, for priestesses always went about barefoot, laughing as she awkwardly put them on.

"It is not funny," she scolded, "I haven't worn shoes in many winters." She straightened herself, and smiled as she dipped into a curtsey. "Well? Am I fit to scrub floors?"

"You surely are," he replied. Caol'nir drank in the sight of her, until his gaze settled on her bracelets. Alluria wore a golden cuff on each wrist, one set with a moonstone and the other with amber, and a jeweled clasp in her hair.

"My lady," he began, as he took her wrist and removed the amber cuff, "forgive me, but *saffira* wear no such finery." He set the cuffs upon the ledge above the hearth, and reached for her hair. "And they do not restrain their hair with adornments fit for a queen." He slid the clasp free, and her hair fell in shining chestnut waves.

"Those 'adornments' are markers of my rank and skill as a priestess," she said by way of protest.

"This morning you're a not a priestess," Caol'nir reminded her with a grin. He led her into the corridor, stopping to grab his cloak on his way out the door; a priestess with a sunburned nose would surely be noticed. When they reached the stables Caol'nir requested two horses. When their mounts arrived, a dark stallion for Caol'nir and a dun palfrey for the lady, Alluria recoiled at the sight of them.

"What do you expect me to do with this beast?" she asked as she glared at the palfrey's hooves.

"Ride it," Caol'nir replied, then he remembered that priestesses were carried everywhere in litters. "You've never ridden a horse, have you?"

"No," she replied, "nor do I wish to."

With a mumbled apology, Caol'nir handed the reins of the palfrey to the groom. "Well, then, you can ride this one with me." She protested, but he held up his hand. "How else are we to get past the gates?" he whispered, and she nodded. He took a deep breath and placed his hands about her waist, trying not to notice her firm hips, and lifted her onto the saddle. He mounted up behind Alluria; no sooner was he seated than she leaned against him, avoiding contact with the horse as much as possible.

"Pretend you're shy, and hide your face against my neck."

"I am shy," she corrected. "We are trained to be demure."

"I disagree, my lady," he said, a smile creeping across his lips. "Remember, you disrobed in my chamber and wouldn't let me leave the room."

Her cheeks were crimson as she glared at him, but before she could respond the horse stepped forward. Alluria threw her arms about Caol'nir's waist, her frightened yelp muffled by his chest. He tried not to laugh, and draped his arm around her waist. No one paid them any heed until they reached the gate, when the guard inquired where Caol'nir was off to.

"She wants to pick some flowers," Caol'nir replied with a nod toward his passenger. "How could I refuse?"

"Flowers, eh?" the guard called back. "If she gets any closer on that saddle, she'll be behind you."

"That's the idea," Caol'nir answered with a wink. The guard cackled as they passed underneath the gate, and once again Alluria glared at her companion.

"Do you often ride off with one of the *saffira*? For flower picking?" she asked icily. Caol'nir looked down at her, enjoying her jealous tone.

"My lady, you are the first maiden I've even taken outside the walls," he proclaimed. "Now, hold on to me."

Caol'nir urged the horse to a trot as Alluria clutched his jerkin. Once they were a short distance outside the walls, Alluria stole a glance toward the palace. "I cannot believe your plan worked."

"Neither can I," Caol'nir replied.

They rode past the foothills toward the eastern forests, stopping at meadow that Alluria claimed might have the herbs she sought. Once Caol'nir dismounted he reached up to help Alluria from the saddle. She stumbled when her feet touched the ground, and caught herself against his chest.

"The shoes," she explained, "I'm not used to them."

"Of course. The shoes." Caol'nir kept his hands about her waist as she steadied herself. Alluria raised her head, and he realized that she was tall for a woman, nearly his own height. He only needed to lean forward to brush her lips with his...

Caol'nir dropped his hands, knowing that it was his duty to keep her body and her virtue intact from all predators, including himself. Alluria didn't notice his inner struggle as she smiled, then stretched her arms up to the sky. Caol'nir thought she was a vision as she spun about, her skirts twirling about her legs.

"It's been so long since I was outside," she said, "I was suffocating inside those stone walls."

"I'll wait here," Caol'nir sat against a tree trunk, intending to take a nap in the shade.

Alluria grabbed his hand. "Oh no you don't," she said, pulling him toward the meadow. "Come, warrior, you will help me find my herbs." Caol'nir smiled, and followed.

They nosed about the field for the better part of the morning as Alluria taught Caol'nir the differences between this herb and that, until he felt like an herbalist himself. Once they had gathered a small mountain of plants Alluria spread his cloak out flat, and set about organizing the herbs into neat little piles.

"What made you want a life in the temple?" Caol'nir asked. Alluria looked at him quizzically, so he elaborated. "You have such a talent with plants. I would think you'd want to work as an herbalist."

"I was born in my little temple," she replied, "and, being that I had no parents to care for me, I was raised by the priestesses. Once I grew to womanhood, I took my vows, as was expected of me."

"That sounds like life in the *con'dehr*," Caol'nir said. "From the time I could hold a sword I've been trained to serve the king. It's what my family has always done; you can trace our bloodline back to the very origins of Parthalan, all the way to Solon." All of Parthalan knew the legend well, that in their hour of need Solon had descended from the skies to defend his brethren and became the fae's first warrior.

"I've wondered if that tale was true," Alluria murmured.

"It is," he replied. "At least, according to my father." Alluria glanced up from her work and noted the wistful expression on Caol'nir's face.

"You desired another life?" she asked.

"To serve the king is a noble calling, one that I am grateful to have," he recited as if the words had been memorized long ago. "But to spend one's days wielding a sword, killing the vermin that encroach upon our borders…it's an empty life."

"Then tell me what a warrior would do with his life, if only he was given the chance?"

"He would take a mate, give her many children, and live out his days in happiness."

"I miss the children from my temple," Alluria said. "There were always so many running about, playing and laughing." She laughed shortly. "No one laughs in this prison of a temple where I am now forced to reside."

"You don't like living in Teg'urnan?" Caol'nir asked.

"I do not," she replied. "I hate being confined inside, surrounded by that horrendous cold stone and by pompous nobles who think the priesthood exists only to send their every vain request to the gods. Why anyone would desire to be here is a mystery to me." Alluria went on to detail her many grievances concerning her relocation to the Great Temple, when she noticed that Caol'nir no longer met her eyes. "You've always lived in the palace, haven't you?"

"Nearly all my life," he confirmed with a tight smile. "I spent a few winters at the Southern Border, but otherwise I've always been at Teg'urnan."

"Why did you go south?"

"All of the *con'dehr* must first serve time in the legion, and that's where Caol'non and I were sent."

"Did you enjoy it?" Alluria asked.

"Mostly we just killed things." Caol'nir stated. "The Southern Border is constantly assaulted by demons." He was silent for a few moments as he studied the clouds overhead. "I've never been so miserable in my life; all the bloodshed, nothing but violence, so violent we hardly dared to sleep. Every time I woke, I was amazed to have survived the night."

"I'm glad you did," Alluria said. Caol'nir's eyes lit up as his grin returned.

"Are you?" he asked, delighted as her cheeks turned crimson.

Alluria ignored his question as she hurriedly asked another. "If you disliked it so much, why did you join the *con'dehr* upon your return?"

"I'm the Prelate's son, what else was I to do?"

"As I was expected to become a priestess." Alluria looked up at Caol'nir, her gaze serious. "Sarelle has forbidden children from the Great Temple. She says they don't understand boundaries and reach out to hold our hands or touch us when they shouldn't. How can one chastise a child for wanting such contact?"

"I thought it was forbidden for anyone, young or old, to lay hands on a priestess," Caol'nir said, acutely aware of his own transgressions.

"It is forbidden to lay hands upon a priestess if you hold ill intent in your heart," she clarified. "But a simple gesture of friendship or comfort is another matter. Remember, my god is a god of love." Alluria reached across the cloak and took Caol'nir's hand, her smile warm.

"And you can tell, just by a simple touch, that I harbor no such intent toward you?" he asked.

"No," she replied softly, "I can see it in your eyes." He tightened his grip on her fingers; Alluria looked away but did not withdraw her hand. "Sarelle is very strict, much stricter than Atreynha was at our temple. Atreynha believed that it was good for one to feel loved, to feel the touch of another. Sarelle has forbidden us from even comforting one another. We live in isolation, islands unto ourselves."

"That sounds like a punishment," Caol'nir observed.

"A punishment when we've done no wrong."

Caol'nir laughed to himself. "You've been forbidden from touching another, and I grab you about the waist and stick you on a horse. A thousand apologies, my lady," he offered as he bowed his head.

"You are forgiven, warrior," Alluria said. She watched his face for long moments, before releasing his hand to resume dividing the herbs. As Caol'nir watched her nimble fingers he saw her tie a neat bundle, only they hadn't brought any string.

"How did you do that?" he asked, leaning close to investigate.

"With magic," Alluria replied with a sly smile one could almost call coy. "You have to catch it in the wind, and stretch it between your fingers. Like this." She made a catching motion with her hands, and then smoothed the air between her fingers while whispering a few words in the old language. In a few moments a red ribbon appeared. Caol'nir stared, awestruck, at what she had done, and she giggled. "It's not so hard. Here, I will show you."

First, she had Caol'nir repeat a few words, and when she was confident he had the order and cadence correct she showed him how to capture magic as it blew past on the wind.

"Now think of a color," she said in her soothing, musical voice. "Think of the most beautiful color you can imagine." He stretched and smoothed until he held a silky sapphire blue ribbon, the exact color of Alluria's eyes.

"An excellent effort, warrior," Alluria said softly. "I'll make a magic handler out of you, yet."

He smiled as he tied the ribbon about her wrist, his smile widening when she blushed. Alluria busied herself with her herbs, giving Caol'nir the opportunity to doze off against that inviting tree trunk. He slept contentedly until the elder sun crested the trees and shone directly on his face. He shifted against the bark, searching for another patch of shade, and felt the soft form leaning against him.

Caol'nir opened his eyes, and saw Alluria napping beside him. Reasoning that he did not want her to be cold, he placed his arm around her shoulders and drew her close. Alluria sighed in her sleep as she settled into the crook of his arm, her own arm finding its way around his waist. Caol'nir stroked Alluria's hair, and her eyes fluttered open.

"Warrior?"

"Forgive me," he said as withdrew his hand, "I meant no disrespect."

"Calm yourself," she said. "I'm not angry with you. And no one is here to inform Sarelle of our indiscretions." He returned her smile, grateful she was not offended, and then looked to the sky.

"It's past midday," he informed her, "I must return you before you're missed."

"A little longer," she said, leaning her head against his shoulder. "I may never get outside those infernal walls again. You don't mind, do you, warrior?"

"Why do you only refer to me as 'warrior'?"

"Would you rather I called you 'guard'?"

"I'd rather you called me Caol'nir."

"You've never addressed me be my name, only as 'my lady'," she countered.

"It's not proper to address a priestess by her name."

"I think we stopped being proper when you brought me to your chamber. And you yourself said that I'm not a priestess this morning."

"Very well, Alluria," he conceded. "No matter what you'd like to be called, we need to return."

"Very well, Caol'nir," she said, not moving from her position. He resumed stroking her hair, enjoying the feel of the soft strands against his skin. Her form fit perfectly against him, her head neatly tucked against his neck.

"I never thought two people could fit so well together," she murmured. "I wish we could stay longer."

Caol'nir squeezed his eyes shut as he clenched his fists. So many times he had dreamed of Alluria saying such words, but now that she had he thought only of his oath to protect her. "This outing was a bad idea," he muttered as he stood. He grasped her hands with both of his as he pulled her upright, rather more roughly than he had intended. When Caol'nir refused to meet her eyes, she bowed her head.

"I'm so sorry," she whispered. "This is my fault."

"Alluria, no," he said, "this was my foolish notion. You've done nothing wrong."

"No, I hold the blame," she said as she stared at the ground. "I was far too critical of the herbs you brought me out of kindness." She leaned her brow against his chest and Caol'nir wrapped his arms around her.

"But what I brought was wrong, remember?" he soothed as he stroked her hair. "Maybe if I'd paid better attention to what you needed we wouldn't be here now."

"I like being here now," she said. "I'm so grateful that you cared enough to help me."

"If you'd like I'll bring you to gather herbs again, perhaps at the next full moon?" Caol'nir wanted to bite back his words for suggesting another of these forbidden ventures, but then Alluria smiled. He would take her anywhere just to see that smile again.

"Inviting me on another outing? My, we are breaking all sorts of rules today, aren't we?" she teased. She placed her fingertips on his face and traced the hard line of his jaw. "Does this mean you'll continue toting me about on your stinking beast?"

"Would you prefer it if I carried you on my back?" he retorted, and she laughed, hiding her face against his chest. "My lady, as much as I would like to hold you all day, we must get back," he said against her hair.

Alluria nodded as she withdrew from his arms, and took his hand as they walked back to their horse. He squeezed her fingers, also sorry that their time together had ended.

"Caol'nir, do you promise to always be my guard?"

"I swear it on my life."

Chapter 3

Their return to the palace took much longer than their journey to the meadow, since Caol'nir took the longer path around the foothills rather than over them.

"Why are we going this way?" Alluria asked. "At the meadow you made it seem as if time was of the essence."

"You should familiarize yourself with the area," he replied. "To know your way around, should you become lost."

"As if that would ever happen," she said. "Unless the king changes the law I'm a prisoner in that palace."

"In that case," Caol'nir began, then he flicked the reins and urged his horse to a full gallop.

"Caol'nir," Alluria shrieked. "Stop, please!"

"As you like," Caol'nir said. "Wasn't that fun?" When Alluria only glared at him, he added, "Look, we've reached the royal road. Teg'urnan is just beyond that rise."

They heard hoof beats behind them, and Caol'nir twisted about in the saddle to see who approached. Caol'nir abruptly pulled up on the reins and dismounted.

"What's wrong?" Alluria asked as he helped her from the saddle.

"The king approaches," he replied. Alluria looked behind them and saw the royal procession; it was quite a sight, with the king's gold standard and streaming blue and red banners. King Sahlgren rode at the head, his guard fanned out behind him.

"I did not know he was away from the palace," Alluria commented.

"He journeys to the south often," Caol'nir explained. He noted that Alluria remained standing, and frowned. "Alluria, you must kneel beside me."

"What? I kneel before no one but Olluhm," she said.

"Do you want the king and his guard to know that a priestess has left Teg'urnan against his edict?" he demanded. "Remember, you're not a priestess this morning." He grabbed her arm and held it in front of her, indicating her *saffira*'s dress. When she still didn't move he pulled her to the ground.

"Be angry with me if you wish," he hissed, "but you must kneel." Alluria glared at him, but bowed her head as the king approached. She had acquiesced none too quickly, for as soon as she bent her head King Sahlgren was before them.

"Good day, Prelate's son," the king stated as he motioned for them to rise. "Which are you?"

"Caol'nir, my lord, the youngest," he replied. "I trust your journey was good?"

"Yes, yes it was. And who is your companion?" Sahlgren asked, looking at Alluria as if she was a leg of mutton.

Alluria peered at the king; she'd never before been in close proximity to him. She noted that he was a small, dark man, with an almost oily sheen to his hair and skin. All of Parthalan knew the tales of Sahlgren driving the demons away from Teg'urnan as he reclaimed it for the fae, yet she could not reconcile that fantastic legend with the little man before her.

"She's from the kitchens," Caol'nir explained.

"Kitchens, eh? I assumed she was your latest from The Swan," Sahlgren taunted. "What's your name, girl?"

"Annalee, my lord," Alluria replied.

"Annalee." The king rolled the false name about on his tongue. "Why haven't I ever seen you?" Sahlgren probed. "A pretty thing like you would certainly stand out amongst those hags. Busy warming the *con'dehr's* beds?" The king and his guard laughed while Alluria forced herself to remain calm. No one, not even the king, would dare to speak to a priestess in such a manner.

"I've only been in Teg'urnan a short time, my lord, and surely you have better things to do than frequent the hot, smelly kitchens," she replied with a coy glance.

"She's a fiery one, boy," the king said as he clapped Caol'nir's shoulder. "I trust you'll take full advantage of that?"

"My lord," Caol'nir acknowledged.

"Don't tire of her too quickly," Sahlgren added with a lewd glance at Alluria. "Not that we wouldn't take up your leftovers!" Alluria's cheeks went scarlet as Sahlgren and his guard laughed. Somehow, she kept herself silent as the procession continued toward Teg'urnan. Once they were out of earshot Caol'nir turned to her.

"I'm sorry you had to endure that," he said. "My lady, if I'd known that we might have encountered—"

"That horrible little creature is our king?" Alluria demanded. "The man who ordered our confinement to this stone prison, yet did not have the courage to attend us upon our arrival?" Alluria remembered well when she arrived at Teg'urnan, and Sarelle informing her that Sahlgren had sequestered himself in his chambers and was thus unable to welcome the priestesses.

"Yes, he is our king," Caol'nir confirmed.

"The way his guard acted," she continued. "They wouldn't have dared laugh if I'd been wearing my robes. And the way he spoke to you, as if you were beneath him!"

"I *am* beneath him," Caol'nir reminded her. He grasped her about the waist to help her into the saddle, but she placed her hand on his chest.

"He may be our king, but you are the better man," she said softly. Caol'nir blinked, then he smiled.

"Up you go," he said as he lifted her onto the saddle. "Let's see if I can manage the rest of this journey without incident." Caol'nir maintained a gentle walk as they approached the palace. Alluria leaned against his chest and mulled over her encounter with the king.

"Do you think I'm fiery?" she asked.

"You're as fiery as the elder sun, my lady," he replied. "The king was wrong. I don't go to The Swan for women. Caol'non does, but I don't."

"Then where do you get your women?" Alluria asked.

"I, um." Caol'nir rubbed the back of his neck. "I think such acts are for mates, not casual dalliances."

"Oh." After a moment, she added, "You didn't have to tell me that. I wouldn't think less of you if you went there for...that."

"I want you to know the truth. Why did you say your name was Annalee?"

"That was my mother's name."

"Do you take after her?"

"I don't remember her," she replied in a small voice. "Do you look like your mother?"

"No, my brothers and I take after our father."

"That is Solon's legacy," Alluria said. "His blood is strong within his descendants."

"You think I look like a god?" Caol'nir asked. Alluria gave him the same coy glance she used on the king.

"Would you blush if I said yes?" she countered. Caol'nir said nothing but the color in his ears answered her. "I know you were trying to embarrass me," she mumbled as she settled against his chest.

"So you do think I look like a god," Caol'nir said.

"Caol'nir, you're incorrigible."

"Lord Caol'nir, to you," he corrected, and Alluria laughed. Then she heard someone call out to them, and she realized it was the gatekeeper asking how their outing was. The guards, impressed that Alluria still clung to Caol'nir so tightly, yelled out a few bawdy comments about what the pair had been doing all morning.

"Does every man in the palace speak this way?" she asked as they passed through the gates.

"They merely wonder why one as beautiful as you would allow an fool like me to tote her about on his stinking beast," he replied. Alluria felt her cheeks warm, and hid her face against his chest.

After returning the horse, they walked to Caol'nir's chamber. They didn't encounter anyone who might recognize them, until they were within sight of his door. Caol'nir heard footsteps and pulled Alluria's hood over her face and pushed her against the wall.

"What are you doing?" Alluria asked as Caol'nir trapped her with his body.

"Hiding you," he whispered, sliding his hand to the nape of her neck.

"Seems like something other than hiding," Alluria breathed.

"Don't tempt me." He traced her cheek with his thumb and leaned his forehead against hers. Alluria placed her hands on his chest, but before she spoke the owner of the footsteps hailed them.

"Brother," called Caol'non. "Where have you been all morning?" Caol'nir blew out a lungful of air, and hoped he could fool his brother as easily as he fooled the gatekeeper. He turned ever so slightly so his twin could see the female form pressed against him.

"She's a little shy," Caol'nir said with a sheepish grin. "I took her to pick some flowers." Caol'non laughed and clapped his brother on the back.

"I told Fiornacht you weren't besotted with any priestess," he proclaimed. "Take your time, I'll tell Father you're busy."

Caol'nir mumbled his appreciation and practically shoved Alluria into his chamber. She watched him close the heavy door and lean against it, wondering what they would have said or done if they were discovered. When he finally turned to Alluria, she caught him in her level gaze.

"A warrior besotted with a priestess?" she inquired. "Anyone I know?"

"Yes," he replied, his eyes not leaving hers.

Alluria speaks...

Gods, gods, gods, yesterday was both the best day since I was dragged to this stone prison, and the worst day I've ever spent. I've always wondered how Caol'nir truly felt about me, if his silly grins were meant for me alone or if he flirted with any woman who crossed his path, and I believe I have my answer. To think that he would risk his very life to spirit me outside the palace, and for such a mundane reason as to gather herbs!

And he was so wonderful while we were in the meadow, remaining ever honorable even as I leaned my head on his shoulder. And the way he helped me on and off the horse... He was so gentle, treating me as if I was made of glass and might crack at any moment. Then, while we rode back to the palace he said I was beautiful—me, beautiful!—and I couldn't even thank him for his kind words. Caol'nir is everything I thought he was and more.

Which is why yesterday was the worst day of my life, for I've never questioned my calling as a priestess so much as when Caol'nir held me. When he tried concealing me in the corridor I was shocked that he would pretend he was kissing me, only to be disappointed when he didn't. He truly is the most honorable member of the con'dehr, and did nothing to endanger his oath or my vows. How I wish he had, how I wish he had.

Knowing that I had to purge these blasphemous thoughts from my mind, I rose as the elder sun did and made my way to Olluhm's shrine. I knelt before his statue—after kneeling before our foul king yesterday I took another vow, to kneel before no one but the gods no matter what awful dress I'm wearing—and contemplated his stone face as I gathered my thoughts.

"My lord, why do I have these desires?" I asked. "I swear to you, I hold you in my heart above all others, but this warrior finds ways to sneak into my soul. Please, help me forget how he makes me feel."

I stared at his unmoving visage for what seemed like eternity. I don't know if I was expecting the statue to answer me or Olluhm himself to descend from the sky and sweep me away. As I knelt in prayer I remembered seeing Caol'non in the corridor, how he was so happy to see his brother with a saffira, thus proving he wasn't besotted with any priestess. Yes, that was the very word Caol'non used, besotted! And here I thought I was the only one who couldn't control her thoughts or deeds, but Caol'nir's smiles must be meant for me alone, he must care for me if...

I caught myself and looked back to the statue's face as shame overtook the joy in my heart. Here I was, begging the god who was also my mate to forgive my wayward impulses, and I still couldn't get this man out of my mind. But then, Olluhm wasn't yet my mate, and that was his doing.

"Why have you not claimed me?" I whispered. "I've always been an ideal priestess, I've followed all the customs...I have endeavored to welcome you to my bed... and you have never come."

The stone god continued regarding me with his blank stare, and I thought I'd collapse into tears right there in the shrine. Most priestesses were claimed within a few moons of taking their vows, and he would return often to those he favored. Why, he had honored Atreynha many times, so many that I could no longer pretend to be happy for her. Olluhm didn't want me, I had no idea why he didn't want me, and if I couldn't get Caol'nir out of my mind he surely never would. I would live out my days an unclaimed woman, alone.

I recited for the hundredth, maybe thousandth time the incantation to welcome Olluhm to my bed, laughing inwardly as I said my name the requisite seven times. 'Servant of the gods' my name meant, and here I was all but begging to serve Olluhm in the most basic way imaginable, yet he remained indifferent. Would I have to dance naked atop the altar in order to fulfill my vows?

"Alluria?"

The voice startled me, and for a moment I thought that Olluhm had finally come for me. But no, it was the novice Sura, peeking her head into the shrine.

"Forgive me for disturbing your meditation," she continued, "but a man is requesting to see you."

"What man?" I asked as I rose. I hoped it wasn't that annoying lord from the north who was pestering me for a spell to convince the neighboring lord to relinquish his lands, all over a few wayward sheep...

"It's that warrior that always follows you about," Sura replied. "I can tell him you're attending to something far more important than dealing with him. Just because his father is Prelate, he thinks you must appear at his command!"

"Sura, we're all in service to the gods," I said sternly. "No matter who requests me, I must hear them out on Olluhm's behalf, regardless of their parentage." I hoped my formal tone would overcome the fluttering of my heart.

"Yes, my lady," Sura said as she bowed her head, sufficiently admonished. I murmured a quick blessing as I swept by her and nearly ran to the central chamber; I composed myself and slowed my gait before he saw me. I found him waiting near the eastern door in a shaft of sunlight, and I wondered if he truly did look like Solon. His back was to me, and his blond hair, caught up as ever in that braid, was a river of sun coursing down his back.

"Again, such an early visit to temple," I said, and he turned to face me. Caol'nir's smile burnt away the lingering feelings of shame and abandonment I'd felt in the shrine. "To what do I owe the honor?"

"I have your herbs," he replied, holding out the bundle I packed less than a day ago; we had agreed that he should bring me the herbs the following morning, lest others wonder how fresh plants appeared in my possession. "The correct herbs."

"Many thanks, warrior."

"Are we back to that, then?" he asked, and I laughed loudly enough for my sister priestesses to look over. I didn't care; let them think Caol'nir made me happy, for it was the truth.

"For now," I replied. Caol'nir made a show of bowing and handing me the bundle, I thought to appease those around me with nothing better to do that stare at us. What they did not see was how he grasped my hand, that gentle squeeze saying more than his words could while in the temple.

I was thanking him when his eldest brother, the Prelate's second, appeared and started ordering him about. I wondered if Caol'non had recognized me and reported what he saw, but my fears were unfounded. Fiornacht is the type of man who enjoys having authority over others, and who better to use that authority on that your younger brother? Not having the slightest desire to listen to Fiornacht's diatribe I took my leave of the two, intent upon working with the herbs.

"My lady?" Caol'nir called after me. I turned and saw that Fiornacht was gone, and that Caol'nir's wide grin had returned.

"Yes, warrior?"

"May I say farewell?"

I knew he didn't mean a farewell with words, and I extended my hand. "Yes, warrior, you may."

As he pressed my fingers to his lips I thought of Olluhm, of how I'd lain awake all those nights hoping he would honor me, of all the rituals I had performed, all the incense I had burned, all for nothing.

I gazed at the top of Caol'nir's head as he kissed my hand, all the while my head telling me that I needed to limit my contact with him, to not entertain these thoughts about him that I hardly admitted to having. Then Caol'nir straightened and I was again awash in the warmth and contentment that I only felt when Caol'nir was close to me, and... and I no longer cared if Olluhm honored me. In fact, I hoped he never would.

Chapter 4

The guard brought Hillel small items that wouldn't arouse suspicion but were useful as weapons. On the first day, he also brought a smooth piece of wood scored with marks denoting how many slaves were willing and able to join Hillel. She was disheartened by the small numbers; she knew of at least thirty women and twelve guards, but the wood bore a total of twenty-seven scratches. On the fifth day he smuggled only a small jar of powder.

"What am I to do with this?" Hillel turned the pot over in her hands. "Throw it in their eyes and blind them?"

"Everything I've obtained thus far has been spelled by my brother," the guard stated. "When the time comes, assemble all I've brought you and sprinkle this powder over it."

Hillel received no further instruction, for at that moment several demons lumbered down the corridor and the guard slammed the cell door closed. She stared at the door and wondered where the guard's brother's true allegiance lay, then she shrugged. All would be revealed in a short time, anyway.

Hillel turned toward the window; she and the guard had agreed to make their escape during the dark moon, three nights hence, and he had rearranged the lots to ensure that the slave taken that night was one of the women beyond help. Hillel hadn't asked, but the guard shared that the woman, knowing she was unable to fight or flee, had volunteered for the right. Hillel silently thanked her for her sacrifice.

As Hillel pondered such a selfless act, her eyes settled on Torim. Even in the dim light, she was pale with fear.

"We will soon be gone from here," Hillel whispered as she pulled Torim into her arms. "I won't let another demon harm you." Torim nodded against Hillel's shoulder, then her shoulders shook and Hillel sank to the floor, cradling her friend against her breast.

"Promise me you won't leave me," Torim whispered.

"We're locked in a cell; neither of us is going anywhere."

"No, once we've gotten away." Torim raised her wide, wet eyes to Hillel. "Hillel, I cannot live without you."

Hillel smiled as she stroked Torim's cheek. "What makes you think I could live without you? I'll never leave you, Torim. You'll never know what it's like to live without me." She drew Torim closer and kissed her forehead. "I will always be here for you."

Torim twined Hillel's pale hair about her fingers. "Promise to stay with me," she insisted as she drew Hillel's face close to hers. "Say it."

"I promise," Hillel swore, and she kissed Torim again to seal the vow.

Three days passed before the moon went dark; three long, agonizing days during where neither Hillel nor Torim saw the guard. They hoped that he was being cautious, the alternative being that he had been found out and put to death.

The cellmates knew it was midnight by the whimpers of that night's female as she was dragged away. Her cries had barely faded when the guard appeared at their door.

"Assemble the pieces," he hissed. Hillel and Torim scrambled to arrange the bits of wood and leather and rusted iron into some semblance of a weapon, then Torim dug the tiny jar from beneath the straw and flung a handful of powder. Before their eyes, the meaningless items melded into two shining, sharp swords. Hillel hefted one, and as she made a practice swing she realized that while her mind had no memory of wielding a sword, her arm seemed to remember the motions well.

"And now, we go," Hillel proclaimed, and she left her cell for the final time.

"My brother," said the guard, "we must free him first so he may break the thrall."

Hillel nodded, and the three of them crept down the corridor. The guards they passed turned away, some quivering with the effort of resisting the magical impetus to recapture them.

They found the *mordeth* where they had expected, in the sole room that could be loosely described as a bedchamber. His back was to the door, and he gnawed on a joint of meat while his slaves cowered in the corners. With hardly a thought Hillel strode up to the beast and plunged her sword into the back of his neck.

Torim screamed as the *mordeth* lunged backward, trying to strike back, but the killing blow was struck. Its great body fell with a thud, and black, caustic blood flowed around floor in small eddies.

Perhaps I was once a warrior. Hillel marveled at the ease with which she had killed the *mordeth*. The creature that had ripped her from her home and destroyed her life, the most fearsome of her captors, was now a corpse at her feet. Filled with newfound confidence, she spun about and grabbed Torim's hand.

"We can do this!" Hillel whispered. Torim nodded, then turned her attention to the slaves in the corner. Hillel stripped the *mordeth's* weapons and started speaking to the guard, when she realized he was no longer behind her. He crouched next to another man bound in chains.

"Your brother?" she asked, and the guard nodded. Hillel found a set of keys on the *mordeth's* body and loosed the magic handler from his manacles. "Can you break the thrall?" she asked as they helped him to his feet.

"I can," he affirmed as he slowly, stiffly crossed the room to what looked like the *mordeth's* sleeping area. He grasped a red sphere, smooth and translucent as if made of glass, and threw to the stone floor. A wave of magic permeated the room, and Hillel saw the thrall fall away from the guard as if he'd cast off a dirty cloak. He looked at Hillel and nodded, her heart leaping at the fire in his eyes.

"Now, the others," she said. When they emerged from the *mordeth's* chamber, they found the other guards' eyes darting about; not only did they feel the absence of the thrall, their free will was returned.

"The spell is ended," Hillel proclaimed. *Gods, how good it feels to be able to speak aloud without fear of a beating!* "To me!" she cried, and the cell doors flew open at the magic handler's command. Slaves and guards alike poured into the corridor, makeshift weapons in hand, slashing and stabbing at any demon who dared approach them.

Hillel did not join the melee in the corridor but instead ran to the chaining room. She wished to rescue the poor, wretched woman who had made their escape possible. Bursting through the door, she killed the one demon inside just as she had dispatched the *mordeth*. She kicked the body aside and began unshackling the woman, then noticed her limp limbs. She was already dead.

"Thank you." Hillel closed the woman's eyes, then she ran back to the fray.

The corridor was a mess of limbs and blood, but the liberated slaves and guards far outnumbered their captors. Quicker than Hillel would have thought possible the demons were subdued, their bodies thrown into a heap in the *mordeth's* chamber.

Once the last corpse was in the room, Hillel looked to the guard. "Now begins the task I most dread."

The guard accompanied her as she made her way to those who could not be rescued, whether they be ruined woman or demon whelp, and performed the ultimate act of mercy.

After all were released, in one way or another, Hillel cast her gaze about the group, seeing some for the first time in her long incarceration. They were ragged and broken, but all stared at her with hope in their eyes. Hillel realized that their expectant gazes meant they were waiting for her instruction, so she straightened her back and moved toward the exit.

"Come." Hillel's voice resonated off the stone walls. "Let us leave this hell."

They took the time to lovingly construct a pyre so those who could not accompany them in body may leave in spirit, and once the pyres had burnt to the ground they set the prison alight. As the flames illuminated the night sky, Hillel looked around at her motley band of survivors. All told, only twenty-four had escaped.

"Are other demons nearby?" Hillel asked the guard as she watched the billowing clouds of smoke.

"I have no idea," the guard replied. "I'm of a mind to leave before we find out."

"Run," Hillel called out. "Meet by the water!"

They did, and it wasn't long before they reached the stream. As the assembled slaves—*No, we will never be called slaves again!*—drank the clear, cold water and washed away the grime of captivity, Hillel's mind turned toward the future.

"Where are we to go now?" asked Torim, her words echoing Hillel's thoughts. "I don't even know where we are."

"Teg'urnan is half a day to the south," offered the guard.

"We're not going there," Hillel said.

Twenty-three sets of eyes turned toward Hillel, shocked that she didn't want to seek asylum in Teg'urnan.

"It's the king who imprisoned us; if we go to Teg'urnan we will likely be recaptured. We must stay away, at least for the time being." Hillel turned to the guard. "Do you know of somewhere we can rest, and regain our strength?" To her surprise, the guard's brother answered.

"There is a cottage we can go to," he said, his voice rusty with disuse. "If we walk through the night, we can be there by first dawn." He pointed the way and offered a few rough directions, and then Hillel turned to the rest.

"You are all free," she declared. "You may go wherever you wish." As Hillel said the words she saw their faces clouded by fear, and she realized that they, like her, might not have anywhere to go. "If you wish to remain with us, you are welcome to do so," she continued. "I don't know what tomorrow will hold for us if we remain together. We may merely wander in the woods, starving and cold. What I can do for you, my friends, is give you my solemn oath that as long as you remain with me no demon will harm any of you, not ever again."

Her impromptu speech ended, Hillel turned on her heel, not looking back as she made her way through the trees. Torim fell into step beside her, followed by the guard and his brother. By unanimous, although silent, vote, the rest decided that Hillel was their leader, whether she wanted them or not. When she glanced over her shoulder, she saw them following her.

After they had travelled in silence for nearly half the night, Torim approached the guard. "Thank you. We never would have been free without you, or you," she added with a nod to his brother.

The guard bowed his head in acknowledgement. "We would not have gotten out without her," he said, jerking his head toward Hillel. "We still don't know what to call each other. I am Harek; I was once a soldier in the king's legion. My brother is called Sarfek."

"I am Torim," she replied.

Harek indicated Hillel with his eyes. "Do you know her name?"

Torim smiled as she watched Hillel's back. "She is the Asherah," Torim proclaimed, "and she will save us all."

They reached the cottage just as the elder sun rose; it was a small and nondescript, situated in a small clearing. It could have belonged to a baker, or a weaver, or anyone who had never been a slave. Torim stopped to greet the elder sun, for it crested the cottage's thatched roof just as the band of survivors stepped forth from the trees, and the rest joined in as she led the prayer. Once the prayer was complete, the survivors followed Hillel as she entered the cottage.

It was small, much too small for twenty-four adults, but to the survivors it was as fine as any palace. There were cots against the wall, chairs to sit upon instead of the floor, and several baskets of clothing off to the side. A wide wooden table, heaped with bread and fruit, took up most of the interior. Miraculously, the cottage held everything the survivors needed, but Hillel had stopped believing in miracles some time ago.

"How did you come by this cottage?" Hillel demanded of the magic handler, who she now knew was called Sarfek. "Is this some sort of a trap?"

"This is a gift from Rahlle," Sarfek replied. "He has seen that the king must be dethroned for atrocities against his kind. He is hoping that you, Asherah, will accomplish this."

Hillel glared at Torim; by the time she learned that Torim had named her Asherah, the entire group was calling her Asherah and there was no convincing them otherwise. She returned her attention to Sarfek, who shrank from her icy stare.

"You speak to Rahlle," she stated.

"Rahlle speaks to me," he corrected. "He is mad as they say, and I doubt he would notice me if I were standing in front of his nose."

"If Rahlle spoke to you, why did he not free you?" Hillel pressed. "Why would he let us remain in our torment when he could just wave his mighty hand and end it?"

"Rahlle has sworn fealty to Sahlgren; he cannot act against him," Sarfek replied.

Hillel pursed her lips as she considered Sarfek's answer; she knew, as did every Parthian, that Rahlle was an ancient and powerful sorcerer, one of Olluhm and Cydia's original twelve children, each so great in their power that they were treated as gods themselves. Their divine parents feared for the safety of all their progeny, for gods were never meant to walk amongst those who were earthbound. As such, the children were bound to serve the rulers of Parthalan, unable to act against them.

It seems they forgot to put such a restraint upon the kings, Hillel thought bitterly, then said, "You're saying that Rahlle remains bound to the king, just as the gods decreed." Sarfek nodded. "If he is, then why speak to you, why give us this cottage? Is that not acting against the king? His actions make no sense."

"These are questions for Rahlle, not I," Sarfek replied as he helped himself to the food. Hillel moved to continue her interrogation, but Torim stayed her with a hand on her elbow.

"Can we not just accept this small piece of fortune?" Torim asked. Hillel looked from Torim to the rest of the survivors, all of whom were watching her exchange with Sarfek; they'd gone so far as to put down their food. She knew they were starved, weary, and possibly dying from their wounds, but still they waited on her word.

"It must bode well that the Master Sorcerer favors us," Hillel said, and the tension abated. Some descended upon the food, stuffing themselves until they could no longer speak or move, while others crawled on to the cots and succumbed to sleep untroubled by demons. Still more searched for clothing, rifling through the baskets as they searched for items untainted by their long imprisonment. Hillel looked at her slave's garb: it was filthy and torn, caked with blood, and decided that she must shed her outer appearance before she slaked her hunger.

As Hillel approached the baskets of clothing, the rest made way for her. This supposed leadership has its advantages, she mused as she selected a tunic and leggings, and sturdy leather boots. She was about to discard her ruined shift in favor of her new clothing, when she turned to Sarfek.

"Is there someplace to bathe?" Hillel asked Sarfek, and he replied through mouthfuls of food that there was a stream nearby. Once he swallowed, he went on to say that it emptied into a pool just past the tree line. Armed with basic directions, Hillel found a cake of soap and left to have her first bath in longer than she cared to consider.

Sarfek's directions left much to be desired; nevertheless, Hillel soon stood in upon the edge of the most inviting body of water she had ever seen. She shed her filthy dress, silently promising to burn it lest it disgrace her flesh again, and stuck a toe in the pool. It was cold, so cold she jumped back before gathering her resolve and flinging herself into the icy water. The small cuts on her feet and the larger wounds across her back and abdomen protested the cold, but her bruises and calluses welcomed it. Hillel made her way to the center of the pool where the water nearly reached her neck, then floated upon the surface, bobbing along with the water lilies.

"If I didn't know better, I'd say you were a water sprite."

Hillel opened her eyes as Torim entered the pool, showing none of the hesitation Hillel had as she submerged herself in the cold water. Torim surfaced and made her way to her friend, cake of soap in hand.

"I brought more soap," Torim said. "I fear we may be too filthy for just the one." She swam toward the opposite edge of the pool. Torim climbed onto a boulder along the edge of the water, and with her golden hair plastered against her head and water droplets clinging to her thick lashes, she graced Hillel with a grin that shone like the suns. Hillel could not remember the last time she saw Torim smile—indeed, if she had ever seen her smile—and as the grin reached her eyes, Hillel thought that she had never beheld a lovelier sight.

They remained at the pool until the child sun rose, scraping away untold moons of grime, then they set about tending each other's wounds. Hillel thought it odd that none of the others came to the pool to wash, to which Torim offered the answer.

"Harek sent them to wash downstream," Torim explained. "He wanted you to have your privacy."

Hillel laughed; after what the demons had done to her, she felt that modesty was a luxury she could no longer afford. "And you just barged in on me," Hillel teased while she gently tugged at a knot in Torim's hair. They sat upon the grassy shore, trying to salvage as much of their tangled tresses as they could. Luckily, the cottage had been stocked with combs as well as with food and clothing.

"Someone had to wash your back," Torim answered. She grimaced as Hillel raked the comb through her hair, only to snap off a few of its teeth. Hillel sighed and began to cut the out the snarl.

Now clean, Torim's golden tresses reflected the light as if they had been polished, and had dried against her back in heavy waves. Hillel regretted every strand she cut as if she was severing rays from the sun. "It's a shame to have to cut this."

"Worry not about something as insignificant as hair," Torim chided as she turned to face her friend. "You did it. You freed us all."

"I didn't do it alone," Hillel reminded her. "I couldn't have done it without you." She grasped Torim's hand and held it against her heart. "I mean it, Torim. If you hadn't befriended Harek, if he hadn't taken pity on us…" Hillel's voice trailed off as she recalled their too-recent torment. "I shudder to think what would have become of us."

Torim's only answer was to nestle herself against Hillel's shoulder, and for a time the two sat together as they had on many occasions. "It is unusual, isn't it?" Torim asked after a time.

"What is?"

"This lack of fear," Torim answered. "Fear has been my constant companion for so long, I almost feel for its loss."

"I do not," Hillel proclaimed. "Now that we know we can kill the demons, I will never fear them again."

Chapter 5

A few days after their outing to the meadow, Caol'nir woke with a smile on his face, having dreamt of a pair of deep blue eyes. At length, he rose and made his way to the hearth. Once the fire was blazing, Caol'nir sat back in his chair and rubbed the bruises on his arms, evidence of Alluria's slender fingers gripping him, and wondered if he could spirit her from the palace a second time. When he raised his head, a sparkling object caught his eye; it was Alluria's jeweled clasp, resting on the ledge where he'd placed it two short days ago.

He picked up the clasp and held it for a moment; then he remembered the prior morning, when he had given the herbs to Alluria. Nothing had been amiss in her appearance, her hair restrained as it always was, however he had only seen her for a brief moment before Fiornacht appeared and gave him a new assignment. Caol'nir had wondered if his brother suspected their venture, but dismissed the thought. Fiornacht liked nothing more than the sound of his own voice, and that was likely all there was to it.

Caol'nir dressed quickly, concerned that Alluria might be reprimanded for not wearing the proper attire. As he made his way across the palace, he was pleased to see his brothers enter the Prelate's chamber. While they were occupied with their father, he could hope for a few moments alone with Alluria. He was so intent on his journey he mistakenly entered the temple from the east, the door used only for the bindings ceremony, which unites those in love.

"Sometimes the heart makes itself known when the head would quiet it."

Caol'nir spun around to the source of the voice, and found that it belonged to the king's sorcerer, Rahlle. As the last of the original fae, first born of the gods and far older than even King Sahlgren, his great power and prophetic visions were balanced by the occasional bout of madness.

"My lord?" Caol'nir inquired, unsure if Rahlle was speaking to him or just walking about the palace rambling away as he was wont to do.

"Your heart, boy," Rahlle replied, "it's trying to get you to come to your senses. All you need do is listen." With that, the sorcerer turned and left, fading to nothingness as he hobbled down the corridor.

Caol'nir shook his head, unsure if he had just experienced a brush with greatness or lunacy. He looked about the temple, grateful that no one else had witnessed his entrance, and found Alluria at the rear of the central chamber, quietly sorting herbs with her sister priestesses. Caol'nir caught her eye and she motioned for him to follow her to the small rooms in the rear of the temple, which were reserved for patrons requiring private counsel. Once inside the room, Alluria knelt on the floor and gestured for Caol'nir to take the chair before her.

"What brings my herb-gathering warrior to temple this day?" she asked brightly.

"The plants you were sorting, are they the ones I brought you?"

"Yes," she replied. "I must say, the others are quite impressed by the quality of the herbs you obtained for me. You may receive more requests for your services—however, please try not to crush them so badly," she added with a smile.

"My companion, she wasn't accustomed to being on horseback," he explained, grinning as he remembered how she had clung to him while the bundle rested on her lap. "She didn't mean to damage your sticks and leaves."

"Perhaps, if you take her to gather herbs again, she'll be more cautious."

"Perhaps," he replied, enjoying their gentle banter. He then remembered the object in his hand, and the purpose of his visit.

"I came to return this to you," he said as he held out the clasp. "I found it in my chamber." Alluria's eyes settled on the object as she murmured that she thought it was lost to her, and then drew free the ribbon from her hair. Caol'nir saw that the ribbon was the one he had created and tied about her wrist.

"Thank you, for bringing this to me" she said softly. She looked at him with an expression he couldn't quite place, a mixture of gratitude and longing that made Caol'nir's heart ache. He became acutely aware of the fact that they were alone, that it was forbidden for any man to look upon one of Olluhm's women with lust in his heart, and that he could not deny how he yearned for her.

"I should go," he said suddenly as he rose to his feet. Alluria also moved to rise, and Caol'nir offered his hand. To his surprise she accepted it, and once she had pulled herself up she stood a mere finger's breadth from him, her eyes staring into his. He snatched away his hand.

"You cannot be so casual with me," he hissed. "I won't risk you being reprimanded, or worse, because of my foolishness!"

Alluria shrank back and bent her head. "I'm sorry," she said, staring at the floor. "I think...I think I became accustomed to you, after being with you at the meadow. Forgive me."

"Please don't be sad," he said softly, "I'm not angry with you, only with myself for putting you in such a situation. Alluria, look at me." Her gaze remained on the floor, so he tilted her chin upward. Unable to resist her soft skin, he traced her cheekbone with his thumb.

"You may touch me, but I cannot touch you?" she asked, arching her brows. "What rules do you abide by, warrior?"

"If I'm seen touching you, it's my head that will roll, not yours," he replied. He meant to comfort her, reassure her that he would not let her shoulder any of the blame for their encounters. Instead, her eyes hardened as she grabbed the front of his jerkin with such force she pulled it open, and dragged his face close to hers.

"They will not harm you," she said, her fierceness taking them both by surprise. "I would not allow it." Alluria twined her fingers in the thick cords that fastened his jerkin and leaned her forehead against his chest. Caol'nir, far more distraught at the thought of Alluria being upset than any possible punishments, placed his arms about her shoulders. She sobbed, and he stroked her hair.

"Hush," He said, his face buried in her shining hair. "No one will harm either of us, you have my word." Alluria clutched Caol'nir's arms, and he felt tears against his skin. "*Dea comora*, don't cry. You know you're safe with me."

"I don't know why I'm weeping," she whispered. "I was so happy to see you this morning, happy to have you return my clasp to me...." They held each other for long moments before she raised her head. Her eyes shone as if ablaze with blue fire, her cheeks wet with tears. "I must look like a fool," she said as she dabbed at her eyes.

"If you weren't a priestess, I'd kiss your tears away." He wiped her cheek with his thumb.

"Then for the second time in as many days, I regret taking my vows," she said, holding his gaze until he could no longer bear it. Caol'nir drew her back to his chest, this time holding her as tightly as he dared while he wished they were somewhere, anywhere but in the Great Temple of Teg'urnan.

"How long before you're missed?" he asked, at length.

"Not long," she replied. "Why? Are we off to the meadow again?"

"Not today, but hopefully soon," he replied. He didn't tell her that he needed to be close to her, more so since they had been to the meadow. In truth, he would have taken her that instant if his brother hadn't suspected them already.

"Maybe you'll teach me to ride a horse."

"The most patient horse master in Parthalan couldn't teach you to ride," he retorted. He felt her laugh against his chest, and smiled as he wound his fingers into her hair. "My lady, you may always ride with me."

Alluria raised her head and smiled at her favorite guard, then she wiped her eyes and straightened her robes. "I must return," she apologized. "Do I look like I've been crying?"

"You're beautiful, as always," he replied, and to his great delight she blushed. Caol'nir realized that he still clutched her clasp, so he pulled back her hair and fastened the jeweled bar at the crown of her head. "I regret to tell you, I may not be able to see you for a time." He drew her hair between his fingers. "My brother, he suspects there is something between us."

"Why ever would he think that?" she asked. "Fiornacht is more bother than brother, if you ask me," Alluria observed as she tied the blue ribbon about his wrist. "So you will think of me whenever you see it."

Caol'nir took both her hands in his and kissed her knuckles, then turned them over and kissed her wrists. "Be assured, my lady, I am always thinking of you." Before Alluria could speak someone called her name, and she frantically looked to him. "Go," he whispered, and Alluria darted from the room. Caol'nir leaned against the doorframe as he watched her bare feet disappear around a corner, and then he turned to exit in the other direction. Once Caol'nir was outside the temple, he nearly bumped into Rahlle.

"The heart knows," intoned the sorcerer, once more fading into the mist.

"The heart knows what?"

Caol'nir turned and saw Fiornacht glowering at him. "What did he mean, little brother?" Fiornacht demanded.

"Rahlle himself doesn't know what he means," Caol'nir mumbled. "He wanders the palace, rambling on to whoever will listen to him."

Fiornacht glared at his brother, his gaze settling on Caol'nir's open jerkin and tear-stained chest. "I've seen you look at her. I'll not have you disgrace our family."

Caol'nir opened his mouth to reply, then closed it. If he tried disputing Fiornacht's words the two of them would end up in an argument, and he knew their voices would carry into the temple. Where Alluria would hear them.

"Yes, brother. I won't." With that, Caol'nir bowed his head and walked away, leaving Fiornacht alone before the temple door.

Alluria speaks...

Gods, what is wrong with me? All Caol'nir said was that he would not let me be punished if we were seen, and in the next instant I became a raving madwoman, only to cry in his arms the next. He must think I've gone mad, running the extent of emotions in the space of a few heartbeats.

I must say, I thought I was insane the way I grabbed his shirt and pulled him toward me. I cannot explain why I did it, other than I have never felt so...strongly. And then these ridiculous emotions overwhelmed me and I wept like a baby. If any other man had seen me cry I would have fled from the room to wallow in shame, for what priestess would ever allow herself to be so vulnerable before a man? But the way Caol'nir held me, the way he stroked my hair and told me that we would both be safe...well, I've never felt as safe in my life as when he holds me.

Then he called me sweetheart and my heart sang, and he said that he wanted to kiss my tears away and I so desperately wanted to let him. Just once, I would like to have the luxury of being a normal girl, with normal desires, who may kiss whomever she wished. Of course, I would only wish for Caol'nir.

I shook my head, confused and irritated by the thoughts that coursed through it. I set out to locate the one sister who would understand my plight: Alyon. She made no secret of the fact that she had taken lovers, and yet she had escaped all punishment. I found her alone in her cell, and she smiled as I explained my dilemma.

"Little Alluria, caught up in love's web," she said, not unkindly. "So Caol'nir is as smitten as the rumors say."

I glanced sharply at her, then relaxed my gaze. I could deny that it was Caol'nir of whom I spoke, but to what end? "Yes, and I may have become smitten in return." She was silent, and I asked her my real question. "How is it that you may take lovers without fear of being chastised?"

"Ah, an accident of fate," she replied. "I was born barren, so Olluhm wouldn't accept me as his mate. That is why I was always called upon to perform the fertility rites; my coupling with a priest meant that no other sister need break her vows." She laughed shortly. "A barren woman, ensuring the lands fecundity! It's a wonder we haven't starved!"

I smiled at her self-deprecating comment, but she hadn't answered my questions. "So Atreynha allowed your encounters?"

"She had no choice. I'm not the god's mate; I may lie with whomever I choose." She regarded me for a moment, and her nature became grave. "It will be different for you, since you were accepted."

"But Olluhm hasn't claimed me," I protested. "You know that. I am no one's mate." I looked at my hands and wondered if it was my destiny to be forgotten, forsaken Alluria. Alyon took pity on me, and offered what advice she could.

"I will tell you this, little sister," she began, "many, many priestesses take lovers, not just those of us who are barren. And no, Olluhm won't strike you or Caol'nir dead if he touches you, but then I assume you've already learned that." I protested but she held up her hand. "Say what you'd like, but I know enough of these matters to realize he's touched you somewhat more than is proper." Sufficiently abashed, I shut my mouth and let her continue. "Also realize that if you decide to pursue something with him, he has his own oaths to consider."

"And his oaths were sworn to the Prelate," I finished. Caol'nir's father, whom I could never ask him to betray. "What should I do?"

Alyon grasped my hand, and smiled at me. "I think you should be careful. You may just be infatuated with him, or with the idea of taking a lover, as he may be with you. Do not throw away all you've learned for this man unless you're sure that what you feel is real. Remember, if you choose to leave the temple you cannot return." I was acutely aware of that, and it was one of my fears. What if I did leave the only life I had ever known, expecting Caol'nir to love me and me alone, and I was wrong?

"And...if it is real?" I asked, for I so desperately wanted it to be.

"Then you should speak with Atreynha. She would help you in anything you wanted to accomplish, even leaving the temple."

I thanked Alyon, and assured her that I would wait at least a moon, maybe more, before I made up my mind about Caol'nir. In that time, we will have gone to the meadow again; well, if he keeps his word we will go again. I hoped he would.

We began to speak of lighter topics when a new question came to the forefront of my mind. "Will you perform the fertility rites here?"

"Sarelle has decreed them unnecessary, since there are no crops grown nearby. And there are no priests in the Great Temple, anyway." Alyon eyed me for a moment, then asked a question of her own. "Do you find it odd that while all the priestesses were relocated to Teg'urnan, the men were left behind?"

"Yes. It is passing strange."

Asherah speaks...

I may as well call myself Asherah now, since it's what everyone else is calling me, thanks to Torim. When I try to correct them, they just smile and say I'm being modest, calling myself by such a mundane name as Hillel (after all, my name does mean cloud, and one can hardly be more common than that), and they go on about their way.

We spent that first day, and the next, at the tiny cottage, which retained its palatial feel compared to the filthy cells we were used to. On the third morning, Harek and I climbed a nearby hill to survey the area. While we could find no evidence of our being pursued, we still made the decision to move on. North was our chosen direction, for no better reason than we were already north of Teg'urnan and it somehow made sense to continue on that path. Once we descended from our perch, we informed the others, and after we had packed up every morsel of food and item that could be carried, we left Rahlle's most generous gift behind.

Our journey north was neither calm nor swift, and we continued our nomadic existence for nearly three seasons. I had been amazed to learn that there were more such slave camps (Harek later told me they were called dojas). My amazement was quickly replaced by determination to burn them all to the ground. We rescued nearly all of the slaves from the first two; sadly, the third camp we encountered held less than twenty women, all of them used without care or mercy. By their leave, I slit their throats and burned them with what dignity we could manage. After the nightmare that was the third doja, the others called me Asherah the Ruthless.

The fourth doja was the largest yet, with more than one hundred fae enslaved to vermin. It was also the most difficult fight we had yet encountered, and we managed to liberate only thirty. Our bittersweet victory was tempered by the fifth doja, where we rescued all sixty of the captive fae. The seventh and the eighth were much the same, as was the next, and the next, until they formed a blur across my memory. While each and every individual was offered the opportunity to take what provisions they needed and a map to their home, invariably they chose to remain with us. In time, our ranks swelled from twenty-four bedraggled survivors to hundreds of rescued fae.

Now, as the lot of us trudged northward, the question remained: where in the north were we ultimately going? Rahlle still left his gift of cottages along our path, filled with food and supplies in quantities that always matched our ever-growing ranks, but I wondered how long his generosity would last. I considered heading to the north and west to the land of the dark fae, our brethren. Yet (if such tales were to be believed) our great and noble King Sahlgren, the very bastard who had ordered our enslavement, was of the dark fae.

That was reason enough to avoid them, for who knew if this demonic pact wasn't a means for the dark fae to usurp Parthalan for themselves? The legends say that Nibika'al, the goddess of night, had grown jealous of Cydia's beauty, and the beauty of her children, and conspired to seduce Olluhm away from Cydia's bed. Nibika'al succeeded, and *thus the dark fae were born of night's union with the sun. Some said that the dark fae had inherited their mother's jealous tendencies and coveted all that Parthalan held dear.*

So, rather than attempting to seek refuge with our distant cousins we continued northward, guided by Harek's excellent navigational skills and maps that Rahlle thoughtfully left in our cottages. We only veered off course to burn more of those accursed dojas to the ground. As winter fast approached, we were so far to the north I worried that we would not be able to find adequate shelter for our ever-growing numbers. Some of the survivors, still healing from their torture, couldn't camp outdoors as Torim and I usually did, and I didn't want to rely on Rahlle's generosity to feed and shelter us all. What if we suddenly fell from his favor?

Yet another reason made me want to find my own solution instead of continuing to rely on our benefactor; no longer merely the survivors, the rescued had become my people. While I will never understand why they saw me as their leader in the first place, I had nevertheless accepted the charge, and I was now honor-bound to guide them safely through this land.

I stood upon a rise one morning, looking out over the valley as the elder sun greeted the earth, and wondered aloud where we were to find shelter before the cold season found us.

"Why don't we go to the elves?" Harek asked. I hadn't realized he was standing there, and I wondered how much of my disjointed rambling he had been privy to.

"Elves?"

"Yes," he replied. He crouched low and drew a crude map of Parthalan's northern border in the dirt with a stick. "The elflands are just beyond this valley. Here is the Seat of the elf king, and here is the southern keep," he added, using small stones to mark their locations. "While the elves are allies with Sahlgren, I doubt they're involved in the dojas."

I studied the faint scratches and considered his words. We had nothing to lose by approaching the elves for asylum; the worst they could do was turn us away. If they did we could continue north and leave behind the lands of elf and fae alike. However, I suspected Harek's true motivation.

"You mean to ask the elf king to rally against Sahlgren?" I asked. The elves were renowned as warriors, their skill and cunning making them such formidable foes that would-be opponents usually surrendered rather than engage. As such, their borders had never been breached by the mordeth-gall, *a fact the elves were more than proud of.*

"Have you a better plan?" Harek countered.

"Why would the elves bother to get involved in fae business?" I pressed. "It would be wiser for them to remain safe behind their borders."

"Do you think Ehkron cares where the border lies?" Harek retorted. "Elves can be enslaved just as fae can, and the horrors no less wretched."

"Very well," I stated, "we go to the elves."

Onward we went, burning more and more dojas until I began to wonder if any fae were left at liberty in Parthalan. As our numbers continued to swell, another phenomenon occurred, one that always happens when a large number of people spend their days together: the former slaves began to pair off and seek cozy, secluded spots to while away the night.

At first, I was shocked that they would be so bold, then amazed that these women wanted to engage in the act of love at all. I couldn't imagine a man's skin against mine—the very thought turned my skin cold and clammy—yet these women practically leapt into bed with whatever warm man would have them. I confided my thoughts to Torim, and she laughed away my concerns.

"They are reminding themselves that they are alive," she replied softly, "in the simplest way possible." We were nestled deep within our bedroll; her touch I did not mind.

Rather, I welcomed it as one parched would welcome a rainstorm.

"But how can they want that?" I asked. "Inviting a man's touch after what was done to us..." My voice trailed off as I spied a solitary figure across the fire. "Harek remains alone."

"I believe there is a special reason for that," Torim whispered, her eyes glinting. "I've spoken with some of the other women, and it seems that our captors went to great lengths to make sure we only bore their whelps."

"What do you mean?" I could not imagine what she was hinting at. What did they need to do other than confine us in a tiny cell and chain us to the floor as they violated us?

"Many of the guards were unmanned," Torim replied. "Not all, but a fair few."

"Ah." My gaze returned to the lone silhouette of Harek as I considered this revelation. "That certainly explains a few things."

Torim grabbed a section of my hair and twined it with hers. "You as pale as the stars, I as golden as the sun," she murmured in a singsong voice. It had a familiar feel to it, as if it was a song I'd learned long ago...meaning in that hazy time before I was captured, when I imagined that I had a family who cared about me and wondered if I still lived.

Or, maybe I'd never been anything but a slave.

"Hillel."

Torim's soft voice snapped me free of my reverie, and as my memories faded away I was met by her soft brown gaze. In that moment she reminded me of nothing so much as a fawn, with her large, innocent brown eyes and golden hair, and I wanted nothing more than to protect her. That overwhelming protectiveness is what made me wonder if I had known Torim before our enslavement; at times, it even made me wonder if she was my child.

"If you question the state of Harek's manhood, I'm sure he'd oblige you with an answer," Torim said, loudly enough for Harek to look towards us.

"I'd like nothing less," I murmured. Torim sat up and stretched, the blankets falling away from her torso as she arched her back. The moonlight outlined her small waist and taut breasts, and I felt a familiar warmth in my belly.

No, not my child, I thought as I wrapped my arms around her. Torim was pliant in my arms and let me drag her deeply into the blankets.

"What are you thinking?" she asked softly.

"About the elves," I replied. "What do you think we'll find there?"

"Help," she replied confidently. "Help, and hope.

Chapter 6

Despite his misgivings, and the danger posed to both him and Alluria, Caol'nir was true to his word. He took her to their meadow so often the palace buzzed with gossip concerning the Prelate's son and his mysterious *saffira*. Caol'nir did nothing to stem the flow of rumors, and to those who dared to ask him the name of his lover he demurred, claiming that she was a modest girl and wouldn't like such attention. What no one realized was the truth of his words.

Summer's heat gave way to autumn's chill, and still no one knew the identity of Caol'nir's girl, least of all his brothers. Caol'nir contemplated this fact as he watched Alluria sort the few herbs they had gathered that day.

"We collected very little today," Caol'nir observed as he helped her organize the meager pile.

"Yes, they typically die back as autumn approaches." Caol'nir almost asked her why they had bothered to take such risks when she might not even obtain what she needed, when Alluria looked up from her work. "I would have told you, but I've so come to enjoy these outings. As soon as you return me to the temple, I look forward to the next." Caol'nir reached across the mound of plants and gently squeezed her fingers.

"Then we will continue to comb this meadow for your plants, and once we have rendered it barren we will move on to the next." She returned his smile as she gripped his hand, and Caol'nir silently thanked the gods for bringing Alluria into his life. After long moments, she withdrew and resumed sorting their measly haul.

"Fiornacht seems to be harassing you less and less," she mentioned, if only to fill the silence. "Has he finally decided that you won't disgrace him?"

"Thanks to your lovely dress he thinks I'm bedding one *saffira* after the other," he replied, nodding at the garment Alluria donned for their outings, "and while he still finds that disgraceful, it's much more acceptable than spending time with a priestess."

"Your brother doesn't even know you. You would never harm one you're sworn to protect," Alluria muttered. "Why is he so hard on you?"

"He misses our mother, and he blames Caol'non and me for her death." Alluria said nothing aloud, but her compassionate, inquisitive eyes made him continue. "When my brother and I were born it was hard on her; she was a small woman, and my father says she never properly recovered. A few winters later, the spring thaw came late and Teg'urnan saw snow for the first time in centuries. She was too frail to withstand the cold, and the healers couldn't save her." His voice trailed off, and Alluria could see that not only Fiornacht blamed the twins for their mother's demise.

She put down her bundles of herbs and took Caol'nir's hand in both of hers. "Do you remember her?" she asked softly as she traced patterns across his palm.

"I do," Caol'nir replied. "She was kind and generous, and she smiled often."

"I'd smile often as well, if I was blessed with a son like you." Caol'nir nodded, but still didn't meet her eyes. "How was she called?"

"Iseult," he replied.

"Meadow," Alluria stated, translating his mother's name from the old language. "Then it is fitting that we speak of her here, now."

"Her eyes were green like a meadow in spring," he explained.

"Like yours?"

"Like mine."

"I would have described them as leaf green," she said, but Caol'nir didn't acknowledge her remark. "You cannot hold yourself responsible for something the gods chose to do. To call your mother home was their choice, no one else's."

He nodded slightly. "My head realizes this. My heart… my heart just knows that she's gone."

Alluria pushed the herbs aside and knelt in front of Caol'nir, placing her palms against his cheeks. "It's one thing to grieve, another to shoulder blame when you've done no wrong. I absolve you of your guilt, Caol'nir." She held his gaze, and again he felt himself falling into her endless blue eyes. "Your mother smiles upon you still, and she wants your heart to be light."

Caol'nir drew Alluria against his chest, and she melted into his arms. It was the first time he held her since the day he returned her hair clasp. She knew that Fiornacht watched the both of them closely, and that Caol'nir didn't want to give his brother any cause to suspect Alluria of compromising her vows. Now, as he took her into his arms, she wondered if he could ever let go.

Indeed, Caol'nir held her so tightly she could hardly breathe, and as Alluria shifted against him he fell backward to the ground. They laughed as the grass in the once-lush meadow, now brown thanks to autumn's chill, crunched beneath them.

"*Dea comora*," he said as he tucked her hair behind her ear, "she who knocks me to the ground with her embrace."

"I suppose I don't know my own strength," Alluria said as she pillowed her head on Caol'nir's chest and gazed up at him.

"You're so lovely," he murmured as he stroked her hair. Alluria looked away, hiding against his jerkin.

"I look like every other priestess," she began, but Caol'nir hushed her as he tilted her chin up to face him.

"No, you don't," he said. "The rest all look the same but you...I could look at you until the end of time."

"Is that why you continue to put up with me?" Alluria asked in a small voice.

"*Rihka*, all this time I thought you were putting up with me!" Alluria laughed, and tucked her face against his neck. Caol'nir ran his hands down her back, pausing when he reached the curve of her hips. His hands were on her waist often—for how else was he to get her on and off the horse?—but now that she was lying atop his chest... Caol'nir kept one hand at the small of her back while he brought the other up to cradle her head as he rolled to his side.

"You never pull away," he murmured as he wound his fingers into her hair.

"I like it when you hold me," she said softly. "You haven't in so long...I thought you couldn't, because of your oath."

"I know better," he admitted. "Somehow, you make me forget." The thick braid of Caol'nir's hair had fallen over his shoulder, and Alluria busied herself with studying the tufted end when she spoke.

"I forget, as well." She hid her face against the hollow of his throat.

"What would Sarelle say if she caught us?" Caol'nir asked at length.

"I don't care," Alluria proclaimed, her voice muffled by his chest. "Let her be indignant and cruel and miserable. I know the truth, and that's all that matters to me."

"And what is that truth?"

"That when you hold me, I wish I was not a priestess."

Caol'nir shut his eyes as he buried his face in her hair. "You make me wish I wasn't sworn to keep you chaste." Alluria's breath caught in her throat. "I'm sorry," he said as he withdrew from her. "I shouldn't say such things." He walked a few paces from her in a futile attempt to clear his head as Alluria gathered the herbs into a sack. Wordlessly they walked to their horse; once Caol'nir had stowed the herbs, he turned to lift her onto the saddle.

"I need to teach you how to mount a horse," he said as he put his hands on her waist.

"What's wrong with mounting this way?" Alluria asked as she draped her arms around his neck. Caol'nir did not respond, and gently placed her upon the saddle. As he took his seat behind her, she settled her body against him.

"Caol'nir?"

"Mmm?"

"Thank you." She didn't elaborate, and Caol'nir didn't ask what specifically she was thanking him for. Instead, he wrapped his arm about her as he coaxed the horse to a gentle trot.

"You are very welcome, *rihka*."

Once they were within the palace walls, they swiftly made their way to Caol'nir's chamber. It was by far the riskiest part of their outings, but it was as necessary as it was dangerous. Alluria could not keep the scullion's dress and shoes in her cell, nor could she just appear in the temple with a bundle of freshly gathered herbs. Therefore, Caol'nir always kept the herbs and brought them to temple the next morning.

Alluria was thoughtful as she donned her sacred robes, her mind centered on her growing affection for Caol'nir. She had always assumed that he would eventually lose interest in her and move on to one he could openly love, but he was nothing if not loyal to his priestess. In fact, the only talk about the palace concerning Caol'nir and a woman was speculation as to which *saffira* he was constantly riding off with.

That news had made her heart light, so light that she had finally garnered enough courage to ask him why he bothered with her; when he replied, he made it seem as if she was doing Caol'nir the favor. Then he admitted his inner thoughts, and Alluria wondered if she had not acted so shocked if he would have gone on to say that he loved her...

She laughed silently, for here she was assuming that Caol'nir loved her when neither had spoken the word aloud. Yet she knew she loved him, and the notion filled her as much with sadness as happiness. Her frustration nearly got the better of her, and she had half a mind to leave her robes where they lay and throw herself at Caol'nir, to declare her love for him and demand that he claim her.

Caol'nir would never do that, she thought as she fastened her robe, *he values his oath too highly.* Alluria sighed, for his sense of honor was one of the aspects she loved best about him, and she resolved to remain silent. She cleared her throat, thus letting Caol'nir know that she was attired. He turned around as she pulled her hair back.

"Wait," he said, "I have something for you." He retreated to the rear of his chamber, and returned with a mirror he placed on the ledge above the hearth. "For your hair, when comb it," he said by way of explanation.

"Thank you," she said, "you're very kind to me." She beamed at him, for not only did he risk his very life for her, he always sought ways to make her happy. Caol'nir merely nodded as he retrieved her scullion's dress.

"I'll need to get you a warmer dress for the winter," he said almost to himself, "and a woolen cloak."

"I always wear your cloak."

"Then what am I to wear?" he asked, and she laughed. "You'll need boots, as well." Caol'nir retrieved a knotted cord and a scrap of parchment, then he knelt on the floor and took one of Alluria's bare feet in his lap. He proceeded to measure its length and width, then he wrapped the cord about her ankle and then her calf, all the while making careful notes on the parchment. She watched in mute fascination as he measured first one foot, and then picked up the other.

"Are boots so specific to their owners?" she asked, for she had assumed he would merely filch a pair as he had done with her dress.

"Good boots are," he replied. "I'll have these specially made for you."

"Won't that be costly?"

"I receive a stipend from the king," he answered. "As do all of the *con'dehr*."

"Caol'nir, no," she protested, and he looked up from his task. "You've earned your coin; don't waste it on me."

"If I've earned it, I will spend it where I wish," he replied as he stroked her ankle. "And, I can't return you to temple with frostbitten toes." She smiled, and Caol'nir resumed measuring her foot. Caol'nir remarked that her feet were cold, and mumbled that he would get the kindling, when Alluria raised her hand and uttered a few words. Before Caol'nir's eyes, a fire sprang to life in the hearth.

"Is there no limit to your talents?" he asked.

"It's not so hard," Alluria replied. She always said that when she did something amazing. "I can teach you, if you'd like."

"Then instead of gathering herbs we can sit before the fire and you will teach me spells," he said as he resumed measuring her foot. "A pleasant way to spend the winter."

"It will take all winter to teach a warrior the finer points of magic."

Caol'nir grinned, then he gripped her ankle and tickled her foot.

"Stop!" she shouted as she tried to yank her foot away, but she was no match for Caol'nir's strength. "Caol'nir, no more!" Finally, he heeded her words and ended her torment, but did not release her ankle.

"That will teach you to tease a warrior," he said as he rubbed her sole. Alluria laughed again, her flushed cheeks scarlet in the firelight. He moved to measure her calf but his light touch made her jump.

"Try it again and you'll be sorry," she said as she jerked back her leg, but to no avail. Caol'nir pulled her toward him, sliding her across the smooth stone floor until he loomed over her.

"What will you do, tie me up in pretty ribbons?" he challenged, glowering down at her. Alluria's elbow slipped but Caol'nir thrust his hand underneath her back, and she grabbed the front of his jerkin. Once Alluria realized she was steady, she let him guide her to a sitting position.

"Thank you, for catching me," she said softly.

"I will never let any harm come to you," he said as he squeezed her hand.

"Do you promise?" Alluria asked, her eyes wide as a child's.

"I do," he proclaimed as he pressed her fingers to his lips. "No one in Parthalan is as safe as you." He reached out to embrace her, then let his hands fall to his sides.

"I need to return you to temple," he said, getting to his feet. "we've stayed here too long." Alluria nodded, and rose as well. Caol'nir carefully folded the parchment with her measurements and said he would speak with the cobbler later that day.

"Caol'nir, I'm serious," she said. "I don't want you to waste what you've earned on me."

"You will need the boots, so it's not a waste," he said firmly. She crossed her arms over her chest and pursed her lips, and he knew she would not budge until she had her way. "Alluria, just let me do this for you," he implored. "I only want you to be warm. Is that so wrong?"

"I suppose not," she replied. She watched the emotions play across his face, and knew he wanted to do so much for her, so much more than their situation would allow. "Why do you always go out of your way for me?" she asked. Caol'nir stroked her cheek before he replied.

"I think you know why."

The next morning Caol'nir arrived at the Great Temple shortly after the child sun rose, only staying long enough to hand over the bundle of herbs to Alluria. He made a point of apologizing for the small amount of plants, then flashed her that grin of his as he mentioned that he had found a new meadow that teemed with everything she sought.

Alluria hid her smile as she brought the herbs to the sorting table, remembering how Caol'nir had gently stroked her hand, his arms about her as they lay together in the meadow. She knew that the entire temple wondered why she let him dote on her, but she no longer cared what her sister priestesses thought. Further, she had long since grown tired of the constant staring she had endured since she arrived at this wretched place, and hoped her sisters would grow weary of her presence and petition Sarelle to send her back to the east.

And Caol'nir would accompany me as my guard... She smiled as she carefully emptied the bundle onto the table and set about examining the plants, much as she had done the prior morning.

"Would you like some help?"

Alluria turned to see one of the younger priestesses, a shy girl called Keena, approach her. Alluria nodded, grateful for the companionship. As Keena set about sorting and organizing the plants, Alluria could not tear her eyes from her midsection.

"Do you know, yet?" Alluria asked, for Olluhm had honored Keena at the last dark moon. *Yet another priestess honored within a few moons of being accepted,* Alluria thought bitterly.

"I carry no child," Keena replied with a sigh of relief, which Alluria found odd. Normally, a priestess was saddened when Olluhm's visit did not result in a child. Keena glanced up at Alluria, and asked, "May I speak freely to you, sister?"

"Of course."

Keena looked about, ensuring that they were alone before she continued. "When he came...I do not think it was a god, but a man."

"What?" Alluria demanded in a loud whisper. "Keena, if this has happened—"

"I know, I should have spoken sooner," Keena said as she watched her hands, "but in truth I didn't think anyone would believe me. I only know what we've been instructed, and Olluhm had never honored me before."

"Why do you think it wasn't the god?" Alluria asked.

"The cruel way he spoke to me...his voice was gruff, like an angry man, not at all how Olluhm should sound. He wouldn't let me look at him, and he was...rougher than I expected." Keena went on, and described in detail the night that left her in such pain she could hardly move from her bed. "In truth I'm glad my womb is still, for I don't know if it would be the god's child or a man's that I bore," she concluded as she stroked her flat belly.

Alluria managed a few words of comfort for Keena, then sent her to rest in her cell. Horrified that a man might have breached the sanctity of the Great Temple, Alluria left in a flurry, her bare feet slapping against the stone floor, to find the one person who would hear her.

She found Caol'nir soon enough, sparring with his twin in the practice field behind the *sola*. They were quite a sight, all flashing silver blades and a blur of wheat blond hair as they circled one another. Caol'non noticed her first, lowering his sword as he nodded to his brother. Caol'nir grinned at the sight of Alluria, and motioned for her to wait on a bench while he whispered something to his twin.

"In need of more herbs so soon, my lady?" he asked once he approached. "You shouldn't be about unescorted."

"The ones you brought are quite fine, as usual," she replied, ignoring his reprimand while marveling at how easy it was for them to slip into their usual banter. "What is Caol'non doing?" He was a short distance away, busying himself with a great heap of practice swords.

"I asked him to stay near. It's better if we're not alone." Alluria nodded, then pursed her lips.

Caol'nir saw her hands trembling her lap, and knelt before her. "Tell me," he implored.

Alluria carefully relayed all that Keena had told her, expecting that Caol'nir would to leap to his feet and capture whoever had done harm to her sister priestess. Instead, Caol'nir all but dismissed her fears.

"Did you consider that Keena is an inexperienced girl, and was thus unprepared for the act of lying with another?" he asked gently.

"We are prepared!" Alluria said indignantly.

"How?" Caol'nir demanded.

"We are shown a statue of a man, and instructed on what to do," she replied, her fury growing as Caol'nir tried not to laugh.

"Alluria, look at my hands," Caol'nir implored as he held both out for her to examine. "My hands are quite different than those of a statue, are they not?"

"Yes," she agreed, "but when I was at my temple in the east and I cared for the children, there were boys among them." She would have continued, but had no desire to talk over his laughter.

"Again, my lady, I assure you that my body is quite different from that of a child's." Alluria felt her cheeks grow hot and she turned away, furious with both Caol'nir and herself.

"You are making me feel like a fool," she said softly.

"No, no, that's not my intent," he said, taking her hands in his. "I don't think you're foolish. I think you're a wonderful, compassionate soul who would do anything to ensure the safety of her temple and that of her sisters." She glanced at his warm smile, and felt the redness fading from her cheeks. "I only want you to understand that there may be a simple explanation, and Keena may not have been prepared for what it is truly like to lie with another."

"We think we are prepared," she murmured. "We are taught that it is a beautiful, uplifting experience."

"I'm sure it is," he said, caressing her wrists with his thumbs. "Also, the doors to the temple are sealed every night, and can only be reopened by a priestess. What man could have entered?"

"I don't know," she answered, thoroughly exasperated and wishing she had not sought him. "But Keena said it was a man that took her, not a god! Surely even we inexperienced girls can tell the difference betwixt the two!"

"If I was a god and sought to lie with a woman, I would take the form of a man," Caol'nir pointed out. Alluria looked away, unsure if she was angry with herself for overreacting, or with Caol'nir for so quickly denouncing her fears.

Caol'nir glanced over his shoulder, noting that Caol'non's back was to them, then he sat next to her on the bench, one hand holding hers while the other went to the nape of her neck.

"I will say this: if any man has violated Keena, I will kill him myself." Alluria's eyes widened, but he continued. "And if anyone so much as lays a finger on you, I'll kill him as well."

"Anyone, save you?" she asked, a hint of a smile returning to her face.

"Anyone, save me," he repeated. "*Mea nalla*, you have my word." He realized what he'd said too late, but Alluria had already heard.

"What did you call me?" she asked as Caol'nir dropped his gaze from hers.

"Something I should not," he mumbled as he tried withdrawing his hand, but she held on to him.

"I know what the words mean," she said, now speaking in the old language for he had called her his beloved in *ahm'ri*, the language of the gods. "Why did you call me that?"

"Because I'm a fool, because when I'm near you I cannot control what comes out of my mouth," he muttered. Alluria ducked her head so she could see his eyes, and once again her gentle gaze drew the truth from him. "Because I can think of no better words to describe you. Forgive me, my lady."

"You are not forgiven, warrior," she said firmly.

Caol'nir bent his head, and tried explaining himself. "Alluria, please don't be angry with me," Caol'nir said. "I mean you no disrespect, and I truly want nothing more than to guard you and your vows…" His voice trailed off at Alluria's gentle laugh.

"You are to call me that often, do you understand?" she said as she pushed a stray piece of hair from his brow. Caol'nir smiled, one of his wide, unpretentious grins that Alluria adored.

"Your mate won't strike me dead for speaking of you in such a way?"

"He didn't a moment ago," she replied. "If I thought he would, I wouldn't be sitting next to you."

"*Mea nalla, mea nalla, mea nalla,*" he said as she laughed. He studied her slender fingers nestled in his palm when he continued. "*Nalla*, am I right in thinking that Olluhm has not honored you?"

"He has not," Alluria said softly; if anyone else had dared to ask about such a private matter she would have stalked off, as much to save her pride as hide her shame. It was unusual for a priestess of her years to not be visited by the god, so much so that Alluria worried that she had somehow displeased him. Atreynha had tried calming her time and again, but those assurances hardly placated her. Until the god claimed her, Alluria was not truly his mate.

As the thought crossed her mind she glanced up at Caol'nir, his face split by a grin, and realized that he also knew she wasn't the god's full mate. Caol'nir didn't try hiding that he was glad she remained unclaimed, and, for the first time, Alluria wondered if her status meant that she could choose another.

"It pleases you that my god has overlooked me?" Alluria asked.

"Your happiness is what pleases me," Caol'nir replied as he squeezed her hand.

"It seems my destiny is to wander this land unclaimed by god or man," she said harshly, no longer trying for the appearance of a complacent priestess. "Alluria: the child no one wanted, grown to a woman no one wants."

"*Nalla*, don't think that," he said as his hand returned to her neck, "not for a moment. You're beautiful, and kind, and... and any man would be a fool to not want you."

"Do you mean that?" she asked without raising her head. He murmured that he did, and she made a soft, frustrated sound that was intended to be a laugh. "Sometimes, I wish I was free to choose my mate the way others do."

Caol'nir shut his eyes, and asked. "What sort of man would you choose?"

"A warrior," she said softly, "with kind eyes and callused hands, who took needless risks to make me smile." Alluria rubbed the calluses that marred Caol'nir's palm, not daring to look at his face. "I would choose him in a heartbeat, if I thought he wanted me."

Caol'nir stroked her wrist with one hand while the other drew her face close to his. "You know I want things to be different." He leaned his forehead against hers. "Alluria, there is so much I want to—"

"Your brother," she whispered as she straightened her back. Caol'nir withdrew his hands and watched Caol'non's approach.

"Others are coming," Caol'non said, as if he regretted the intrusion. "You should return her to the temple."

"Alluria has cause to think that the temple is not secure at night," Caol'nir stated as he rose. "Will you accompany us and help me see to the sisters' safety?"

Caol'non agreed, and as the twins escorted Alluria through the palace complex they discussed the various points of entry to the Great Temple, and how one or all could be breached. Alluria noted that they took her request seriously, and realized that Caol'nir had been attempting to calm her fears earlier, not treat her as a silly girl. Then he had called her his beloved…

She glanced over her shoulder, pleased that she caught his eye almost immediately. He flashed her a quick smile before resuming his discussion with Caol'non, and Alluria looked ahead with the austere mask worn by all those in service to the gods. *If only I was not a priestess,* she lamented, *then everything really would be different.* She knew Caol'nir would never break his oath, and she would never ask him to do so. They returned to the temple through the northern entrance, the symbol of Parthalan's strength, and as they passed through the carved stone doors Alluria decided that she would find a way to undo the vow she'd sworn those many winters ago.

The brothers examined every entrance to the temple, and spoke with each member of the *con'dehr* currently on duty. They even spoke with the High Priestess, who denied that any of her priestesses claimed to have been taken by a man. To their credit, the brothers did not divulge Alluria or Keena's identity to Sarelle, stating that they wanted to preserve the privacy of the girl in question. Sarelle, who believed that as High Priestess she was privy to all information, didn't care for such a response and threatened to go to the Prelate.

Once Sarelle had been calmed and the entrances were verified secure, Caol'nir found Alluria alone in her cell.

"My lady, we can find no signs of an intrusion," he said. "Of course, if it happened at the last dark moon such evidence could have been hidden by now. I will speak with my father about adding additional guards."

"I'm sorry I was angry with you earlier," Alluria said, staring at the floor. "I know you were only trying to be kind to me. I should not have bothered you."

Caol'nir knelt in front of her and took her hands. "I'm glad you came to me. If you ever suspect that you, or anyone, are in danger I want you to come to me."

Alluria nodded, then said, "But this turned out to be nothing, and I took you away from your duties just to quell my fears. I wasted your time."

"My duty is to keep you safe, nothing more or less." He looked toward the door, and noted that Caol'non remained just outside; his brother would alert them if anyone approached. "Alluria," he murmured, "promise me that you'll come to me if you're frightened. Even if you think it's nothing, even if you worry it's a waste of time."

"Caol'nir," she began, "what if something really did happen to Keena?"

"You think I'm giving up just because my father and Sarell ordered it?" he countered. "You know I'm more stubborn than that." When Alluria smiled, he continued, "We're posting extra guards, and I'll press Father to investigate further. We will keep you safe." Caol'nir kissed her hand. "I'm always here for you, all of you, you have my word." With that, he stood and walked toward her door.

"*Nall?*"

She said the word so quietly Caol'nir almost didn't hear her, then assumed he merely imagined it. He slowly turned to her, perched on the edge of her cot as if she wished to ask him something. He crouched before her and took her hands in his. "What is it, *mea nalla*?"

"In the arena," she began, "you started to say something, then your brother interrupted. What did you want to say?"

Caol'nir wondered if anyone could look into those sapphire eyes and tell a lie. "That there is much I wish I could tell you, and do for you, and…there is just so much." Alluria placed her palm on his face and ran her thumb over his cheekbone.

"I know," she whispered. She smoothed the hair from his brow, and then straightened the collar of his jerkin. "You had better go, before your brother knows as well."

"I'll be back before nightfall," he promised. Alluria nodded as she turned away, hiding the single tear that escaped her lashes. Caol'nir moved to wipe her cheek with his thumb, then changed his mind and kissed it away. "Just so much," he murmured against her skin.

He left her cell without another word, and rejoined Caol'non in the corridor. Caol'nir was silent as he and his brother made their way to the Prelate's chamber, his mind churning with Alluria's fears. What if someone had violated the temple, what if Keena really was in danger? Caol'nir wouldn't be able to live with himself if any of the sisters were hurt. He would request—no, he would *demand*—additional guards be placed outside the temple at night, and perhaps one of the *con'dehr* should remain within in case of—

"She is your *saffira*," Caol'non said, rousing Caol'nir from his thoughts.

"Yes," Caol'nir admitted.

"Where do you take her?"

"Past the eastern hills, to gather herbs." Caol'nir stepped in front of his brother. "We do not…I don't take her outside the palace for any other reason. She is untouched."

"I believe you," Caol'non said, more than a little taken aback. "I know you too well to think otherwise." Thus satisfied, Caol'nir moved aside and the two resumed walking down the corridor.

"You love her," Caol'non observed.

"More than I can describe."

"You should find a way to be with her."

"What way is there? She's the god's woman, if I do more than touch her hand he'll strike us both dead."

"He didn't smite you while you were on horseback," Caol'non said with a sidelong glance at his twin. "You forget, I've seen you two ride off with your arms around each other. Not to mention the time outside your chamber door, when you tried hiding her face from me."

"I didn't want to lie to you. I just...I don't want Alluria hurt. She doesn't know how to ride, and the horses scare her. That's the only reason she holds on to me."

"She holds you because she returns your feelings." Caol'nir opened his mouth, but Caol'non continued. "Why else would she put up with a lovesick guard? Any other man who behaved in such a way would have been turned over to Father by now."

Caol'nir grumbled, then remained silent until they arrived before the Prelate's door. Before Caol'nir could enter his brother placed his hand on the door, and offered his last piece of advice.

"If you have the chance to be together, you should take it. Love is a gift to make you happy, not a curse to make you miserable."

"But she is—"

"Do you think Father would have let a god stand in his way?" Caol'non asked. Caol'nir remembered his early years, how even as a small child he could look at his parents and see the great love they shared. In the many decades since his mother's death Tor had only lived for her memory, never once seeking the companionship of another as he kept his mate alive in his heart.

"No."

"Then neither should you."

Chapter 7

Lormac shifted upon the wooden throne, which had been crafted for a much shorter man than he. It was not a throne in the strictest sense of the word; it was nothing more than a large chair that was dragged atop the dais whenever Lormac held court at his keep, which was rarely. He much preferred the Seat of Tingu—the lavish palace that sat atop his ancestors' birthplace— to the damp and drafty keep, which was little more than a military outpost. Lormac came to the keep to handle matters that occurred near Tingu's southern border, and only when another could not adequately handle the matter.

This trip had come about after Lormac was advised of some sort of unrest in Parthalan, and he found the lack of suitable information infuriating. All his advisors had gleaned from passing rumors and gossip was that the strife centered on a revolt against the king. Furthermore, this revolt was supposedly led by a band of renegade fae, who were determined to burn out Parthalan's legion, one encampment at a time. Lormac did not for a moment believe these reports, for in his dealings with Sahlgren he had always found the faerie king to be fair and just. Why any of the fae would seek to dethrone their king was a mystery.

Indeed, the meek fae involved in any sort of an uprising was a mystery in and of itself. Faeries were certainly not fighters, not like his strong elfin warriors. They were a peaceful race, devoted to their gods of the moon and sky, content to putter around their temples. Such an existence would drive Lormac mad, for he loved nothing more than the military campaigns he had embarked on since he was a small boy. Lormac's father, the quasi-legendary L'hirre, had expanded Tingu's borders far to the north and west, and had eventually become lord over all seven of the elfin kingdoms. While Lormac had not needed to personally engage in a battle in well over a century, he still regularly travelled about his lands. As his father had often said, a show of force now and then went a long way toward keeping his subjects compliant.

If Sahlgren did the same, there would likely not be such unrest now. Lormac had no sooner formed the thought than his *saffira-nell*, Aldo, advised him that the leaders of this band of faerie rebels wished an audience with him. The king entertained the notion of having them wait until tomorrow, for he did not want to give the impression that the Lord of Tingu had time to waste upon the fae, but agreed to see them regardless. As he shifted again on the uncomfortable chair, he imagined what sort of throne he would request for the keep; possibly one of stone, a mirror image of his throne at the Seat, or perhaps polished metal encrusted with gemstones to match his crown and the Sala.

He absently touched the Sala, the heavy metal band he always wore upon his left forearm. It was the creation and legacy of the first elf, Nexa, whose power over the earth was said to be so great that the stones leapt into the metalwork at her bidding. Lormac's own power was not as strong, yet it was stronger than his father's had been. Lormac decided that when he returned to the Seat he would test his own power by willing stone to reshape itself into a throne, imagining himself as a stone carver who needed no tools.

He had become quite lost in his plans when four of the most wretched faeries he had ever set eyes on were ushered into his presence; to call them bedraggled would have been a kindness. Lormac thought to himself that he had never seen the fair and proper fae looking anything less than pristine, even during the heat of battle. These four, however, looked as if they had been living in a rubbish pit.

The first to enter his hall was a woman with golden hair that must have shone like the sun when it was not so dusty from travel. She bore an impressive gash across her neck. The two men who followed her were just as filthy, with dirt caked into the creases of their ill-fitting gear. Lormac looked again and realized that none of their clothing fit correctly; in fact, they looked as if they had happened upon a pile of cast-offs and each had put on whatever was closest. Then the fourth faerie, also a woman, began to speak, and she so absorbed his attention that Lormac did not think of the men or the golden-haired woman again.

She must be their leader, he realized, and while she was just as grimy as her companions her pale hair reflected the light and her eyes sparkled despite her weariness. She stepped forward and told his court an unbelievable tale of faerie slaves and demon masters. Lormac noted that her dignified bearing and manner of speech marked her as one of noble breeding, regardless of her tattered garments. Her charisma drew glances from across the hall, and she held his court in the palm of her hand. When she concluded by implicating Sahlgren in a plot with the *mordeth-gall,* many called out for the faerie king's punishment.

Lormac looked pointedly at Aldo, who had the source of the outbursts silenced. No matter how lovely she was, Lormac did not need a wayward faerie inciting his men to violence. He turned back to the pale-haired woman and watched her while he mulled over her words. Surprisingly, she did not flinch under the royal gaze.

"How are you called?" Lormac asked. The leader cast a quick glance toward the golden-haired woman before she replied.

"Asherah, my lord."

"Asherah," he repeated. Lormac stood, startling the faeries as he rose to his full height. "Very well, Asherah, come with me so we may speak in private." The four of them followed Aldo when Lormac pointed at Asherah. "You. Alone." Asherah remained rooted to the floor and nervously looked to her companions, the first time her composure had faltered. "Your companions will be well cared for," Lormac assured her. "You have nothing to fear in my court."

The golden-haired woman whispered something to Asherah. Whatever passed between them boosted Asherah's confidence, and she strode toward the elf king. They didn't speak as Asherah followed Lormac and Aldo to a private room, then the *saffira-nell* shut the door and left the two of them alone. Lormac removed his crown, heavy gold set with green and blue gems, and hooked it on the back of chair, then he poured two goblets of strong northern brandy and sat in that same chair, indicating that Asherah should sit across from him.

"Drink," he said as he handed her the goblet, "you look as though you could use it." Asherah nodded her thanks as she took the goblet and rolled it between her hands, staring at the liquid within.

"*Ish h'ra*," Lormac said, accenting her name with archaic *ahm'ri*. "The deliverer." Confusion crossed Asherah's face, and Lormac was in turn confused; surely, this woman knew the meaning of her own name. "Well? Would you call yourself a sort of savior?"

"Yes, I suppose so." Asherah said nothing further, and Lormac was torn between frustration and curiosity. While he wanted to know what was happening to the south, this disheveled faerie seemed intent upon wasting his time.

"You were so eloquent in my hall, only to fall silent when you have my full attention," Lormac commented. "I give private audiences to very few, and never to travelers without title or lands to their name."

"Forgive me, my lord," Asherah apologized. "I was not prepared to speak privately with you." Asherah looked up, and Lormac realized that she was hardly a woman; in fact, her youthful face made him wonder if she was a maiden still living under her father's roof. Lormac smiled at her, clearly not what she had expected from the king, and Asherah's shoulders visibly relaxed.

"You've made serious accusations against your king," Lormac continued, "if such things were said about me I would have the treasonous bastards flayed and hanged. What proof do you have?"

"I am proof," Asherah replied softly. Lormac's brows knit together, and he examined her appearance more closely. She was grimy, yes, but that could be due to travel, nothing more. As Lormac's eyes moved over her, he noted horrible, healing wounds that were just visible on her neck and forearms. He returned his eyes to her face and considered the defiant set of her jaw, how her black eyes shone.

"You were one of the slaves," Lormac concluded, and Asherah nodded. "As were your companions?"

"Yes, but there are many more of us, more survivors," she replied. "We are now over five hundred strong."

"If what you say is true," Lormac asked carefully, "how did you escape?"

"I always thought that we would be rescued, that our imprisonment was only temporary," Asherah began, once more staring into her goblet. "When I learned that it was the king himself who ordered our enslavement...enslavement to demons! The vilest of creatures, who used us for their vile purposes." She again fell silent; this time, Lormac did not prompt her to speak before she was ready.

"Our king was supposed to protect us as if we were all his children, but instead he sent us to lie with monsters," Asherah continued, then raised her head and faced Lormac. "So I rallied my wretched companions, we killed our captors and ran out into the night. We've been running ever since, only pausing now and again to burn a doja to the ground."

"Then the targets are not the legion," Lormac said. Asherah asked what he meant, but he waved away her question. Lormac now had bigger items to sort through than a few faerie rumors. "You've killed what, *scores* of demons over the past few seasons?" he asked.

"Yes."

Lormac leaned back in his chair and emptied his goblet. The maiden before him, with her slender, delicate limbs and soft voice, expected him to believe that she and her companions had killed more demons in so many seasons that his entire legion had killed in the past decade. That, coupled with her charges against Sahlgren, made him suspect she was mad.

But fae never turn against one of their own, he mused. Fae also never turned elsewhere for help; the significance of the fact that she had come to Tingu, rather than the dark fae, to seek help was not lost on Lormac.

"Why are you here?" Lormac pressed. "What do you expect me to do for you? Sahlgren has never caused any strife among the elves. He has always been my ally."

"I'm begging for your help," she replied. "When we escaped I thought all of the enslaved fae were free, but we've liberated twelve doja*s* since then. Twelve! And these were only what we encountered on our way north; I've been told that Parthalan is now littered with these prisons. I cannot allow the fae to become subservient to demons!" Asherah, having realized that she was shouting, lowered her voice as she continued, her black eyes gleaming. "I cannot allow Sahlgren to do this."

"Again, my lady, I ask why I should help you. No elf has been so enslaved."

"Not yet," she replied, "but if Ehkron gains a strong enough foothold in Parthalan, who's to say he won't look north to Tingu? Elfin women can be enslaved just as easily as faeries."

Lormac moved to drink from his goblet, realized it was empty, and ran a hand through his hair instead. He rose and crossed the short distance to where Asherah sat. "May I?" he asked, indicating her hand. She nodded and he took it, then he pushed up her sleeve as he examined the wounds on her forearm. "Did you sustain these wounds as you liberated a doja?"

"This is from the most recent," Asherah replied, indicating a raw burn, then turned her hand over to expose a badly healed abrasion. "This is from the second."

"And this?" Lormac asked as he traced a jagged scar on her inner wrist.

"That is from…earlier," she replied. By her reticence, Lormac understood that she had gotten that wound during her captivity.

"Do you have many such injuries?" he asked gently, to which she nodded. Lormac rose and went to the door, where he instructed Aldo to fetch salve and bandages for Asherah and her companions, and to make rooms ready for them.

"You will help us?" Asherah blurted out.

"I did not say that," Lormac stated. "You will mark on a map where these dojas are located, and I will send out riders to verify your words. If it appears that what you have told me is true, we will speak again. Until that is done, I cannot have you skulking around my keep like a filthy urchin, and while I'm sure you have tended your injuries as well as you are able, my elfin healers are without equal."

"My lord, words cannot express my gratitude," Asherah said as she rose.

As hope burned away some of the weariness in Asherah's eyes, Lormac realized she was beautiful. Not only in face and form, for that had been apparent the moment she entered his hall, but in character as well. To have endured such torment without breaking was achievement enough, but most would have taken their freedom and been done with it. Not Asherah, for she had made it plain that she would not be content until every faerie was free, and the king made to answer for his crimes. She was a delicate beauty with the soul of a warrior, the kind of woman Lormac had ever hoped to meet.

"The way you're looking at me is thanks enough for now," Lormac said. Asherah's cheeks darkened, but her happy glow remained. "Once we have word from the riders, we will discuss what is to be done. Now gather your companions and rest while I find lodging for a half thousand fae."

Asherah speaks...

 I had initially refused Lormac's gift of lodging, attempting to convince him that it wasn't right for the four of us to sleep indoors while the rest remained out in their bedrolls, but the man was stubborn (Torim said he was almost as stubborn as I) and insistent. He claimed that once his riders returned he would want to speak with us immediately and didn't want the inconvenience of slogging through mud in order to do so. To my surprise Torim also sided with the king, claiming that since we had asked for Lormac's help the least we could do was accept what we were offered.

 I was again surprised when Lormac's own saffira-nell *was tasked with finding each one of us a private chamber; even so, I elected to remain in Torim's for the time being. And what well-appointed rooms they were! Lormac's well-trained* saffira *drew us a bath, the first bath, both hot and indoors, that we'd had in longer than either of us cared to dwell on. They politely acquiesced when I refused their assistance, for as a grown woman I was quite capable of bathing myself. Even so, they shook their heads while murmuring about this strange faerie as they left us to our bath.*

"Hillel, the elfin custom is to have attendants," Torim soothed once we were submerged in the enormous tub. The saffira had strewn flowers across the surface of the water, and Torim batted them toward me.

"It's different for you," I murmured as I scooped up the petals. "Your wounds healed cleanly." I glanced at the unmarred skin of her breast, now pink from the water's heat. My own breasts were crisscrossed with scars, some silvery pale while others remained red and thickened, like blood soaked twine against my flesh. My disfigurement didn't end there, as my belly and thighs also bore similar marks of cruelty. Torim leaned forward and traced a silvery line that followed my collarbone.

"All gotten on my behalf," Torim murmured. I protested but Torim hushed me. After I had begged to take Torim's place in the doja, the mordeth punished me for my kindness by slicing first my flesh and then his own, letting his caustic blood drip into my wounds.

"And I'd get them all again," I affirmed as I leaned back and closed my eyes, and let myself succumb to the small luxury of the steaming water. Our repose ended all too quickly, and when I allowed the saffira back into our chamber they brought with them armloads of clothing, more clothing than Torim and I ever could have imagined, in more colors and fabrics than we had thought possible. Torim was drawn to the fine silks and deep colors of the dresses, but I was only interested in basic leggings and tunics, not wishing to take advantage of our host's generosity. Torim laughed as I proclaimed my feeling, and assured me that Lormac wouldn't have sent the items if he didn't want them worn.

I suspected that Torim's assurances were driven by a motive other than her quest to not offend our host, and she flitted from one lovely dress to the next like a hummingbird unsure of which flower to alight upon. The saffira fawned over her, draping her in one vibrant color after the other, and I it warmed my heart to see her so enjoy herself. While

I gazed upon Torim's loveliness, the saffira-nell gently suggested that I might want to choose at least one dress. No sooner had she laid out a few perfectly awful creations than there was a knock at our door, announcing Aldo's return. He advised us that Lormac had requested our presence in the hall that evening, thus damning me to a night spent wrapped in finery and lace.

I was surprised by the invitation, since I'd gotten the impression that the elf king wouldn't suffer our presence again until he verified our tales as true. I also couldn't comprehend why Lormac was treating us as if we were visiting nobility rather than the fugitives we were. Before I could share my feelings with Torim, the saffira-nell proclaimed us suitably attired to appear before the king and we were whisked back to his hall.

So there they we were, standing in the entrance, being stared at by every elf in Tingu as they wondered if we were the same filthy faeries that had shown up on the king's doorstep earlier that day. Torim was resplendent in pale orange silk edged with gold. Against her golden hair, it made her resemble a midsummer sunset. Lormac (or the saffira-nell he sent) had thought to bring jewelry along with the clothes, and sparkling blue drops dangled from her ears. As Torim moved through the hall all eyes turned to her and the assembled guests murmured of how lovely she was.

I, however, felt (and looked!) like a fool. The kindly saffira-nell insisted that my pale coloring meant I was suited for darker hues, and she ended up stuffing me into a heavy velvet gown dyed such a dark purple it was nearly black. The bodice was cut so low that I worried my scars would be visible, but she brushed off my concerns and quickly stitched in a lace edging, black and stiff and impossibly scratchy for such a small bit of fabric. The saffira-nell had then taken it upon herself to select further adornments for me in the form of ruby eardrops and a matching pendant, which felt cold and alien nestled in my cleavage.

At least Torim is enjoying herself, I thought to myself. It gave me such joy to see my dear friend happy. As she laughed and shyly offered thanks for the many compliments she garnered, I could have believed that Torim was never a slave. I scanned the room and found Harek near the center of the hall, Sarfek close beside him, speaking with the commanders of Tingu's legion. Harek certainly seemed destined to avoid women for the rest of his days. I wondered if a similar fate had also been thrust upon his brother.

Satisfied that they were suitably entertained, I turned my attention back to Torim, intent upon following her to the women's hearth. I didn't understand why elves would divide genders within the hall, since faeries did not view women and men as anything but equals, but I was in no position to question our host's customs. As we neared the hearth, I saw that all of the women in attendance were bedecked in finery that matched our own, and I later learned that elfin women were always expected to dress as if the gods themselves may appear at their table. How glad I was to have been born a faerie and not need to concern myself with such foolish customs.

Chapter 8

"And you believe her?"

Lormac glanced at his second, Balthus, who withered under the king's icy glare.

"I believe I should at least look into her claims," Lormac replied. "What if they prove true? I'd prefer engaging Ehkron in Parthalan rather than risk my own lands."

Balthus voiced his agreement, but something at the far end of the hall distracted him. Lormac turned and saw that Asherah's entrance was the cause of the disruption. While Asherah and Torim had been attractive when they first arrived, now that they were bathed and attired as women should be, they were radiant. Most of the whispers centered on Torim, but Lormac's attention fixed upon Asherah as she walked with her back straight and head held high.

Lormac left Balthus and strode toward the women's hearth, causing a few confused murmurs. Men didn't approach the women's hearth until after the meal, and even then, the king would never deign to do so. Many eyes watched in amazement as Lormac approached this taboo portion of his hall, not to speak with a lady born of a strong elfin bloodline, but a homeless faerie in a borrowed dress.

"My lady," Lormac said. Asherah looked behind her, as if expecting the king was greeting an actual lady, not her. "Yes, I'm speaking to you."

"Forgive me," she said hurriedly, bowing her head, "I'm not accustomed to being referred to as a lady."

"Surely I'm not the first to address you as such," Lormac commented, noting her formal language and dignified gait. "Your bearing marks you as one with noble blood. But then, all you fae think you're nobility, don't you?"

Asherah's head snapped up, only to relax once she saw his teasing smile. "If you say so, my lord," she replied, and moved toward the smaller hearth.

"Lormac," he corrected, "and as my guest, you'll sit to my right."

"What of Torim?" Asherah asked.

"She is welcome as well," Lormac assured. "Come, my lady." He extended his arm and Asherah took it, glancing at their many observers.

"Should a king have a slave on his arm?" Asherah whispered.

"Afraid you'll sully my honor? I'm told I have very little of that left." Lormac's merry eyes once again put her at ease. He leaned close to her ear and murmured, "I told no one what you shared with me in my chambers. I thought you'd prefer that."

"Thank you, my lord," Asherah said. "Again, I am indebted to you."

As they crossed the hall to the main hearth and the king's table Lormac shot a look toward Aldo, and jerked his head toward Asherah. Aldo, long accustomed to Lormac's ever-changing temperament, set a chair and plate beside the king's.

Lormac nodded to his thanks to Aldo, and as he and Asherah took their places he informed her of the state of her followers. Harek had led Balthus to their encampment, and five hundred faeries were now camped upon the plain before the keep. Before Lormac could continue, Balthus took his place at the king's left, intent upon discussing a matter concerning the trolls.

After a time, Torim took her seat next to Asherah, and Lormac noticed how Asherah's agitation calmed. He also noticed that the women had managed to captivate every man in his hall; even Balthus commented on Torim's lovely golden hair. He also noted that Asherah had only consumed a bit of bread and none of the meat.

Once the meal was complete and the platters had been removed, dancers and musicians came forth to entertain those seated with the king. Lormac ignored them and turned again to his guests.

"Have a look at this." Lormac placed a map in front of Asherah and Torim. "Harek has marked the locations of the dojas. Does this seem accurate?" Asherah nodded as she traced their route with her fingertips, lingering over the southernmost mark.

"This is where we were held," she murmured, mostly to Torim, "and this was the next to burn." Asherah touched each mark in turn, explaining to Lormac how they had lived since their escape, until she settled on a mark close to Tingu's border.

"That was the most recent?" Lormac asked, and she nodded. "How long did it take you to reach my keep after you burned it?"

"Ten days," Asherah replied. Lormac leaned back in his chair and pressed his fingers together; if it had taken hundreds of faeries ten days walking to reach the keep, a host of demons could be upon them at any moment.

"Very well." Lormac rolled up the map and handed it to Balthus. "Riders will leave on the morrow, and we should have confirmation of your claims shortly." Asherah thanked him again, when one of Lormac's commanders begged the king's attention.

"My lord," began Belenos, "by your leave, I would like to ask your guest to a dance." Lormac's initial reaction was to deny him, for how dare he ask to take Asherah from his side, when he realized that Belenos's eyes rested on Torim.

"That leave is not mine to grant," Lormac said with a sidelong glance at Torim. Belenos looked expectantly at

Torim, who ignored him and whispered in Asherah's ear. Lormac chuckled softly; Belenos was counted amongst the most powerful of his warriors, and yet he seemed unable to find his tongue.

"My lady?" Belenos asked awkwardly. Torim finally looked at him, then smiled coyly and followed him before the musicians. Asherah and Lormac watched the two for a time, graceful Torim trying to navigate around Belenos's awkward movements. Eventually, Lormac leaned close to Asherah.

"My lady, if you would accompany me, there are things I must discuss with you," Lormac said as he rose.

"What sort of things?" Asherah asked as she took his arm.

"Things you have kept from me."

"I have kept nothing from you," she said tightly, her fingers tightening on his forearm.

Lormac said nothing as he led her amongst the assembled elves, most of whom bowed to the king as he passed while others just stared at the faerie on his arm. He ignored them all and did not speak again until he and Asherah were atop the battlement.

"My lord." Asherah spoke louder now that they were alone. "I have done nothing to—"

"Hush." Lormac swept his free arm toward the plain. Asherah looked over the edge of the battlement and saw her followers camped before the keep; not the muddy, disorganized camp they usually set up but an orderly affair with rows of tents and fires.

"Oh," Asherah gasped at the hundreds of tents and small fires that occupied the plain. She reached out a hand as if to touch one of the tents, then let it fall to her side. "My lord, you are a kind and generous man."

"What you kept from me," Lormac began as he moved to stand next to her, "is that they call themselves *Ish h'ra hai*. The delivered ones."

"Do they?" Asherah asked. "I had no idea."

Lormac explained that many were sleeping three and four to a tent, for they only had so many stored at the keep, when Asherah shook her head.

"This is more than they have had in a long, long time," she whispered, her voice low with emotion. "In giving them this, a warm place to sleep, you've shown them more care than our own king."

"And me, nothing but an elf."

"Why do you make such comments?"

"You fae are full of yourselves. 'Born of gods', you claim, and remind all within your hearing."

"We are born of gods. Olluhm—"

"I am aware of the tale," Lormac interrupted with a dismissive gesture, "and I do not dispute. However, being born of the earth has its own merits."

"By your actions this day, you have shown that to be true." Asherah turned to Lormac, her black eyes shining in the ruddy moonlight, and Lormac was unprepared for the effect her gaze had upon him. For the first time that evening, he allowed himself to look at her. Seeing her freshly washed hair and ornate gown, he felt something stir within him.

"Come." Lormac took her arm, this time not waiting for her to accept his invitation. "I will see you to your chamber."

"Does the king often escort his subjects?"

"Only my honored guests," he replied. "I must say, you look like an elf in that dress." Asherah pursed her lips. "You don't like the compliment?"

"No, no, I appreciate your words. The dress is just heavy, and dark... I'm not used to such a garment. I will, of course, return the jewels." Asherah moved to unclasp the pendant, but Lormac stayed her hand.

"Keep them," he said. "At the Seat of Tingu, there are rooms full of jewels with no one to wear them. Would you like me to send you a dressmaker?"

"Again, your generosity knows no bounds, but I have little use for dresses."

"Then what will you wear when you sit beside me?"

Asherah looked at her hands. "I will sit beside you often?"

"As often as you wish." Lormac's eyes moved to the pale skin of her breast, and an even paler line beneath her collarbone. "Do not misinterpret my words, but I hope that your claims about Sahlgren prove false. Going to war on a beauty's whim never ends well."

"They won't," she whispered. She turned her face up to his, but before Lormac could speak again, there was the sound of movement inside Asherah's chamber.

"Who waits for you?" he demanded. "Harek?"

"No, it is Torim."

"My instructions were for you to have a private room," Lormac stated.

"Oh, I always sleep with Torim," Asherah replied. Lormac's expression told her that he was not satisfied with her answer, so she elaborated. "We shared a cell in the doja."

"Ah." Lormac stepped back. "We will speak again in the morning." With that, the elf king turned on his heel and left. He resisted the urge to look back at Asherah, and didn't know that she watched him until he disappeared from her sight.

Chapter 9

Alluria woke with a start, not realizing what had disturbed her rest. Then she heard it again. Terrified cries emanated from the cell beside hers.

He has come, she thought dejectedly as she shrank back in her cot. Knowing that cowering would accomplish nothing, she rose and threw on her robes. Swiftly and silently, she made her way across the darkened temple. At the northern entrance, she whispered the words to unseal the door—if only Sarell knew how many were aware of her spell—and ran down the corridor. After a frantic search, she reached Caol'nir's chamber.

"He will help," Alluria whispered as she soundlessly opened his door with her magic. "Caol'nir will help."

Alluria eased the door shut, her hand remaining on it for an extra moment as she cast a simple charm; now, the door would only open for her and Caol'nir. As Alluria approached the bed, she saw his sleeping form and was grateful beyond reckoning that he was in his room alone. She knelt next to him and whispered his name, only to jump when his eyes snapped open and he sat straight up.

"What's wrong?" he asked. "Alluria, you're shaking."

"He has come," she whispered, her eyes wide with terror.

"For you?" Caol'nir asked, his voice betraying that his heart had fallen. He reached out to her then abruptly stopped; both knew that if she was now the god's full mate he would never be able to touch her again.

"No. For another," she replied softly. "I heard her scream."

"If he is with another, why did you run?" Alluria did not answer him, preferring to study her hands. "I thought he only came to one woman each moon."

"That is how it has always been," she conceded, "but…" Alluria fell silent as she gathered both her thoughts and her courage. "Caol'nir, I don't think it is Olluhm that visited the temple tonight."

"Alluria, how can you know it is not Olluhm that honors your sister? He won't be pleased if his priestess runs from him."

She covered her face with her hands, her shoulders shaking. "It's not him," she whispered. "I don't know how to explain it, but it's not my god. I've asked Atreynha what it was like when Olluhm honored her. She said it was like a beautiful, loving light filled her with happiness. Before, when Olluhm attended one of us, we could all feel such contentment. Now, it's as if a pall hangs over the temple, and not one of us welcomes his touch." Caol'nir took her hands, but remained silent.

"I know you think I'm mistaken," she murmured, having discerned Caol'nir's thoughts from his pained expression. "I wish you could believe me."

"It's not that I don't trust your word," Caol'nir said. He brushed her chestnut waves back from her eyes; in her haste to reach him she had forgotten to tie back her hair. "*Rihka*, I do believe you, and I'm glad you came to me. You can always come to me." Caol'nir fell silent, but Alluria already knew what he wanted to say.

"Caol'nir, I cannot go back to my cell."

"It isn't safe for you to be here," he continued. "If you'd been seen leaving the temple, or entering my chamber, I fear for what your punishment would be. Even my father might not be able to intercede." Caol'nir took her hand and stroked her wrist. "I must return you."

"Please, don't." Alluria's voice cracked as her tears fell anew. "Even if it is really Olluhm that has come, I don't want to go back."

"Alluria, you cannot hide from—"

"I don't care if he's displeased with me!" she said harshly. "I don't want to bear his child! *Nall*, please hide me from him, whoever he is!"

Nall. The word halted Caol'nir as surely as a stone wall, and he gathered her beneath the sleeping furs, cradling her against his chest. "Hush, *nalla*," Caol'nir soothed as he stroked her hair. "Don't cry. Stay as long as you wish, and I'll watch over you. No man or god will find you here."

Alluria pressed her face against his chest and realized he was bare. She hesitantly moved her hand down his side and felt nothing but skin as she reached his hip. Caol'nir remembered his nakedness, and mumbled that he would rise and put something on.

"I don't care about that," she said as she gripped his arms, "just hold me."

Caol'nir enfolded his arms around Alluria, murmuring that no one would harm her while she remained with him. He noticed how Alluria trembled, and he silently berated himself for attempting to return her to her cell. Whatever she had heard had frightened her enough to make her flee the temple in the dead of night.

There must be something in the temple; the question is what. Whatever it was had thrown her into a panicked state, making her hands shake and her breath ragged, and Caol'nir couldn't fathom what had caused such terror.

But she came to me. Alluria should have gone to Atreynha, or even the High Priestess, with such fears, but she'd come to Caol'nir instead. The idea filled him with a sort of grim happiness. *She cares for me, she must. She would only have risked so much if she cares for me, as I care for her.*

Then, she had called him *nall*. Beloved. Alluria had called him that only once before, and Caol'nir hadn't realized how desperately he'd wanted to hear it again. After the word had been spoken, it no longer mattered to him who or what was in the temple, only that his beloved needed him.

He wrapped the furs around her, nestling her against him. After a time, her shoulders ceased shaking and her breath came evenly, and he knew she was asleep. Caol'nir removed his arms from her now quiet form, pausing to stroke her cheek before he left the bed to pull on his clothes. He needed to think, and he could not do so while in bed with Alluria.

The fire had burned low, so he grabbed a poker and stabbed at the embers. Alluria's words bothered him. *I do not think it is Olluhm that visited the temple tonight.* While he and Caol'non had verified that the temple entrances were secure and Sarelle assured them that she sealed the doors every night, he was not so naïve as to discount some sort of magical influence. Yet, he had no means to combat a foe who wielded sorcery. His whole purpose in life had been to ensure that only the god had access to the priestesses, and if they were somehow being violated, then the entire *con'dehr* had failed.

He turned in his chair and watched Alluria, peaceful as she slept in his bed. Caol'nir smiled as he looked upon her, content in her slumber, and he resolved to eradicate the source of her fear, whatever it was. His life had had a new purpose, one greater than anything the *con'dehr* or even the king could devise for him: that of keeping Alluria safe.

Caol'nir turned back to the fire; it had reduced itself to glowing coals, and he retrieved a fresh log. As flames licked the wood, he considered what Alluria had told him. The priestess who Olluhm honored had cried out, and no priestess now wanted to suffer the god's presence. In times past, when Olluhm had come, there were no screams. In fact, when Caol'nir had seen the priestesses in question, they were invariably ecstatic from the experience, hoping that they carried the god's child. Something must have changed if the coming of Olluhm was now heralded with fear rather than joy.

Caol'nir knew of the many gods that vied for Parthalan and wondered if one of those gods had somehow usurped Olluhm's place in the Great Temple. Caol'nir rubbed his forehead, then jabbed his sword into the fire. If another god truly was the source of Alluria's fears, he might as well walk away from Teg'urnan and never look back. He had no idea of how to fight a divine battle, but for Alluria he would.

Alluria woke in the twilight before first dawn, alone in the furs. She opened her eyes, fearful that Caol'nir had returned her to her cell while she slept. *It would be for the best,* she thought as her heart sank, *I don't want him punished for my actions.* Then she recognized the wall of his chamber, the cheerful tapestry that hung near his bed, and relief washed over her.

"You woke quite early," she said when she joined Caol'nir before the hearth.

"I didn't sleep." Caol'nir stared at the fire, his fingers pressed together beneath his chin. He did not shift his gaze as Alluria knelt before him.

"Whoever was in the temple didn't find me," Alluria said, gazing up at Caol'nir. "I knew you would protect me." Caol'nir offered her a small smile, but said nothing as he stared into the flames.

"Forgive me," she said, her eyes downcast, "I shouldn't have come. It was foolish of me to risk leaving my cell." She rose and moved to leave, but Caol'nir caught her wrist.

"I'm glad you came. I only wish you hadn't felt the need." He nodded to the chair opposite his, but Alluria knelt at his feet instead, just as a priestess would do when counseling a patron. Caol'nir shook his head and sat beside her on the floor.

"You say you heard screams last night?" he asked, and she nodded. "Alluria, I need you to tell me everything, everything Atreynha told you about her encounters with Olluhm, everything you've been taught about being honored by him, and tell me again what happened to Keena."

Alluria recounted as best she could, beginning with what every priestess learns about giving herself over to Olluhm, body and soul. Atreynha's experiences closely matched this description, for the Mother Priestess claimed that each visit filled her with a loving presence that permeated her soul and left her in a dazed, ecstatic state. Keena's experience was markedly different, having left her bloody and unable to leave her bed. Alluria's voice faltered as she spoke of Keena's nightmarish encounter, and she turned away, not wanting to weep again after the tears she shed the night before.

"*Rihka*, don't be upset when I ask you this, but I need to know," Caol'nir said gently as he stroked Alluria's wrist. "How do you know it was not Olluhm that came to the temple last night?"

"It may have been *a* god, but it was not *my* god," Alluria replied, her voice hardly more than a whisper. "My god is of love and happiness, and would never hurt those sworn to him. If you had heard her last night, shrieking in terror…"

Caol'nir took her hands in his. "I don't understand what could have breached the temple. Could it have been a sorcerer, or another god?"

"I don't know," she choked out. "I only know that whatever it is chills me to my soul." Caol'nir wiped her cheek with his thumb, then took her hands.

"I will find out what is happening," he vowed. "Whether this is a god or a man, I will not let it harm you. *Rihka*, you have my word." Alluria smiled at the endearment; "beauty", he had called her. Add that to the list of pet names he had for her: sweetheart, darling, and her favorite, my beloved. Since that first secret outing to gather herbs, whenever Alluria was distraught Caol'nir would call her affectionate names in the old language. It was one of the many ways Caol'nir sought to make her happy, and one of the many reasons she felt so strongly for him, why she looked forward to seeing him every day.

Alluria stared at her hands, noticing how small they seemed in Caol'nir's, before raising her eyes to his face. His eyes were not their usual pale green, but had darkened to the color of pine boughs. Alluria reached out to touch his sandy hair, bound as always in a tight braid. While the texture was much rougher than hers, it was pleasant against her skin, much as Caol'nir appeared to be a hardened warrior but was truly a gentle soul. Alluria gazed into his eyes and put words to a choice she made long ago.

"Caol'nir," she began, "I am going to break my vows, but before I do, I want you to know that it is not your fault. They are mine alone to break." Caol'nir began speaking, but Alluria leaned forward and caught his lips with hers. At first, he remained still, then he wound his fingers into her hair as he kissed her back.

"I love you, Caol'nir," Alluria whispered as she leaned her forehead against his cheek. "I know it is foolish of me to say so, for I've hardly spent a good deal of time with any man, save you. But I've met many men, and none pull at my heart as you do, or make me smile just to be in their presence, or make me feel as if the most horrible things in this land cannot harm me. If that is not love, then I don't know what is." Caol'nir remained silent. "And I don't want you to concern yourself with my vows," she continued hurriedly. "If they're broken, they're broken, and I won't let you suffer for my actions."

Caol'nir still had not spoken, and Alluria's throat burned with unshed tears. *He doesn't love me,* she lamented, *he is only protecting me because it's his duty, and I'm a fool.* Her back straightened as she gathered what pride she had left. Before she could pull away, Caol'nir drew her face to his, and kissed her so tenderly he took her breath away. He kissed her cheeks next, then her forehead, and gently brushed his lips against her eyelids before returning his mouth to hers.

"I've loved you long," Caol'nir murmured. "I never thought you'd love me in return." His lips traveled to her neck, eliciting her soft laughter. "Why tell me now?"

"I needed to, though I can't say exactly why." She leaned her head against his shoulder and toyed with the end of his braid. "I tried not to love you, believe me, I tried. I told myself that you weren't worth breaking my vows, that my one mate was Olluhm and no other, but I cannot deny the hold you have over me. Even after I accepted that it was love, I still assumed that you would lose interest in me after a time, and that once you moved on from me, I would return to my quiet life in the temple."

"How could I lose interest in you?" Caol'nir asked.

"You're so young, Caol'nir, hardly more than a boy," Alluria replied. "Someone like you should be with one he can love openly, not one he needs to sneak out of the palace just to hold her hand."

Caol'nir chuckled at her assessment. "I may be young, and foolish," he began, pausing to silence her with a kiss, "but my heart wants you alone. Besides, our little outings were fun."

"Caol'nir, my selfish needs could have gotten you killed!"

"A risk I gladly took, and I would take a thousand more just to see you smile. *Dea comora,* I've always been happy just to be in your presence. I would have warded you until the end of time, never having felt your touch, and it would have been enough. I'll never forsake you."

"I know that now," Alluria said, smiling at her warrior. "I daresay, I've known for some time."

Caol'nir tucked her head against his neck, much as he had during that first morning at the meadow. "I need to ask you something," Alluria said after a time.

"Ask me anything."

"Why do you always have your hair in this braid? I've never seen men with such braids, save you, your brothers and the Prelate." She ran her fingers over the length of it, marveling that it was woven as tight as a rope.

"It's an old legend," he replied. Alluria unwound the leather thong that tied off the end of his braid, noting how he watched her hands. "It says that a warrior's strength in battle can be measured by the length of his hair."

"And you believe that?"

"My father believes it, so my brothers and I have always worn our hair long." He watched her slender fingers unraveling the braid. "What are you doing?"

"I've never seen your hair loose," she replied, "and I think it will be lovely, long and pale as it is."

Caol'nir stayed her hand. "The legend also says that a warrior's hair is unbound for only one act."

"What act is that? Bathing?"

"Well, that, and another we're not likely to engage in."

Alluria smiled tightly, for he had reminded her that as long as she remained Olluhm's unclaimed mate she could not truly be his. "Well, now you know not to place such faith in stories." His hair now unbound, she ran her fingers through the long strands. "What will happen when we leave this room?"

Caol'nir smoothed back her hair and drew her against his chest. "I will escort you to the temple."

"You mean you will walk two paces behind me, and I may only touch you on pain of death," Alluria said bitterly. Caol'nir tightened his embrace but said nothing, while she imagined a life of clandestine meetings and stolen kisses. "Do you remember the day I found you in the arena?"

"Of course I do."

"What...what were you really going to say?" When he pursed his lips, she added, "You can tell me, now."

Caol'nir was silent for long moments, and Alluria did not prompt him. She understood that it was no easy task to bare one's heart. "I asked you what kind of man you would take as a mate, and you described me," he began. "At least, I hoped you described me." He caressed her cheek, bringing her face close to his. "I want things to be different; I wish I had never sworn this accursed oath that keeps me from you... Say the words, *nalla*, and I will leave the *con'dehr* behind and bind myself to you."

"You would do that?" she asked incredulously. "But your father, and brothers... What would they do if you left?"

"They would get over it," he said, though she didn't believe that for a moment. "If I'm with you that's all that matters."

Alluria nearly wept as he said the words; all her life she had wanted to be mated, to have someone to wake up with, share her thoughts with, watch the suns rise and set. She realized that she was wrong to take her vows as a priestess, for Olluhm wasn't her true mate, he never had been.

But, she had taken those vows.

"*Nall*, I would still be a priestess," she pointed out. "Another's mate."

"Another's mate," he repeated. A god's mate. Caol'nir kissed her forehead and said nothing, for he had long ago accepted that she would never be his.

"What if I left the Great Temple?" Alluria asked.

"Where would you go?" he asked. "Would you return to your temple in the east?"

"I would stay with you." She placed her hands against his cheeks, and looked deeply into his eyes. "By leave, I mean renounce my vows."

"Can that even be done?"

"There must be a way," she replied. "I've been trying to learn how to leave for some time now."

"Alluria, I don't want you to give up your life for me," he began, but she pressed her lips to his.

"I'll give up nothing but that which keeps us apart," she murmured against his lips. "Do you not want me to do so?"

"*Dea comora*, all I desire is you." Caol'nir nestled her against his chest. "Have you never noticed how well you fit in my arms, how you are the perfect height for me to kiss, how my hands fit around your waist? I wonder if you weren't made for me." He stroked her hair for a moment, smoothing down the soft strands. "You were meant to be mine; I've thought that from the first moment I saw you. I will stand by your side, no matter what sort of life you choose."

Alluria smiled. "I chose you long ago."

Chapter 10

Caol'nir and Alluria left his chamber once the child sun had risen. Caol'nir first checked the corridor, ensuring it was empty, then he beckoned her to follow. With Alluria walking a few paces ahead of Caol'nir it looked as if he was merely escorting her though the palace, not returning her to the temple after a night spent in his chambers. As they approached the temple's northern entrance, they noted a flurry of activity, and Caol'nir stepped in front of Alluria.

"What has happened?" he demanded of the *con'dehr* at the door. The guard indicated the cells and stated that the god had come, but it had gone...badly. Caol'nir strode toward the cells, ignoring the pleas of others to keep back. When he entered the tiny room, he lost his breath as his stomach heaved.

Whatever had been with the priestess had ripped the girl to pieces, most of which were smeared across the walls. The girl's cot was demolished, the sleeping furs rent apart and so blood-soaked it looked as if dead animals littered the floor. Caol'nir could only stare, unable to comprehend what could have caused such carnage, when he heard Alluria's stifled scream.

"I told you to stay back," he snapped, regretting his harsh words when he saw her terrified eyes. "I need to get you out of here." Taking her elbow, he guided her out of the cell lest her bare feet touch what was left of the girl.

"Ethnia," Alluria murmured.

"What?"

"Ethnia," she repeated. "Her name was Ethnia."

Caol'nir frowned, then turned to the *con'dehr* he'd last spoken to. "Who knows of this?"

"Only the two of us," he replied. "I was waiting for another guard before I advised your father."

"Bar the room, and keep all others from entering until me or my father declare otherwise," Caol'nir ordered. The guard assented, and Caol'nir added, "I'll see Alluria to her cell."

Once they were inside, Caol'nir pulled her into his arms and carried her to her cot as she collapsed in sobs.

"Is this to be my fate as well?" she wailed. "Murdered within my own temple?" Caol'nir hushed her and stroked her back.

"I will find you a safe temple," he promised. "I will take you away from here."

"I don't want another temple," she said, her musical voice hoarse with sobs. "I want to be released from this servitude." Alluria raised her eyes to his, and he was struck by their beauty, even swollen and streaked with tears. "I want to be with you."

"I don't know what to do," he whispered. "*Nalla*, I only want you to be safe."

"Just claim me and end this nightmare," Alluria said bitterly. "Olluhm hasn't only forsaken me, he has forsaken us all."

Caol'nir drew Alluria against his chest and kissed her hair. He wanted her as well, but had no idea how he was supposed to claim a priestess, or a former priestess for that matter. "Before we do anything, we need to go to my father," he murmured against her neck. "He needs to know what is really happening here."

Once Alluria had progressed from hysterical to despondent, the priestess and her guard made their way to the Prelate's chambers. They came across Caol'non on the way; somehow, the brothers were never far from one another. Caol'non asked why Alluria was so distressed, but his twin replied he would tell him while he told their father.

Upon entering the chamber they found the Prelate conferring with Fiornacht. The two fell silent when they saw the twins, one grim-faced and the other confused, and a priestess who had obviously been crying.

"Has something happened within the temple?" demanded Tor.

"Have you heard what befell a priestess last night?" countered Caol'nir.

"I know that Olluhm came. Is she with child?"

"She's dead."

Caol'nir's father and brothers were stunned, and Alluria whimpered as she covered her face with her hands. Tor told her to sit and she obeyed; as Prelate, he held more authority that the High Priestess and was second only to the king.

"How did she die?" Tor asked slowly.

"She was ripped apart by whatever took her," Caol'nir replied.

"Why am I just learning this now?" Tor demanded.

"Because the fool you assigned to the morning watch saw fit to wait for another before informing you," Caol'nir shot back. "I've seen her cell, and there is very little left of her." Alluria's shuddered, and Caol'nir whispered, "Be strong, this will be done soon."

"Why are you in the company of a priestess?" demanded Fiornacht.

"Alluria heard the girl screaming last night, and came to me for protection," Caol'nir replied.

"Came to you in your chamber? And you're calling that protection?" sneered Fiornacht.

"It's my duty to protect all of the priestesses!"

"Then why didn't you seek out the one who was screaming? Too busy 'protecting' this one?"

"Maybe if she'd come to me as well, this wouldn't have happened!"

"Enough," shouted Alluria. "She has a name. Her name is Ethnia!" She glared from Caol'nir to Fiornacht, before approaching the elder. "Do not fault Caol'nir for his actions. He is right; I went to him. Ethnia's screams terrified me, and I didn't know where else to turn. I surely couldn't have gone to you, Fiornacht. You would have just as likely taken me as sent me back to my death."

Caol'non laughed and Fiornacht blanched, for once with no rebuttal, and Alluria turned to Tor.

"Prelate, I beg you not to hold my actions against Caol'nir. I was frightened, and acted foolishly. I can assure you that he remained honorable while I was with him." Tor regarded the priestess and his son, his eyes hard.

"I have no doubt that my son is honorable. A priestess should feel free to approach any member of the *con'dehr*, at any time, for any reason; therefore you, Alluria, have done no wrong." He leaned back in his chair and rubbed his chin. "Now, on to Ethnia…Alluria, would you like to step away as we discuss this?"

"No," she stated firmly. "I will hear you out, my lord, in the hopes that none of my other sisters are so harmed." With that, Alluria went to Caol'nir's side and stared defiantly at Fiornacht, almost challenging him for the right to stand near his brother.

The discussion was swift, if one could even call it that. Tor gave Fiornacht the assignment of speaking with Rahlle's apprentices in order to learn what, if anything, could have breached the sealed temple doors and done harm to a priestess. However, he declined posting additional guards in the temple.

Alluria disagreed. "My lord, I believe I speak for all of my sisters when I say that we no longer feel safe in the temple at night. May we be moved to rooms in the palace until whoever has breached our sacred space has been caught?"

Tor rubbed his chin as he regarded the priestess. "Your words have merit," he said at length. "I know I wouldn't sleep a stone's throw from a recent murder. Caol'nir, can you see to finding accommodations for the sisters who wish for such?"

Caol'nir bowed his head as he agreed to his father's request. Fiornacht glared at Caol'nir, but held his tongue after a quick look at Alluria's face. As the two left the Prelate's chamber, Caol'nir did not remain two paces behind Alluria but walked at her side.

"You know something of my brother and a priestess?" Caol'nir quietly inquired.

"I know nothing at all," Alluria replied with a knowing smile. "I only wanted him to stop shouting at you. His reaction was interesting, wasn't it?" Her innocent eyes gazed into his, and he fought the urge to wrap her in his arms right there in the main concourse.

"I've been trying to quiet him for years without success, and you do it with a few words. My lady, I could not love you more."

Caol'nir escorted Alluria back to the temple, and as she gathered her things, he spoke with the High Priestess, Sarelle. She was not pleased to hear that the Prelate had decreed that her priestesses could sleep outside the Great Temple, if they chose. She insisted that removing them would only anger Olluhm. Caol'nir placated her as best he could, but in the end, Sarelle had no choice but to concede to the Prelate's authority.

Once his conversation with Sarelle had reached its inevitable conclusion, the High Priestess stalked off to give Tor a thorough tongue-lashing. Caol'nir found Alluria in her cell, her belongings neatly packed.

"I'll put these in your new chamber," Caol'nir said, taking the sachel.

"What part of the palace will I be in?" she asked.

"You'll stay with me," he replied. "Once the suns go to rest, you will not leave my sight."

With that declaration, Caol'nir had bowed his head and left the temple, promising to return before nightfall. For the remainder of the day, Alluria performed her duties as best she could, all the while shadowed by Caol'non. She appreciated that Caol'nir had sent his brother to watch over her, but being followed about by the twin of the man she loved was quite unsettling.

To distract herself from Caol'non, She wondered where Caol'nir and his father were. Maybe Caol'nir was trying to learn what had befallen Ethnia, Tor was speaking with Rahlle, and Fiornacht...

Alluria laughed inwardly as she looked at her fellow priestesses, wondering whom Fiornacht had bedded. She was well acquainted with men like him, who thought the rules did not apply to those in such high positions. The way he belittled Caol'nir, only to disguise his own indiscretions... yes, she knew the type. Now, she just needed to know the girl in question.

As the elder sun went toward his rest, Caol'nir reentered the temple, speaking with his twin for a few moments before he motioned Alluria toward him. Wordlessly she followed, her heart in her throat as they traversed the long corridor to his chamber. She didn't know how to tell him what she had learned when she had spoken first with Atreynha, and then with Sarelle, or how he would react to hearing it.

Caol'nir opened the heavy chamber door for Alluria, and nervously scanned the room. "I don't know how to do this," he confessed. "I know we should just act as we always do, but I've never been faced with the possibility of having you for the entire night." He squeezed his eyes shut. "Forgive me, I didn't mean that I would have you, I meant…" Caol'nir shook his head. "Gods, I sound like a fool."

"It's fine," Alluria mumbled. "I'm just so glad I'm here, not where…" She cleared her throat. "Thank you, for allowing me to stay."

"Of course," he said. "It's just that no woman has ever spent the night here. Well, except for you."

"Well, I promise I won't try to seduce you."

Caol'nir smiled as he pulled her against him, shaking his head at her candor. "I should be making you comfortable, not the other way 'round." He kissed her forehead and led Alluria to the hearth, but as he sat in a chair she again sat on the floor. Caol'nir shook his head as he got down on the floor across from her, watching her as she stretched out on the thick rug. "How is it that you always go about barefoot, yet your feet are always pristine and white?"

"I practice an ancient art," Alluria said mysteriously.

"Is it some sort of a spell?" Caol'nir asked

"It is called bathing," she replied, nudging him with her foot. "You should try it, warrior; it will work for your feet as well." Alluria laughed at his indignant face.

"Exactly how often do you wash your feet?" he asked.

"Obviously more than you do."

"You enjoy teasing me, priestess," Caol'nir rebuked as he crawled toward her on his hands and knees, not stopping until an arm was on each side of her hips and his lips were a hair's breadth from hers. "I thought you were trained to be demure."

"I never claimed to be a good student." Caol'nir brushed his lips against hers; Alluria wound her arms around his neck and kissed him hard and they slowly sank to the floor.

A knock at the door roused them. "I expect that will be our supper," Caol'nir said; he had thought to speak with the kitchens earlier in the day, knowing that the sight of him and Alluria dining together in the hall would cause rumors neither wanted to deal with. Caol'nir grabbed his cloak and draped it around Alluria's shoulders, hiding her priestess robes. Fortunately, the *saffira* who attended them that evening was polite enough to not stare at the woman reclined before his hearth. After she left, they shared a simple meal of bread and stew. Once the bread had been reduced to crumbs, Caol'nir poured two measures of wine. He had no sooner handed it off to Alluria than he caught her smiling into her goblet.

"Does wine always make you smile?" Caol'nir asked.

"I was remembering the first time you brought me wine. I'd just come to Teg'urnan, and I was miserable. Everyone kept saying that I should be glad to be here, that it is a privilege to serve the Great Temple, and that I didn't know how lucky I was. I just wanted to go home." She stared into her goblet for a moment, swirling the wine. "I even hated my cell, barren and cold with no windows. My prior cell had beautiful, wide windows, and I could always see the sky."

Caol'nir tucked Alluria's hair behind her ear. "I had no idea you were so sad. If I'd known, I would have tried to help you."

Alluria turned to kiss his open palm. "You did. It was my fourth morning in Teg'urnan, and as I lit the censers a warrior had the audacity to approach me, his face split by a silly grin."

Caol'nir laughed softly, remembering their awkward first conversation. "I was afraid you'd shout at me, and send me away."

"I nearly did! But then you held out a jug of golden eastern wine, not the horrible red wine they have here in the palace, and said you thought I might like something of home." She looked at the pale liquid in her goblet as she smiled. "You were the only one who understood that I might be homesick, and I had never even spoken to you. How did you know?"

"I didn't. I only knew that if I was suddenly taken away from the only home I'd ever known, I would miss it terribly." Caol'nir dipped his finger in his goblet and stroked Alluria's lower lip with his damp fingertip, then bent to kiss her. "All I knew of the east was that their grapes are white, not red. If I had to do it again, I would bring you herbs instead."

"The wine was perfect," she said as she stifled a yawn.

"Are you tired?" he asked, and she nodded. "You may have the bed, I'll stay here."

Alluria raised her head, her brows peaked. "You don't want to share your bed with me?"

"I didn't think you'd want that."

"Well, now you know better," she said as she rose. Caol'nir quickly stood behind her, and then he swept her into his arms and carried her to the mound of furs. Alluria squealed as she twined her arms around his neck, and he murmured for her to be silent lest someone come to her rescue. Caol'nir sat on the edge of the sleeping platform, holding Alluria in his lap while avoiding her eyes.

"Is it true?" He asked; tradition dictated that if a man was so bold as to claim a priestess Olluhm would strike him dead before he completed the act.

"While I personally do not know, I can tell you that most priestesses are not nearly as chaste as they pretend to be."

Caol'nir raised an eyebrow, and she giggled. "Many here in Teg'urnan are certainly not virgins, regardless of whether they have been honored by our god."

"You mean to tell me that I, and my father and brothers, have dedicated our lives to keeping you women untouched, and we are failing miserably?"

Alluria nestled herself against his chest. "The incidents I know of have not happened here, under your watchful eye, but at the outlying temples. Why, Alyon has had many lovers."

"And you, fair maiden?"

"No man but you has ever interested me." She pulled the thick cable of hair over his shoulder and fingered the leather thong that bound it. "Do you not believe me?"

"I believe you," he replied softly, cradling her against his chest, "I love you, and I cherish you." Caol'nir kissed the top of her head and rubbed his cheek against her soft hair, drinking in her sweet, wildflower scent. Alluria's fingers migrated to the neck of his jerkin and traced the edge of the thick leather.

"Are you…going to…?" Her voice trailed off, leaving the question unfinished but her meaning clear.

"I can sleep in my clothing," he replied.

"Won't you be uncomfortable?"

"I'll be fine." Alluria tugged at the laces of his jerkin, twining the cords around her fingers.

"I liked the feel of your skin against mine," she said softly. Alluria turned her face up to his as he kissed her, and Caol'nir forgot that she was a priestess, only recognizing her as the woman he loved. He lay back on the furs as Alluria drew the cords free and parted the heavy leather.

"I wish…I wish I could share one night with you. Just one perfect night…" As Alluria's voice trailed off she touched his chest, then let her fingers travel to the hard muscles of his abdomen. Caol'nir arched his neck as he moaned; she had no idea that her gentle touch was driving him mad.

"I wish for the same," he said, his voice hoarse with wanting her. Emboldened by her words, Caol'nir ran his hands down her back, pausing to squeeze the swell of her hips. "You say Alyon has had many lovers?"

"And none are dead." Alluria placed her cheek against his chest and took a deep breath. "I've spoken to the High Priestess."

"About what, *nalla*?"

"About being released from my vows."

Caol'nir rubbed his eyes as he imagined Sarelle's stern, judgmental face as Alluria sought guidance. "What did she say?"

"That it can be done honorably."

He raised himself up on his elbows, his shock nearly outweighing his joy. "How?"

"I don't know yet. I am to go into the vaults; the information is contained within." She dropped her gaze. "I'll be sequestered for five days and five nights, beginning at second dawn."

"Tomorrow?" Caol'nir was not pleased about being separated from Alluria for five days; he had seen her, spoken to her, every day since she arrived in Teg'urnan. Now, when he finally knew that she loved him, he wouldn't see her for a small eternity.

"Tomorrow," Alluria confirmed.

"Why will it take you five days to find your answer? I thought the vaults were a sort of library, full of scrolls and such."

"One cannot just enter the vaults. I must be purified before I enter, and again after I leave." Alluria wrapped her arms around Caol'nir. "If I present my question, and the answer is no…"

"What will they do to you?"

"I may never petition to be released again."

"But you won't be harmed?" he asked, tracing her cheekbone with his thumb. "Tell me you'll be safe."

"Of course, they won't harm me," she replied. "I'm still the god's mate. To harm me would mean their deaths."

"Then this is not so bad," he said. "I'll be lost without you for five days, but you'll be returned to me soon enough. If the answer is no, we will remain as we have been, and I'll guard your sacred chastity until the end of my days."

"And… if it is yes?"

"Then you're mine."

Alluria speaks...

That night was indeed perfect, although not in the way I'd imagined. Nestled deep in the furs, Caol'nir rained kisses onto my face, my neck, my breast. He let me unbind his hair again, and I loved how it fell around us like a sun-colored curtain hiding us from the rest of the world. Even though I had no right, I prayed and prayed for that night to last forever, but all too soon the elder sun sent his rays to rouse us. I pressed my face against Caol'nir's neck and squeezed my eyes shut, willing the sun to halt.

"Alluria," he said softly. I hadn't thought he was awake.

"Another moment," I whispered, and he tightened his arms around me. I still hadn't told him what I truly feared: that if my request was denied I'd be forbidden from seeing him ever again. He didn't know Sarelle as I did; every resident of Teg'urnan saw her as the all-powerful High Priestess, favored by the gods to know and execute their will. I saw her for what she truly was: a cruel, vindictive woman who sought retribution rather than forgiveness. I clutched his arms as if he could be taken from me at any moment, and thus betrayed my thoughts.

"Tell me," was all he said, and my fears poured forth like a waterfall. He was silent as he stroked my hair, and when I finished he kissed my forehead. "That won't happen."

"How can you know?" I asked. "If Sarelle orders it, it will come to pass."

"If she orders such, I'll abduct you in the night and take you where we will never be found." He pulled me up so that my face was directly over his; I daresay he also enjoyed it when my hair fell around us. "Nothing will keep us apart, I swear it. Whether I spend my life as your mate or your guard, I will spend it with you."

I couldn't believe he said that, I couldn't believe how loyal he was...I couldn't believe he loved me that much. In that moment, my heart swelled near bursting and I kissed him with more fervor than I'd thought myself capable of. He returned it with his own passion, then held me for another all-too-brief moment.

As we readied ourselves for the walk back to the temple, I convinced him to leave his hair loose. At first, Caol'nir protested. Anyone who knew the legend (which was most of the palace, and certainly all of the con'dehr) would assume he'd claimed me, and he did not want me to suffer their idle gossip.

"Let them talk," I replied. "I'm the one going to my trial within the vaults, not them. If I want to hold the image of you as such in my heart over the next five days, I will."

Caol'nir frowned. "What if they try disgracing you, forcing you from temple?"

"Well, then, that will solve everything." His frown deepened, so I added, "Nall, please."

"You know I can't resist you when you call me that."

"I know," I replied, and we left his chamber.

Indeed, we were the recipients of a few startled glances as we walked side by side to the temple thanks to Caol'nir's wild mane of hair, and that he didn't stay the required two steps behind me. No one questioned us, and one look at

Caol'nir's face told me why: his jaw was set as if for battle, warning others to stay clear of our path.

Once we reached the temple, we entered through the southern door which represented knowledge, for knowledge was what I sought. Waiting for me was Atreynha, who had cared for me since I was a baby. I had steeled myself against Sarelle's inevitable presence, assuming she would greet me and oversee my purification. When I saw Atreynha's kind eyes, I nearly wept.

"Mother Priestess." I knelt at her feet, overcome with relief. Surely if Atreynha was there, nothing bad could come of this; surely she wouldn't let Sarelle take Caol'nir from me. She stroked my hair for a moment before she bade me to rise, and I followed her without question as she led me away. If Caol'nir had not spoken, I wouldn't have looked back.

"My lady," he began, "I'd like to accompany Alluria, as far as I may."

Atreynha glanced over her shoulder, not slowing her pace as she replied. "You will not be with her long. Come, warrior."

Atreynha led us to a small cell that adjoined the baths; I smelled the humid air, heavy with lavender, and knew that my first purification awaited me. Atreynha sat and I knelt at her feet while Caol'nir stood in the doorway. She spoke as if he wasn't there, first explaining the purification I needed to undergo, then what I would experience in the vaults. As she recited the third day's trial, Caol'nir interrupted her.

"No, Alluria," he said, so forcefully Atreynha was too startled to be offended. "I won't have you subject yourself to this, it's too much. Leave this room, remain a priestess, and I'll remain your guard."

"Caol'nir," I said, "I want to do this. I'll be all right."

Caol'nir's gaze moved from me to Atreynha. "Mother Priestess, have any entered the vaults and not returned?"

"Yes. Not often, but it has happened."

Caol'nir knelt before me and took my hand. "Mea nalla, I won't have you suffering, not for me, not for anything. I beg you not to do this."

I gazed into his green eyes, fraught with concern and fear, and overriding all other emotions, love. I knew that he'd remain with me for the rest of our lives regardless of whose mate I was. I also knew that as long as I wasn't truly his, neither of us would be happy.

"You think I won't be suffering if I spend my days mated to another? Do you think you wouldn't suffer?" I asked.

His gaze briefly returned to me, and for a moment, I thought he would protest again. Instead, he looked to Atreynha, and she replied to his silent question.

"Alluria is strong," she said softly, "much stronger than we ever thought she'd be. There is nothing in the vaults that can harm her. If she doesn't return, it will be of her own doing." She leaned forward and stroked Caol'nir's hair, much as she had stroked mine a moment before. "And you, young warrior, have answered many questions for me. I pleaded with Sarelle to let me prepare Alluria for her journey, my intent to question her resolve. Now I see that you are willing to forego your own happiness to keep her safe, and I'm confident that she has chosen well."

"I'd undertake this journey for her, if you'd only let me," he said.

"I know, my son," she replied, "but you will be judged in your own way."

At last I dared to look at Atreynha and saw her smiling at my beloved. To have her blessing for these trials meant so much to me.

"Thank you, Mother Priestess," I said.

Atreynha resumed her explanation of my coming travails and Caol'nir remained at my side, his hands clutching mine. When her recitation was complete, she rose and placed her hands on my head.

"Now that you know what your journey entails, are you still willing to undertake it?" Atreynha asked.

"Yes, Mother Priestess."

She smiled her familiar, kind smile that made the corners of her eyes crinkle, and motioned for us to rise. She bade me to follow her. Caol'nir automatically fell into step beside me. "No, warrior," Atreynha said, "you've come as far as you may. The purification is for Alluria alone."

Caol'nir nodded, then asked, "May I say goodbye?"

"Of course," she replied, bowing her head. He cupped my face with his hands and murmured that he loved me, that he would continue to love me no matter what the result of this trial may be. Then to my sheer and utter amazement he kissed me, right there in front of the Mother Priestess! It was not a chaste kiss on the back of my hand. Caol'nir pressed his lips to mine as if I hadn't been adorned in the sacred robes of a virgin priestess. And I, I kissed him back.

"I love you," I murmured once we parted, and he kissed my forehead.

"Forgive me, Mother Priestess." He gazed at her over the top of my head. Atreynha's only response was to touch my elbow. I left my beloved and followed the Mother Priestess to the baths.

Atreynha prepared me herself, not allowing a single novice to touch me. She was silent as she removed my robes and adornments, then she bound my hair in a loose braid. I nearly wept as she tied off the end, remembering Caol'nir's heavy blond cable. As I stood before her, she poured blessed oil over my head and shoulders, then scrubbed me raw with salt. Finally, she bade me enter the bath. I did, and as I submerged myself in the scalding water I wondered if the oppressive heat was intended to make me welcome the cold air of the vaults.

Neither of us spoke during the purification, which was repeated six times with various oils and abrasives. When I was led to the final bath, I noticed it was steeped with chamomile and the water was tepid, a moment's comfort before my hardships began.

"The elder sun will soon rest," Atreynha said and she held out a length of soft linen. "You will descend soon."

I merely nodded as I rose and accepted the linen. I patted dry my raw skin and wrapped the fabric about myself and sat as Atreynha combed out my hair.

"Are you angry with me?" I asked, unable to look her in the eye.

"Why would I be?"

"For turning my back on you." Atreynha was the one who had always cared for me, the one who had been there for me when even my own mother had gone, and now I was leaving her and all she had taught me.

"I think you're doing nothing of the sort," she replied, then bent to pick at a tangle. "Life within the temple is difficult in ways that others can hardly imagine, and it is not for everyone. Just because you were born in a temple does not mean you need to reside in one for your entire life." She was silent for long moments while she ran her fingers through my damp hair. "I think that love is a gift from the gods, and we merely serve their will. If they have decreed that Caol'nir is your soul's true mate, who am I to dispute their wisdom?"

"Caol'nir's brother told him something very similar," I mused.

Atreynha laughed softly, then came around to face me. "Child, I love you as if you were born of my own body, and I know you better than anyone. Well, anyone except your warrior." My cheeks grew hot and I ducked my head, but she turned my chin to face her. "I also believe that you must love him very much to attempt this, as he must love you very much to risk kissing you right in front of me." For the first time that day, I smiled, and Atreynha smoothed back my hair. "If nothing else, you deserve a chance to be happy. Now come."

She held out a rough garment of undyed wool, as shapeless as it was uncomfortable, all I was allowed to wear. Once it was about my shoulders, she took my hand and led me down a long corridor until we stood at the mouth of the steps that disappeared into darkness. Atreynha murmured a quick blessing as she squeezed my hand, and I descended to the most sacred spot in Parthalan.

Chapter 11

Lormac stood atop the battlement as dawn broke over the mountain range called the World's Spine. Spread out upon the plain before the keep was the *Ish h'ra hai*, and Lormac enjoyed watching Asherah walk among her people. During the past moons Lormac had hosted the *Ish h'ra hai*, her daily walk had become something of a ritual, so much so that many now lined her regular path. As Asherah made her way about the encampment, asking how one was faring, offering a few reassuring words to another, her regal bearing once again impressed the Lord of Tingu.

Someone, somewhere has taught her the art of leadership. He noted how she rallied those around her, how her eloquent speech both calmed and inspired her followers. Lormac was reminded of his youth and of the many hours he sat at his father's knee, learning how to present himself, how to speak in such a way that people hung on his every word and would clamor to follow him. Lormac wondered if Asherah undergone a similar tutelage, and who'd been the teacher.

Her.

The word rumbled through Lormac's mind, heard not with his ears but deep within his being. Lormac absently rubbed the Sala, the silver armband set with green stones that marked him as Lord of Tingu, and wished he could quiet the nagging urges it manifested in him. While the elf king readily admitted, albeit only to himself, that he was somewhat captivated by Asherah, he had no intention of taking matters any further. He was Lord of Tingu, a larger and more ancient land than Parthalan, and he would not let his emotions be swayed by one lone fae. It didn't bother him that she was once enslaved; in fact, her escape and subsequent leadership of the *Ish h'ra hai* only increased his opinion of her. But, if Lormac was to contemplate taking a mate, the woman should be an elf.

Not that Asherah wouldn't be a worthy mate. In addition to watching her morning walks, Lormac had also observed Asherah as she practiced swordplay. She had little in the way of formal training, but she fought with an innate speed and grace. Such was her skill that Lormac wondered if she had once been a member of Parthalan's legion.

Trust the fae to make their women into warriors. Elfin women had long ago ceased to be warriors, save for a few with hereditary titles such as the Lady of Thurnda. Elves counted it among their strengths that their prowess in battle was such they could leave fully half of their numbers behind and still be victorious. Of course, if faeries fought as well as elves they could also leave their women safe at home.

Lormac returned his gaze to the faerie below and was certain that Asherah wouldn't suffer a man to leave her next to the hearth. In fact, after her first night in the keep he hadn't seen her in another gown, despite the many he sent. In truth, Asherah needed no finery to enhance her appearance. He watched her move, enjoying the way her lithe muscles stretched like a cat stalking its prey. Lormac wondered if maybe faeries had it right, that a woman warrior might be a source of untold pleasures.

Her.

Lormac shook his head and willed the Sala to silence, at least for the time being, and summoned Asherah. By the time he had unrolled the maps in his chamber, Asherah joined him.

"My riders have returned," Lormac began, forgoing a greeting, "and your claims have been confirmed. We may now discuss what kind of assistance you're expecting of me."

"What sort of assistance you will offer?" Asherah asked. "You've already done so much, and I don't want you to compromise your people."

"I may not have a choice," Lormac replied. "While I have no wish to war with Sahlgren, I am afraid that the situation is far worse than you described, or than I imagined." He leaned over a long table and pushed a map toward Asherah. "The blue marks were made by Harek, but I want you to make note of the black marks."

"There are many," Asherah said as she scanned the parchment. The map was of not only Parthalan, but also the elflands and the dark fae. The markings were abundant throughout. "What do they signify?"

"Dojas."

The blood drained from Asherah's face. Her hand trembled as she ran her fingertips across the map. "There are hundreds."

"Yes. In some regions, such as the west and the south of Parthalan, entire villages have been emptied." Lormac eyed her for a moment. "I've also learned that the demons only want those of pure blood, no mixed races. Do you know why?"

Asherah shook her head, still staring at the map. "So we're all pureblooded."

"What?" Lormac asked. Asherah kept her attention on the map, which so agitated Lormac he grabbed her chin and turned her face to his. "You act as though you do not know you own heritage."

Asherah knocked his hand away. "Don't touch me like that."

Lormac remembered the scars on her wrist. "Forgive me, I acted without thinking." When she nodded, he said, "Answer my question. Do you know your heritage?"

Asherah stared at him for a moment, her eyes burning with indignation. "I do not," she ground out.

Lormac's brows knitting together as he contemplated this new layer to the enigma of Asherah. "Leave us," he ordered, and his varied attendants filed out of the chamber. "How is that possible?"

"My earliest memory is of being taken by the *mordeth*. I remember sitting at a table—or maybe before a hearth—then this great beast burst in and grabbed me. My next memory is of waking in my cell alongside Torim." Asherah wrapped her arms around her waist and crossed the room to the window. She leaned upon the frame and gazed toward the *Ish h'ra hai*. "If I concentrate I can almost see who I was with, almost remember their faces…but almost only takes you so far, doesn't it?"

Lormac leaned upon the opposite side of the window and reached for her hands; this time, she let him. "That's your only memory of your time before the doja?"

"Yes," she replied, then shook her head. "No. I…I remember many things, but nothing important. I shouldn't trouble you with my ramblings."

"You're not troubling me," he assured. "I want to know."

Asherah glanced at his face, and then resumed staring out the window. "Well, I remember how to walk and ride and speak. I can speak the old language as though I studied it for many years. I can wield a sword with a measure of skill. What I don't know is how I learned these things. Did my father teach me swordplay? Did my mother teach me *ahm'ri*?" She continued staring out the window, her gaze focused far beyond the faerie camp. "It's as if I'm a book and someone has ripped out the important pages. No, they made me a blank page, filled with nothing but emptiness."

"Then the only life you have ever known is that of slave or fugitive." Lormac traced her cheekbone. "How do you find the strength to go on?" Asherah stepped back, out of his reach.

"I cannot let this happen to others," she replied. "If I don't stop him, who will?" Fire leapt in the dark depths of her eyes, and while Lormac couldn't be certain of her noble blood, it was her strength of character, her conviction to protect others that made him want to discard his crown and follow Asherah to the very edges of this realm and beyond.

Her.

Lormac no longer willed the Sala to silence; instead, he acknowledged his desire for Asherah, for the Sala's urges were merely a reflection of the king's own. There was a noise below; as Asherah looked toward her people Lormac saw a scar against her hairline. This further evidence of what she had endured strengthened his conviction, and Lormac grabbed her hands and drew her close.

"I will," Lormac declared, his voice raw with emotion. "No elf or faerie will be so treated, not if I can prevent it, and Sahlgren must be made to pay for his crimes. Who better to bring the fae king to justice than an elf?" he added with a wry grin. Asherah returned his smile, and Lormac realized that she had doubted his aid.

Very well, he thought, I will prove to her that an elf's word is law. He was about to swear an oath, proclaiming him her savior just as she had saved her followers, when Asherah again glanced to the camp. Several individuals had noticed the king and Asherah speaking, their faces as close as lovers, and were intently watching the two. Lormac had quite forgotten that they were in front of the window. She stepped back and out of his reach, and the Sala protested their lack of contact.

No! rumbled the voice in Lormac's mind, so loudly his head throbbed. He winced at the sudden pain and rubbed his eyes as one would do after drinking too much rum, when he felt a soft touch against his forehead and the pain vanished.

"My lord, are you unwell?"

Lormac opened his eyes, and saw that Asherah had placed her hand alongside his temple, her face a mask of concern. Her simple touch had ended his pain as if it had never existed.

Her, the Sala claimed smugly. *Mine.*

"I'm fine," Lormac assured. He grabbed her hand, holding it before him as he continued. "My lady, will you accept my offer of aid?"

"Of course, my lord," Asherah replied in that same formal tone, smiling so brightly her dark eyes sparkled. Lormac kissed her hand, and tried not to notice how uncomfortable it made her.

"Then it is settled," he said. "We will journey to the Seat of Tingu. I'll have Aldo determine what you'll need."

"I have a request to make of you, my lord."

"Another?" he asked, though he didn't mind her requests. He would relocate the World's Spine if Asherah asked it of him.

"Please stop sending me dresses."

Lormac's brows peaked. "You don't like them?"

"Each has been more beautiful that the last, and I appreciate them all. However, if we're going to war I need to dress as a warrior should, not like a pretty maiden studying embroidery or the harp. I'm afraid your elfin custom of wrapping women in bright colors and using them to adorn your halls like so many gems is not for one such as I."

Lormac chuckled; here she was, worried that she had offended him, when her statement had pleased him beyond measure. "Any other woman would be thrilled with gowns and jewels, but not Asherah. Very well, my lady, no more finery." Lormac strode to the door and summoned a *saffira*, instructing them to retrieve riding gear for Asherah.

"My lord, I did not mean you needed to replace what you have offered me," Asherah said, but he chuckled again.

"I'm not offended," said the king, "but you will need the gear. We will leave on the morrow for the Seat of Tingu. I'll summon my lords to the Seat, and we will plan what's to be done next."

"How long will it take to reach the Seat?"

"Three days, if the weather holds." He observed her expression, and answered her unasked question. "I've never marched with an army of fae, but I imagine it will take your *Ish h'ra hai* at least ten days, possibly longer. I'll leave a contingent to guard your followers and guide the way."

"I'll travel with them," Asherah proclaimed.

"No." Lormac watched Asherah's eyes flame, but she held her tongue. "Asherah, I'm doing this on your word. You will accompany me." His tone made it evident that he was issuing an order, not making a request.

"As you wish, my lord."

Asherah speaks...

Despite Lormac's insistence that he and I should travel on ahead, we all made the journey together. The logistics of splitting up the king's guard, half to escort him while the other half made the much slower march alongside the Ish h'ra hai proved more troublesome than Lormac had anticipated.

And so we marched across the semi-frozen plains and mountains. When I commented that we might have made better time if we had waited for the spring thaw, Lormac laughed. He said that the cold and snow were something you learned to appreciate when you lived in the north, not things to be avoided. He went on to say that if I remained in Tingu long enough, I'd grow to enjoy the cold just as much as an elf.

The march took twelve long, cold, wet days. To his credit, Lormac never once chided me for declining his offer of the two of us traveling on ahead, even though my miserable state was plain to see. He understood that I couldn't leave my people behind, my Ish h'ra hai, not even for a few days, since all we had was each other.

Every morning, I rode among them as they readied themselves for the coming march, breaking down their tents and rolling up their bedding, and every morning I was amazed by their fortitude. While I knew that they must have hated the journey as much as I, not one of them complained (at least not within my hearing), and we all trudged on to our goal of the Seat of Tingu, the ancestral home of the elves.

Lormac remained cloistered with his commanders for the first few days, and I saw precious little of him. On the fourth evening, I received an invitation to sup in the king's tent, delivered personally by his saffira-nell, *who made sure I understood that the invitation was for me alone.*

"Torim may not come?" I asked.

"My lady, I assure you that she will be well fed in your absence," Aldo replied, and so I readied myself to dine with the king.

After a minor wardrobe crisis, which involved me searching through my trunk and wondering if I should wear one of the dresses I so disliked, to which Torim told me I was being foolish and Harek called me something slightly more colorful, I arrived at Lormac's tent wearing the cleanest riding gear I possessed. I was surprised to find him alone with the makings of a feast.

"Do you always eat so well while traveling?" I asked upon my entry.

"Of course," he replied with a smirk. "Actually, the table is set for my commanders and me, but I sent them away for the evening."

"Why?"

"They distract me, and I wish to give you my full attention," he replied. Lormac didn't expand on his statement, and after a moment I joined him at the table.

"I've seen you walk among your people every morning," he continued. "You rally their spirits. You inspire them to go on, even after such horrible experiences as they, and you, have endured." He leaned toward me, searching my face.

"I ask you again, my lady, how do you find the strength to continue?"

"I'm not strong," I replied. "Far from it." I meant to continue, but memories chose that moment to well up in my mind. Memories of burning pain and fear and starvation. Trying to distract myself, I looked to the food spread before me and saw a plate of roasted meat. The memories the smell evoked were even worse, and I almost retched right there at the king's table. Instead, I got to my feet and walked away from the table.

"What's wrong?" Lormac demanded.

"Nothing," I replied, but my voice wavered with the lie. Lormac was suddenly behind me, so I elaborated, *"The meat, the smell of it reminds me of...things."*

Lormac didn't ask what I was reminded of, but summoned an attendant to clear away each and every morsel of meat. Once the stench of flesh was gone, I took a deep breath, and vowed never to consume meat again.

"You didn't need to do that," I said in spite of my silent oath. *"What will you eat?"*

"Something else," he replied. We returned to the table and he poured wine into my goblet, then filled his plate with assorted fruits.

"You're very kind." I stared at the table.

"You amaze me more every day." His compliment caused me to look up. *"You're like no woman I've ever encountered. You don't want gowns and gems, preferring instead leather tunics and boots. You turn away the finest foods, you refuse to let my healers cosset you—"* I hadn't known he was aware of my refusing to let his healers examine me, but I was loathe to disrobe, even for them *"—and rather than travel at the king's side, you march along with the masses."* Lormac leaned forward and when he continued, the teasing tone was gone from his voice. *"I will admit, Asherah, I don't quite know what to make of you."*

The rest of our meal was passed amicably, with Lormac being polite enough to pretend that I hadn't ruined his dinner. I surreptitiously studied his face while we ate. Lormac wasn't what you would call a handsome man, far from it in fact. His eyes were set a bit too deeply beneath his brow, his nose and chin jutted out a bit too far, and he was taller than any elf should be. Yet, despite his flaws, or perhaps because of them, I found it difficult to look away. Perhaps it was his innate charisma that I was noticing; perhaps it was his kind and generous nature that was plain for anyone to see.

"Asherah?"

That roused me from my contemplation of his features. "Yes?"

"Is there something you wish to ask me?"

I fixed my eyes on my plate and examined the remains of a pomegranate. "I was wondering how you procured such fresh fruit this late in the season." I couldn't care less where the king obtained his fruits!

Lormac, not fooled by my ruse, laughed deep in his chest. "If you'd like, I'll have a basket of them waiting for you in your room at The Seat."

"Thank you, my lord, but that won't be necessary." I didn't even like pomegranates, with their many seeds crammed into pithy compartments. Blissfully, Lormac let the issue drop and our conversation returned to the much more pressing matter of our journey to the Seat.

Eventually, I retired for the evening. When Torim and I emerged the next morning, we found Lormac waiting outside our tent, wearing the most ridiculous cloak I had ever seen. It was brown and coarse, so much so that I assumed it was caked with dried mud but no, that was how it was supposed to look. He merely smiled when I commented upon it, which I felt I had the right to do since he had spent the better part of the prior evening criticizing my taste in riding gear.

Then he made a request of me. "Perhaps you'll allow me to walk among your followers with you."

And so we slogged through the mud, the redeemed slave upon the king's arm. At least half of the fae didn't recognize Lormac, while those who did dropped to their knees in supplication. Lormac tried to keep as many out of the mud as he could, and he helped to dry off those who were too quick in their praise of our benefactor. As he walked among them, helping break down their tents, pack up bedrolls—once I even caught him stirring a cooking pot—he proved to the fae that he thought himself no different than they, regardless of his noble birth.

Once fae and elf alike were prepared to march onward, Lormac made another request of me: would I consent to ride at his side?

"I believe it will hearten your people to see their Asherah riding at the head of our procession," he explained. "Also, this fight now belongs to elf as well as faerie; should we not approach it together?" His tone was jovial, but his gray eyes implored me to accept.

We mounted up and made our way to the front of the procession, the mud sucking at the horses' hooves. While I wondered how long we would be able to travel before we would need to stop, Lormac called out to me.

"We may have a dry day," he said, indicating the parting clouds. "It is too late to help overmuch today, but with any luck the roads will improve tomorrow."

As I watched the elder sun's rays break through the gray haze, and then the child sun follow suit, I smiled. Yes, things would be better; I was free, Torim was free, all those behind me were free. Surely better days lay ahead.

Chapter 12

It was a lovely day, the air crisp with winter's promise, birds singing in defiance of the coming cold. Caol'nir didn't notice any of it as he wandered throughout Teg'urnan, ignoring his assigned tasks. His beloved was sequestered in the vaults for the second day, and he could think of nothing else. Atreynha's descriptions of the trials which Alluria would undertake rang in his ears. He should have forbidden her from the vaults, pleaded with Atreynha to dissuade her; hells, he should have grabbed Alluria and forcibly removed her from the temple.

Caol'nir uttered a short, mirthless laugh as he gazed at the sky. His restless feet had brought him to the northern tower, and he leaned against the crenellated edge. *How can I have let her do this?* He cursed himself, cursed his oaths and the *con'dehr*, but stopped before he cursed the gods themselves. Alluria had been confident that she would find a way for them to be together honorably. Caol'nir hoped she was right.

He smiled, imagining a home all but overrun with his and Alluria's children, sobering when he realized what a far-off dream that was. Caol'nir turned to watch his ancestor, Solon, ascend skyward in the guise of the child sun, and asked for guidance.

His prayer complete, Caol'nir ran his and over the stone battlement, and wondered if the vaults were made of the same stone. He doubted it, and imagined Alluria kneeling on a rough floor of packed dirt while she shivered.

Maybe if I speak with Atreynha she will halt Alluria's trial. Maybe I'll just follow her into the vaults and retrieve her myself. Caol'nir spun about but stopped short when he saw Rahlle standing an arm's length from him.

"To enter the vaults unpurified is not advisable," Rahlle opined.

Caol'nir stared at the sorcerer, wondering how long he had been standing there, how Rahlle knew what he was thinking, if he knew how to help Alluria. Before Caol'nir could give voice to his questions, Rahlle spoke again.

"The floor is stone, not dirt, and while it is cold she'll not freeze to death." Rahlle moved to stand next to Caol'nir and gazed across the northern plain. "Alluria will return to you unharmed."

"You know much of the ways of the temple?"

"More than I ought."

Caol'nir realized that the Rahlle might be the only one who had the means to discover who—or what—had visited the temple the night of Ethnia's death. "Master Sorcerer, do you know what happened in the temple recently?"

Rahlle turned to the warrior. "You speak of the girl who claims she was taken by a man, and of the girl that was killed." Caol'nir nodded, and Rahlle bowed his head. He was silent for so long that Caol'nir didn't know if Rahlle was contemplating his answer or if he had forgotten what they were speaking of. "The girl who claimed a man came to her spoke true. As for the other, it was likely a demon that killed her, possibly even a *mordeth*."

The words shocked Caol'nir; a man entering the sacred space without leave was blasphemy enough, but a demon set loose in the Great Temple was a horror beyond reckoning. "Is Alluria in danger?"

"No, no, she's alone in the vaults. Neither man nor demon can reach her."

Caol'nir exhaled a great sigh. "How could a man enter the temple after nightfall? Sarelle seals the doors at night, and they remain so until morning."

Rahlle attended the brocade trim of his sleeve before replying. "You've been told that the four doors of the compass are the only entrances," he said at length. "There is another."

All temples had four entrances, no more, no less, in honor of how the fair folk came to be. Olluhm came from the east and carried Cydia to where they lay together in the west. Once Cydia was heavy with child, she went to the north to gain the knowledge to teach her firstborn of the world he would inherit, then to the south to gain the strength to bear him. Anything different would negate the temple's sacred geometry; a fifth entrance not only made the Great Temple vulnerable to intruders but also compromised the integrity of the space.

"It was through this entrance that a man came and violated Keena," Caol'nir stated, but he received no acknowledgement from Rahlle. *What if that man had taken Alluria instead? And demons—what if they had entered Alluria's cell?* Caol'nir regarded the ancient fae before him, and asked his next question. "My lord, you say Ethnia was killed by a *mordeth*?"

"Oh, it was most certainly a demon," Rahlle said as if a demon walking the halls of Teg'urnan was a normal occurrence. "I mention *mordeths* because of the way the girl died. The warlords are, shall we say, rather more intense than the lesser demons."

"How could a demon make its way to the temple? It would need to pass the gate, pass the guards… hells, it would need to pass everyone in Teg'urnan." Caol'nir had never felt so distraught. His beloved had never been safe; she had slept near rapists and demons alike. Rahlle turned his grey eyes, wild and churning like a gathering storm, to the warrior, and Caol'nir spied a measure of calm amongst the madness.

"A portal." The clouds in Rahlle's eyes shifted, as if lightning had struck its mark. "The king, he has invited these things into our home."

Caol'nir was nearly struck dumb. The great King Sahlgren was a living legend amongst his kind for deeds performed near three millennia past, when Parthalan had been overrun by demons, Teg'urnan lost to the *mordeth-gall*. Sahlgren had rallied the gentle fae to become warriors, much as Solon had once done, and drove the monsters back to the underworld. If Rahlle was to be believed, Sahlgren had committed the ultimate betrayal.

"Why?" demanded Caol'nir.

"He seeks power, more than the gods have bestowed upon him, more than I can provide." Rahlle paused for a moment, his voice hardly more than a whisper when he continued. "He would gladly trade us all for such power."

"What does he mean to accomplish with such power?" Caol'nir asked. Sahlgren was stronger than any prior king of Parthalan, and Caol'nir couldn't imagine a prize so great that he acted in collusion with demons.

"He seeks to conquer," Rahlle said, then made a quick gesture with his hands. Before him an ethereal globe appeared, then eight more orbited it. "He seeks to conquer all the nine realms. We fae cannot freely cross the veils that separate our worlds, as we are bound to our gods. Demons, however, are bound to none and may cross as they will." Rahlle laughed shortly. "Olluhm saw to that when he cast the old gods from the sky."

A memory of the first winter he spent at the southern outpost burst across Caol'nir's mind. The wind had blown unusually cold one morning, and while Caol'nir had known that demons preferred the cold, he hadn't known that the chill air would make them appear in droves. His outpost had been besieged for many days, the white sands blackened by their foul blood. He looked to the swirling orbs before Rahlle and imagined such carnage spread across not only Parthalan, but all of existence.

"If you know what he is about, why don't you stop him?" Caol'nir asked. It was known far and wide that Rahlle was the most powerful sorcerer to ever live, his abilities matched only by the gods. It was Rahlle's great power that created the oaths faeries swore to each other when they bound their souls, pledged their swords to the service of the king, and vowed to mate themselves with a god.

Or, in Rahlle's case, pledged to support and serve the ruler of Parthalan.

"I cannot overtly work against him," Rahlle replied. "I do what I may, but it is not enough. You must help with the rest."

Caol'nir stared at the central orb, representative of the world he lived in…the world he wanted to share with Alluria. "How can I stop him?"

"Tomorrow, the king leaves for the south. Follow him. When you've learned all you need, go north to the elflands. There, you will find those who will remove him."

Caol'nir accepted his charge and swore to do whatever was necessary to ensure Alluria's safety. If her safety involved the death of the king, so be it. Rahlle called upon the gods to bless Caol'nir's coming journey, for he would certainly need it, then the mad sorcerer faded from view. Caol'nir looked to the child sun, who by now had moved far from his zenith, and wondered if Solon had heard his plea.

Just as Solon had never acted without first obtaining the blessing of his father, Caol'nir descended from the tower and made his way to the Prelate's chamber. His determined stride dissuaded all from approaching him. He had no interest in the petty concerns of others, not when the safety of not only his beloved, but all of Parthalan hung in the balance. Caol'nir entered the room without knocking, though that was a privilege not even Tor's son could claim.

Caol'nir found the Prelate involved in a meeting with three men. Two were lords from the west currently involved in a dispute with the dark fae, and Caol'nir didn't recognize the third. All eyes turned toward Caol'nir, the lords aghast at the disturbance.

"Is something amiss?" Tor inquired, his tone betraying his annoyance.

"Yes," was Caol'nir's simple reply. What Caol'nir was about to say bordered upon high treason and meant for his father's ears alone.

Tor dismissed the three, then he glared at his son. "Given your behavior I'm assuming this is a matter of much importance."

"I've just left Rahlle's company," Caol'nir said. "He told me that there is a fifth entrance to the Great Temple, through which both men and demons have violated the sisters and made fools of the *con'dehr*."

His father appeared neither surprised nor outraged. Instead, he seemed well aware of the situation. "Caol'nir, sit and we will discuss this. There are things I need to explain to you."

"You knew of this," Caol'nir accused. "You knew that a man had taken Keena. That a demon had killed Ethnia, and yet you said nothing."

"I only know of the fifth entrance," Tor replied. "It's called the King's Door. As for Ethnia, I examined her cell myself. A demon could have been responsible, but I don't know how one lone creature could have breached every defense we have."

"And what of the girl who claimed she was taken by a man?" Caol'nir demanded.

"That man is the king." Caol'nir stared at his father in shock, and Tor continued, "Son, it has ever been this way; either Olluhm chooses to honor a priestess or sends the king in his stead."

"I've never heard of this custom."

"Sahlgren was once rarely summoned to the task, but Olluhm no longer honors the sisters as he once did."

"They why do the sisters still perform the summoning rites?" Caol'nir asked. "Seems like a waste of time if they know Olluhm won't appear."

"Only I, the king and Sarelle are aware of this," Tor replied. "Sarelle thought it best to not let all of Parthalan know that our god finds his pleasure elsewhere."

"Alluria was right," Caol'nir murmured. "Olluhm has forsaken us. How long has he been absent from the Great Temple?"

"Many winters," Tor gravely replied. "Sarelle believes that Cydia has again allowed him to share her bed, but the king believes the god has found love elsewhere."

"And you?"

"I don't presume to know the heart of a god."

"When we heard the sisters' concerns, when Caol'non and I drove Sarelle mad examining the temple for evidence of intruders, you dismissed us because you knew it had been the king!"

"Yes."

"Then why didn't you say something?" Caol'nir demanded. "Why didn't Sarelle send for you? And the sisters, they do *not* know that the one who honors them may not be the god they're mated to!" Caol'nir's fury had gotten the better of him, and without realizing it he had leapt to his feet. "Forgive me, Father," he muttered as he sat.

"Which priestess told you a man was coming to their beds?" Tor asked.

"I told you, Keena."

"I did not ask which girl suffered. Who told you?"

"Alluria." Caol'nir raised his head and met the Prelate's gaze; his outrage had taken him far past Tor's ability to intimidate. "After Keena told Alluria of her ordeal, Alluria confided to Caol'non and me. That was what, three moons ago? I had assumed she was a scared girl. Now, one has been killed—under our very noses, she was killed—and I wish I'd paid her more heed."

"Then Alluria does remain untouched."

"By man, god, and king, yes." Caol'nir leaned back in his chair and rubbed his eyes. "It doesn't seem right, the king visiting the sisters. It's a breach of their trust." He again fixed his gaze on his father. "If I had a mate, I'd not send another man to get her with child."

"Caol'nir, what would you have me do?" Tor asked. "Forbid Sahlgren from entering the Great Temple, which is his right as king? When my father was Prelate, and his father before him, this custom existed. What right do we have to question it?"

"Perhaps it should have been questioned long ago," Caol'nir said. "Father, do you know of a portal in the Great Temple?"

"I do not. I only know of the four compass entrances and the King's Door, which is hidden to all but Sahlgren."

"Something very wrong is happening in the temple." Caol'nir rose to his feet. Now that Caol'nir knew of the king's deceptions, he needed proof of Rahlle's other claims. "And I plan to stop it."

Once he had extracted a promise from Caol'non to guard Alluria in his absence, Caol'nir and his horse spent a cold night on the eastern foothills, waiting for King Sahlgren to depart. He didn't allow himself the luxury of a small fire; his anger kept him both alert and warm. If what Rahlle said was true, if the king had somehow allowed demons entry into the temple…

He shook his head, unsure if he wanted to prove the sorcerer's allegations true or false. What really he wanted was to speak with Alluria, partake of her wise counsel, and ask her if the king really did visit the priestesses at Olluhm's behest. He considered asking Atreynha, but that would risk sending the temple and all of Teg'urnan into an uproar. If Caol'nir were wrong, he would surely lose his head. No, better he follow Sahlgren and learn for himself, then he could relay what he learned to his father and ask for guidance.

The moon had just set when the king's procession passed through the iron gates. *If they aren't doing anything wrong, why are they leaving under cover of darkness?* Usually, when Sahlgren ventured forth from Teg'urnan he was accompanied by a good deal of fanfare, sometimes even a feast. As Caol'nir watched them travel down the royal road he realized that this was the king's third trip south in as many moons, and wondered why. Most avoided the region, because it was where the *mordeth-gall* was rumored to reside.

Caol'nir forced himself to think on something else, and felt more than a little foolish as he shivered upon the small hill. He had worked himself into such a state he was ready to believe Rahlle's ramblings over the slightest evidence. He pulled his cloak close and watched the procession until they were out of view, then he mounted his horse and pursued.

For two days Caol'nir shadowed the king. He kept himself well out of sight until the third morning, when he crested a hill and saw the royal camp spread out in the valley below. Quickly he backtracked, and once he had seen to his horse Caol'nir began the long process of watching, and waiting. Nary a soul entered or left the camp for the remainder of the day, and Caol'nir wondered if the king was merely enjoying a royal whim. When night fell, Caol'nir's patience was rewarded.

Torches were lit as the child sun went to rest, outlining a walkway to the king's tent. A hush descended over the bustling camp as Sahlgren emerged. Others were approaching from the south, and Caol'nir nearly cried out when he saw them.

Striding toward King Sahlgren was Ehkron.

Ehkron!

Ehkron, the reigning *mordeth-gall* and sworn enemy of the fae, the demon that had killed Caol'nir's grandsire, was welcomed by the king as an honored guest. Fae and demon entered the tent together, and the king's private guard stood watch.

Caol'nir rolled onto his back and stared at the sky, his blood beating in his ears. Tor had confirmed that the king had his own entrance into the temple; if he could enter, then a demon could as well. He thought of Keena, how she had claimed her experience left her bloody and hurt, how he had dismissed her. He thought of Ethnia, a priestess he hardly knew who'd been torn to shreds within her cell. And he thought of Alluria, who had narrowly avoided such fates.

As Caol'nir thought of his beloved, he realized that she would emerge from the vaults that morning, and he was two days south of the palace. As he lay beneath the stars, he remembered the night they'd shared, his arms wrapped around her as he finally had said everything he'd wanted to say. He could still feel her against him: her soft lips exploring his neck, her shy glance when she unlaced his jerkin. He was careful with his hands, but she didn't protest as he stroked her neck, her back. She moved toward him as his hand crept up her thigh…

Caol'nir woke; he'd been dreaming of making love to Alluria. Frustrated, he groaned, an emotion echoed by his swollen shaft, and gritted his teeth as he rolled onto his side. The king's camp was quiet, the torches having burned low. Light still emanated from the oiled silk tent Sahlgren occupied. Caol'nir could not determine if the *mordeth-gall* remained, but he had learned all he needed. Rahlle had been correct; their king had invited the enemy into their home. As Caol'nir mounted his horse and rode toward Teg'urnan, he hoped he could find a way to stop him.

Chapter 13

Alluria crept up the frigid, dark stairs from the vaults, shivering and starving but also elated. She had the answer she sought: she could depart Olluhm's service honorably. She stumbled as she ascended the stone steps, her feet long since numb. Two novices appeared and helped her to the bathing chamber. Once inside, Alluria breathed deeply of the humid air as the girls removed the woolen shift from her shoulders, and led her to a pool filled with steaming water with petals strewn across the surface. Alluria sank into the water, enjoying the warmth after kneeling against hard stone.

The older of the novices, a soft-spoken girl called Serinha, quietly moved about the chamber lighting incense, while the younger girl, whose name Alluria did not know, rubbed a salve into her chilled hands. Once the incense permeated the air, Serinha drew Alluria's feet from the water and rubbed a separate ointment into the chilblains on her soles. Alluria leaned back against the stone basin and wondered if they were going to bring her any food, and contemplated eating the flowers floating atop the bathwater.

No sooner had Alluria formed the thoughts when she heard the rustle of heavy silks; Sarelle had entered the chamber. The High Priestess carried a golden ewer and a plate of fruit, along with her usual air of displeasure.

"Leave," Sarelle commanded, and the novices silently disappeared. Alluria said nothing as Sarelle sat on the edge of the bath, unsure why the High Priestess was really there.

Sarelle was loathe to complete any task she considered beneath her, including the offer of comfort to another, even one who'd recently been in the company of the gods.

"Well?" Sarelle asked as she filled a goblet and handed it to Alluria. "Tell me what transpired." Alluria drained the goblet, learning too late that it was not water the High Priestess offered but a strong brandy.

"I'm able to leave the sisterhood with honor," Alluria rasped, the brandy having burnt a path down her throat. "But it won't be simple."

"Things worth having rarely are," Sarelle observed.

Alluria proceeded to describe what she had learned during her confinement, all the while struggling to keep her emotions in check. Despite her many years of training, Alluria's austere mask cracked when she mentioned Caol'nir.

"You have a natural talent for magic, near to Rahlle's own gifts," Sarelle said. "Why leave it behind for this boy? Is he worth all this trouble?"

Alluria considered the past days she'd spent alone in the cold and dark, of the aches she was just now feeling as the warm water thawed her frozen limbs, and admitted to herself that this was indeed a lot of trouble. She had a secure existence within the temple, where her needs were met and she was able to indulge her passions for spellcraft and herbals. Her life was comfortable, and there was no reason to change it.

Her thoughts turned to Caol'nir, how he always went out of his way to make her happy, either by simply bringing wine or risking everything to smuggle her outside the palace. During the last night of her confinement, by far the most arduous, Alluria had thought the still, soundless vaults would either kill her or drive her mad. Then the very thought of Caol'nir's smiling face, his kind eyes, his gentle touch, gave her the courage to go on.

"Yes," Alluria replied, "he is worth this, and more."

Sarelle soon took her leave. Alluria endured six additional baths, and while each was far more pleasant that those just five days prior, Alluria wished for their end. Once the baths were done and Alluria was allowed to robe herself, she was given sliced melon drenched with honey, the same food Olluhm had once fed Cydia when she was heavy with child; legend claimed that Olluhm fed sweet foods to his beloved to ensure that their children would share their mother's temperament. Atreynha joined Alluria for her ritual meal, and the Mother Priestess reassured her that she would always have a home among the sisterhood, as a priestess or otherwise.

Atreynha accompanied Alluria as she ventured into the temple's main chamber, and was surrounded by her sisters asking about the trials. Alluria answered as best she could, hiding her disappointment when Caol'nir wasn't there to greet her. Alluria reasoned that he had not expected to see her until the following morning and made her way to Caol'nir's chambers, excited beyond reckoning to share what she had learned, yet nervous for his reaction.

The moon had not yet risen, and Alluria found the room dark and empty. *Caol'nir must be finishing his duties,* she thought, *he will return soon.* Alluria sat on the edge of his bed, intending to wait up for Caol'nir's return, but she was exhausted. She yawned and lay back on the soft furs, telling herself that she would only sleep until her love returned and woke her.

It wasn't Caol'nir but the elder sun that woke Alluria, invading her slumber with his bright rays. She wondered if Olluhm was punishing her for wanting to leave his service. She'd assumed that Caol'nir slept beside her, having quietly slipped into bed so as not to disturb her, but when she rolled over she realized that she remained alone. Alluria rose and looked about the room, finding it as empty as the night before.

Where is he? she wondered, her mood having gone from concerned to frantic. Alluria went to speak with the only one who always knew of Caol'nir's whereabouts.

Alluria entered the small bathing chamber that adjoined Caol'nir's room and passed into his twin's bedchamber. As she looked upon Caol'non in the morning light her breath caught in her throat; he looked so like his brother, from his strong jaw to his sun-colored hair, also bound in a thick braid.

"Caol'non," Alluria whispered. As his eyes opened, she saw the one aspect of the brothers that differed: Caol'non's eyes were blue as a summer sky, not the pale green of her love's. Caol'non blinked and then stretched in the early morning light.

"Alluria?" he yawned. "How did you get in here?"

"Through the bathing chamber," she answered. "Caol'non, I must find your brother."

"He's gone," Caol'non replied, rubbing the sleep from his eyes.

"Gone?" Alluria's voice wavered. How could he be gone, gone now when she needed him the most?

"Only for a short time," Caol'non replied. "He said he would return in a sennight or so, and that was five days ago. He's not been gone long enough to worry." He watched Alluria's hands tremble as he continued. "Caol'nir made me swear to guard you until he returned."

"Do you know where he went?"

"No, he wouldn't say." Alluria turned her face to the wall in a vain attempt to keep Caol'non from seeing her tears; the only man that had ever seen her cry was Caol'nir, and she meant to keep it that way.

"My lady, don't be sad," Caol'non soothed. "My brother loves you very much; he will return as soon as he is able."

"He told you that?" she asked, pleased that Caol'nir had confided to his twin.

"Yes, my lady."

"You needn't be so formal," Alluria said, "I won't be a priestess much longer." *If Caol'nir returns and accepts the terms for my release*, she silently amended.

"Then you have the answer you sought," Caol'non observed.

"He told you about that, too?"

Caol'non nodded. "It's quite hard to keep things from your twin. I remember the day you came to Teg'urnan; when you arrived with our father and Fiornacht, Caol'nir and I were there by the gates. Caol'nir was complaining about the extra work with the priestesses being brought to Teg'urnan. Then he saw you step out of the litter. Nothing has ever quieted him as quickly as the sight of you." Alluria smiled at Caol'non's recollection and remembered her first encounters with a young member of the *con'dehr* who had annoyed her with his constant staring and foolish smiles.

"He loved you in that moment," Caol'non continued, "and he's loved you ever since."

"You never told him it was folly to pursue a priestess?"

"Never."

Caol'non and Alluria shared a smile, and she noted that Caol'non was as kind as his brother.

"Are you staying in Caol'nir's chamber?" he asked, to which she nodded. "If you'd like, once the child sun rises, I will escort you to the temple."

"Thank you, Caol'non," Alluria said as she rose. "That would be very good."

Chapter 14

Caol'nir entered his chamber, halting just inside the door. The moon's red glow illuminated the room, and he could just make out Alluria on his bed. His heart beat faster, for surely she had been released from the temple if she was here. Surely she was a free woman… Caol'nir knelt on the steps of the sleeping platform and kissed her forehead, smiling as her eyes fluttered open.

"Where have you been?" Alluria demanded as she threw her arms about his neck. "When I emerged, you were gone, and not even Caol'non knew where you were."

"Forgive me, *nalla*," he soothed, stroking her back. "I didn't think I would be gone so long. I've only just returned." Alluria didn't loosen her grip, clinging to him far more tightly than his short absence should warrant. "I was only gone for seven days, surely you didn't miss me this much." When she only gripped him harder, he said, "Tell me."

"I have learned how I may be released with honor, but there is only one way," Alluria began. "My vows can only be undone if the one who would claim me makes his intent known to the gods."

"Then I'll make it known, to every god in every land, that I want you as my mate."

"It's not so simple." Alluria took a deep breath, assuming the calm mask of a priestess. "You'll need to challenge Olluhm, and prove that you love me. If your heart is pure, he will bind our souls. If he deems you unworthy, he will likely kill you."

"How do I perform this challenge?"

"You will need to claim me in the old way, atop the altar."

Caol'nir was silent for a moment, watching as the moonlight imparted a pinkish glow to Alluria's skin. He was confident that he could withstand whatever challenge he faced. "You say we will be bound afterward?"

"Yes."

"Then you'll be mine, truly, irrevocably mine, forever?" he pressed.

"Yes, if you prevail." Before she had finished saying the words his lips were on hers. "You will do this?"

"Of course I will," he affirmed. "Alluria, I swore I'd take you as my mate if you were released."

"But you could die," she whispered. "*Nall*, I don't want to lose you."

"If I'm judged based on my love for you, I'll be fine. *Nalla*, I won't fail." He sat next to her and took her hands in his. "Alluria, will you let me undertake this challenge and become my bound mate?"

"Yes," she breathed, elation flooding her voice, "yes, Caol'nir, yes." Alluria fell into his arms, his confidence having allayed her fears. They held each other for a time, then Alluria rose to her feet and pulled Caol'nir along with her. "Come, we will go now while the temple is empty. I have no desire for my sisters' to look upon your naked form."

Caol'nir caught her wrist. "When you said claim you atop the altar…"

Alluria met his eyes, and she did not flinch or blush as she replied to the unfinished question. "I mean that you will need to make love to me in the temple, upon the altar stone, and that is where Olluhm will judge your heart."

Caol'nir's brows knit together. "I thought it wasn't done that way any longer," he said.

Alluria shrugged. "Perhaps not in Teg'urnan, but it is what we must do."

"I cannot lay you on the hard stone," he murmured. "You'll be bruised, and cold, and—"

Alluria pressed her lips to his, silencing his protests. "If you are so concerned, I will bring one of the furs." With that, she grabbed a fur from his bed and tossed it around his shoulders on her way toward the door. "Are you coming?" She glanced over her shoulder, looking at him through her lashes.

Caol'nir grabbed her, trapping her between his body and the door as he kissed her, thrusting one hand into her shining hair while the other slid to the small of her back, pressing her hips against his. He surprised both of them, for even when they had laid in bed Caol'nir was mindful of her chastity. Now his careful touch was demanding, and Alluria responded with passion of her own. When at last Caol'nir released her, his eyes were dark with emotion.

"Afterward, I'll make love to you properly," he said as he stroked her cheek. "I will kiss every part of you, from the top of your head to your pretty toes, and prove how I have longed for you."

"Then we should make haste, my love," Alluria breathed.

They walked in side by side to the Great Temple, as they had the day Alluria descended to the vaults. Once they reached the eastern door Alluria unsealed it, then Caol'nir kissed her forehead and led her inside.

"Did you know," Alluria began, "our entrance is part of the ritual."

"Is it?" Caol'nir asked. "Did I do well?"

"If you show tenderness to your mate upon passing through the eastern door, it means you'll treat her well all her life." Alluria glanced at him. "What else do you know of bindings?"

"Not much, beyond that you must enter from the east to receive Cydia's blessing," he replied. "No one observes, save the gods?"

"No one but Olluhm," she confirmed. Alluria strode across the central room and halted a few paces before the altar.

"We will leave our clothing here," she stated, and her hands moved to the stays of her robe. Alluria hands fumbled when she attempted to undo the delicate knots. "It is for you to disrobe me, anyway," she grumbled as she hid her hands in the folds of her garment.

Caol'nir noted that she would not meet his eyes; the confident priestess was gone, and in her place stood a trembling, chaste girl. He reached for her, not for the simple ties beneath her bosom but for her chin, and tilted her face up to his. "Alluria, it doesn't have to be now. We can wait until you are ready."

"But I want to be yours," she replied. To prove her words she unlaced his riding tunic and pushed it from him, his shoulders so broad she needed to stand on her toes and stretch to bare them. She brought her hands back up the length of his arms, then across his shoulders and down the smooth expanse of his chest as she lightly stroked his skin. Alluria's fingers then traced a path across his back to that rope of sandy hair, and she tugged at the thick braid.

"Around," she ordered. "Help me undo this."

Caol'nir didn't turn but took his hair from Alluria's hands, his gaze never leaving hers as he unwound his hair. Once his hair was loose Alluria smoothed it across his shoulders, then she placed his hands on the ties of her robe.

"If you would claim me, it is your right," Alluria said huskily, and Caol'nir tugged the knot loose and pulled the thin garment from her. He gasped as her robe fell to the floor; he had known she would be beautiful, but to look upon her naked was almost more than he could bear. *She is perfect*, he thought, gently tracing the curve of her shoulder. Mindful of the fact that she had never bared herself before another, he wrapped the fur about her shoulders, then he shed the remainder of his clothing. Alluria shyly watched him, only to look away once he was naked as well.

"Do we approach the steps now?" he asked softly.

"Yes." Alluria took his hand and led him to the base of the altar. He was about to climb the steps, but she halted him. "You must wait, and then follow me," she whispered as she shrugged the fur from her shoulders.

As Alluria ascended to the sacred altar, Caol'nir was entranced by the sight of her smooth skin. Her chestnut hair fell in soft waves against her back, the contrast between her dark hair and pale skin exquisite. When Alluria reached the uppermost step she paused, and glanced over her shoulder at Caol'nir.

"Come, warrior," she commanded. "Our god awaits us."

She disappeared onto the altar, and Caol'nir climbed the remaining steps. When he reached the grand, wide platform, he found Alluria standing before the altar stone, extending her hand to him. When their skin made contact, Alluria began reciting the binding ritual in the old language. Caol'nir responded in kind, swearing his body and soul to his beloved as he laid her atop the altar. Alluria's voice resonated throughout the temple and light swirled about the altar, at first like lightning bugs on a hot night, then blindingly powerful. It was not only light but a sentience, and Caol'nir realized that Olluhm, himself, had come to pass judgment.

Who dares to claim my child? demanded a booming voice they heard not with their ears, but within their thoughts.

"I do," Caol'nir replied, "look into my heart and know that I love her!"

Alluria paused in her recitation and grasped Caol'nir's hand. He mounted the altar and knelt between her knees, but when he reached toward her the light thrust him backwards, almost off the stone. Alluria gasped as he caught himself on the edge.

You think you are worthy, boy? Worthy enough to claim a god's child?

"I love her!" Caol'nir shouted. "I love her as no other ever will! I would forfeit my life to keep her safe!"

The light was joined by a wind that whipped into a frenzy atop the altar. Caol'nir struggled against it as it tried to push him off the stone, clinging to the edge as he pulled himself toward Alluria. He felt the light examining him; tiny needles of pain speared through his flesh and into his bones. Finally, Caol'nir reached Alluria and grabbed her hips; she pressed her face against his chest, gasping against the wind.

What say you, my daughter? Do you accept this man?

"I give myself to him, freely and completely," Alluria declared. To Caol'nir's amazement, the light paused, listening as the priestess spoke. "I do not seek to disavow what I have learned from you, but your central lesson has always been love. Would you deny your child the opportunity for a love of her own?"

"She is mine," Caol'nir proclaimed in the old language. "She is yours no longer. Her heart belongs to me, as mine belongs to her." The light surrounded them, enveloping them in a sensation of shelter and warmth, and Olluhm's voice was benevolent when he spoke again.

Then go into his arms, my beloved daughter, and may your union be blessed.

The light became brighter, so strong that it could have been solid, until all Caol'nir could see was a pair of blue eyes looking up at him. He gazed into those sapphire orbs as he claimed her, and she him.

Afterward, when the light had faded but power still coursed around them, Caol'nir held his mate close as he nuzzled her neck. Alluria reached between their legs and then pressed her wet fingers to Caol'nir's forehead, and recited the final words of the ritual.

"Your heart is true, Caol'nir, son of Tor. I mark you with the seed of a warrior and the blood of a virgin, as the gods have marked our souls. You challenged Olluhm, and you prevailed. You've claimed you mate, warrior."

He kissed her, his heart swelling for she who gave so selflessly, she who had just renounced everything she had ever known for him. "All I ever wanted was you."

"And you are all I ever truly wanted." Alluria shifted against Caol'nir, and laughed softly.

"What's so funny, beloved?"

"You left the fur on the floor."

"So I did." With that, Caol'nir rose and carried his mate down the western stairs, traversing the sacred path without missing a step. He brought them to where their clothes lay in a heap and set his mate on her feet. They dressed quickly, but when Alluria turned to leave, Caol'nir wrapped her in the fur and scooped her into his arms. He carried her through the empty corridors, not releasing her even after they entered his chamber. Caol'nir brought Alluria, his mate, his beloved, to bed, and they lost themselves in each other.

Chapter 15

When he woke Caol'nir felt Alluria's soft hair against his face, breathed in her sweet wildflower scent. He brushed her hair away from her neck and kissed the tender skin over her spine. She moaned softly, and Caol'nir's lips made their way across her neck before gently nibbling her earlobe. Alluria moaned again, and his tongue continued to travel across the edge of her ear; as he gently drew the pointed tip between his lips she shivered, and Caol'nir smiled. "How much longer are you going to pretend to be asleep?"

"As long as you keep doing that," she replied without opening her eyes.

Caol'nir rolled her onto her back and kissed her neck with abandon, now that he knew she was awake. Alluria laughed as he pulled her against him, wrapping her arms around his neck.

Once they parted, he held her face close to his. "You're every dream I've ever had come to life before me."

"Then I look forward to waking in your arms every morning, my love."

Caol'nir nestled his mate against him, and took a deep breath. "I never got to tell you where I was these past few days."

"It's understandable. You were distracted." Alluria kissed the hollow of his throat. "In truth, I care not where you were as long as you're here with me now." She felt him tense, and leaned back to regard Caol'nir's face. "You can, of course, tell me."

"I followed the king when he left Teg'urnan," Caol'nir began, and recounted all that had occurred while she had been in the vaults, from his conversation with Rahlle to observing the king meet with Ehkron.

"Why would Sahlgren engage in any sort of a meeting with the *mordeth-gall*?" Alluria mused.

"There's more," Caol'nir said, stroking her hair. "Did you know that Sahlgren goes to priestesses in the guise of the god? Apparently, he is sent by Olluhm."

"That's blasphemy," Alluria said. "My god would never send another in his stead! It goes against everything we believe!"

"My father claims it is the way of things, and has been this way for many years."

"I cannot say what has happened in this temple, but in my temple that would never occur." Alluria met Caol'nir's eyes. "There are certain rituals that involve a priest, fertility rites and such, but no priest or king has ever been granted leave to act on Olluhm's behalf. Someone has lied to your father."

"I know," Caol'nir said softly. "I believe it is the king." He nestled her head against his neck, and steeled himself to continue. "Rahlle has told me that there is a resistance."

"And you want to join them," Alluria concluded. "Very well, I will go with you."

"You cannot, it won't be safe."

"As your mate, my place is at your side."

"Not if it puts you in harm's way." They stared at each other, and Caol'nir was the first to look away. "I don't want to be apart from you, but I must learn what they're about. If their cause is noble, as Rahlle believes, I'll help them. If they're nothing more than treasonous rabble rousers, I'll inform my father and they will be apprehended."

Alluria traced the line of his jaw. "If it's not safe for me, how can it be safe for you? Am I only to be your mate for one night?"

Caol'nir tightened his embrace. "*Nalla*, you're mine for eternity. This resistance is in the north, near the elves. It would be foolish to attempt the journey before the spring thaw. I won't depart for a moon, perhaps two."

"It is not you departing that worries me, but whether you will return."

"I will," Caol'nir promised. "Nothing will keep me from you."

"Swear to be back by midsummer," she implored. "No, the first day of summer. I cannot be parted from you longer than that."

"I'll return long before if I can," he said as he kissed his mate, thus sealing the vow.

"Am I to assume that our seclusion will not be longer than one moon?" Alluria inquired, and Caol'nir grinned. He had all but forgotten the custom of seclusion, where a newly bound pair hides themselves away from the world, ensconced in their love and nothing more.

"I must speak with my father today," he replied, "and then I will arrange for our undisturbed time together." He nibbled her neck, his words muffled as he continued. "Of course, we cannot leave our bed until we have greeted the child sun together. How will we pass the time until second dawn?"

Alluria laughed as she twined her arms around his neck.

Shortly after the child sun rose, the pair left the warm furs and made their way to the Prelate's chamber. They found Tor conferring with Fiornacht over a document, but the sight of Caol'nir and Alluria together made the men forget the parchment.

"What have you done? You've finally disgraced us all," Fiornacht said.

"I've disgraced no one," Caol'nir replied. "Alluria and I—"

"Have come to beg Father's protection," Fiornacht interrupted.

"Silence, Fiornacht; you've come begging for my help often enough," Tor interjected, stunning Caol'nir into silence. Fiornacht, sufficiently abashed, stormed to the far corner of the room. Caol'nir turned to his father, intending to tell him of his and Alluria's binding, but Tor's harsh gaze silenced him. While Tor was not as tall or broad as Caol'nir, one did not hold the title of Prelate without learning to intimidate.

"You weren't seen in the temple for some time, Alluria," Tor stated. Alluria began explaining, but Tor ignored her. "And you," he continued, turning to Caol'nir, "have been gone from Teg'urnan for days without my authority. Apparently you only deigned to tell Caol'non of your little journey." Tor leaned back in his chair and pressed his fingertips together. "I want a full accounting of your whereabouts, both together and apart."

"We weren't together, not until yesterday," Caol'nir said. "I followed the king when he left Teg'urnan—"

"And I had entered the vaults, by leave of Sarelle," interjected Alluria. Tor cast a stern glance toward the priestess, then he addressed his son.

"You followed the king because of what Rahlle told you?" Tor asked.

"Yes."

"Well? Is the sorcerer as mad as I thought?"

"I saw the king meet with the *mordeth-gall*."

"The royal guard engaged him in battle?" Tor demanded.

"No. The king and the *mordeth-gall* greeted each other as old friends would and spent the evening in the royal tent."

Caol'nir waited for their reaction, expecting his father and brother to leap to the king's defense. Instead, they shared a knowing glance, and Fiornacht retrieved a map. He unrolled it across the desk and beckoned Caol'nir to examine it along with him.

"We have heard reports—all unconfirmed, mind you—of pureblood fae being captured as slaves," Fiornacht explained. He indicated several points on the map, which Caol'nir recognized as legion outposts. "We have sent squads to investigate these sites but each was found destroyed. All they have found are burned out structures and corpses."

"Slaves?" Alluria asked. "Who would enslave us in our own land?"

"I don't know," Tor replied, "but I mean to find out."

"The king knows; it's why he was meeting with Ehkron," Caol'nir said, giving voice to what Tor and Fiornacht had suspected for some time. He was silent for a moment, regarding his father before he continued. "There is a resistance, in the north. They believe the king has been corrupted."

"Yes, I know," Tor said, "Rahlle informed me. It's led by an escaped slave."

"I mean to go north and learn what this resistance is about," Caol'nir stated. Tor and Fiornacht shared an uneasy glance, which irritated Caol'nir. He was ever the little brother, having been born the day after Caol'non. He used to take advantage of other's low opinion of him, shirking his duties as a silent protest of his life in the *con'dehr*.

No longer would he look the other way, not now that he was tasked with keeping Alluria safe. "Someone needs to learn more of what's going on, especially if you believe we are being enslaved," Caol'nir said. "We cannot go to the king since he is involve—"

"You do not know—" interrupted Fiornacht.

"I know what I saw," Caol'nir shouted. "What reason would the king have to meet with Ehkron?" Fiornacht held his tongue, and Caol'nir continued. "With your leave, Father, I'll go after the thaw."

Alluria looked away. Caol'nir turned to Alluria and murmured a few soothing words.

"Why do the two of you come before me now?" Tor asked. "Surely, Caol'nir, you didn't need to bring a priestess when you informed me of this."

Caol'nir placed his hand on Alluria's shoulder, and she covered it with her own. "Alluria has bound herself to me. We are mated."

"That's not possible," Fiornacht shouted, leaping to his feet. Caol'nir also stood, but it was Alluria's calm voice that gained the Prelate's attention.

"It is more than possible," Alluria said, "it has come to pass. I went into the vaults for this reason alone, to find a way to be honorably released from my vows. Caol'nir challenged Olluhm for me, and he won."

"It cannot be," Fiornacht muttered.

"Can't it?" Tor asked. "What is less believable, our king breaking bread with the *mordeth-gall* or Olluhm allowing Alluria her freedom? It seems that both are possible." Fiornacht grumbled, but Tor ignored him as he watched his son and his mate.

"The morning after your binding you came to speak with me?" Tor asked, drawing Caol'nir's attention away from Alluria. "Your mother and I weren't seen for a full moon after we were bound."

"My lord, you needed to know of my whereabouts, and this resistance, and—" Caol'nir fell silent as Tor held up his hand, the he rose walked around his desk. He leaned against it as he regarded the pair before him.

"When did you begin to address me as 'my lord', rather than 'father'?" Tor asked with a wry grin.

"When I thought you would be angry with me for my transgressions," Caol'nir replied.

"You, daughter, are not to refer to me as your lord, either," Tor said to Alluria, who offered a small smile. "I will see to procuring a proper chamber for the two of you."

"But I like Caol'nir's room," Alluria said. "I've become accustomed to it." A smug grin spread across Fiornacht's face, and Alluria looked away. Now, they all knew that when Caol'nir was charged with finding Alluria a room, he looked no further than his own.

"Nevertheless, my dear, it is not suitable for a bound pair," Tor continued. "What if you were to have children?" Alluria blushed at his suggestion. "And, may I ask, will you still work in the temple?"

"I-I don't know," Alluria stammered in reply. "I will need to speak with Sarelle, and learn if she still has need of me."

"Would you like me to speak on your behalf?" Tor offered.

"No, thank you," Alluria replied. "The High Priestess knew it was my intention to renounce my vows. She will want to learn of the outcome. The wonderful outcome," she added.

"Very well," Tor stated. "However, I forbid you to speak with her for the next moon." Tor laughed at their shocked faces. "Do you young ones not understand the concept of seclusion?"

Alluria's cheeks darkened as Caol'nir objected, sputtering that they needed to discuss the resistance, and the king's meeting with the *mordeth-gall*, when Tor silenced them. "That all can wait. I've always believed that duty to your mate comes before all else, even duty to your king." Tor stepped forward and took Alluria's hands. "My son challenged a god for your heart?"

"Yes," she replied. "And I gave it to him freely."

"I have no doubt," he said softly. "Now, off with you both. I don't want to see either of you until your seclusion has ended."

The pair thanked Tor and left the Prelate's chamber for their much-anticipated time together. Once in the corridor Caol'nir swept Alluria into his arms; already, she had been too long from his embrace. The Prelate's door opened again, then Caol'nir felt a hand on his shoulder.

"Brother," Fiornacht said, "I...I am very happy for you."

Caol'nir merely nodded—the pride in his brother's tone was not something he was accustomed to—and led Alluria back to their chamber. He forced himself to forget about the king, forget about demons, slaves, and all the realm's evils that could harm his beloved, and concentrated upon being her mate.

Chapter 16

Caol'nir never realized what a short span of time a single moon encompassed, and his seclusion with Alluria ended all too quickly. The morning they returned to their regular lives found Alluria venturing to the Great Temple, a cloak over her sacred robes lest she offend Olluhm. While she was gone, Caol'nir busied himself with leatherworking.

"Were things well?" he asked when she returned. Alluria had wanted to speak with the High Priestess alone regarding her position in the temple, if such a position still existed. Caol'nir knew that Sarelle was reticent to trust those outside the temple; her distrust extended to the *con'dehr*, and she merely tolerated the Prelate.

"They were," Alluria replied. "While Sarelle expressed her extreme displeasure over the abandonment of my calling," Alluria paused to roll her eyes, "she did admit that my knowledge of flora is without equal. She asked me to remain as the temple's herbalist." Caol'nir had risen while Alluria spoke and wrapped his arms about her, kissing her as if she'd been gone much longer than half a day. "Thank you for sending your brother to guard me."

"He was supposed to remain unobtrusive."

"You think I would not notice a man that looks exactly like my mate?" Alluria freed herself from his arms and held out a dark green garment. "I even have a proper herbalist's robe."

Caol'nir felt the fabric between his thumb and forefinger; the weave was tight, and it would take a seam well. "Will you put it on for me?" he asked.

"Um, certainly," Alluria replied, then she exchanged her usual blue robe for her new herbalist's garb.

"Do you like it?" she asked, twirling her skirts while she fluttered her eyelashes. The dress was loose, cinched at her waist with a gold brocade belt. Matching brocade edged the bodice and hem, and over the dress she wore a loose robe of the same green fabric.

"You are lovely as ever," Caol'nir replied, sliding his hands about her waist. "This dress only pulls over your head?" he asked, feeling the belt.

"Looking to disrobe me already?" Alluria asked coyly. Caol'nir smiled as he grazed his hands across her back, confirming that there were no other fastenings. He kissed her again, then released her as he retrieved the leather he'd left in his chair.

"I made this for you," he said as he buckled a weapon belt, complete with a dagger the length of her forearm, around her hips. "I meant for you to wear it inside your robe, so you could carry it unawares, but that won't work with this dress. Although..." his voice trailed off as he ran his fingers across the edges of her belt. "Can you get more of these dresses?"

"I believe there are many in the storeroom," Alluria replied. "What are you planning?"

"I can make the dress into two pieces, and you can carry the dagger in secrecy," Caol'nir answered as he sat, drawing Alluria onto his lap. "Or, perhaps I can add a pocket for the dagger."

"My warrior knows how to sew?" Alluria asked with a raised brow.

"Father believed we should be self-sufficient," he replied. "He would say, 'What if you were stranded, and needed to mend your gear?' And so my brothers and I were taught the art of the needle, by one frustrated nursemaid after another."

Alluria was silent for a moment before she continued, "When I asked what you were planning, I meant why are you putting this dagger on me?"

"I want you able to protect yourself while I'm gone," he said softly. "My father and brothers will watch over you, of course, but I want an extra bit of assurance that you'll be safe."

"I thought you weren't leaving before the thaw," Alluria whispered.

"I won't," he said. "I swear I'll return as soon as I'm able, and from then on you'll have to suffer my endless presence." She smiled, but her eyes remained somber. "*Nalla*, I only made it now to test the fit, and now I know I need to work on your pretty green dresses."

"I don't know how to use a dagger."

"I'll teach you."

Alluria nestled into his arms. "I wish you weren't going."

"So do I." He kissed her forehead. "So do I."

They held each other for a time, staring into the flames, until Alluria remembered something. "I found the king's doorway."

"Alluria, I asked you not to involve yourself," Caol'nir said. "I don't want any suspicion to fall on you while I'm away and can't protect you. It would kill me if anything happened to you."

"Then you should stay here and watch my every move."

"*Nalla*," he began, but she waved away his words.

"Well, I found it nonetheless. It's between the northern door and the statue of Olluhm. The statue casts a shadow over the doorway, making it nigh invisible. On the exterior of the temple, it is covered by a tapestry." She laughed shortly. "The tapestry is of our mighty king driving the demons away from Teg'urnan."

"Can you seal the door?" Caol'nir asked, to which Alluria nodded. "Will anyone know it was you who did so?"

"No," she replied. "I can bind the opening with a poultice of strangleweed, hide it behind the tapestry. Like as not, no one will look for a few leaves. There are advantages to being a master herbalist."

Caol'nir kissed the hollow of her throat. "Always keeping your sisters safe."

"Oh, I've something else to keep them safe," she said, and leaned forward to retrieve her blue robe.

"Get back here," Caol'nir said as he grabbed her hips, and Alluria laughed as her mate yanked her onto his lap. "You're not to leave my arms." While he nuzzled her neck, she produced a small leather pouch.

"For you." Alluria placed a shiny white stone in Caol'nir's hand. "This stone is charmed against the spell Sarelle places on the temple doors every night. With it, you can unseal the doors, should you need to."

Caol'nir turned the stone over in his hand. To him, it looked like one he would skip across a lake. "Does anyone know you've taken it?"

"No, because I made it," Alluria replied. "It is not so hard, once you know the spell she uses for sealing them."

"Is there anything you cannot do?" He pulled the clasp from her hair and let her chestnut waves fall about her face. "Magic must course through your veins." He kissed the pulse in her neck.

"Unfortunately, I'm limited to charming stones and lighting candles," she said. "I wish I could uncover what the king was truly doing. Then you and your father could stop him." Alluria shuddered and burrowed further into Caol'nir's embrace. "The notion of faeries being enslaved… it chills me."

"I know," he said as he smoothed her hair, "I know."

The thaw came, as did the day Caol'nir left for the north. While Alluria said nothing as she helped Caol'nir pack, her sorrow was plain. They walked slowly toward the palace gates, Caol'nir leading his horse with one hand while the other rested on Alluria's waist.

"Do you know how much I'll miss you?" Caol'nir said against Alluria's hair. They stopped to let a merchant's cart pass, and he took the opportunity to kiss her temple.

"I can imagine," Alluria replied. Instead of her herbalist's robes, she was clad in a simple blue dress, her hair loose about her shoulders. As she leaned against Caol'nir, she wondered if anyone recognized her as a former priestess. The cart passed and they resumed walking, neither spoke until they reached the shadow of the stag's antlers, eternally frozen as he made his mighty leap across the gates.

"Two winters ago, I saw these gates for the first time," Alluria said. "I didn't pass under these gates again until one winter passed, when a young warrior dressed me as a *saffira* and spirited me away on his horse." Alluria turned to her mate and smiled, but her eyes were sad. "And now you pass under them again, and I remain behind."

Caol'nir pulled her against him and buried his face in her hair. "*Mea nalla*, you know my heart will remain here with you."

Alluria nodded; she had wanted to be strong for him, to make his departure as easy as possible, but the thought of facing the next moons without him was devastating.

Caol'nir understood all too well; he remembered well how hard it was to spend seven days without Alluria. Now that she was his mate—against all odds, she was finally his—he was leaving her. Many times, he had wanted to request his father send someone else north for recognizance, some trusted member of the *con'dehr*, but this could not be done. The fact that the Prelate and his sons knew of a resistance and had not told the king was treason. Anyone they sent to the north would be also guilty. Moreover, what if this individual went to the king and spoke against Caol'nir's entire family? No, better that he went himself.

Not that these facts made leaving Alluria any easier. Caol'nir drew back and gazed at his mate, the woman he'd never dared hope would love him. "Remember everything I taught you," he said, stroking her cheek. While his remaining family would watch her, he had also spent the winter teaching her how to wield a dagger.

"I will," she promised, "and remember what I taught you." In addition to the firestarting spell, Alluria taught her mate to discern direction, as well as a glamour to hide him while in plain sight. "And don't lose the stone!" she added; she still couldn't say why she had charmed a few stones to override Sarelle's spells, but she felt better having done it.

Caol'nir promised that he would forget nothing, and she straightened the laces of his jerkin. "And, *nall*, do not forget to return." Alluria's voice caught in her throat.

Caol'nir tilted her chin up and began to say his goodbye, when Alluria caught sight of something over his shoulder and smiled. He turned and saw his father, leading a horse packed for travel.

"It seems I'm going with you," Tor said in response to his son's startled face. "Alluria's forced me to watch over you, and return you to her in one piece."

Caol'nir turned to his mate, who explained, "I couldn't let you go alone," Alluria explained. "What if those who would enslave us captured you?"

Caol'nir protested, for removing the Prelate from Teg'urnan for several moons would garner more attention than was prudent. "So you cajoled my father into watching over me?"

"No, I begged him," she clarified. "Be angry with me if you wish, but know that I only went behind your back out of love." She continued in a low voice, "You've kept me safe often enough; can I not return the favor?"

Caol'nir tangled his fingers in Alluria's hair as he drew her close; he would take her hair with him if he could, he so loved the feel of it against his skin. "As I was saying before we were interrupted," he continued, now wearing that rakish grin she loved so much, "I need you more than the air I breathe. You're my soul, Alluria. I'll count the moments until we are together again." With that, he kissed her, hard and long and passionately enough that even the gatekeeper stayed silent. When they parted, Caol'nir regarded his father while he held Alluria. "What of your duties?"

"Fiornacht is more than capable," Tor replied, "and he will enjoy the authority." Tor swung into the saddle and urged his horse toward the gate.

Caol'nir turned back to his mate. "*Nalla...*"

Alluria hushed him. "Don't. Just know that I love you and that it rends my heart to be without you. I too will count the moments until we're together again."

Caol'nir kissed her again and mounted his horse. Leaning down, he kissed her a third time. As he was about to bestow a fourth, Alluria said that the sooner he left the sooner he could return. He kissed her anyway, and then rode north to save Parthalan from its own king.

Chapter 17

As the elder sun approached his noonday apex, nearly a thousand weary faeries and elfin warriors crested the World's Spine and beheld the Seat of Tingu, the ancestral home of the elves. The Seat was made of polished green and purple stone that looked as if it had been coaxed from the earth as one would tend a seed. While the palace was smooth as a river stone, the emerald and amethyst mountain from which it was carved jutted toward the sky at sharp angles, uncut or polished and yearning for a jewelers touch.

Home.

As Lormac looked upon the Seat, he agreed with the Sala; it was good to be home. While all elves preferred to live near the northern mountains, he felt the pull of earth and stone stronger than most. Like all those of Nexa's line, he felt the Seat call to him, a call magnified by wearing the Sala.

Lormac mused on his long life as he neared the Seat; while elves were an immortal race, as were the fae and trolls, Nexa's blood afforded him a much more enduring nature. He was never ill, unlike the trolls who had retreated far beneath the surface to avoid illness millennia ago, nor was he easily injured like the fragile fae. His stoic nature meant that he afforded precious few a glimpse at his true self, but when he did choose to let go and love, he loved them deeply.

And for eternity.

The thought was not his own; rather, he would not admit to it being his, and he rubbed the Sala to quiet it. Lormac had long ago grown accustomed to its voice within his mind, but lately it had grown louder and more persistent. Almost without realizing his actions, Lormac looked over his shoulder and saw the object of the Sala's interest riding next to Torim.

"What do you think of my home?" Lormac asked Asherah.

"Amazing," she replied, her eyes fixed upon the Seat. "I don't know if amazing is the proper word. No, it's splendid!"

"It is half again as large as Teg'urnan," Torim murmured. "I did not think so big a structure could exist."

"It's larger than it appears," Lormac stated. "You can only see the outer walls now, but the Seat travels deep into the mountain."

"Like a cavern?" Asherah asked.

"Nothing like a damp, dark cavern," Lormac replied. "It is full of light, and warmth, and…" Lormac realized that he was waxing on about the Seat, evidenced by Asherah and Torim's bemused faces. "I'll just have to show you."

"I would like that," Asherah said.

Lormac smiled—no, the elf king *grinned*—as Asherah spoke the words, the Sala's approval singing in his mind. Before he could continue, Balthus approached him.

"My lord, the Gatekeeper waits," Balthus proclaimed. Lormac murmured his apologies to Asherah, and followed his second to the Gate.

The Gate of Tingu was largely a ceremonial object, for while it rose to three times Lormac's height, it was only a gate, without an attached wall or fence. As Lormac approached the Gate he brought his left hand to his right shoulder, the Sala resting over his heart.

"Ancestors, I beg your leave to enter," Lormac said, his voice reverberating off the Seat. The elves turned as one from their king to the Gatekeeper, a wizened old man in a grey robe, and the faeries quickly followed suit. The Gatekeeper nodded to Lormac, and with a strength that belied his frail form he dragged the Gate open and allowed the king's procession to pass through to the Seat.

As soon as he entered the palace, Lormac was whisked away to deal with matters that had been waiting for him during his long absence, and couldn't send for Asherah until the following morning. Lormac paced about his chamber as he waited for her arrival, the Sala humming her name inside his head. Finally, he heard Aldo admit her and he rushed to the front room.

"My lady," Lormac said as he took her hands, "how do you find the Seat of Tingu?"

"Magnificent," she replied. "I had no idea that such a palace existed."

"Good," he said. "I'm sorry I didn't summon you sooner, but I've learned some unsettling information." Lormac kept hold of her hand as he led her to a long table and indicate a map, yellowed and crumbling at the edges, which took up nearly the entire surface. "We have reports of Ehkron in Thurnda. It seems that your fight has become mine, after all."

Asherah studied the map, tracing Thurnda's border with her finger. "Do you know why he's here?"

"I've been told precious little," Lormac replied bitterly. "I hope to have word soon enough."

"I didn't want to bring trouble to your door," Asherah said softly.

Lormac gently squeezed her fingers. "It's not your fault that an evil creature behaves in an evil manner. If it is truly the *mordeth-gall's* intent to enslave all he can, he would have breached my lands sooner or later. Your coming here alerted me sooner rather than later, so I'm better able to protect my people."

Asherah nodded. "Have many been harmed in Thurnda?" she asked, but was interrupted when a small child burst into the room.

"Da!" cried a boy with Lormac's gray eyes and wiry frame, bounded across the room and flung himself at the elf king. Lormac swept the boy into his arms, then brought him before Asherah.

"Asherah, this is my son, Leran."

Leran wrestled free of Lormac's grasp and offered Asherah an elfin salute.

"Hello," Asherah greeted, crouching before the boy. "Did you make this for your father to play with?" She indicating the small wooden horse he clutched, crudely carved with splinters sticking out from every angle.

"I did. I finished it yesterday. You're pretty," Leran said, then he hid behind his father's legs.

"And you are very handsome," Asherah said, laughing when Leran blushed. Lormac marveled at Asherah's easy manner with his son; Leran was not comfortable with many people outside of Lormac and his two nurses, yet he interacted with Asherah as if he had known her all of his short life.

Her.

"Thank you," Lormac said as he accepted the tiny horse. "Now run along, and I'll join you soon." Leran nodded and bounded from the chamber.

"He is a wonderful boy," Asherah said. "Have you others?"

"There is only Leran," Lormac replied. "He is the center of my world." Lormac had placed his hand on Asherah's shoulder as he replied. He found that he needed contact and kept touching her without asking, his only reward being Asherah's stiff limbs as she moved out of his reach. "I don't mean to make you uncomfortable."

Asherah smiled tightly. "I know you don't."

"Come, I want to show you something," Lormac said as he extended his arm to Asherah. "Only to help you along," he added.

"Thank you," she said, accepting his arm. He led her to a small door in the rear of his receiving chamber, grabbing his cloak along the way.

"We're going someplace cold?" she inquired.

"It is much cooler than the rest of the palace," Lormac replied as they entered a stone passageway.

"The floor slopes upward?" Asherah asked.

"Yes, this lead's toward the mountain's peak."

"And what is at this peak?"

"You'll know soon enough."

Lormac smiled when Asherah frowned, then turned her attention toward the passageway itself. Initially, the walls had the look of masonry, as did the walls of Lormac's chamber, but they quickly gave way to smooth, undulating stone in the same rich greens and purples as the exterior of the palace. A swirl of white metal, broken up so it resembled windblown pollen, was imbedded in the stone.

The passageway opened up to a large gallery. The walls and floor continued in that green and purple stone, but now veins of other gems and precious metals also swirled together. The ceiling was not solid stone but rather a field of white crystal, transparent enough to let sunlight illuminate the interior as bright as day. Toward the rear of the chamber, the crystals became larger and adorned the floor as well as the ceiling, giving the appearance of a chamber decorated with crystalline furniture.

"Oh," Asherah breathed, "what is this beautiful place?"

"This is the Seat of Tingu," Lormac replied with a sweep of his arm, "birthplace of all elfkind. Remember when I told you that we were born of the earth and stone?"

"Elves were born from this very spot?" she asked.

"Yes," he replied, placing his hand on the small of her back and turned her toward a large, flat crystal. "It's said that this crystal was Nexa's bower." Asherah trailed her fingertips along the edge of the glowing stone, then she noticed similar formations.

"And what do these signify?" she asked.

Lormac explained that each elf descended from Nexa was represented by their own stones, those of the living glowing, as did the crystal ceiling, while the stones of those who had passed took on an iridescent sheen. Lormac named them all, until they reached the tiniest stone that was Leran's. Lormac's heart swelled as he took her interest as yet another sign that she was his true mate. Then Asherah uttered words that removed the few lingering doubts he possessed.

"Thank you, for sharing this with me," Asherah said. "I've never been to a place as sacred and magnificent as this." She traced the stone that was Lormac's, and he felt her touch along his back, warm and soft and utterly calming. "Of course, I don't remember most of the places I have been, but I don't think anyone could forget being here."

"It does leave an impression in one's mind," Lormac agreed. Asherah still had her hand on his stone, and Lormac was enjoying every moment. "When you touch my stone, it's as if you're touching me."

"Oh," Asherah said, dropping her hand. "I-I didn't know."

"Not to worry," he said. "I didn't mind." Asherah smiled, then she dropped her gaze to the Sala.

"The stones in your armband, they are from here?" Asherah asked.

"Yes," Lormac replied, further pleased by Asherah's interest in his heritage. "This is called Sala, and it was created by Nexa herself. By wearing it, I proclaim my right to rule Tingu."

"I thought your crown signified that."

"The crown is just a decoration," Lormac said, "but this is who we truly are."

"You've always reminded me of a mountain, but I could never say why." Asherah again looked about the gallery, her eyes filled with wonderment as she murmured, "Truly, I've never seen a lovelier sight."

Nothing is lovely, compared to you. Lormac could not say if the thought was his or the Sala's, but it no longer mattered. "You remind me of the night sky," Lormac said.

Asherah glanced over her shoulder. "How is that?" she asked, the same bemused expression on her face as when Lormac went on about the Seat. He loved that look of curiosity and fascination that she frequently wore, just as he loved so many other aspects of her.

"Your eyes are black as a moonless night, your hair pale as starlight," he said as he stepped toward her. "You are a star, a shining beacon of hope for your people."

Asherah stared at Lormac for a moment, then she turned away, mentioning a vein of silver that coursed about the Seat, but Lormac refused to let her distract him again. "Little star, where will your light shine next? Where will you go once your people are free?"

"They are not my people," Asherah said.

"The *Ish h'ra hai* are most certainly yours," Lormac insisted. "They look to you in all things. You are their light, their savior. Any one of them would die for you."

"As I would die for them." Asherah rubbed her arms, and Lormac draped his cloak about her shoulders. "A king should have a nicer cloak," she commented, feeling the lumpy fabric. "You adorn others in silks and velvets, yet you go about wearing this sackcloth."

"You have not answered me. Where will you go?"

"I don't know," Asherah answered truthfully. "I have no home, no family...I suppose I'll find a place for myself."

"You could remain in Tingu."

"I'm not an elf," she said hurriedly. "There is no place for me here."

Lormac closed the short distance between them and took her hand. "As long as I'm king, there will be a place for you here, little star." He kissed her hand, rigid in his.

"What place?" she gasped.

"At my side," Lormac replied. He noted her nervousness and stepped back, but did not release her hand. "I can give you a home."

"What of Leran's mother?" she demanded.

"I forget, you fae only have children if you are bound," Lormac said. "His mother was one of the house women, but now she is gone." Asherah expressed her condolences, but Lormac continued, "Not gone as in dead; gone as in she left Tingu."

"Left?"

"I couldn't give her what she wanted," Lormac replied, somewhat harsher than he'd intended.

"I'm sorry."

"Don't be," he replied with a tight smile. "She gave me the gift of my son, for which I am ever grateful." Lormac still held on to Asherah, and he wrapped a fold of his cloak around her hand. "You asked me where I obtained this—what did you call it? This sackcloth—and the answer is that Leran made it for me."

Asherah stole a glance at his face, and her curious expression bade him to continue.

"After his mother left, Leran was inconsolable. No one could comfort him, for what substitute is there for one's own mother? Finally, one of the *saffira* decided that Leran needed distraction rather than coddling, so she taught him to weave." Lormac drew the coarse fabric across her skin as he concluded, "As you can see, he is not very good with a loom."

"That is noble of you, to wear what your son made for you," Asherah said.

"It's a small act on my part, but it brings him much joy," Lormac replied. "I'll do anything to keep those I love happy."

"Oh." Asherah looked at the floor. She withdrew her hand and Lormac, having said all he could for the moment, led her back to his chambers. The return was notable for its silence, in sharp contrast to the banter they had enjoyed during their ascent to the Seat.

Lormac watched Asherah look around the room, noting details she overlooked earlier such as the shelves that lined the walls full to bursting with maps and tomes, the small toys scattered about that belonged to Leran, then she saw the entrance to his bedchamber.

Asherah removed his cloak and thrust it toward him. "I will not become your concubine," she said. "If that is the price for your help, I will find another way."

Lormac took the cloak, his laughter rumbling low in his chest. "Do you think that's what I was asking you? I can assure you, there's no shortage of pretty things to warm my bed. If that was all I desired, I wouldn't have bothered bringing you to the Seat." Asherah frowned and turned her back. Lormac tossed the cloak aside and placed his hands on her shoulders, his thumbs caressing the skin over her spine. "Your place would be one of honor."

"You speak as though this is a business transaction."

"Forgive me; I'm accustomed to speaking so." He put his arms around her waist and tried to draw her against him, but she resisted. "Do you not want me?" he implored. "Do you want Torim instead?"

"You should not want me," she whispered. "I am ruined."

"You're nothing of the sort."

"I am!" she insisted. "I am."

Lormac rested his chin on her shoulder and reached for her wrist, tracing the jagged scar. "Tell me how this happened."

"You...you do not want to know." Asherah hid her face against her shoulder.

"I do." Asherah sighed, and pushed up her sleeve. Lormac saw three more scars, raised and thickened as the first, fanned out like fingers.

"These are from claws," she said hoarsely. "It didn't want to use the chains; at first I was happy about that and thought that maybe I could escape. How I don't know, for even if I got out of the room, there were still the guards to contend with... If they caught me escaping, I would have been boiled."

"Boiled?"

"When we were used up, or if we proved to be trouble, they boiled us down to broth. Those were the days we had meat."

Lormac rested his forehead against the back of her head. "Is that why you don't—"

"Yes. I-I don't want to talk about that."

Lormac raised his head, turning his attention back to her wrist. "Then tell my why you didn't attempt an escape."

"I couldn't. It pulled my arms back and hooked its claws into my flesh. The scars are jagged because I pulled and tried to get it off me, but it wouldn't budge. It ground itself into me, laughing and taunting..." Asherah's voice trailed off as she rubbed the marks. "And would you know the worst part of it all? Not that it raped me; I was used to that. Not that it broke my ribs, for bones heal. It pulled my shoulders out of their sockets. My arms were useless, so useless I couldn't pick up my shift from the floor. I couldn't even cover myself once it was done with me."

Asherah stared at the wall as she related her tale, her body as unyielding as a statue. Lormac tightened his arms about her waist and said, "I'm so sorry. If I could take your past from you, I would." His shoulders shook, and Lormac turned her around.

"Little star, little star," Lormac whispered, "weep now if you must, but while you remain with me, I'll see to it that you never weep again." Asherah cried against his chest as Lormac stroked her hair. Once she had calmed, Lormac tilted her chin up and he gazed at her, her black eyes that were like molten pools of darkness. He opened his mouth to speak but thought the better of it. He was a man of action, a king who inspired his followers with deeds, not speeches, and he slid his sacred armband onto her wrist.

"What?" Asherah asked, shocked out of her despair. "No, Lormac, nonono, you don't want to do this." She tried to pull the Sala from her arm, but his hand closed over hers.

"I do," Lormac insisted, "and it's done." He grasped her hands and held them against his chest. "Wear it, and be mine." Asherah looked from the armband to Lormac's face, his eyes telling her what this simple act meant more than words ever could.

"My lord." A *saffira* rushed into the room.

"Leave!" Lormac shouted over his shoulder.

"My lord, the Prelate of Parthalan is here!"

Asherah speaks...

Of the many things I'd never expected to encounter in the elf king's home, the arrival of the Prelate of Parthalan, the right hand of Sahlgren, was one. Gods, I hoped he didn't have legion at his back along with orders to return us to the dojas.

"No one's taking you anywhere," Lormac declared when I voiced my fears. "The Prelate has much power, yes, but not over me."

"Should you wear this when you meet him?" I asked, and again tried giving back the armband. I was shocked that Lormac asked me to stay with him, shocked that he would put the Sala on me... and despondent, that he'd regain his wits and realize what a mistake he had made.

"I'm well acquainted with the Prelate. He will recognize me without it."

"But Lormac—"

"We will speak of this later," he said. "Now, I must deal with my guests."

Lormac left his chamber in a flurry of motion, calling out commands to his advisors as they scurried around him.

I located Torim and Harek; both were as shocked as I to hear of the king's visitors. They both eyed the Sala but said nothing, which was good, since I myself didn't know what I thought about wearing the most sacred object in Tingu. Worse, I understood all too well what my wearing of the Sala meant.

I was jolted free of my musings when we entered the hall and saw the two men standing before Lormac's throne. The one speaking was short for a faerie, but solidly muscled, his yellow hair shot through with strands of silver. I knew he was the Prelate; his authority hung around him like a royal mantle. The man next to him bore an uncanny resemblance, though he was a head taller and his hair more the color of the sun.

As we approached, the Prelate was attempting to berate Lormac for offering us aid without first consulting with Teg'urnan. I wanted to shout at the Prelate, accuse him of complicity in the enslavement of our kind and indifference to our plight. I also suppressed a wave of guilt, for while I'd come to Lormac for help I hadn't wanted to cause him or his kingdom strife.

"When I learned that there were faeries plotting rebellion against Sahlgren I expected that they would hide beyond our borders," the Prelate was saying, "but I didn't expect to find them camped before the Seat of Tingu."

"As always, an elf to clean up a faerie's mess," Lormac replied. The jibe made the taller man's eyes flame, but the Prelate remained composed. "History does repeat itself often amongst your kind."

"They're all guilty of treason," the Prelate continued. "I can have them executed where they stand." Torim gasped and clutched my arm; Harek set his jaw as if he were about to be sentenced; I tried very hard not to faint. Lormac, however, was unaffected by the threat.

"You forget, Parthalan's border is a two day ride south," Lormac stated. "These are my lands. You'll be executing no one, and you'll speak to none without my consent." Lormac and the Prelate glared at each other, but before the threats could escalate further the taller man spoke.

"We're not here to punish them," he said. "We believe their cause is sound!"

The man's outburst, an unthinkable breach of propriety before a king, effectively silenced the entire hall. Torim, Harek, and I exchanged glances; none of us had anticipated that the Prelate might also be against the king. Lormac met my eyes, and I gave him the slightest of nods. Had the Lord of Tingu just looked to me for approval?

"Here are those who would remove your king," Lormac stated, rising from his throne, "perhaps you'll find their claims interesting." Lormac brushed past the men as if they weren't there and strode toward us. "This is Asherah, who was herself a slave by Sahlgren's leave and now leads her followers, along with her companions, Torim and Harek." Lormac's hand hovered over the small of my back, careful not to touch me; I noted that he positioned himself in such a way as to display the armband I wore. The Prelate must have been familiar with it, for he eyed it silently.

"My lady," Lormac continued, "if you're willing, the Prelate would like to discuss your claims against Sahlgren." He then shifted his stance so my face was hidden and spoke softly, only to me. "If you don't wish to speak to them, say the word and I'll handle it."

In that moment, as Lormac stood between us and the Prelate, willing to defend us against those who could—and possibly should—make us answer for our deeds, I felt the tough shell around my heart crack. I'd already known that Lormac believed our claims—hells, his riders had seen the evidence firsthand—and he had already pledged his aid. But this was different. Never before had anyone put themselves bodily between me and harm, nor had anyone ever had such faith in me.

Gods, how I would miss him once he came to his senses and realized what a pathetic shell of a person I was.

"I am willing," I replied, fighting the urge to smile. Something in my voice must have told him how I felt, and he drew me closer.

"Very well," he said, and then turned back to the Prelate and his man. "Once you've refreshed yourselves, we will meet in my chambers. A private room will better suit our needs."

"We need no refreshment," said the Prelate. "We're ready to discuss this now."

"You may be ready, but I am not," Lormac said. "I'll send for you shortly."

With that, Lormac dismissed the Prelate, albeit against his wishes. As one of the saffira led them away, I turned to follow Torim and Harek, believing that we all had a short reprieve.

"Asherah."

Lormac spoke as a king, and his tone made me stop instantly. Torim also stopped; I could only imagine what my dearest companion was thinking, perhaps why was I wearing the Sala? Had I forsaken her for the elf king? But she asked nothing, and after she squeezed my hand, she followed Harek from the hall.

"My lord?" I turned to face Lormac. He beckoned me to follow, and we entered his much smaller receiving chamber.

"I meant what I said," he said once we were alone. "I will handle the Prelate and send him on his way. You do not need to be so indisposed."

"His man said that they also question Sahlgren. What if they know of the dojas? What if they also want to stop him?" I paced the room, speculating on how they may have learned of the king's transgressions.

Lormac shook his head; it seemed that my behavior amused him. "Little star, you are a woman like no other."

"Will you forever call me little star?"

195

"Tell me you'll stay in Tingu, and I'll call you many other names." He reached for me, stopping before he made contact. "May I?"

I watched his face for long moments; here was a man who was accustomed to getting whatever he desired, taking whatever he wanted, yet he made sure to check himself before he touched me. In his every action, Lormac was sensitive to who I was and what I'd endured. To this day, I wonder what he saw in me.

I didn't answer with words; instead, I went into his arms and let him hold me. No, I let myself be held, and I availed myself of all the comfort he was willing to share. It was more than enough.

"If you stay, I'll call you my beloved," Lormac murmured. "You'll be my companion, my advisor, my equal in all things. My star, my light, my love." I leaned back and watched him for a moment, taking in his craggy brow and merry eyes that were suddenly so somber.

I touched his face. "Why do you want me so? You already have everything. I have nothing to offer you."

"You're wrong," he replied, "I see what you really are, not what others have done to you. You can give me the one thing I truly want."

"What is that?" I asked, fearful of his reply.

"You."

While Tor sat calmly, Caol'nir paced the small chamber for easily the hundredth time; it seemed like they had been left rotting in that room for days. It bothered Caol'nir that Lormac had shoved them aside while he went off with his faerie mate, his face smug as he forced them to wait.

"You miss her," Tor observed, and Caol'nir had to admit that his unsettled state owed little to Lormac's tardiness.

Caol'nir scrubbed his face with his hands, the image of Alluria standing before the gates as he rode away still sharp in his mind.

"I hope I wasn't wrong to leave her," Caol'nir said. "I told her that she must remain in Teg'urnan for her safety, but now I wonder if she would have been better off here, with me."

"Fiornacht is there, and Caol'non," Tor reminded him, "they won't let anything happen to Alluria." Caol'nir wished to dispute his father's words. Ethnia and Keena had thought themselves safe, too.

Lormac arrived, and his second and an advisor laden with maps closely followed. "Asherah will be with us presently," Lormac stated as he selected a map. He unrolled the parchment and spread it across the table.

"Congratulations on your new queen," Tor stated. "I see that she wears the Sala." Lormac acknowledged Tor with a nod, then returned his attention to the map. "Tell me, old friend, did she bend your ear and convince you to war with Sahlgren?"

"When were we ever friends?" Lormac asked without looking up. "I will remind you, Prelate, you only remain here by her leave. If I had my way, you would have been gone shortly after you arrived."

"Then your consort does advise you," Tor said as he baited Lormac. Caol'nir did not understand what his father hoped to accomplish, but he didn't think antagonizing the Lord of Tingu was wise.

"Father," Caol'nir began but fell silent when Asherah, Torim, and Harek entered the room; Sarfek remained skulking in the corridor.

"She does not," Asherah stated as she took her place at Lormac's side. "My lord has his own opinions."

"You claim an elf as your lord?" demanded Tor. Asherah's eyes flamed at the Prelate, but it was Torim that spoke.

"Lormac is not the one who sent us to the dojas," Torim said softly. "He's trying to put right all the harm that Sahlgren has done."

Caol'nir watched his father as Torim spoke. It pained Caol'nir to think that such a seemingly gentle creature as she had been a slave; he guessed that Tor felt the same. Torim's words had the desired effect, and the Prelate turned his attention back to Lormac.

"This is a map of Thurnda," Lormac began, "where Ehkron was sighted this past Winter Eve, and this," he traced a path across the mountains, "is the trail of carnage he has wrought among my people. As you can see, Prelate, your king's actions have brought strife to my lands as well."

"You're certain it was Ehkron?" Caol'nir asked. "Seven days prior to Winter Eve, I saw him meet with Sahlgren in the High Desert. He couldn't have made the journey so fast, unless..." Caol'nir looked to his father, and then continued. "Rahlle mentioned that the king has use of a portal."

"And a portal would allow Ehkron to journey from the High Desert to the World's Spine in the blink of an eye," Lormac concluded. "Did the mad magician say what the portal is used for?"

"By demons, to gain entry to Teg'urnan and the Great Temple." Caol'nir leaned forward and covered his face with his hands. "One of the priestesses was torn to pieces." Torim gasped, and even Harek's immovable features were touched by the image of an innocent priestess's murder. "Rahlle said it was likely a *mordeth* that killed her."

"Was she marked?" Torim asked quietly.

"Marked?" Caol'nir asked.

"*Mordeth's* mark their property by burning their handprint into flesh," Torim replied. "They use their own blood, so they may always know where the bearer lies. It makes escape near impossible unless the *mordeth* is killed."

"Blood burns heal," Caol'nir said. "I've had many, yet I bear no scars. Why do the handprints remain?"

"I don't know why a *mordeth's* blood is different," replied Torim. "I only know that it is."

"There was no way to know if she'd been marked," Caol'nir said, remembering the gore that had once been Ethnia. He did not remember any pieces of her being large enough to carry such an imprint.

"May I ask what has given you cause to believe these claims against Sahlgren?" Lormac asked, breaking the pall of silence.

"Rahlle claims that Sahlgren wants a new legion that carries demon blood in its veins," Tor said. "Apparently, once he has conquered this realm, he will use them to conquer the rest."

"Is that why only the pureblooded are enslaved?" Lormac asked. Tor and Caol'nir looked quizzically at Lormac, and he retrieved another map. "My information states that the demons only take those of pure faerie blood for enslavement. You'll notice that most of the dojas are in the west and south, where few other races live. There are almost none near the dark fae, and few to the north."

Tor studied the map for a time, and then retrieved a scroll of his own. "We had reports filtering in of slave camps, but we could only verify the location of a very few," he said as he unrolled the parchment. "By the time we reached them, they were burnt out."

"This is where we were held," Asherah said, indicating a spot on Tor's map. "And these are dojas that we burnt." She traced their route northward.

"You engineered the destruction of each of these dojas?" Tor asked incredulously.

"I did," Asherah answered. Tor looked at her with a new measure of respect, while Lormac looked on her with an abundance of pride.

"What I still don't understand is how we've only learned this of late," Caol'nir stated. "Based on your information there are dojas all across Parthalan, yet we have received no reports of trouble. How could so many faeries be captured and no one come to the legion for aid?"

"Your legion was the first to be compromised," Harek stated flatly. "We were kidnapped from the legion and tortured nearly to death, then put under a thrall that kept us from helping the women, no matter how they screamed or fought."

"Helping the women?" Tor repeated, and Harek nodded. "One thing I do need said plainly, what was the purpose of these dojas?" Asherah squeezed her eyes shut, and Torim looked away. Caol'nir did not know why Tor needed an explicit description; perhaps his loyalty to Sahlgren ran too deeply. Perhaps he just needed to hear it with his own ears in order to believe it.

It seemed that Lormac thought such talk unnecessary as well, and he whispered something in Asherah's ear, to which she shook her head and assured him that she was fine. Caol'nir then remembered that Lormac had said that Asherah was a former slave—*He took a slave as his queen?*—and realized that this delicate girl had been subjected to the same horrors he was trying to keep from Alluria.

"Our purpose was to get demon heirs," Asherah replied. "We were to be the source of Sahlgren's new legion."

Tor shoved back from the table and walked to the far side of the chamber; Caol'nir stalked after him.

"Now you have confirmation of what the king plots under our very nose," he hissed in his father's ear. "I told you that things were wrong. I told you that there should not be a fifth door to the temple." Caol'nir gestured wildly and the blue ribbon about his wrist caught his eye. "Is this why all the priestesses were brought to Teg'urnan? As a final offering for the *mordeth-gall*?"

"Sahlgren said he brought the priestesses to the Great Temple for safety," Tor replied, "likely to keep them away from this plan."

"You believe that?" demanded Caol'nir. "Ethnia—"

"Was a great tragedy," finished Tor, his tone letting his son know that the matter was finished, at least for the moment. The Prelate of Parthalan strode back to the elf king, and addressed the consort who was once a slave.

"How long has this gone on?" Tor demanded of Asherah, but it was Sarfek who answered.

"It began fourteen winters past, when Ehkron raided my master's home," Sarfek began as he hobbled in from the corridor. "He only kept us novices alive. He ate my master's heart before our very eyes. Were dragged about the edges of the kingdom for three winters, enthralling the legion to send reports that all was well while we forced the soldiers to build dojas. Any home within a day's travel of a doja was burned. The men, we killed; the women were not as lucky." Sarfek sank into a chair, as if speaking for so long had sapped his strength. His words hung over the room like a cold fog, chilling all in attendance.

"I will rip Ehkron's heart from his chest and shove it beating down his throat," Caol'nir vowed. "We've failed you all." He spoke to the faeries before him, but he was only thinking of his mate, alone in Teg'urnan.

"My lady, you have my deepest regrets," Tor said to Asherah, "you all do. I know words said this late are useless, but had I known of your plight I would have retrieved you myself." Asherah murmured an acknowledgement as Tor resumed his seat. "Well, Lormac, what are we to do? It seems my king has run amok, and we are begging the elf lord's help."

Lormac acknowledged Tor's words with more grace than Caol'nir had expected, and looked to the map before him. He studied it for a moment, then, oddly, he smiled.

"We need to know what Ehkron ultimately wants," Lormac said, his eyes glinting. "We certainly cannot ask him, so we will learn his plans another way."

"What way is that?"

"We capture a *mordeth*."

Asherah speaks...

Tor and Caol'nir both argued against Lormac's plan to capture a mordeth, but to no avail. While capturing any demon was fraught with risks, snaring a warlord was surely nothing but folly, they said. When I indicated the burnt dojas on the map—dojas that I and my Ish h'ra hai *had* personally destroyed—even the Prelate fell silent.

They selected a doja that was uncomfortably close to the Seat for their attack, so close that they hoped to be there and back in the space of a day. Tor and Caol'nir rode out to the doja, accompanied by Harek, and returned with detailed drawings of the camp and the surrounding landscape. It was decided that a small force would be best suited to the endeavor, and that Lormac would lead the Prelate, Caol'nir, and ten of his personal guard. Oh, and five healers for the slaves who'd survived their torments.

"No one has more of a right to see this doja destroyed than Torim and I," I declared when they tried to dissuade us from accompanying them. "You would deny us our retribution?"

"I'd rather spare you the sight of it," Lormac began, when Harek spoke up.

"If not for Asherah, none of us would be free," Harek stated, looking at me with such appreciation it made me uncomfortable. "We are no longer of Parthalan, but of the Ish h'ra hai. We are loyal to Asherah alone, and we will see her safely to the doja and back."

There was no arguing after that, and Lormac's advisors assembled supplies. We would leave four days hence, and attempt to take the doja by noon. While others were making decisions, I went with Torim to her chamber. As soon as the door shut behind us, she looked at the Sala on my arm.

"Forsaking me so soon?" she teased.

"I did not ask for this," I replied. "He just put it on me. I had no idea what he was doing!"

"And yet, you're still wearing it." I protested but Torim held up her hand. "Do you want to wear it?"

"I...I don't know."

"Then go to him and find out."

I don't know how long I stood outside Lormac's door, debating whether I really wanted to enter. It would be so much easier to just return to Torim, to hide away in the familiar warmth of her arms...but she would know that I hadn't spoken to Lormac and just send me right back. Eventually a saffira came down the corridor, and rather than have her think I was skulking about outside the king's chamber, I finally knocked on his door. Lormac's manservant admitted me, then announced my presence.

Lormac hurried from the rear chamber and enfolded me into his arms; he was bare to the waist, his skin damp and warm. He must have been bathing. "My star," he murmured into my hair, "don't ever knock on that door again. My chamber is yours." He nodded to his attendants and they left, and I was alone with the man who would be my mate. I pulled out of his arms and crossed my own over my chest.

"Forgive me," he said, indicating his state of dress, "I didn't expect to see you tonight. But I'm glad you're here."

"Torim sent me," I said shakily. I glanced at his chest, his wiry muscles limned in firelight. The amount of skin on display made me uncomfortable, and I turned away.

"You don't want to look at me?"

"I don't remember ever being alone with a naked man." Lormac chuckled as he wrapped his arms around my waist.

"I'm far from naked," he commented, "and I'm honored to be the first."

"I didn't say you were the first, just the only one I remember." I didn't move or turn around, and Lormac released me. I peeked over my shoulder and saw him pull on a tunic.

"Sit with me," he said, and I took my place next to him. He placed his arm around me and I rested my head on his shoulder; it unnerved me, how natural it felt to mold my body to his. "Torim sent you?"

"Yes." I fell silent after that, and we sat together for what seemed like half the night before I got the courage to go on. "You just put this on me without asking."

"If I'd asked, what would you have said?" Again, I was silent, and Lormac read volumes into what I'd left unsaid. "You're free to say no."

"I am?" I must have sounded too eager, for his face was pained as if I'd struck him. "It's not that I want to deny you. When we escaped, I swore that no one would ever know me in that way again. All I wanted was to be free. And to free the others. I never imagined that I might one day have a mate." I leaned against him as I traced the stones of the Sala. "And then you put this on me, and now everyone assumes that I belong to you. I don't want to belong to anyone."

"Asherah, it won't be like that," he said.

"I heard the Prelate call me 'your consort.'" I said. "That certainly sounds like belonging."

Lormac held my wrist with one hand, while the other moved my fingers to the oval stone of the Sala, the only stone that wasn't green; it was dark pink and smooth, warm to the touch. "This stone signifies the king's heart," he explained. "Until I met you, it was white and cold, but it warms and the color darkens as my feelings for you grow. Once you are my mate, it will be a deep red. If you take me as your mate." He turned my face to his, his gray eyes reflecting orange in the firelight. "You wouldn't be my consort, or my lover, if you accept me. You'll be my queen."

"I cannot be a queen."

"Why not? Who's to say you aren't one already." He pushed my hair back and held my face close to his. "You know, I haven't even kissed you."

"You've never asked," I retorted, feeling bold despite my anxiety.

"May I?"

I searched his face, and try as I might I could find nothing but affection. And compassion. And hope. Having decided to no longer sabotage my own happiness, at least for the rest of the evening, I leaned toward him and pressed my lips to his. It was sweet and gentle, and Lormac made no demand to take things further. Once we parted, he held me close against his chest and said something or other, but I felt something strange against my arm.

"The stone, it's darker!" I stared at the Sala, feeling the warm gem under my fingers, surprised beyond reason to see such a tangible representation of Lormac's affection for me.

"Let's see if we can make it darker yet," he murmured as he kissed me, harder and longer than before. Afterward, he tightened his arms about me and I rested my head on his shoulder.

"I don't know how to want a mate," I said softly. "I don't know how to want you. Yet here I am, and I don't want to leave. I won't lie; the idea of you claiming me fills me with terror." I didn't speak of my real fear, that if he saw *the horrible wounds that covered me from neck to knee, permanent reminders of what I had been, he would be sickened and never wish to look at me again.*

"Are you filled with terror now?"

"No."

"Then stay, and let me hold you. We can work out the rest later."

Chapter 18

Asherah stayed with Lormac that night, thought she tried slipping away just before first dawn.

"I thought you were asleep," she explained when Lormac caught her elbow. Asherah sat beside him. "I only wished to return to my chamber."

"I can have your things brought here," Lormac offered, but Asherah shook her head.

"That won't be necessary." Asherah leaned forward, her elbows propped up on her knees as she traced the heartstone with her fingertip. "Am I truly free to refuse you?"

Lormac brushed his fingers across her cheek, hoping it wasn't the last time he would do so. "Yes."

Asherah was silent as she stared at the heartstone. "Will you be angry if I say no?"

"No. I'll be heartbroken, but I won't be angry." He was already heartbroken, mostly because Asherah had not fallen into his arms as he had hoped. Lormac cursed under his breath; in his eagerness to proclaim his feelings for Asherah he had managed to put her so ill at ease she could hardly speak to him. "Forgive me; I went about this the wrong way. I should have…" Lormac shook his head as he leaned forward, copying Asherah's posture. "Nexa save me, I've no idea what to do. I've never asked someone to become my mate."

"I'm honored to be the first," Asherah quipped.

"The only," Lormac said.

"Among faeries, a man would never ask a woman to be his mate," Asherah offered. "The woman is the one who chooses."

"And the man just abides by her decision?"

"I suppose." Asherah rested her head against his shoulder. "It's not the same with elves, is it?"

"It's not." Lormac cupped her hands and pressed her palm against the heartstone. "Will you do something for me?"

Asherah leaned back and regarded him.

"What do you need?"

Love. Companionship. You spread naked atop my bed, screaming my name. "Keep wearing the Sala. Touch it, feel it, think on a life wearing it. Then tell me your answer."

Asherah smiled at him, not one of her usual, tight smiles that were more of a grimace, but a genuine smile. "I can do that."

Asherah spent the next four nights in Lormac's chambers, though they had confined themselves to his parlor. Asherah had looked over maps, eager to find some clue that would remind her of her former life, and Lormac told her tales of elves, of past battles, and of his ancestors. He told her about the Sala, of the magic that coursed through it born of earth and stone, and how he held a measure of power over both.

During these long nights Asherah mostly listened in rapt attention. Lormac had worried she would find his stories boring, but she claimed to enjoy them all. When he felt that he had talked enough, she told him tales of faerie gods and of how Parthalan had become a kingdom, but faltered when she realized she had no stories of her own ancestors.

"Worry not, little star," he soothed, "we'll make our own memories."

Asherah smiled and settled back into his arms; she had grown somewhat comfortable with him holding her, and Lormac embraced her whenever he could. Lormac had already known he enjoyed being with her, but he looked forward to those evenings as if he was spending time with Nexa herself. After his attendants left for the evening, Asherah let her guard down, and he learned that she was funny, intelligent, and even slightly mischievous. What she was not, however, was eager to give him an answer.

"Little star," he asked on the fourth night, "have you thought about what I've asked you?"

"Must I answer you so soon?" she asked. She laid her head against his chest and looked up with wide, black eyes. "I know you need my reply, but I so enjoy this time with you. Being here with you, like this, makes me happy, and I don't want that to change just yet."

The Sala railed inside his mind, but Lormac ignored it. He understood why she was putting him off, and he could hardly blame her. Moreover, he wanted Asherah to come to him willingly rather than see their mating as nothing but a course of duty.

"I'm glad you're happy," he said as he stroked her hair. "You'll tell me soon?"

"Soon ."

As he led the small band of warriors toward the doja, Lormac had difficulty concentrating on the battle that lay ahead. Being as much a warrior as a king, Lormac had never before let his concentration falter when he was about to engage an enemy, whether it be for a small skirmish or a full scale attack.

Not so on this morning, which had dawned clear and cold with a biting wind. Lormac preferred fighting in the cold, for the stench of spilled blood quickly turned rank in the heat. He glanced to his side at the woman who occupied his thoughts, the woman who stared straight ahead, her knuckles white where they clutched the reins. Lormac had wanted her to remain at the Seat, but she had refused him outright.

She refuses me often. Never had it taken Lormac more than a moment to get a woman into his bed; then again, whenever he'd been refused in the past he'd just moved on to another. That had changed when his star strode into his keep with more concern for her people than herself. Lormac had loved her that day for her compassion, and for something new every day since.

He glanced back at her, fearlessly heading toward a nest of demons. *Fearless, as a warrior queen should be.* Lormac imagined their life together as she travelled with him on campaigns, fighting by his side. The soldiers that fanned out around them, all handpicked by Lormac, cast sidelong glances at Asherah and Torim, for in the elfin lands women were rarely warriors and would never be sent against a known grouping of demons.

That will change, Lormac thought, smiling at Asherah. His soldiers watched as Asherah smiled back, just as they had also noticed that Asherah wore the Sala. No one would dare to question Lormac, for as Lord of Tingu the Sala was his to bestow as he chose. Still, Lormac knew that Asherah felt their curious glances. He also felt her growing sense of disquiet as they approached the doja so unbearably close to the Seat.

"How can this doja be so close, yet the elves have no idea of its existence?" Torim whispered to Asherah as they closed in upon their destination.

"How can half of Parthalan's legion have been enslaved and the Prelate have no idea?" Asherah countered.

"I think those in positions of power grow complacent and deny that such evil can not only exist but flourish in their lands," Torim continued. "Hillel, I don't want you to grow complacent." Asherah looked at Torim, but before she could question her, Lormac approached.

"My ladies," he said, "come, the doja can be seen from this hill."

They followed him to the crest, and Torim's breath caught at the sight of the doja. "It's smaller than most," Asherah said. "Perhaps no more than twenty are held inside."

"How many demons?" Lormac asked.

"Maybe as few as five, along with the *mordeth* and magic handler," Asherah replied. "Who knows how many fae guards they have." Harek began explaining the layout of the doja, when something caught Caol'nir's eye.

"That guard," he said, pointing at a man dragging something from the doja, "he's called Olwynn. I served with him at the Southern Border. How is he enslaved here?"

"Once you're put under thrall, you're moved far from anything familiar," Harek replied. "It's to keep you docile, under their control."

"Docile, eh?" said Tor. "I'm of a mind to agitate them."

Lormac called for his soldiers to assemble. "I will lead the charge," Lormac proclaimed. "My lady, will you ride beside me?"

"Of course." As she took her place next to Lormac the soldiers now murmured with approval. They still found it odd to have a woman warrior in their midst, but a warrior queen who rode beside the king deserved respect. Once they were in position, Lormac grabbed Asherah and kissed her hard; he attributed her stiff limbs first to surprise, then embarrassment as his gesture caused a great whooping cheer from his soldiers.

"Tradition," Lormac explained with a glint in his eye, "the longer the kiss between the king and queen, the swifter the victory."

Asherah glanced over her shoulder at the cheering elves. "Shouldn't we be trying to surprise the enemy?"

"Surprise is for lesser warriors," Lormac declared. "Elves fear no foe!" With that, Lormac let out a war cry and the warriors of Tingu hurtled down the hill toward the doja. Despite their clamor they did surprise the demons, lazy in their role as torturers. Only four stood watch, and the flashing elfin swords quickly cut them down. The elves leapt from their horses as they flowed inside the doja.

"This way!" Asherah yelled as she ran toward the rear of the structure, looking for the *mordeth's* chamber. A door crashed open and Asherah saw the *mordeth's* arm behind the door. She raised her sword to strike, then the demon stepped out from behind the door. Standing before her was the largest demon she'd ever seen.

The *mordeth* roared, and Asherah ran.

"Out of my way," she shrieked, and elf and demon alike leapt from her path. She found the main corridor and saw an open cell door. Asherah darted to the side once she reached it; the much larger *mordeth* did not. Asherah slammed the heavy door shut and slid the bolt into place, panting as she leaned against the rough wood.

"My lady," Balthus yelled as he ran into the corridor.

"Get Lormac," she gasped. "The *mordeth* is in the cell!"

"You captured him alone?" Balthus asked incredulously.

"Me alone," Asherah replied, then the beast roared. "Go!"

Balthus ordered three soldiers to guard her while he fetched Lormac. The *mordeth* threw himself against the door, rattling the walls.

"Let us," said one of the elves. Asherah stepped aside and they pressed their shoulders against the door; as soon as they did, a lesser demon launched itself down the hall.

One of the soldiers leapt in front of Asherah, but didn't land a blow before the beast tore out his guts. Two more demons appeared in the blink of an eye, these nearly as large as the *mordeth* in the cell. One of the soldiers attacked the demons, chasing them from Asherah, while the other soldier was flung into the wall and landed unconscious at Asherah's feet.

More demons entered the corridor and Asherah raised her sword. Before she could another entered, whether elf or fae she couldn't tell. Then she saw a blade flash as Caol'nir killed all three of the demons. When the last dropped he strode toward her, heedless of the bodies around him.

"Only five demons?" Caol'nir smirked. "I've killed seven myself."

"I said *maybe* as few as five," Asherah clarified. "Did you find the magic handler?"

"Harek is searching for him now." Caol'nir eyed Asherah's sword hand, and frowned.

"Here," he said, grabbing Asherah's arm and adjusting her grasp. "Grip it like so, your swing will have more force." He stepped aside so she could take a test swing. "Get a heavier blade as well, that way even if you don't kill your opponent you can maim it."

"And all this time I thought I had a talent for swordplay," she said.

"You do," Caol'nir replied, "but even the best needs practice."

She took another swing. "Lormac wouldn't let me carry a true warrior's sword," she said with a rueful smile. "I don't think he found it ladylike."

Caol'nir laughed, then Lormac burst into the corridor, closely followed by Balthus. His gaze swept over the scene: a disemboweled soldier, another two unconscious, three dead demons and his would-be mate smiling at the Prelate's son while a *mordeth* bellowed from a cell.

"Are you hurt?" he demanded, ignoring Caol'nir as he strode to Asherah's side.

"I'm not," she replied. "Caol'nir killed them."

"Many thanks," Lormac said to Caol'nir.

"You should get her a real sword," Caol'nir added. "The one she's holding won't protect her from a frightened rabbit."

Lormac frowned, and the *mordeth* picked that moment to throw himself against the door.

"Brace the door," shouted Caol'nir.

"Don't bother," Lormac said. "I'll seal him in."

"How?" demanded Asherah, dust falling from the rafters.

"Remember the power I told you of?" Lormac asked, and Asherah nodded. He strode to the door, held by four elfin warriors but still looking like it could give way at any moment. "I will require the Sala," Lormac looked at Asherah almost apologetically. "I must have access to all of my power if I'm to encase the beast."

Asherah immediately slipped the sacred object from her arm and returned it to the elf king. Lormac touched the Sala with one hand and Asherah with the other, and Asherah gasped as the power of the Seat coursed through the both of them.

"I also require my mate at my side," he murmured, so that no one but Asherah heard him over the beast's wailing. "Later, I'll return it to you properly." Asherah nodded, and placed her hand over his.

Lormac knelt and placed his hand over the metal bolt—*raw iron, good*—then placed his other hand into the earth. Those assembled felt the room waver. The earth crawled up the wooden door until it met the metal hinge, the two substances becoming a swirling gray pool. When Lormac finished, he stood back to reveal a layer of earth and iron that covered not only the door but the surrounding walls as well. They could still hear the *mordeth* raging within, but Lormac's mound didn't budge.

"You expect a pile of dirt to hold a *mordeth*?" Caol'nir asked.

"It will hold until I release it," Lormac proclaimed as he dusted off his hands. "Leave him to rot while we see to the others."

The soldiers followed Caol'nir and Balthus from the corridor, and began breaking apart the wooden cells that held the slaves. As they did so, Lormac stayed Asherah with a hand on her elbow.

"When I touched the earth, it spoke to me," he began. "It told me the story behind every drop of blood, every broken body that touched it." Asherah looked away, and walked toward a room at the end of the corridor. Lormac followed and found a windowless room, slightly larger than the cells. A rough-hewn wooden table occupied most of it. At first, Lormac thought the heavy manacles bolted to the table were rusty; he looked closer, and saw that they were caked with blood.

"What does the earth tell you here?" Asherah asked, tracing a manacle. Lormac knelt and touched the ground. He saw women dragged across the dirt and thrown onto the table, broken and bloody and some barely alive. Then Lormac saw demons ravaging them until they were nearly dead, and he snatched his hand from the earth.

"This...this is what is done in all of them?" he asked hoarsely, and Asherah nodded.

"All these places are the same," she said, staring at the manacles. "If they're in a mood to play they cut themselves, bleeding all over you. I remember it pooling under the chains, burning like fire..."

Lormac had known she was a slave, but he never imagined anything like what the earth had shown him. "Were these things done to all the women? To you?"

"When you're first taken, it's every day," she said quietly. "To break your spirit. When you're nearly dead, they leave you for a time. Then, if you aren't carrying a whelp, it starts up again."

Lormac put the manacle against her palm, then he placed his hand atop hers. "Never again," he declared, the room wavering as the metal crumbled under his influence, "not here, not anywhere, and never to my mate." He wrapped his arms around Asherah's waist, but she remained distant.

Lormac turned her around and cupped her face with his hands.

"My star..." he began.

"I understand if you want me to leave," she said.

"What?" Lormac asked. Before he could continue, they heard Torim shouting for Asherah. They left the torture chamber and found Torim among the healers, tending to the freed women.

"Asherah," Torim said as she rushed forward, "only four can be saved."

"How many to be killed?" Asherah asked.

"Killed?" Tor roared. "We'll kill no one; we will get them healers."

"They don't want to be healed. Death is their only solace." She noted Tor's appalled face, and added, "Why do you think they call me Asherah the Ruthless?"

Torim had been mistaken; out of the twelve women the healers saved nine, and all ten of the guards were loosed from the thrall. Asherah dispatched the three who needed it quickly, holding Torim's hand all the while. After seeing the inside of a doja even Tor didn't argue against Asherah's methods, and offered his sharpest dagger.

The elves and fae established camp far too close to the doja, and the bellowing cries of the *mordeth*, than any cared for. The mood at the camp was somber, for while they had been victorious, none but Asherah, Harek, and Torim had been prepared for the wretched conditions. The death of the three women and the elf soldier hung over the survivors like a damp fog, chilling them to the bone. Adding to the pall was that three of the women had been elves, which neither Lormac nor his warriors had expected.

Once Lormac's grand tent was erected he, Balthus, Tor, and Caol'nir sat inside for nearly half the night, discussing how the *mordeth* was to be questioned and eventually disposed of. Ultimately, the decision was made to leave the *mordeth* be for the night in the hopes that he would be willing to bargain for his freedom come morning.

Lormac emerged from the meeting to find Asherah sitting before the fire. She leaned heavily against Torim, her arms wrapped around her waist. Harek, still acting as their guard, stood behind the two while the newly freed slaves fanned out about the three, as if they were a beacon of safety.

He studied the two women, noting how peaceful Asherah seemed in Torim's arms. *Why doesn't she relax like that when I hold her?* Asherah's behavior both confused and frustrated him; when he had placed the Sala on Asherah he had assumed she would be overjoyed by the honor of being the king's mate. Instead she had acted like a cornered animal. And her face, when he'd told her that she was free to deny him…

But she hadn't denied him; she'd remained in his chamber and had let him hold her. She'd admitted that she was scared. Lormac understood Asherah's hesitation, more so now that he had seen a doja, and he was enraged that his mate had been subjected to such torment. He even understood why Torim's touch calmed her so; he just wished his calmed her as well.

She thought I wouldn't want her once I knew. Lormac admitted that he was both disgusted and disturbed by what the women suffered, but he didn't hold those acts against Asherah. In fact, as he imagined his star rallying her fellow slaves and turning on their captors, he smiled. Asherah truly was the warrior he thought she was, and her triumphs only strengthened his love.

Lormac approached the fire and learned the true reason for Asherah's peaceful state: she was fast asleep. He sat beside the two and met Torim's soft doe eyes above Asherah's head.

"Have you noticed that no matter where she is, the scent of her hair is cool and green like a meadow?" Torim asked quietly. Lormac was irritated that Torim would say such a thing, mostly because he had no idea what Asherah's hair smelled like.

"She does not like being close to me," Lormac confessed.

"She does," Torim reassured. "You must be patient with her, for as terrible as the wounds upon her skin are, her soul was cut much more deeply."

Lormac remembered the images shown from the doja, of what the earth told him, of what was done on that table. "Let me take her."

Torim released her friend into the king's arms. Lormac carried Asherah into his tent and gently laid her on his bed, then pulled off her boots and unbuckled her sword belt. He tucked a blanket about her, and kissed her forehead before dragging a chair next to the bed.

"You're mine, and I'll see all the fae gods in hell before I allow anything to harm you."

Asherah woke soon after Lormac had placed her on the bed. She heard the *mordeth* wail and flinched, but relaxed when she saw Lormac beside her.

"How did I get here?"

"I carried you," Lormac replied. Asherah's eyes widened, and he explained, "You fell asleep before the fire. I couldn't let you catch a chill." Asherah nodded, so Lormac took the opportunity to lean forward and grasp her wrist. When Asherah saw the Sala in his hand, she pulled away.

"You still want me to wear it?" she asked.

"Did you think I would hold your captivity against you?" he asked. "I don't."

"Truly?"

"Truly." He again tried placing the Sala on her arm, but still she evaded him.

"Shouldn't it be replaced when I become your mate?" Asherah asked, refusing to meet his eyes. His initial thought had been to tell her that they could take care of that immediately, but Lormac remembered the images from the doja.

"I won't lie with you until you're ready," Lormac promised. Asherah nodded but wouldn't look at him, and Lormac worried that there was another reason for her hesitation.

"If your answer is no, just tell me. I swear to you, you'll have my aid regardless. I will not renege on my words."

Asherah shook her head and took his hand, lightly stroking the heartstone. "It's not that," she insisted, "I just don't want it to be here, in the shadow of a doja, with that creature wailing away."

Lormac smoothed back her hair. "I understand, love." He kissed her forehead, and then stood. "Rest now."

"But where will you sleep?" Asherah asked. "This is your bed."

"I had a second made up," he had replied, indicating a curtained-off area at the rear of the tent. "I thought you'd want your privacy. I'll sleep there." Asherah smiled at him, the first time he had seen her smile since they arrived at this accursed spot.

"Lormac, you're as wonderful a man as you are a king."

He went to the second bed, which, in accordance with his instruction, was just as sumptuous as his, and lay on top of the blankets. He stared at the roof of the tent; whenever he closed his eyes he was met by images of Asherah telling him no. After a time he heard the curtain rustle, then felt a tug at the bedclothes.

"I hope you don't mind," Asherah murmured as she slid underneath the blanket. "I missed you."

"Did you?" Lormac asked. "I worry that you haven't yet found a way to gently refuse me."

"I don't want you to think that," Asherah said. "This morning, when you told me you don't know how to do this... Well, neither do I. I've never before been a former slave who caught the king's eye... never before..." Her voice trailed off, and when she continued, Lormac heard a lilt to her words. "But if you'd like to get under this blanket with me, I'm willing to try."

Lormac kicked off his boots and did as she requested, his bare feet finding hers beneath the bedclothes. "What has made my little star so bold tonight?"

"The darkness," she replied. "It's less scary in the dark."

"Are you scared of me?"

"Not you," she replied softly.

"Then I'll order every lamp in Tingu extinguished, and we'll bump around in the dark until you say otherwise," he proclaimed. Asherah laughed, and he wrapped his arms around her. "Come here, you," he murmured as he tucked her against him; he buried his face in her hair, and yes, she did smell like a meadow in the first flush of spring.

"Tell me, my star, what will happen tonight?" Lormac asked.

"Tonight, I'd like to pretend we're a thousand leagues away," Asherah replied. "A thousand leagues, and a thousand winters. I want to pretend we've been mated so long we know everything about one another." She propped herself up on an elbow, her black eyes searching his. "I want to sleep in your arms like it's the safest place in all the nine realms."

Lormac pulled her down and tucked her head underneath his chin. "For you, it always will be."

Chapter 19

The following morning they began the arduous task of questioning, or rather torturing, the *mordeth*. Tor and Caol'nir took on the brunt of it, being that they both spoke the demon tongue, and they used fire, since demons seemed to hate it.

"Why fire?" Torim asked. Tor had ordered fires set around the perimeter of the doja, slowly encroaching on where the *mordeth* was held. "Why not use water, or something else?"

"Long ago, Olluhm banished demons to the burning underworld," Tor replied. "I imagine they're tired of it."

When only the cell around the *mordeth* remained, Lormac stepped forward collapsed the walls, then restrained him with manacles of earth and stone. When Lormac was done he saw Asherah chewing her lip. She said nothing as she laced her fingers tightly with his, and Lormac tried not to smile; he liked that she worried over him.

After much bellowing, blood, and screams that made everyone's spine cold as ice, Tor stepped aside and shared what the *mordeth* had revealed. It was indeed Ehkron's plan to get as many whelps by fae women as possible, however (and to no one's surprise) the *mordeth-gall* had reneged on his agreement with Sahlgren and keep these half-fae warriors for himself. Only a few moons past, the faerie king had sweetened their deal.

"But why only pureblooded fae?" demanded Lormac. "That is what makes no sense, since demons have taken whatever female they could in the past."

"Ehkron's whelp, Asgeloth, is born a pureblood fae," Caol'nir replied. "It's said that he ripped himself from his mother's womb. Since then, Ehkron believes that a fae and demon are the ideal mix to produce warriors." Caol'nir rubbed his eyes, and continued. "The *mordeth* claims that Sahlgren has put aside a woman, supposedly Olluhm's daughter, as an offering to Ehkron, but claims he doesn't know where she is."

"That old rumor?" Lormac asked. "Two, perhaps three centuries ago there was talk of Olluhm siring a daughter. They said that her mother was so beautiful Olluhm descended from the skies for the first time in millennia to know a woman who wasn't already in his service. Once the girl was born, he took her mother to the skies with him and left the babe to be raised by priestesses in the east."

Caol'nir stared at the elf king; he knew of only one orphan woman raised by kind priestesses. "How would the *mordeth-gall* know this?"

"It was the talk of Parthalan for many winters," Lormac continued. "Whenever I traveled to Teg'urnan, it was all anyone spoke of. Sahlgren himself looked for the girl, saying that he desired a god's child to be his queen, but those priestesses hid her well."

Caol'nir looked at his father, his face a mask of fury mingling with disbelief. "Not well enough. Now we know the true reason Sahlgren moved all the priestesses to Teg'urnan."

"You know who Olluhm's child is?" Lormac asked.

"I have an idea." Caol'nir stalked away, and Lormac turned to Tor.

"Well? Do you know as well?" Lormac demanded.

"Caol'nir worries more than he knows," Tor replied. "I've heard the rumors, but I have no hard facts."

"This *mordeth*, then, how believable is he?" Lormac asked. "How do we know he isn't just spouting lies to keep himself alive?"

"We know, because the *mordeth* we captured is Mersgoth," Tor replied. Very few knew the names of any demons, but Mersgoth, the right hand of Ehkron, was known throughout all the realms for his brutality. Lormac asked what was to be done with Mersgoth—as far as Lormac was concerned, the demon had outlived his usefulness—when an approaching party distracted him. He looked to the small hill and shielded his eyes against the suns, only mildly surprised when he recognized them.

"Their standard marks them as a delegation from Thurnda," Lormac said, remembering how he had summoned all of his lords to the Seat; if they'd chosen to follow him rather than just wait for his return, things must be dire. A tiny elf girl dismounted from her horse and ran down the hill, calling his name.

"Sibeal!" Lormac called once he recognized her. She reached Lormac and halted, panting. "Little cousin, why have you come all the way here? And where is Elvasla?"

"That's what I've come to tell you," gasped Sibeal. "We need not war against the demons. Ehkron is dead!"

Sibeal told them how Ehkron had appeared in Thurnda the prior winter, cutting a path of destruction across her homeland. Elvasla, Sibeal's older sister and the Lady of Thurnda, led her legion against the *mordeth-gall* and destroyed his force, but he escaped. Undaunted, Elvasla and her mate tracked Ehkron through the underworld, emerging in the mortal realm where Elvasla at last killed him.

"If Ehkron is dead, then he wasn't our true foe," Lormac observed.

"No, Sahlgren is," Caol'nir insisted.

Sibeal frowned at Caol'nir. "The fae king? What threat is he?"

"A large one," Lormac said. "I will apprise you of everything that's happened shortly." Lormac rubbed his chin, then said to Tor, "Perhaps this does means we don't need to war."

"There is still Asgeloth to contend with," Tor said. "Have you news of him?"

"I don't," Sibeal replied. "He retreated to the underworld with Ehkron, but wasn't sighted in the mortal realm."

Lormac nodded. "Is Elvasla tracking him?"

"My lord, Elvasla has perished," Sibeal gravely replied. "The *mordeth-gall* struck a death blow, and she died mere moments after the beast." Sibeal turned away and dashed at her eyes.

"Nexa save her," Lormac murmured. "And what of Tarac?"

"He returned to advise us of Elvasla and Ehkron's deaths, but he couldn't remain," Sibeal replied. "He said he couldn't bear to be in Thurnda without his love, so he and their children returned to the mortal realm." She raised her head, her gaze mixed with despair and hope. Lormac knew exactly what she wanted him to say; Sibeal was his cousin and Elvasla's sister, and the rightful heir to Thurnda.

"This would make you the Lady of Thurnda," Lormac said carefully; until he named her as such, she was merely Sibeal. "When we have returned to the Seat we will discuss what this entails."

Sibeal smiled brightly at Lormac, making her appear that much younger, and went on about how she would need to find herself a mate, for an unmated Lady simply would not do, until a terrible creaking noise silenced her.

What was left of the doja crumbled and Mersgoth burst forth, dragging the manacles behind him. Lormac pulled Asherah into his arms as the elves attacked. The *mordeth* swung the chains about like a flail, striking one warrior in the head. As the elf crumpled to the ground, two more squared off to face the demon, but it was Caol'nir who launched himself at the *mordeth*.

He had fire in his hands, and shoved it into the demon's face. Mersgoth screamed, and Caol'nir leapt back and drew his sword. He swung at the demon, but Mersgoth grabbed the blade with his bare hand.

"I will finish what my lord left undone," the demon growled, then he dropped a silver disc at his feet. In the blink of an eye, Mersgoth was gone and another of Lormac's soldiers lay dead, two others injured by the makeshift flail. Caol'nir's sword was bent, his neck and torso scored by the demon's claws. Lormac called for healers while keeping Asherah in his arms.

"I promise you, I'm fine," Asherah insisted, after the third time Lormac questioned her. Lormac picked dirt and pieces of metal from her hair as she added, "You bore the brunt of it, anyway." He stepped back and Asherah helped him brush the debris from his cloak, murmuring that Leran would not be pleased if his handiwork were damaged.

"You said it would hold," Caol'nir muttered as he stalked past Lormac to the healer's tent. Lormac pursed his lips; normally, he wouldn't accept such blatant disrespect, certainly not within his own lands, but Caol'nir was right, the wall should have held. Worse, he was afraid he knew why his power had faltered; after he'd tried replacing the Sala on Asherah's arm and she refused him, his mind had been wound up in knots. While Asherah had slept in Lormac's arms the Sala had insisted he claim her, and it took all his willpower to resist. Willpower that should have held the demon's prison fast.

"Should it have held?" Asherah asked. "Perhaps the *mordeth* was too strong."

"Yes, it should have," Sibeal replied for Lormac, "regardless of what was inside. Are you unwell, cousin?"

"No," Lormac snapped; regardless that Sibeal understood the Sala, it was not her place to answer for him.

"You're sure?" Sibeal pressed. "Is there anything I can do to assist you, my lord?" Lormac noted that as Sibeal spoke her eyes rested on the Sala, and a quick glance at his forearm told him why: the heartstone was a rich red, which meant the Lord of Tingu loved another. He remembered talk from many winters past about uniting the bloodlines of Tingu and Thurnda by having Lormac take either Elvasla or Sibeal as a mate. Based on Sibeal's interested gaze, she remembered the same.

"I assure you, I'm quite well," he replied, his hand resting on Asherah's back. "Sibeal, allow me to introduce my mate, Asherah."

"M-My lady," Sibeal said, bowing her heard. "Forgive me, word had not yet reached us in Thurnda."

"We met while I was at the keep," Lormac said. "We've not yet made the formal announcement." Sibeal nodded, and returned to Thurnda's delegation.

"Will everyone refer to me as their lady?" Asherah asked.

"You don't mind when I call you my lady," Lormac countered, wrapping Asherah in his arms.

"You're right. I don't."

Torim gazed at Asherah, laughing at Lormac's words, and wondered what had happened overnight to make her so relaxed in his arms. Then Lormac pulled Asherah close and said something that made her blush; Torim turned away, not wishing to intrude upon their newfound closeness.

She went to where the *mordeth* last stood and crouched. The dirt was blackened as if burnt, but didn't smell of smoke. Torim picked up a small silver disc and turned it over in her hands; it was mirror-smooth and cool, like metal encased in glass. She went to where the healers tended Caol'nir and showed him the disc.

"You spoke of a portal?" Torim asked, presenting him the disc. "Is it like this?"

"I don't know," Caol'nir admitted as he turned the disc over in his hand. "Rahlle only said there was a portal; he didn't say how it would appear." Caol'nir threw it to the ground as Mersgoth had.

Torim leapt back, the fact that nothing happened not lessening her anger. "Watch yourself," she hissed. "You know not what foul devices these beasts carry!"

"I know enough of what they're like," Caol'nir replied hotly. "I spent many winters trying to stem the flow of them into Parthalan."

"Perhaps if you'd been successful, these dojas wouldn't exist," Torim spat.

Caol'nir bowed his head. "Forgive me. I shouldn't let my temper speak for me."

Torim noticed that he rubbed a ribbon tied about his wrist as he spoke. "Who is it?"

"Who is what?"

Torim traced the blue ribbon. "Surely a warrior would only wear a ribbon at a lover's request."

"My mate," he replied. "The first morning we spent together, she taught me how to catch magic from the wind." Caol'nir rubbed the ribbon between his thumb and forefinger. "You know, the only reason I undertook this cause was for her."

"Then it seems we're all in her debt," Torim replied.

Chapter 20

The march back to the Seat took far longer than the march to the doja had. The wounded slaves necessitated that Lormac's party travel more slowly on the return trip. While all of the guards could walk or ride, six of the women needed to be transported in litters.

Caol'nir kept the silver disc on his person, showing it to no one, not even his father. To his knowledge, only he and Torim were aware of the disc's existence, and he meant to keep it that way. His needed to show Rahlle the disc, needed to know if it was the same portal demons used to access the Great Temple. Caol'nir remembered the bits of Ethnia's corpse littered about her chamber, and that her chamber shared a wall with Alluria's. His fist clenched around the disc, and he resolved that he would destroy whoever was responsible for Ethnia's death. If that someone was Sahlgren, so be it.

He said as much later that night. Caol'nir, Tor and Lormac stood apart from the others, discussing what they might encounter when they arrived at the Seat.

"The rest of my lords will be there," Lormac said. "Sibeal tells me that when she arrived, only Drustan the Dark had yet to make an appearance."

"You're certain they will heed your call to war?" Tor asked again.

"Ehkron has murdered the Lady of Thurnda," Lormac said gravely. "For that reason alone, vengeance belongs to the elves."

Tor nodded, and indicated Sibeal with a jerk of his head. "She is the new Lady of Thurnda?" Tor asked.

"She will be, once I name her," Lormac replied. "I'll do so at the Seat."

"Should she be included in this talk?"

"Sibeal is young, as yet untried," Lormac said with a shake of his head. "She'll follow my orders, but I don't relish the thought of bringing her to battle."

"And the troll king?" Tor asked.

"Grelk will complain, and threaten, and in the end he will sulk, but he too will do as I command," Lormac replied almost offhandedly. Caol'nir followed the elf king's gaze and wasn't surprised that it rested on Asherah. She was making her way among the newly rescued, offering what hope and encouragement she could.

"She's amazing," Caol'nir commented. "Not only does she have the strength to get herself out of a living hell, but enough to rally the spirits of those around her."

Lormac nodded. "She has strength for that, and more." With that, Lormac left the Prelate and his son.

"He really loves her," Tor said. "I never thought the old elf had it in him"

Caol'nir snorted. "I'm sure no one said that about you after you met Mama."

"They did not," Tor said. "I'm an old fae, not an old elf." Caol'nir scowled, but Tor laughed. "Enough of this. Let's see what's for supper."

Lormac strode toward Asherah, Caol'nir's words ringing in his ears. If he only knew how amazing Asherah really was, with her sharp wit, intelligence, the way her back arched when—

Lormac shook his head; those thoughts were the Sala's, not his. Despite the constant pressure in his mind Lormac refused to claim Asherah until they'd returned to the comfort of the Seat. It would take more than a priceless elfin relic to make him see otherwise.

Lormac caught Asherah's attention and she left the wounded. She met him halfway, shrouded in a darkness that was not pierced by light from either fire.

"How are they?" Lormac asked.

"I wish Tor had let me kill them," she replied bitterly.

"You don't think they'll recover?" Lormac asked. His healers claimed they could treat even the most grievous of wounds the women had sustained.

"They don't want to," Asherah replied. "Their minds are intact, including their memories. To know that those who professed to care for you never came to rescue you from such a fate... I supposed the *mordeth* did me a favor in stripping me of my life." Asherah wrapped her arms around herself and turned her face to the wind. "I often wonder if I had a mate that never came for me."

"You don't," Lormac replied. Asherah's head snapped around to face him. "Part of the power of the Sala is when I am in the Seat, I can see if one's soul is tied to another."

"You cannot see these things now?"

"No," he replied. "It is why I brought you there before I asked you to stay with me. I never would have asked you to be my mate if you already had one elsewhere."

"And...if I had?"

"I would have helped you find him."

"And if I'd chosen a woman?" she pressed.

"Then I'd have brought you to your woman," he said, and pulled her into his arms. As they laughed, he saw movement across the camp. "Is that your woman?" he asked, angling himself so both saw Belenos holding his tent flap aside for Torim.

"She's Belenos's woman now," Asherah said. "Just as I'm yours."

Lormac kissed her forehead, then drew her forearm between them. "Does it speak to you, too?" he asked, tracing the Sala's heartstone.

"The Sala? No, never. Should it?"

Lormac breathed a sigh of relief; if Asherah knew of the Sala's demands, she'd probably run and never look back. "No, but one never knows with these things. Always best to ask."

"What does it say?"

"It's a link to my ancestors. They lend me their wisdom, help me guide Tingu."

Asherah regarded the Sala for a moment, then she slid her arms around Lormac's waist. "When you were at the Seat, did you see if I had any children?"

"I saw no one tied to you," Lormac replied.

"Then I really am alone in the world," she murmured. "I don't know if the knowledge that my family didn't forsake me makes me glad, or if I should be sad that I have no family to speak of."

"You have me." Lormac kissed her temple.

Asherah looked up at him and smiled. "Lormac, my mountain. My strength."

The next morning the Lord of Tingu's party arrived at the Seat shortly before noon. Lormac's call to arms had indeed been answered, and the legions of the six elfin kingdoms that surrounded Tingu were in orderly rows around the Seat. The Parthian soldiers who had avoided the thrall had also arrived. Lormac saw Tor hang his head when he saw how few remained.

"Don't blame yourself," Lormac said. "Evil tends to hide its tracks well."

"Who are they?" Caol'nir asked, pointing toward a group close to the palace gates that looked less like a well-trained legion and more like a drunken mob.

"Those are the trolls," Lormac replied, his long frustration with Grelk evident. "Go to any forge and not a tool is out of place, but they show no such order when they're summoned to my home." Lormac scanned the assemblage, and noted the absence of the dark fae. He turned to mention this to Tor, but Leran chose that moment to break free from his nurse and dash toward his father, heedless of the marching warriors and horses' hooves. Lormac reached down and snatched the boy, admonishing his reckless behavior as he swung him onto his shoulder, where he remained as they entered the gates.

Once inside the Seat, Lormac instructed Aldo that all the elfin lords were to join him in the hall. As the lesser lords arrived with their retinues, they found their king standing upon the dais, surrounded by elf and fae warriors alike.

"Where is Grelk?" Lormac asked Aldo as he surveyed the throng.

"Here," called out the troll king as he lumbered to the front of the hall. He was a large creature, not overly so from a troll's perspective, but easily half as wide as he was tall, with a beard that hung to his knees. Ever the smith, his hammer hung from his belt where others would carry a sword.

Lormac acknowledged the troll, then seated himself on his throne. Leran remained on his shoulder, leaning against the high back.

"My lords," Lormac began, "on this day I bring you great and terrible news. Demons—nay, the *mordeth-gall* himself—have availed themselves of our lands and people."

The hall buzzed with the hushed tones of the lords talking; for the *mordeth-gall* to have breached elfin lands was without precedent. Lormac went on, detailing how he had been first alerted to the existence of the doja*s*, and that one was less than a day's ride from the Seat.

"My lord," began Aish'inn of Nugt, "forgive my ignorance, but how did the Lord of Tingu became involved in matters that seem only the fae's concern?"

"My lords," Lormac said, extending his arm to Sibeal, "I was informed just three days past of Lady Elvasla's death at the hands of the *mordeth-gall*." A murmur rolled over the crowd, and Sibeal turned to them with sad eyes.

"It is true," Sibeal proclaimed. "Ehkron burst into our lands not two moons past, intent upon erecting more of his foul dojas. My sister would not suffer him his life and tracked him—through the underworld she tracked him!—to the mortal realm. She fell, but not before she killed the *mordeth-gall*."

Sibeal's words silenced the throng; Elvasla was a kind and just ruler and would be mourned by many.

"And now, Sibeal, you take up your sister's mantle as Lady of Thurnda," Lormac proclaimed. "I trust you will lead your people well."

"I will," Sibeal affirmed.

"If Ehkron is dead," called out a soldier from Rael, "why do we need to war?"

"Ehkron's death did not end Sahlgren's foul plot with demons," Lormac answered. "The dojas are still in operation. Do you think the *mordeths* overseeing them care if their overlord has fallen? Do you think Sahlgren will abandon his plans to raise an army and conquer us all?" Lormac paused as his lords talked amongst themselves. He surveyed the room of elfin nobility, wondering how much more convincing they would need, when Aish'inn stepped forward once again.

"My honor and my blood to you, my king." Aish'inn knelt, reciting the ancient elfin oath of fealty. One by one the rest swore their aid. The last was Sibeal; she retained that honor due to Thurnda being the largest of the elfin lands. As soon as Sibeal pledged her loyalty there was a low, angry grumble.

"I not swear," rumbled Grelk. "Fight belong to fae and elf, not troll. We in ground, forge and furnace far below your war. Why should troll die? I say no."

Lormac rose to his full height, taller than any elf or fae, and towered over the troll king. The very walls rumbled with his words. "If you refuse aid, I'll use the power of my birthright to close up every troll hole within my borders. Every furnace will be extinguished; every den will be filled with earth. You'll use my lands no longer, Grelk!"

Grelk shifted on his feet, for while he claimed independence of both elf and fae, the trolls needed them not only for trade, but defense. "Meaningless threat!" Grelk accused. "Your power not so great!"

"Isn't it?" Lormac asked. The hall fell silent as all, even young Leran, awaited Grelk's response.

"Fine," Grelk shouted at length. "Aid you have, but only weapons! Lormac know I no leave my dens," he continued in a low tone.

"We can make do with just the weapons," Lormac said as the corner of his mouth quirked. He'd only wanted the fine blades trolls were known for throughout the nine realms. The image of trolls lumbering across the battlefield was certainly amusing, as long as they were on the side of his opponent. Lormac descended from the dais, Leran still clinging to his shoulder, and approached the troll king.

"I am grateful for your acquiescence," Lormac said to Grelk, "we would likely not prevail without you, friend."

Grelk grumbled about elves being lost without the trolls in general. Lormac pretended not to notice the troll's complaints as he moved to stand in the midst of the hall, surrounded by his nobles and peers.

"Whether our blood is of elf or fae or troll, we have united to rid our lands of this evil," Lormac proclaimed, extending his arms as if to hold them all in his sheltering embrace. "As an elf, the urge to protect is strong in my veins. We were conceived by the Earth herself, to protect our mother from those that would ravage her. Now, we ride forth not only in her defense, but to strengthen the bonds of all races that tread upon her soil!" He looked to find Asherah and found her standing next to his throne, radiating confidence as she met his gaze. *We can win!* he thought, and she smiled as if she'd heard him.

Her.

"Today, we begin our preparations. Soon, we ride to war," Lormac declared to the cheering throng. Elves were true warriors; the thrill of battle coursed through their veins. As Asherah held Lormac's eyes above the cheering mass he felt—no, he *knew*—that she was warrior born as well.

Her!

Lormac winced, but the Sala kept up the pressure in his mind, the insistence that Asherah be his. And, Lormac no longer wanted to resist.

Intent on a new purpose, Lormac navigated his subjects as one would walk among waves crashing against the rocky coast. Once he reached the dais, he sank to his knees before Asherah, and as Leran climbed down from his father's back Lormac held out the Sala before him.

"My queen," he said, gazing up at her. The cheers died away, and the hall fell silent as every set of eyes fixed on Asherah. Lormac suddenly wished he had not chosen this moment to publicly declare her as his mate. He knew how she hated the weight of others' stares, but it was too late to take back his action.

Nor did Lormac want to; all his days he had wanted a woman like Asherah, beautiful as the night sky, her fierceness with a sword adding a sharp edge to her lovely features. It had been many generations since Tingu had had a proper queen, and one as fearless and sharp-minded as she was the ideal woman to help lead his land of warriors. Lormac fantasized about their life together, riding off to battle side by side, the strong sons whom he would teach to wield both sword and spear...

However, none of that was likely to happen as Asherah remained rigid, uttering not a sound, her eyes locked upon the Sala. He heard the whispers of his people, wondering if this strange fae woman had the audacity to refuse Lormac, why they should go to war when one lone wench couldn't accept the great honor bestowed upon her.

Please don't refuse me. Just this once, please do as I ask.

Slowly, cautiously, Asherah reached out and ran a finger along the edge of the Sala; Lormac thought it odd, for she had already worn it for some days. Her fingertips lingered over the heart stone, tracing its edge for long moments until she returned Lormac's gaze. Asherah brushed her hand over his jaw as she spoke.

"My honor and my blood to you, my king," she declared, but it might well have been a whisper for the cheers that drowned out her words. Lormac solemnly placed the Sala on Asherah's forearm, then let out a whooping cry of his own as he swept her into his arms and swung her about.

"My people, I present your queen," Lormac proclaimed, his eyes never leaving the faerie in his arms. He loosened his hold only enough for Asherah to slide down to his eye level, and Lormac kissed her passionately enough to elicit a second, much louder cheer.

"My star," he murmured, "you will be our greatest queen."

Asherah speaks...

The preparations for our march to Teg'urnan moved swiftly, though not swiftly enough for Lormac's liking. Grelk attended upon him as though he was Tingu's most loyal subject, always agreeing and nodding to whatever Lormac said. The troll king took Lormac's threat quite seriously, and after a few weeks of his constant prostrations, I asked Lormac if he really could have closed up the troll dens. Lormac had laughed heartily, and claimed that he didn't even know where most of the dens were located, much less how to fill them in, and he imagined that the troll's network was so vast it would take the whole of the World's Spine to close them off.

Despite Grelk's desire to please Lormac (and keep his dens open), the production of our weaponry crawled along like so many turtles in a race. The sluggish pace irritated Lormac, his irritation growing whenever he brought up this lack of progress to Grelk's attention. The troll king had asserted that all would be completed within five days. Five became ten, then fifteen, and Lormac had stopped asking for fear of murdering Grelk in a fit of rage. In the event of the troll king's death, we would likely get no weapons at all.

So Lormac had tasked Sibeal with overseeing the troll's progress, and she either incited them to work or put the fear of death behind them, for after she began her daily discussions with Grelk the piles of swords and spears grew more quickly. They even managed to turn out a shield or two.

One morning Lormac took advantage of a lull in the preparations (by lull I mean Grelk's painfully slow progress with our weaponry) to take Leran and me on a short ride from the Seat. Leran was thrilled (it seemed that he hated being cooped up as much as I) and he squirmed excitedly as he sat on his father's saddle. When we came upon a quiet, sun-drenched pond, the boy insisted we go swimming.

"Isn't it a little cold for a swim?" I asked as we dismounted.

"Perhaps for a faerie, but we elves are made of stronger stock," Lormac teased. With that, he and Leran stripped down to nothing.

"You haven't a shred of modesty, have you?" I asked as I sat upon the grassy bank. While I had no intention of going about naked, I certainly enjoyed looking at Lormac.

"Not a bit," he replied as he stretched in the sun. He called after Leran to stay near the shore, and then knelt before me. "All my life I've been surrounded by attendants at every moment, helping me to bathe, dress, do anything they can think of to assist Tingu's scion. The first time I lay with a woman a council of seven observed me." Reading my shocked expression, he explained, "An elfin custom, in case I'd gotten her with child."

"You elves and your customs."

"Don't worry, we'll be quite alone," he said, then he kissed me. Sitting there in the warm sunlight with Lormac naked beside me was...exhilarating. "Will you join us, my star?"

"I-I don't think so," I murmured. Lormac didn't press the matter, but then he didn't have to since Leran, soaking wet and wearing only mud, ran up to us.

"Aren't you coming?" he asked, seeing me fully clothed.

"Asherah doesn't want to," Lormac replied.

"Why?" he asked, his wide, innocent gray eyes staring at me. "You don't want to be naked?"

My cheeks went hot at Leran's candor while Lormac chuckled. "Um, no," I answered as I shot his father a withering glare.

"Then just wear your shift," Leran said matter-of-factly. "It's what Lukka does when she takes me swimming." I looked to Lormac and he shrugged, so I stripped down to my shift and soon enough the three of us were laughing and splashing away.

After a time, I dragged myself back to the shore, exhausted by our games, and lay flat on the grass to let the suns dry my soaked shift; wearing it was pointless, the water having made it nearly transparent, but I needed that layer between myself and the world. Lormac crawled up the shore and lay next to me.

"Where's Leran?" I asked.

"Trying to catch a fish," he responded, jerking his head toward the water.

I propped myself up on my elbows and saw Leran flailing about in the mud, trying to leap upon the fish unawares. "I think he's scaring them away."

Lormac said nothing and a quick glance told me why; he was staring at my scars through the thin, damp fabric. I tried distracting him with my babbling speech, but fell silent when he touched me.

"This is why you won't let me look at you," he murmured.

"Mostly. Somewhat."

Lormac's gaze followed the trail of one, then another. "Why are some raised?"

"That's where the mordeth bled into me," I said softly. Lormac pushed up my skirt and examined the scars on my thighs. I made no attempt to stop him; thanks to my soaked shift I was practically naked, anyway. Lormac rose and went to the shore, returning with a handful of mud. He knelt between my legs and positioned my thigh so the scarred inner skin was facing him.

"What are you doing?" I asked as he spread the mud across my thigh.

"You'll see," he murmured. Lormac placed one hand over the Sala while the other massaged the mud into my skin. Then he withdrew his hands and the mud moved of its own accord, shifting and bubbling until black, oily spots appeared. Lormac tore off a piece of my shift and soaked it in the pond, then used it to wipe the mud from my flesh; the sensation of the cold water on my hot skin was amazing. As he revealed my skin I saw something else amazing: while my scars were still there, they were no longer raised, red cords against my flesh. They were flat, and silvery and...well, they looked like scars. Ordinary scars.

"How did you do that?" I asked. "The Sala gives you the power to heal?"

"It's not a healing," he replied, pressing a kiss onto my newly smooth skin. "The Earth took the demon blood, because it doesn't belong." Lormac retrieved another handful of mud, then he resumed his place between my knees and pushed my skirt up farther (without asking, mind you!) as he plastered more of the cold, wet earth against me.

"Please, wait," I whispered.

"Is it too cold?" When I remained silent he glanced at my face; whatever he saw there made him drop his handful of mud. "I'm sorry, I don't mean to make you do anything you'd rather not." He set his hands on his knees and stared at the ground. "Ever since the doja, all I've wanted is to take those memories from you. All my power as king, yet I can't make my mate feel safe..."

He shook his head, then he took my hands. "This, fixing your scars, this is something I can do. Please, let me help in my small way?"

I gazed at him, the king who'd covered himself in mud, all for me. "You wish to help me so much?"

He kissed my knuckles. "More than anything."

"Well, I suppose," I said. Lormac grinned, then he scooped up more mud and went to work between my legs.

"They seem to have avoided your womb," he said calmly, as if it were perfectly normal for me to be sprawled in front of him with my skirt hiked up to my waist.

"They wanted that intact," I said bitterly. Once the black blood had bubbled to the mud's surface Lormac soaked the cloth again, this time wringing it out to rinse away the mud. I gasped when the icy water splashed over me, and again when he pulled me to a sitting position and yanked my shift over my head.

"Lormac!" I warned.

"How else am I supposed to help the scars on your breast?" he asked.

I glared at him as I leaned back on my elbows, then looked away so as not to let him know how much I enjoyed his hands upon me. He worked slowly and methodically, being sure to massage even the areas without scars.

"I wish you'd told me." He cleaned away the last of the mud.

"I didn't know you could help," I said simply. Lormac's gaze was heavy upon me, and I turned from him as I reached for my shift. "I...I need it," I mumbled when he stayed my hand.

"No, you don't." When I dared to look up his gray eyes gazed lovingly into mine. "You're safe. Those that hurt you are dead, and I'll never let anything harm you again. My star, do you believe me?"

"I do," I said, then I leaned my forehead against his shoulder. "Gods, Lormac, how did you fall in with my wretchedness? You deserve a beautiful mate, not one like me."

"Another thing," he said. "I don't want you to think of yourself as anything other than beautiful."

"I look a lot better now, thanks to you."

He cupped my chin in his hand and drew my face close to his. "You were always beautiful." He kissed me. "Now, you're just a little less lumpy."

I laughed along with him, and as I leaned my cheek against his shoulder I realized how comfortable I had become with Lormac, despite that we were naked. I let the torn and muddy shift fall from my hand because Lormac was right, I didn't need it. He saw it drop but said nothing as he kissed me again, one hand tangling in my hair while the other made my breath catch in my throat.

"What are you doing?" I gasped.

"Making sure I got to all of the scars."

"You said there weren't any there."

"So I did," he murmured as he nudged me to the ground. My breath came quicker as his mouth moved to my neck, then the colors of the sky began to swirl together as I arched my back and...

"Asherah!"

And Leran ran up to us with a squirmy, smelly creature in his hands. "I caught you a fish!" he cried as it flopped down onto my belly.

"T-Thank you, Leran," I said raggedly. What else was I supposed to say?

We didn't stay at the pond much longer, and once we had washed away the majority of the mud, we returned to the Seat. Leran insisted upon riding with me, snuggled before me on my saddle. Lormac smiled every time he looked at us.

I went to Lormac's chamber that evening as I always did, only this time I felt an air of trepidation, for I worried that he would want to continue where we left off at the pond. While I had enjoyed myself (immensely!), I was still nervous.

My anxiety must have been plain to see, since Lormac commented upon it as soon as I entered his chamber.

"Little star, do you really think I'd do anything to hurt you?" he asked, seeming somewhat hurt himself.

"No," I replied as I fell into his arms. "But you could have asked at the pond."

"Forgive me?" he asked with that smile that could melt all the ice caps atop the World's Spine.

"Forgiven," I replied. We kissed then, long and hard, and Lormac began asking me something, and once again the Seat's tiniest resident interrupted us. I felt a tug at my hair and looked down to see a sleepy-eyed Leran at my feet. An exhausted Lukka hurried after him.

"It's fine, Lukka," Lormac said when she apologized. "Leran knows he's always welcome in my rooms." As Lukka returned to the nursery, Lormac asked Leran what was so pressing he needed to tell us in the middle of the night.

"Can I sleep with you?" he asked me, his eyes hopeful. I was about to tell him that I actually didn't see a bed while in his father's rooms, when he added, "I used to sleep with my mama, but then she left." He held out his arms and I picked him up, loving how he clung to me.

"Of course you can stay with us," I said, then I followed Lormac into his bedchamber for the first time. The walls and floor were the same green stone of the rest of the palace, but the ceiling was covered in iridescent crystals, much like the larger crystals that populated the Seat, emitting a soft glow. The king's enormous bed was piled high with silk cushions and surrounded by purple velvet curtains edged in gold thread. We nestled Leran between us, then Lormac cupped my chin in his hand.

"I finally have you in my bed," he quipped. For once, his joking manner didn't make me uncomfortable and I leaned over to kiss him, only to be interrupted by a giggling Leran.

"What's so funny?" Lormac asked. Leran kept giggling, until Lormac told him he would need to settle down if he wanted to stay.

And so began our new sleeping arrangements, with Lormac and me spending every night since with Leran wedged between us. I can say truthfully that I enjoyed his presence more than Lormac, since it further delayed the consummation of our mating. Lormac must have suspected my motives but said nothing, preferring instead to sneak up and ravish me for a few moments, then abruptly leave and carry on with his duties.

One morning Sibeal asked me to accompany her as she went to meet with Grelk in the great hall. I thought it odd that she would request my presence, but soon enough her motives were revealed.

"Tell me," Sibeal began, "how are things with you and my cousin?"

"Well," I replied. "Lormac is a wonderful man."

"Once, we thought to unite the royal lines of Tingu and Thurnda. I see our chance has passed." Sibeal gave the Sala a rueful glance.

"You and Lormac?" I asked as my heart fell. Sibeal would be an ideal mate for the Lord of Tingu, what with her noble blood and title. She almost looked like an elfin version of me, with her thick white hair and slender frame, albeit on a more diminutive scale. I imagined that she had never been a slave.

"No," Sibeal replied, "perhaps he would have accepted my sister, but Lormac has never seen me as anything other than his little cousin." There was an edge to Sibeal's words, and I suspected that Sibeal had long aspired to be Lady of Tingu. And why shouldn't she? Lormac was every elf woman's ideal mate. He was strong, fearless, and powerful. And he was mine.

Well, not yet.

Not that anyone knew.

As I looked about the hall, bustling with the preparations for war, I wondered if anyone would dare to suspect that Lormac had yet to claim me. Since our return from the doja, all had treated me as his mate and Lady of Tingu. Neither Lormac nor I had done anything to dissuade them; indeed, how could we, for Lormac would look like a fool if anyone knew the truth.

And while I still wasn't his mate, it was not for lack of trying on Lormac's part. I spent every night with him, though with Leran between us. I'd even stopped sneaking out to crawl into bed with Torim, mostly because the last time I attempted it she refused me and sent me back to Lormac. It seemed that she was as eager as Lormac to get me into his bed.

I knew that it was difficult for Lormac to hold himself back, and the strain was evident to all who looked at him. I imagined that others thought it was the pressure of war, but I alone knew the truth.

"The strain of these preparations is showing on his face," Sibeal commented and gave me a sidelong glance. "Is my cousin sleeping well?"

"As well as one could expect," I replied sweetly. Did she really think that I was going to discuss what happened in my bedchamber with her?

"Good," she replied. I couldn't decide if I was furious with her for being so nosy, or frustrated with my own reticence to make love to Lormac. I looked across the hall and saw Lormac speaking with Balthus, their heads hunched over a scroll that detailed provisions or weapons or something for the coming march to Teg'urnan. The strain he was under was plain for anyone to see. His hands trembled where he held the map, and there were dark smudges underneath his eyes. I resolved to send Leran to the nursery that evening, though I knew he would pout. I had no idea if I really could give myself to Lormac that evening, but I wanted to. I owed it to myself to try.

"Now, what is it you wanted to discuss about Grelk?" I asked. If this fool asked me here merely to question my and Lormac's relationship, she would get a piece of my mind. Before Sibeal could either defend herself or admit guilt, a voice startled us.

"Mama!"

Sibeal was just as shocked as I to hear the word, and we turned in unison to see Leran run toward me and leap into my arms.

"He calls you Mama?" she asked, shock evident on her face.

"He never has before," I murmured. "Leran, why did you call me Mama?"

"I asked Da if you could be my new mother," he replied.

"And what did he say?" I pressed.

"He said he would like that very much," Lormac replied. The man was always sneaking up behind me, but this time I did not mind. In fact, I minded less and less each day. "What do you say, little star?"

Two sets of gray eyes looked at me expectantly and I sighed; Leran wasn't going anywhere but to bed with us that evening, and I was more than a little relieved. "I would like that as well."

Chapter 21

The elfin custom of Madoc'na was a celebration of life in the face of death, where everything was permitted and nothing taboo. In times past in had always occurred on the eve of battle, but later generations had found wisdom in letting warriors rest for a sennight after the revelry.

As Lormac exited his chambers, clad in his king's regalia, he remembered his first Madoc'na, when he had just barely been a man. The feast had begun as any other held within the Seat, with an endless array of food and drink for all to partake in. There had been music and dancing, but as the food dwindled men sought to quench other appetites. At that Madoc'na Lormac's intent had been to lie with as many women as possible, and at each subsequent Madoc'na he had succeeded in adding to those numbers.

Then there had been Leran's mother, with eyes like a doe and a tongue soaked in acid; he'd had first lain with her at a Madoc'na. While most hadn't been able to see past her sour demeanor, the fact that she hadn't been impressed by his royal status had intrigued Lormac. That, and parts of that bitter girl had been as sweet as honey. Lormac's fascination had been short lived, and after she had left Tingu he'd sworn that at the next Madoc'na he would lie with more women than he'd had at the last to atone for the time he devoted only to her.

Now that feast was upon him, and Lormac thought not of the many women who would eagerly take him to bed, but of one faerie that he couldn't get out of his mind. He still hadn't claimed Asherah, and he feared his quest to make her comfortable had only succeeded in making it impossible for them to be intimate. If they weren't in the presence of the Prelate or Balthus planning war, they were in his chamber with Leran glued to Asherah's side.

Lormac smiled when he thought of Asherah and Leran together. He had wanted his son's acceptance of Asherah, though he never dreamed Leran would be so taken with her. Asherah managed to fill the void left by his true mother, and Lormac enjoyed having a complete family.

Make her yours.

Lormac shook his head, ridding himself of the Sala's influence. Lormac reached Torim's chamber and knocked brusquely. He had rearranged his schedule before the feast in order to spend time alone with his mate, but Asherah had insisted upon being with Torim instead. Lormac would never admit to such a base emotion as jealousy, but he had every intention of sharing his displeasure with Asherah.

Torim opened the door bearing a smug grin, which only added to Lormac's annoyance. He stepped past her into the chamber and called Asherah's name, determined to tell her once and for all she was to leave Torim be, but when she emerged, he promptly forgot what had angered him so.

If Asherah had been beautiful before, as she stood before him she looked like a goddess. Her pale hair was swept back from her face with a circlet of pearls and flowed down her back, small crystals woven into the length of it. She wore a simple gown of white silk edged in silvery blue embroidery, the diaphanous fabric trailing and dragging across every soft curve. The long, full sleeves were slit from shoulder to elbow and she wore the Sala on her left arm, the only jewelry that so adorned her.

"You're a vision." Lormac took her hand, then spun her around to admire her from every angle. He glanced toward

Torim, who smiled as she slipped from the room. "This is why you wouldn't spend the afternoon with me?"

"Forgive me?" she asked, fluttering her lashes. Lormac's heart skipped a beat when he realized she was flirting with him.

"Forgiven," he replied. "I've never seen a woman attired so."

"You're always trying to dress me up like an elf, but the fae style suits me so much better," Asherah said, to which Lormac heartily agreed. He grasped her about the hips, the silk of her gown so fine it was as if nothing lay between his skin and hers. Asherah rested in his arms for a moment, then pulled him toward the door. "They're waiting for us," she reminded him.

Lormac captured her in his arms again. "We can be a little late." He brushed his lips over her neck.

"They cannot begin without the king," Asherah said, and he let her lead him toward the door. The Sala screamed inside Lormac's mind to bolt the door before throwing Asherah to the floor, feast be damned. His skin tingled and his heart pounded with wanting her, so much so that he wondered if one could die from unrequited desire. Lormac also knew that if he did throw Asherah to the ground, even in jest, he would lose every ounce of trust he had built with her.

Lormac quieted the Sala and extended his arm to his queen, and they made their way to the grand hall of the Seat. As they walked, Lormac told her of the first battle he faced, when his father pushed Tingu's northern border past the World's Spine and to the land of ice and fire, home of the mountain trolls.

"And you sought not to conquer them as well?" Asherah asked.

"The land is inhospitable, home to such beasts as orcs and gryphons. Our only interest there was to establish an alliance with the mountain trolls, but they proved much less cooperative that our friends of the forge," Lormac replied.

They arrived at the hall, and took a moment before they entered.

"Your first Madoc'na as my queen," Lormac murmured as he traced her cheekbone. "Tell me, mother to my son, where will Leran be spending the night?"

"With us, of course. Why would he spend it anywhere else?" Asherah asked, black eyes wide and innocent. "Is there something of this feast you haven't told me?"

"If you keep looking at me that way, we'll never make to this feast," Lormac replied, then worried he had gone too far. He did not want to do or say anything that would jeopardize the carefully constructed trust that now lay between them. To his relief, she was unoffended.

"And that simply wouldn't do," she said, stretching to kiss his chin. With that, the Lord and Lady of Tingu entered the grand hall, and the sacred feast of Madoc'na commenced.

As Lormac and Asherah entered the hall, Caol'nir and the rest watched the king and queen make their way toward the dais. Their progress was slow as every lord and lady in attendance stopped to congratulate them, and swear allegiance to the new queen. Caol'nir wondered if others found it odd that the elf king would take a faerie as his mate, especially since Lormac was rumored to have the purest bloodline in Tingu.

Some claimed that the king's son wasn't a pureblood elf, and that Lormac had a penchant for women of other races. The rumor was that Leran's mother was a nymph who had enchanted the king to get with child and dilute the royal elfin bloodline, but when the boy was born the spell shattered and Lormac cast her out. While Caol'nir could believe that Leran's mother was a nymph, he doubted that Lormac had been enchanted in any way. Men were men, regardless if they were kings or swineherds, and if Leran's mother was as lovely as they said Caol'nir understood exactly what Lormac had seen in her. Caol'nir smiled to himself as he felt the ribbon on his wrist, and knew that Alluria had been right: people readily believed in legends.

As Caol'nir thought of his mate, he absently brushed his new sword, the hilt set with a blue gem that matched Alluria's sapphire gaze. Grelk had impressed twining herbs upon the length of the blade, an amazing feat for one with fingers the size of saplings. Caol'nir had been specific about the six herbs he wanted represented and in which order. Grelk had grumbled and complained, but the finished product had been well worth it. Grelk had also insisted on making Caol'nir's new sword himself; trolls have long memories, and Grelk remembered when Solon had descended from the skies. Caol'nir had been flattered by the troll king's insistence, but that quickly gave way to frustration.

"None of these are blue enough," Caol'nir said when Grelk had shown him the thousandth blue gem. "These are blue like the sky, blue like the sea, but her eyes are so much… richer." Caol'nir sifted through the stones while Grelk looked on. "Forgive me," Caol'nir apologized, worried that he had offended the troll. "I just have an idea of how I want it to look. I don't mean to trouble you so."

"No trouble, Solon-son," Grelk said. "Blade difficult to make, but no trouble."

"That's what I meant. I don't wish to make things difficult for you," Caol'nir said. He had long since stopped trying to get Grelk to refer to him by his actual name. "Any sword will do."

"No, Solon-son. I make Solon's sword, I make his son's sword." With that, Grelk produced a pouch from beneath his beard. Caol'nir wondered what else was buried in there, being that he could see a few mushrooms and what might have been a bird's nest huddled in the depths. "I keep this special for you."

Caol'nir opened the pouch and tumbled an assortment of stones into his hand, not the smooth stones that were in the basket but gems cut and polished to a brilliant shine, each a deeper blue than the last. He selected one that was half the size of Alluria's palm and held it up to the light.

"This is it," he proclaimed, grinning at the troll. "This is the color of her eyes."

"I put in hilt," Grelk said as he took the stone, then turned away.

"Wait!" Caol'nir grabbed the troll's shoulder. "That gem must be priceless. Let me select another."

"Worry not, Solon-son. I make for you." Caol'nir protested, and counted out gold coins. "Coin no good. I make, you kill."

"How can you not charge me for such a weapon? You time, your effort; you deserve to be compensated!"

"When Solon come from sky, he save not only faerie and elf, but troll, too. Grelk no forget. You get new sword, Solon-son."

"I am not his son," Caol'nir explained for the hundredth time.

"Fool me," the troll said, smiling so his grizzled teeth poked through his beard. "Look like him, act like him, could be him." Grelk lumbered away, then called over his shoulder, "You have sword five days."

"That's what you said ten days ago," grumbled Caol'nir. Five days was in truth twenty-three, but in the end, Grelk produced the finest sword Caol'nir had ever seen. He couldn't wait to show it to Alluria, tangible proof that though they had been apart, he never stopped thinking of her.

Caol'nir was itching to leave the Seat and march south, back to his home and to his love. While he had not attended a Madoc'na in the past, Caol'nir was well aware of the purpose of the feast: it honored Nexa's firstborn, Madoc, who had feasted his enemies with endless casks of ale, then bedded their women while his enemies slept and conquered them the next day. Nowadays the king wasn't expected to lie with all the women, but Caol'nir knew the feast would become little more than an orgy by midnight, and he had no intention of participating. Three winters ago he would have eagerly anticipated the event, but that was before. His mate brought out the good in him, and he wanted nothing more than to be the honorable man she deserved.

"How long are we expected to remain?" Caol'nir whispered to Tor.

"Don't worry, things will be quite calm for most of the night," Tor reassured him; earlier he had told Caol'nir that this was the fourth Madoc'na he had attended. Caol'nir wondered how long his father planned to stay during this feast. "Lormac has just now reached his throne."

Caol'nir watched Lormac and Asherah as they wound their way through the throng of well-wishers, finally reaching the dais. Lormac had asked Grelk to construct a throne for his new queen in white metal, studded with blue gems and polished to a mirror sheen. Lormac had wanted to surprise Asherah with it, and judging by her shocked expression, he had.

"I don't think Asherah was expecting that," Caol'nir said to his father. "Look at her smile."

"Lormac is nothing if not a good man," Tor proclaimed loudly enough for the elfin warriors seated around them. "And a good man seeks to please his mate," he added with a wink. Caol'nir's thoughts returned to Alluria, not that his thoughts were ever far from her. He knew that Alluria disliked living at Teg'urnan, and Caol'nir resolved to take her to wherever she would be happiest, even if it meant the cold north surrounded by elves and trolls. He began to tell his father, but there was a commotion at the far end of the hall.

"What is happening?" Caol'nir demanded.

"Lord Drustan." Tor jerked his head toward the rear entrance. Caol'nir's gaze followed; the king of the dark fae's arrival was causing an uproar during Lormac's Madoc'na. "He has always enjoyed making an entrance."

Drustan the Dark looked a great deal like Sahlgren in that he was short for a faerie, with slick black hair and a stocky build. Tor was easily a head taller than Drustan, Caol'nir more so. Drustan swaggered as he approached the dais, as if he was doing Lormac a favor with his attendance.

Lormac, not sharing his sentiment, cast him an icy glare, settling his queen on his knee rather than upon her new throne. When Drustan arrived at the base of the dais, Lormac eyed him with thinly veiled contempt.

"My lord," Drustan said as he and his men bowed low.

"You're interrupting my feast, Drustan," Lormac said, his voice booming across the crowded hall. "Have you come to congratulate me?"

"I'm here in response to your summons," Drustan replied.

"I summoned you nearly a season past," Lormac stated. "You've ignored me until now."

"That was in the depths of winter," Drustan cried. "We needed to wait for the thaw."

Caol'nir chuckled as Lormac tormented Drustan the Dark; it was well known that Lormac's father had struck a bargain with Drustan's grandsire so that the dark fae might retain their lands under Tingu's rule. Tor shot his son a quieting glance.

"No matter," Lormac said, waving away Drustan's apologies. "Come sit beside me, Drustan, I've much to tell you."

Lormac did indeed tell Drustan many things, from the appearance of Ehkron in Tingu to his mating with Asherah. Before long, Drustan was swearing fealty to Asherah, in such an embarrassing display that Lormac had him removed to the farthest table in the hall.

Once the king and queen had eaten their fill, they rose and made their way down opposite sides of the table, Asherah accompanied by Torim as she spoke with the elfin noblewomen while Lormac accepted congratulations from his lords. Caol'nir noted that others were leaving their meals behind as they called for more of that strong elfin brandy that made one's gullet burn. Once the king stepped down from the dais, it would signify the commencement of Madoc'na, and Caol'nir was of a mind to depart the hall long before that happened.

"Enjoying yourself, Prelate?" Lormac asked once he made his way to Tor's side. "I trust you and your boy will avail yourselves of all the pleasures Tingu may provide," he added. Normally Caol'nir would express his displeasure over being referred to as a boy with the back of his hand, but he had come to like the elf king. He understood why his father held Lormac in such high esteem.

"I think we'll depart long before we have the chance," Tor replied.

"I was sorry to learn of Iseult's passing," Lormac said with a kindness Caol'nir had not expected. "She was a good woman, a true warrior's mate."

"As is your mate," Tor said. "Look at how she glides among your people as if she has been their queen for many winters. They already respect her."

"Mmmm," Lormac nodded in agreement, gazing at his mate. "Do you recognize her?"

"Should I?" Tor asked with a raised brow.

"The *mordeth* that took her did something to her mind," Lormac replied. "He took her memories."

"Does she remember what part of Parthalan she's from?"

"She does not, but suspects she came from the east."

"Alluria may know of her," Caol'nir offered. "My mate was a priestess in the east for many winters and had dealings with much of the nobility."

"Your mate was a priestess?" Lormac said with a sly grin. "As *con'dehr*, aren't you supposed to keep them virgins?" Caol'nir felt his anger rise, mostly with himself for divulging such a detail, but Lormac clapped him on the back

255

and called for more brandy. "Boy, I grow to like you more than I ever thought I'd like the stodgy Prelate's son. Come; let us drink to your mate, lovely she must be!"

Lormac grinned as he quaffed the brandy with Tor and Caol'nir; to think, the Prelate's son took a priestess as his own! He had never understood why the fae valued virginity as they did. Elves saw the pleasures of the flesh as pleasures to be had, and availed themselves whenever they had the opportunity.

As the thought crossed Lormac's mind, he watched Asherah, pale and lovely as she made her way among the elves. Despite his earlier sentiments, he knew that he would never seek another's bed, not so long as Asherah deigned to stay with him. His loins practically groaned as he imagined her beneath him, her hair fanned out around her head as she called his name.

"What of your mate?" Tor was saying, and Lormac turned to him. "Will she ride beside you in this war?"

"She will," Lormac assured. Tor commented but Lormac hardly heard him as he turned back to Asherah. He was transfixed by her, the way her slender limbs moved beneath her impossibly thin gown. The Sala called to him, maddening in its insistence that he claim his mate, shouting inside his mind that until the union was complete the power of the Seat would falter and he would be unable to hold his kingdom together. Moreover, he physically needed her; his hands shook, his throat was dry and raspy, and the Prelate asked him if he was well.

Lormac muttered a response to Tor as he rose, well aware of what would cure his affliction, nearly salivating at the thought of getting it. Lormac strode across the hall to where Asherah stood, surrounded by admirers—*Who would not admire her? She is perfect!*—who declared their loyalty to their new queen. He caught a *saffira's* elbow and gave a few quick instructions to be carried to Lukka, detailing that she was to take Leran to the nursery immediately and keep him there until first dawn. As she scurried off Lormac saw Asherah conversing with his lords as easily as if she had been born into royalty.

She is loved already, Lormac marveled as he caught her eye. No one had loved Leran's mother; not one of his subjects, none of her fellow *saffira*, and least of all Lormac. He had regretted getting her with child every day, wondering how he could have been so foolish as to tie himself to one such as her, until the day she bore Leran. When Lormac first beheld his son, who had his father's eyes and his mother's fine-boned beauty, he resolved that he would do anything for her, she who had bestowed this great and wonderful gift upon him.

What she had wanted, however, was to be away from Lormac and their son. So once Leran was weaned he let her go, sending her off with all the gold and jewels she could carry to fund her new life, along with his solemn oath that she was forever welcome in Tingu. Lormac had never missed her, not for a single moment.

Now, as he gazed upon his queen he knew why. Asherah was what he had always desired, a true warrior, not one to shy away from sharp steel or the call to battle. His subjects flocked to her like moths to the flame, entranced by her quick wit, her charm, her pale beauty. In every way, she was the opposite of Leran's mother, and Lormac wanted her in every one of those ways.

"My king," Asherah said as he approached, that mischievous glint dancing in her eye. She bowed her head, those around her amused by her supplication.

"My lady, there are things I must discuss with you," Lormac began, then leaned close as he continued, "in my chamber."

Fear flashed across her eyes, gone in an instant. "As my lord wishes," Asherah replied and took his arm as they walked from the hall. Lormac took note of her rigid shoulders, her stiff gait.

She cannot still be frightened of me, Lormac mused. *She must realize how much she means to me, that I value her life above mine.* As the thoughts crossed his mind they were all but drowned out by the growing need in his body, a need so great he knew that he must claim her that evening.

"What would you like to discuss?" Asherah asked.

"What I would like to discuss," he replied as the arm that linked with hers traveled around her waist, "is the completion of your queenmaking."

Asherah speaks...

Queenmaking.

He said it as if it was some sort of a ceremony performed in a hall, complete with guests and wine and a crown, but that's not what he meant. I wore the Sala, I had publicly acknowledged that I would be his queen, and now he meant to claim me and make me his.

I glanced at his face and saw a hunger that would no longer be placated by my halfhearted excuses. Lormac had been both patient and indulgent as I fended him off. In hindsight, I wish I had not done so but jumped into his arms. I now realize how much time I wasted being foolish, refusing to relinquish my fears, the many moments gone that I could never reclaim.

And why was I so afraid of him? Of all the men I have since met in my long life, Lormac was certainly the kindest, gentlest soul one could hope to meet. One can hardly expect to meet two men like him in one lifetime.

I stopped to gaze out a window into a walled courtyard; the thaw had come to Tingu and multicolored petals and leaves poked through the melting snow, all outlined in the rich, red moonlight. I began to say how lovely the scene was, how I had never imagined that the cold, frozen north could generate such beauty, when Lormac's hands slid around my waist.

"Asherah," he murmured, his breath hot against my ear. I turned and looked up, up at this elf that was impossibly tall thanks to his mountainous heritage, and tried not to tremble.

"My lord?" I was relieved that my voice held steady. Lormac drew me against him, tangling his fingers in my hair, crystals tinkling to the floor as he covered my face in kisses.

"I need you tonight," Lormac said against my skin. "Tell me it will be tonight."

Tell him? What choice did I have since he had publicly proclaimed me his mate? It irritated me that he (again!) decided that I was his mate without first asking me, that he not only stuck the Sala on me (again!) but that he had done it before the whole of elfdom. Luckily, my irritation burnt away just enough fear for me to answer him.

"Tonight," I began, but his mouth was on mine before the word was fully spoken. I hadn't realized how much he held himself back until that moment, and for the first time, I was fully awash in his passion. His desire ignited some of my own, and as I kissed him back I thought that Tingu was where I was meant to be, that I really was Asherah of the north, that my past no longer mattered...

Until he tried to lift me and I screamed. I shrieked, I kicked, I yelled, then there was pain, pain so great that all I could see was red, and then darkness took me.

I awoke in Lormac's chamber, ensconced in his enormous bed with a head that throbbed as if the troll king had used me in place of his anvil. Someone, most likely Lormac, had tucked me under the heavy velvet coverlet and drawn the curtains that encircled the bed, making the interior dark as a moonless night. My lovely white gown was gone, and I wore only the Sala. I lay still for a time, straining to hear movement outside the curtains. When I was certain that I was alone I sat up and stretched.

Apparently, my hearing is not as sharp as I imagined, for as soon as I moved I heard a wooden chair scrape across the floor. In another instant, Lormac snapped open the curtains and sat at my side. He had removed his ornate coat and sword belt, and he looked exhausted and harried. With a pang of guilt, I wondered if he had been watching over me for half the night.

"How do you feel?" he asked as he smoothed back my hair, concern mingling with confusion across his face. I relayed my analogy of my head and Grelk's anvil, and he chuckled.

"Why am I in your bed?" I asked. While I understood that this had been our ultimate destination, Lormac remained clothed and I remembered nothing after kissing him in the corridor. Before he could answer, the force of nature that was Leran burst into the room.

"Da," Leran cried as he bounded into bed with us. His nurse, who was proffering her usual apologies for Leran's behavior, closely followed him.

"He's been waiting up for the two of you," Lukka was saying. "As soon as he heard your voices, he ran faster than I could catch him."

"Shouldn't you be in bed?" Lormac asked as he ruffled the boy's hair. Leran pouted, for not only had he been forbidden from attending Madoc'na, he had been sent to sleep in his own bed for the first time in more than a fortnight. I had expected him to be cross, but what he said next took both Lormac and me by surprise.

"This can't be mine anymore?" he asked, and I realized that he was staring at the Sala. It had never occurred to me that I was wandering around the Seat with Leran's birthright on my arm. Me, one with no claim to the elfin throne, one who really did nothing except convince the king to fight in a war that shouldn't be his.

"Maybe he should have it," I blurted out, only to have Lormac glare at me as if I'd suggested we leave Leran out for vultures to pick at. Thoroughly abashed, I shrank back against the cushions and let Lormac deal with his son.

"It belongs to Asherah now," Lormac said gently. Leran continued to pout and Lormac continued soothe, reassuring him that he would still rule Tingu one day. Once the boy had been sufficiently placated, Lormac nudged him toward Lukka and extracted a promise that he would remain in his own bed until sunrise. Then Lormac turned back to me and tried drawing me into his arms, but I remained stiff.

"You haven't told me how we ended up here," I reminded him. "Did you make love to me?"

"Do you really think I'd take you unawares?" he asked, hurt evident in his voice and on his face.

"No," I said truthfully, "I don't."

"Good." Lormac reached for me again, and again I evaded him.

"Then why am I naked?" I asked, full of irrational shame when I realized that Lormac was likely the one who removed my gown. Irrational, because we had seen each other naked before, and hells, it wasn't as if I was the first woman to wander into the king's bedchamber. "And why does my head ache so?"

"I was trying to be gallant and carry you to bed, but you fought against me and struck your head on the door," Lormac said with a smirk. "Once I got you up off the floor and made sure you weren't bleeding, I settled you here to rest. I thought you'd be more comfortable without your dress." His brows knit together as he took in the image of me cowering under the bedclothes, and he removed his tunic. For a moment, I thought he would remove the rest of his clothing and climb *into bed. Instead he offered me the garment and went so far as to turn his back as I pulled it over my head.*

"I hate being carried," *I said as my head emerged from the too-large neck; his tunic would likely reach my knees when I stood.* "They never let us walk to our torment; they took even that small dignity from us." *I shuddered as I recalled how the demons would carry me down the dark corridor, their disgusting hands and hoofs and claws raking over my skin and tearing away my pathetic shift even before they chained me to that table.*

"I'm so sorry," *Lormac said, his voice little more than a hoarse whisper.*

I hadn't realized that I'd been speaking aloud, and a new wave of shame washed over me. While Lormac was well aware of my time as a slave, and of the many atrocities that I endured, there were still details I did not want him to know. I realized that Lormac was still speaking, and I wrenched myself from my horrible past to my confusing present.

"You know I would never... force you," *Lormac was saying. He had taken my hand and was tracing the scars on my wrist.* "I could never hurt you."

"I know," *I replied. We sat in silence then, neither of us looking at the other, and I sighed. While my captors were long dead, they were still ruining my life.* "I should go."

"Stay." *He pulled me into his arms, and I was just on edge enough to be annoyed.*

"Lormac, I've already ruined your evening," *I said as I squirmed free.* "I'll return in the morning."

"No!" *Lormac said, tightening his arms.*

"Lormac! Don't hold me down!" *I shrieked. Being naked and unable to move threw open the deadbolted gates of my memories. I fought him as I'd fought against my captors so many times before. I must have shocked Lormac to immobility. I tore myself from his arms and scurried to the far side of the enormous bed, my back against the wall and the coverlet yanked up to my neck. The crystals that had* taken Torim almost a full day to weave into my hair sprayed across the bed, catching the light and refracting patterns across the darkened velvet. I drew my knees to my chest as I broke out in a cold sweat, willing my limbs to stop shaking.

Lormac's saffira clambered into the bedchamber, having heard my hysterics, and Lormac quickly assured them that all was well. Once he had quelled the commotion and we were alone again, he returned to my side, this time keeping a careful distance from his crazed bedmate.

"I'm sorry," I said softly, "I did not mean to shout at you. It's just..." I didn't trust myself to finish my thought, since I'd already shared things I'd never wanted Lormac to know. Hesitantly I glanced at him; his lip was swollen, and blood darkened the corner of his mouth.

"Gods," I croaked as I covered my face, screaming having roughened my voice. While I'd never gotten a demon off me, I did succeed in giving the only man I cared for a bloody lip. That, coupled with my earlier outburst, left me truly mortified.

"It's all right," Lormac soothed. "May I take your hand?" I barely nodded as he did so, holding my fingers lightly so I could withdraw it at a moment's notice. I stared at the Sala, the symbol of Lormac's kingship, symbol of our mating, and I sighed again.

"You should not have given this to one like me," I said as I traced the green stones. "I remember little of my life, and what I do remember seems intent upon ruining the lives of those around me." I leaned back against the bedpost and stared at the ceiling. "Hells, I can hardly let you touch me without going into a panic."

"You don't need to remember anything," Lormac said. "We can make new memories. Once you are fully my mate—"

My mirthless laughter rattled between us. "When is 'once'?" I asked. "Once will never come. Can't you see that this need you have to possess me will only destroy you? You should find someone whose memory and mind is whole, not a hollow shell of a woman. A hollow shell, and even the shell is cracked and crazed."

"I don't want another," he insisted for the hundredth time; this wasn't the first discussion we'd had on the subject. "I want you."

"How could you want me? You don't even know me! Do the gods themselves need to tell you that this does not work? We do not work!" Before he could stop me, I removed the Sala and placed it on the coverlet between us. "This is not meant to be mine."

Lormac looked from the Sala to me, fury boiling behind his eyes. "I have bestowed upon you the greatest honor my people can give, and yet you only want to give it back." He growled the words, anger making his voice low and thick.

"You never asked me if I wanted it," I retorted. "You just expect me to be yours until you tire of me! Your faerie mate, proof that an elf could destroy an evil that the fae could not! You only want to thumb your nose at my people!"

"Is that what you think?" he bellowed. "I don't see you as a prize or a symbol of power or anything other than Asherah!"

"Don't call me that!"

"What am I to call you other than your name?"

I glared at him and spat, "You do not know my name."

I immediately wished I hadn't.

Telling Lormac that he did not know my true name hurt him, and I would have sooner scratched out my own eyes. I was trying to save him from a life bound to me, though it hurt to do so. Lormac leapt from the bed and paced for a moment, his hands flailing about as he muttered to himself. After a moment, he stopped and spoke, his voice having regained its calm.

"I understand why you don't want me to claim you as yet," he said softly. "Truly, I do. What I cannot understand is why you accepted the Sala, not once but twice, agreeing to be my mate and my queen, yet now you only push me away."

He turned and walked from the bed, then stopped and spoke over his shoulder. "All I want to do is love you, but you won't let me."

Love?

Lormac loved me?

That was why he was so insistent that I wear the Sala, why he wanted me to remain in Tingu?

"What?" I assumed I had misheard him. "What do you mean?" I received no answer, for he was already gone.

I hadn't seen which door he exited, his departure having been hidden by the bed curtains, but I knew that he had retreated to the Seat. I got to my feet and followed, wearing only his tunic as I made my way down the passage, my bare feet surprisingly agile on the cool stone.

I found him standing at the rear of the great chamber with his back to me; thanks to his being bare to the waist I could see the tension in his neck and shoulders. He remained still as I approached, his head bowed.

"Lormac," I began.

He clenched his fists and leaned forward, his forearm braced against the wall. For a time, I just stood there staring at him. Why hadn't I known that Lormac loved me? Many, many nights, I had lain awake wondering why he so desperately wanted to be with me, why he couldn't manage to find a nice elf for a mate, what I had done to deserve a man like him...but love never once entered my mind. I could probably blame my oversight on my time in the doja, some torture visited upon me had destroyed some innate sense to know when someone loved you, but that was not the case. I had only myself to blame.

"I never knew," I murmured. "You never told me."

"Told you what?"

"That you love me."

"I didn't think I needed to," he said. "But if you need it said, I love you. So much so I would relinquish my lands, my birthright... everything. If it meant I would have you."

"Why me?" I pressed. "Why not someone else?"

"For me, there is no one else," Lormac said softly. In that moment, I finally accepted that he loved me, that I deserved to have him love me. And I knew that I loved him just as madly and deeply and truly as he loved me.

I grazed my fingertips over his skin, feeling the knots in his muscles pull even tighter. Emboldened by his words, I took the final step toward him and rested my cheek against his back. My hands, palms flat against his skin, moved to his chest as I pressed my body to his.

Lormac turned to face me, and held my face close to his. "Little star, will you stay? Will you stay and let me love you?" Lormac's eyes searched my face. He was surprised when I kissed him, the blood I'd drawn earlier salty against my tongue. I believe he thought I'd followed him up to the Seat to say my final goodbye when in truth I could no longer imagine being apart from him.

"Yes," I said against his lips.

"Yes?"

"Yes, I will stay with you," I replied. "Yes, I love you. Yes, I'm honored to be your mate." Then I kissed him again, not as a scared girl who could not bring herself to forget the abuse she had endured, but as a woman who wanted to utterly possess him. Lormac responded to my newfound passion with his own, his hands roaming over my body as if to memorize my form. Then his hands were on my waist and he again tried to lift me.

"No," I cried, my voice reverberating off the stone walls, and he immediately halted. He touched my cheek, whispering soft, soothing words. "No," I repeated in a softer tone, realizing that Lormac wouldn't harm me; not then, not ever. "Here. Now."

"Here?" he questioned, falling silent as I shed my tunic. Lormac tossed it aside and we tumbled to the ground; in another heartbeat he was thrusting into me. I hardly noticed the tears squeezing out of my eyes, but Lormac did.

"Love," he murmured. "You're safe." When I remained silent, he added, "I'll stop."

"No," I said, pulling him down against me. "Now."

I steeled myself against the coming pain, the humiliation I'd always felt in the past, but there was none of that now, not with Lormac laboring above me. I realized that I wanted him, wanted this, and I arched my back as I came, digging my nails into his buttocks as waves of pleasure cascaded over me.

Lormac slowed his pace just long enough to kiss me deeply, then he rolled onto his back and let me control our pace. I leaned back as I rode him, his hands firm on my hips, guiding me. I called his name as I reached my peak for a second time and collapsed forward on to his chest; I didn't realize that he'd peaked as well until I noticed his slowed panting.

The Seat had reshaped itself to accommodate our lovemaking and we were ensconced in a stone cocoon, remarkably soft and comfortable considering its construction. Lormac had heaped our discarded clothing on us in lieu of a blanket. We didn't speak and hardly moved as we held each other; after a time, I fell asleep in his arms. When the elder sun's rays illuminated the crystal ceiling, I opened my eyes and saw Lormac smiling at me.

"You're mine now," he murmured as he smoothed my hair. "Well and truly claimed."

"Does this mean I'm now your mate?"

"If you still wish to choose me, then yes."

"That is backwards," I pointed out. "Among faeries, the choosing comes first."

Lormac propped himself up on his elbow and gazed down at me. "Then choose me, and I'll claim you again. And again and again, if I need to," he proclaimed as I laughed, my face pressed against his neck. "Will you?"

I looked up and met his pensive gaze. "Will I what?"

"Choose me."

I propped myself up, too, and regarded him His soft gray eyes that were usually so merry but were now somber. "Are you sure you still want me?" *I asked.* "You would really prefer a scarred, broken faerie to a beautiful elf?"

Lormac pulled back my hair where it had fallen over my shoulder and traced some of the cruel marks. He followed one to its terminus near my collarbone, then kissed the hollow of my throat. "My star, I think you're lovely as you are, but even if you were the scarred monster you believe you are it wouldn't matter. I love you for your heart, not your body."

"You really mean that?"

"I really mean that."

"Then you are my choice," *I declared.*

Lormac drew me to him and kissed me, and felt him stir against me. "And you are my only choice," *he said between kisses.* "Asherah, my love, my queen."

"Asherah is not my name," *I said.* "I am Hillel."

"Hillel. I love you, Hillel."

Alluria speaks...

I stood outside the southern door of the Great Temple, clutching my basket of herbs and tapping my foot while I waited for it to open. It was still new for me to wake in Caol'nir's chamber—no, *our* chamber—instead of within the Great Temple. Of course, there was no need for me to rush the temple door at dawn's first light (in all my years, a patron had never experienced a dire herb-related emergency before noon), but in Caol'nir's absence I felt the need to busy myself rather than dwell on the lack of him in our bed.

Caol'nir... the mere thought of him warmed me. We'd known each other for such a short time, and we were mates for only a moment before he left on his quest. While I'd understood that I'd miss him terribly, I wasn't prepared for the constant ache of his loss. I rubbed my neck, stiff from waiting overlong outside the temple, remembering how he would trail his lips across my throat...

Sarelle picked that moment to open the doors, me standing there with a foolish grin on my face. She glared before stalking away, a rustle of haughty golden silk in her wake. I entered the temple and gazed at the priestesses and novices lighting the morning incense. I didn't miss my life as a priestess, not one little bit. The way the girls rushed about, subjected to the wills and whims of a god who may or may not answer them, not to mention Sarelle's mood swings... No, I much preferred my role as an herbalist. I happily worked in my quiet corner, assisting those in need with poultices and teas.

I made my way toward the aforementioned quiet corner, intending to assemble little muslin bags of tea, when I caught sight of a familiar pale braid. My heart nearly stopped beating, but no, it was only Caol'non going about his morning duties. I sighed as I gazed upon my mate's twin; I would truly give anything just to be in Caol'nir's arms at that moment. So lost I was in my memories that I bumped into my mate's eldest brother, dropping my basket of herbs at his feet.

"Forgive me, I did not see you." I knelt to retrieve the small bundles. Fiornacht watched for a moment, then bent and helped.

"Is everything all right?" he asked. I looked up, more startled than I ought to have been by his simple question. It was the first time Fiornacht had spoken to me in the short slice of forever since Caol'nir had departed. I had the impression that he still didn't approve of my union with his brother, and I was perfectly fine with avoiding him. The fact that he now seemed concerned only unnerved me.

"Yes, yes," I answered, "I just..." I stopped speaking, took a deep breath and decided to finish my thought. I did not need the acting Prelate wondering if something was amiss in the Great Temple. "I saw Caol'non, and for a moment I thought—I hoped—he was Caol'nir."

Fiornacht stood and helped me to my feet. "When they were small, it was near impossible to tell them apart. At times, we simply guessed who was who."

I laughed, and Fiornacht took the basket from my hands and escorted me to the sorting table. He set the basket down, his eyes downcast. I waited for him to say whatever weighed upon his mind. It seemed that no matter what my role in the temple, I was still acting very much the priestess.

"You miss him a great deal, don't you?" he said at length.

"I do," I replied, but Fiornacht still wouldn't look at me. "Do you not approve, Prelate?" Using the title got the desired reaction, and his head snapped up.

"I am not Prelate," he clarified, "I just perform Father's duties until his return." He took a few steps away from the table, then stopped and stared off into the distance. Having had much experience with reluctant patrons, I began arranging my herbs and waited.

"I've never disapproved of you and Caol'nir," Fiornacht said softly. "We all knew how taken he was with you, but to expect a priestess to forsake Olluhm for a man, is foolish. I..." His voice trailed off, and I glanced up. "I did not want him hurt."

"Well, luckily for Caol'nir I'm just as foolish as he is," I commented. Fiornacht was still staring off at nothing, or so I thought. I followed his gaze and saw that it rested upon a head of brown curls that I knew all too well.

"Serinha?" I asked, more than a little taken aback. I'd always suspected that Fiornacht was the type to entice a priestess into his bed, but the way he looked at her... Well, it was the same way Caol'nir used to look at me.

"You think less of me now?" he asked, a bitter edge to his voice. "That I spoke against Caol'nir only to hide my own misdeeds?"

"I think nothing of the sort," I said. I probably should have at least thought him a hypocrite, but I didn't. I knew well that love blossomed where it wished, not where it was convenient. "Fiornacht, she is still a novice. If she chooses to be with you, she is breaking no vow. You're not doing anything wrong." I placed my hand on his arm.

"I'm not doing anything right, either," he said with a rueful smile. "How could I ask her to leave her calling? What if she said no?" He was silent for a moment, then he asked me something that had apparently been on his mind for some time. "How did my brother ask you?"

"Caol'nir never asked me to give up being a priestess."

"He didn't?" Fiornacht asked, and I shook my head. "Then why did you?"

"I wanted, more than anything, to be his," I replied.

"Caol'nir never told you?"

"He said you went into the vaults to learn how to be released. I assumed that you'd gone because he asked you."

"Actually, he tried to forbid me from the attempt. He worried that the trials would be too much." I gently squeezed his arm. "Love is stronger than any vow or oath, of that I am certain."

Fiornacht glanced at me, then looked again toward Serinha. His Serinha. He caught her eye and she flashed him a quick smile before returning to her duties. Fiornacht's face lit up; indeed, it was the happiest I have ever seen him.

"Well, ask her," I said. "Don't you want to know if she feels as strongly as you do?" His smile faded, and he bent his head. "You're so like your brother," I huffed. "Always being the noble one, always trying to sacrifice your own happiness. Did you ever once think that she may want to be with you as well?"

"If I was truly like my brother, I would dress her up as a saffira and spirit her out of Teg'urnan this very morning."

My cheeks went hot. "He told you that?" I asked in a small voice.

"He didn't breathe a word of it, at least not to me. It was quite apparent what was happening when neither you nor Caol'nir were anywhere to be found and the gatekeepers were jesting about the many women my brother was riding off with." He softened his gaze. "You may have fooled them, but you did not fool my father or me."

"Why didn't you stop us?" I asked, only to follow his gaze back to Serinha. He didn't stop us because Caol'nir was willing to take a risk that he feared. In that, at least, *the younger brother's bravery shone brighter.* "Fiornacht, would you like me to speak to her?"

"If I cannot talk to her myself, then I must not deserve her, eh?" *he countered.*

The more I spoke with Fiornacht, the more he seemed like my mate in both word and deed. I wondered if his overbearing nature was really just protectiveness toward his younger brothers.

"I've taken up too much of your time," *Fiornacht said,* "and I was sent to fetch Sarelle for the king. I bid you a good day." *I nodded, and he bowed his head.* "I will say, my brother is quite lucky."

"As am I."

Chapter 22

At least the storm is holding off, Caol'nir mused as he looked toward the sky. His horse fidgeted, a reflection of his rider's state of mind. After what had seemed like an eternity of preparations, the *Ish h'ra hai* were finally ready to march to Teg'urnan. The name now encompassed not only the freed slaves but the elfin warriors who wished to honor of their new queen.

The small group of dark fae led by Drustan the Dark kept themselves apart from both fae and elf alike. Caol'nir was not impressed by the dark fae nor their leader. He felt that they didn't believe Sahlgren guilty of any wrongdoing, and that they had sent their puny force only to placate the Lord of Tingu, who held rights to their kingdom. As Caol'nir looked over their meager legion, he wished they had remained in their own land.

The trolls, still insisting they couldn't leave the north, nevertheless came to see the *Ish h'ra hai* depart from the Seat. Grelk's forges had turned out gleaming swords and shields, as well as arrows and spears. Caol'nir's own sword, with its engraved blade and jeweled hilt, looked more a piece of art than a weapon. Grelk had assured Caol'nir that the sword could cleave a *mordeth's* head in one clean stroke. After a few practice sessions that decimated many wooden targets, Caol'nir believed him.

While Caol'nir was eager to return to his home and his mate, he was not eager to return to the *con'dehr*. He had become something of an instructor, teaching the *Ish h'ra hai*, and not a few elves, better ways of combat. Caol'nir feared he would not be able to indulge his newfound passion once things returned to normal at Teg'urnan, if indeed that even happened. He wondered how his father, and Fiornacht, would react when he told him that he wished to leave the *con'dehr* and carve out a quiet existence for him and Alluria.

Alluria... Caol'nir wished for he thousandth time that he had brought her along. His insistence that she remain in Teg'urnan was for her safety, but he now felt that she would be safest at his side. Of course, he wouldn't have let her accompany him to the doja, but that would have been a separation of six days rather than these many moons without her touch. She would have found the Seat beautiful, from the gem-encrusted mountain that housed it to the thick blanket of snow upon the World's Spine. Caol'nir imagined his mate's first encounter with snow, and wondered if Alluria would enjoy a short journey northward.

A sound akin to a thousand beating drums broke Caol'nir free of his reverie. The elfin warriors were beating their swords against their shields, battle cries piercing the air as they worked themselves into a frenzy. Lormac climbed atop the Gate and knelt, holding the Sala before him. Asherah approached and accepted the Sala, then bestowed a kiss upon Lormac's forehead, further inciting the crowd.

"He is pledging himself to his queen, and therefore all of Tingu," Tor explained, having noticed his son's perplexed face. "He is swearing to give his life in her defense."

"Like a binding," Caol'nir murmured, and Tor nodded. "Only he is bound to the land as well."

Caol'nir's voice was drowned out by the ever-louder shouts from the elves, who were cheering as Lormac led Asherah from the Gate to their horses. The royal pair turned toward their people and Lormac said a few words, then he grabbed Asherah and kissed her in such a way that made

Caol'nir wonder if Lormac considered the Gate an extension of his bedchamber.

"Lormac is promising his people a victory," Tor stated.

"Does every custom in Tingu involve Lormac kissing her?" Caol'nir asked.

"The longer the kiss, the swifter the victory," Tor said with a gleam in his eye. Caol'nir shrugged and wished for them to get on with it; the sooner they were done with their elfin rituals, the sooner they would be on the move, and the sooner he would be kissing his own mate.

"Da!" shouted Leran. Lormac ended his kiss to Asherah far earlier than he had intended, but his warriors shouted and cheered nonetheless.

"My boy!" Lormac swept his son into his arms and squeezed him against his chest; every time he left Leran at the Seat, he missed him so dearly he swore he would never be apart from him again. Leran, however, was used to his father's long absences, and was much more distraught with the departure of his new mother.

"Don't go," Leran pleaded, staring at Asherah with mournful eyes.

"I'll only be gone a short time," she assured the boy, smoothing back his hair. Leran leaned forward and wrapped his arms about Asherah's neck, so tightly she could hardly breathe. Asherah took him from Lormac and gazed worriedly at her mate over the boy's head. Lormac shook his head; despite Asherah's pleading and Leran's pouting, he would not take his son from the safety of the Seat. They were all just going to have to miss one another, which would make them appreciate the reunion all the more.

"Don't worry," Asherah soothed, rocking Leran back and forth as if he were still a baby. "Soon, Da and I will return and we will never leave you again."

"Do you promise?"

"I promise."

Asherah speaks...

Most kings ride in the center of the march, with strong warriors on either side to protect them from unforeseen foes. Not so Lormac, who proudly rode at the front, almost daring his foes to strike. I'd heard many tales about his prowess in battle (mostly from Lormac's own lips, but a few came from Balthus), and I wondered if my mate believed himself invincible.

His prowess was also the subject of another topic within the camp, which involved our sleeping arrangements. I couldn't bear the thought of Torim alone in her bedroll, and adopted the habit of sneaking out of the palatial tent I shared with Lormac and into her bed. I always intended to return to him before dawn, but I did tend to oversleep while in her embrace. After Lormac had awakened without me a few times, and Belenos complained that there wasn't room for him in Torim's bed, Lormac followed me to my not-so-secret encounter and proclaimed that our bed was more than large enough for three, and thus we became the most discussed bedmates in Parthalan. Belenos, to his great disappointment, was not invited.

Others tried not to speculate on what went on in the king's tent within our earshot, but when Lormac heard such comments he merely joked that whether we were home at the Seat or marching to war, he couldn't manage to sleep alone with his mate.

Our newest bedmate created another small but manageable problem in that we needed to find someplace to make love. Lormac spun a yarn about needing to bed me often now that we were outside Tingu's borders (as if he had let me alone while we were in them!) so he could freely draw upon the power of the Sala. While I didn't think his reasoning was sound, neither did I protest, and we became adept at finding secluded locations to share a few moments.

Initially, I'd been reticent to be intimate with him out of doors, fearful of someone happening upon us, but the cool air and warm sun on my skin was an aphrodisiac like none other. I also learned that Lormac had handpicked his most trusted, closed-mouthed soldiers to set up a discreet perimeter and keep anyone from disturbing us. Despite his warriors' skill, on one such day I couldn't escape the sensation of being watched.

"I do hope you're mistaken," Lormac murmured after I'd shared my suspicions with him. He had found a sunny clearing for us to while away the afternoon and had even brought furs and cushions, lest anyone wonder what we were up to. "If anyone looks upon my queen unclad, the punishment is to have their eyes struck from their skull, and we will need all the sighted warriors we can manage."

I had laughed as he described a bevy of blinded elves trudging toward Teg'urnan, and we languidly passed the afternoon together. We returned to the same spot the next day (a bridge needed fortification to allow our massive force passage, and it ended up taking eight days to complete). As I sank into the soft grass with Lormac, I again felt an uninvited presence.

But who could have evaded Balthus? Whoever it was needed to have unsurpassed tactical knowledge to know where the sentries would be stationed and how they moved. It had to be someone stealthy enough to evade...a demon.

"Love, would you fetch me some wine?" I asked.

"Now?" He gave me the most frustrated of faces, to which I smiled as sweetly. "I'll be back in an instant." I watched Lormac disappear through the trees, and then I turned toward the opposite side of the clearing.

"Are you going to come out?" I asked, and Harek emerged. "How many days have you skulked about, spying on Lormac and me?"

"Only since yesterday," he replied "And I wasn't spying." His eyes were downcast, and I suspected that there was more to this than simple curiosity.

"Here," I said, indicating that he should sit beside me; he did, and I wrapped the thick fur about me in spite of the warm day. Of all people, Harek should have known not to watch me during such a moment. "If not spying, then what?"

"As always, I watch over you," he replied.

"I'm surrounded by those sworn to die for me," I stated. "Further, if Lormac or his warriors had seen you, you would have been punished first and questioned later."

"Those boys cannot catch me," he scoffed. I pursed my lips, and waited for him to explain himself. "I just wanted to know that you were safe with him."

"Of course I am. He's my mate."

"I had to know for myself," Harek said. "It's unlikely for the Lord of Tingu to take a faerie to bed, let alone as his mate." I took no offense at Harek's argument, for I'd thought the same. Lormac, however, had proven me wrong. "I had to know you were well cared for."

I heard the softest of footfalls and saw Lormac on the edge of the clearing, cask of wine in hand; Harek was deep within his contemplation and hadn't noticed him. I motioned for Lormac to wait and questioned Harek.

"Care of me concerns you so?"

"I've always sought to care for you, even when I could not," Harek said quietly. "I remember the day they brought you to the doja. You were so young, the youngest taken at that time, but you fought against them like a caged animal. No one had ever fought the way you did. I couldn't move but I silently praised for you, hoping you would wound one of them and escape..." Harek fell silent, staring at the ground.

"Then what?" I prompted. While I'd known that Harek was present when I was brought to the doja, I did not know that he had witnessed my first agonizing day. I hoped his recollections would stir my own long-buried memories.

"It became clear what they were going to do... First, you pleaded with them to spare you... You claimed to be maiden still, and promised to another... Your claim only angered the mordeth; he wanted you for his own, but he thought you were lying. He choked you until you fainted and left you for the lessers." Harek turned to me then, his face that never betrayed emotion now drowning in anguish. "I've never felt as helpless as I did in that moment, watching them..."

His voice broke, and he turned away. When he continued, he had regained the stoic timbre that only comes from years of observing such torment. "Afterward, I carried you to Torim's cell. I couldn't do anything else for you, but I hoped the two of you might help one another."

I smiled wanly as I remembered waking in that cell for the first time; Torim, filthy and huddled in a corner, terrified of the new woman that stared at her from across the tiny room. Disregarding my own plight, I had coaxed Torim from her hiding place behind the straw and... and you know the rest.

"I'm glad you left me with her," I murmured, realizing that he had placed us together because he worried that neither of us would have survived alone. "Thank you, for the care you took with us."

Harek grunted. "You call that care? I returned you to them, time and again!"

"You had no choice. But you were as kind as you were allowed to be, and we wouldn't have lasted long without you."

Harek faced me, and I flinched under the weight of his gaze. "We of the Ish h'ra hai have you to thank," he said gravely, "you alone." Then he pulled me toward him and kissed me; I was too shocked to evade him. "I'm yours to command, deliverer." Then he rose and walked away.

I touched my fingers to my lips and momentarily considered following Harek, but not for the reasons he would have wanted. I worried that he saw me as something I wasn't, someone to be placed upon a pedestal...but I was only Hillel. I put my concerns aside when I heard Lormac approach, having left his hidden spot at the edge of the clearing. He sat next to me, and I opened the fur, wrapping him in its warmth as he wrapped me with the comfort only he could give.

"Did you hear?" I asked at length.

"I did."

"Now, you know how it began," I said softly. "Now, we both know."

He squeezed me against him, and I could sense that his mind was filled with the images Harek had described. "Do I tell you that I love you often enough?"

"You could tell me every moment of every day, and I'd never tire of it," I replied. "Are you angry with Harek?"

"I'm certainly not pleased," Lormac snapped. "If Harek had kissed you in front of my warriors, any one of them would have struck him dead for the affront. I will deal with him." I looked up at him, pleading without words. "You don't want me to?"

"Many of the guards were made eunuch," I explained. "We suspect that he was as well."

"If he wasn't, I will arrange it," Lormac muttered. He went on to mention nearly a hundred arguments for Harek's punishment—that in Tingu he would be put to death for touching me, that as queen I could demand his torture and eventual death, that being cut was a lesser punishment than he deserved—and I declined them all.

"Please, ignore it this once," I asked. "If not for Harek and his brother, I'd likely be dead in that doja. The least I can do is spare him for this single transgression."

Lormac's eyes softened. "For giving me the gift of my beloved queen, I will suspend action against him. However, I still wish to speak with him."

"Lormac," I began, but he held up his hand.

"As you wish," he grumbled. "The traitorous bastard who dared touch my mate will escape all retribution."

"Now, none of that," I scolded. "I expect pouting from Leran, but not from his regal father." I rose, and tugged Lormac along with me.

"Where are you taking me?"

I glanced over my shoulder, and saw the mischief in my eyes reflected in his. "I'm suddenly of a mind to take a swim."

Chapter 23

On and on they marched, until Torim wondered if she would ever see the world framed by aught but her horse's ears. Every joint in her body ached, every muscle was sore; no, she had transcended beyond sore days ago. What was more amazing was that the *Ish h'ra hai* had walked all the way to Tingu, herself included, and she didn't recall being in such discomfort when they arrived at Lormac's keep.

This creature hates me. She glared at her horse, all but convinced that its uneven gait was merely a tool to cause dull, throbbing pains across her body. Torim glanced over her shoulder at the marching warriors and sighed; it was an honor to have use of a horse, but she would be so much happier moving under the power of her feet and nothing more.

Her opinion was strengthened when camp was made that evening; her bones audibly creaked as she dismounted. Torim handed the reins to a handler, then Asherah approached her.

"The Prelate wishes to speak with us," Asherah murmured, "all of us."

Asherah laced her fingers with Torim's, and together they entered the Prelate's hastily-erected tent. Torim blinked at the darkened interior, then observed that everyone of note was in attendance. In addition to herself and Asherah, Tor Caol'nir, Lormac, Balthus, Belenos, and Sibeal were present; even Drustan the Dark was there. A moment later Harek slipped inside the tent, narrowly evading the daggers thrown by Lormac's eyes. When all were present, Tor spoke without preamble.

"There is one matter we've yet to consider. What is to be done with Sahlgren once he's been captured?"

"He will be judged," Lormac said, as if the matter was obvious, but a quick glance at the faeries that surrounded him said otherwise. "How else do you propose we deal with him?"

"It's not a question of whether or not Sahlgren should be judged, but who shall judge him," Tor replied. "He has ruled Parthalan for three thousand winters, none are his equal."

"I am his equal," Lormac replied. "I haven't ruled near as long, but Tingu is a larger land than Parthalan. Drustan is fae and king of his land. And," he added, placing his hand on Asherah's back and drawing her toward him, "my queen is fae. We three may act as a council and decide his fate."

"Aye," Drustan agreed, "we will hear his crimes, right on Teg'urnan's steps so all may know what he's done."

"Well and so, once he is judged, what do we do with him?" Tor pressed.

Lormac eyed Tor. "I would sentence the traitor to death, but your manner makes me wonder what you aren't telling me."

"Rulership of Parthalan is passed by blood, either through birth of an heir or the spilling of the king's blood," Tor explained.

"In three millennia, Sahlgren has not managed a single heir?"

"No," Tor replied flatly.

"Does he have a cock?" Belenos demanded.

"As far as I know," Tor replied. "We fae don't get children as often as elves."

"Apparently not," Belenos grumbled.

Lormac ran a hand through his hair; the situation had just become unbearably complicated. "I wish you'd explained this to me in Tingu," he grumbled. Balthus and his men still did not understand, and Lormac gestured for Tor to explain.

"Since Sahlgren has no heir, whoever spills his blood will become the next king of Parthalan," Tor stated.

"What if he's killed without bleeding, say strangulation?" asked Balthus.

"Then there is no king, and Parthalan will remain without a ruler until Solon appoints a new one."

"You cannot fight for the throne?"

"No, and I am beholden to stop anyone who tries. As Solon's heir, I cannot work against him" The elfin warriors stared at the Prelate, as did Torim and Asherah. Sahlgren had ruled longer than most had lived, so the rites of succession weren't widely known.

"This is the most foolish custom I have ever heard," grumbled Belenos as Drustan muttered a similar opinion. "Among elves, if there is no heir the strongest warrior becomes king."

"We aren't like you," Tor said. "Parthalan was given to us by the gods, and they choose the ruler, not we. Therefore, per their design, the old king must be beheaded by the new."

"Why don't you behead him?" asked Balthus, but Tor shook his head.

"I'm sworn to defend the king. I cannot break my oath."

Balthus threw his hands up in the air. "You fae have effectively hobbled yourselves," he said. "What are we to do? Capture Sahlgren and hold him somewhere until we find a suitable ruler? Or is there an oath to keep that from happening?" A sharp look from Lormac silenced Balthus.

"While I do not condone such outbursts, Balthus is correct," Lormac stated. "If rulership is passed by blood, we need to find Parthalan's next ruler." Lormac looked to Caol'nir. "What about you? Who holds your oath?"

"My father," Caol'nir answered. "As *con'dehr* I'm bound to the Prelate."

"You could rule, Solon-son," Lormac stated gravely. "The scion of a warrior god's line is a good choice."

"No," Caol'nir replied without hesitation, then elaborated, "My mate, she would not be pleased."

"Your priestess will mate to a warrior, but not a king?" Lormac asked with a raised brow, chuckling as indignation rose in Caol'nir's eyes. "Calm yourself, I mean no ill will. But the question remains: who will take Sahlgren's head?"

"Asherah will."

All eyes turned to Harek, heretofore silent during the deliberations. Fury rose in Lormac's eyes, and he opened his mouth, but Harek had the audacity to speak over him. "There is no better choice," he insisted. "Dojas burn because of Asherah, slaves are free because of Asherah. Who better to rule Parthalan than she who has saved it?"

"She is Lady of Tingu," Lormac snapped.

"That she may be, but she is also a faerie," Harek continued. "If she is to rule, it should be over the fae, not elves."

"Who are you to decide where she should rule?" Lormac demanded. "You merely wish to separate her from me, her mate!"

"That is preposterous!"

"Is it? I heard what you said to her, you pathetic gelding—"

"Enough!" Asherah glared from Lormac to Harek. "If you consider me fit to rule not one, but two lands, show me enough respect to not discuss my fate as if I were not standing before you!"

"Forgive me," Lormac said, "but the idea of you in Parthalan and while I remain in Tingu upsets me greatly." Asherah's eyes widened, then she walked out of the tent. Lormac moved to follow her, but Torim stayed him.

"I'll go," she said quietly. "You're needed here."

Torim found Asherah a short distance from the tent, staring at the *Ish h'ra hai* camp. The sight reminded Torim of a time not so long ago, when Asherah had gazed out over a haphazard gathering of freed slaves and wondered where she should lead them. *And now she leads them home to Teg'urnan.* She stood behind Asherah and grasped her hand, resting her chin on Asherah's shoulder. Asherah relaxed against her, and Torim felt her tension to ebb.

"You think you would be such a horrible queen?" Torim asked.

"I think Parthalan can do better," Asherah replied. "I don't know how to lead."

"You already lead Tingu."

"I'm no leader. I'm only Lormac's mate."

"I don't believe Lormac considers you only his mate," Torim said. "His people don't, either."

"Torim, this is absurd. Why Harek even suggested me, I don't know."

"I do." Asherah turned to look at her friend. "All of the *Ish h'ra hai* know."

Asherah sighed. "Leading a group of slaves is different that ruling a land."

"There is one who can teach you, one who has already welcomed you into his life," Torim said.

"Lormac? He cannot leave Tingu without a leader."

"Who says he has to? Perhaps it's time for the land of elf and fae to become one."

Asherah sighed again. "Why don't you lead, Torim? You're as qualified as I."

"No," Torim said quietly. "I'm destined to be a companion, nothing more." Torim gestured to the ranks of fae and elfin warriors. "You see, we already fight together."

"That we do," Asherah murmured.

At length, Lormac emerged from the tent. Torim moved aside as he put his arms around Asherah and kissed her temple, then she leaned against them both. Torim found that she enjoyed the solidity of the two, the mountain and his mate.

"What has been decided?" Asherah asked.

"Sahlgren will be captured, and while he is held prisoner, we will decide what to do with him," Lormac replied. "Belenos brought up a good point in that we need to ensure there is no heir before a replacement is chosen. A man can have many dalliances in three thousand years, and it's unlikely that no children have resulted." Lormac chuckled. "Or perhaps he's cockless like Harek."

Asherah thumped his shoulder, hiding her smile against his chest. "Stop."

"Solon never intended for a king to be chosen the way one chooses a mate," Torim said. "He wished for a strong warrior to take the king's head in battle, not for Parthalan to be caught up with councils and such over the lack of an heir."

"I forget your Solon was a warrior," Lormac mused. "Elves are the same; a king is made on the battlefield, not in a closed-off council."

"You see, Hillel, elf and fae are more alike than different," Torim said.

"Perhaps," Asherah murmured as she settled against Lormac's chest, "perhaps we are."

Chapter 24

"Sunbonnets?"

Caol'nir looked up from his flower gathering and met Torim's soft brown gaze. "They are my mate's favorite," he explained. "She'll enjoy these."

"I'm sure she will," Torim replied.

The *Ish h'ra hai* chose to camp beyond the eastern foothills. The natural topography shielded them from view of Teg'urnan, and the sorcerers had magically obscured them from view. Caol'nir waited impatiently for its completion, for until the shield was established passing through it would shatter the illusion. He'd taken a walk to pass the time and happened upon a patch of his mate's favorite blossoms.

"For you," Caol'nir said as he proffered one of the tiny blossoms to Torim. She tucked it behind her ear, then the two made their way to the Prelate's tent. Tor glanced toward them, the handful of flowers telling him what was on his son's mind.

"I wish you'd reconsider," Tor said. "It will be difficult to take the palace unawares if you're recognized. Questions will be asked."

"And I won't leave Alluria inside a palace that's about to be attacked," Caol'nir countered. "Wouldn't you do the same for mother?" Tor glared at his son; Caol'nir knew that drawing a comparison between Alluria and his mother wasn't fair, but he was adamant that Alluria be far from Teg'urnan before the *Ish h'ra hai* began their assault.

"Don't you see how this is foolhardy?" Tor continued. "Why don't you beg an audience with Sahlgren and explain our plans to him in detail?"

"No one will know I've returned. Remember, I have a twin."

Before Tor could respond, a shout announced that obfuscation of the camp was complete. Without another word, Caol'nir left his father, mounted his horse, and galloped toward the palace, his blood singing in anticipation of being reunited with Alluria.

Caol'nir entered the gates without incident; the gatekeeper even hailed him with his twin's name. Once his horse was stabled, he entered the palace and moved directly toward the Great Temple.

While he was most anxious to see Alluria, being within the smooth gray walls that had sheltered him nearly his entire life eased him. As he walked the corridors, he realized how much he loved Teg'urnan and resolved to ask Alluria if she'd consider making it their permanent home.

The lack of activity near the heart of the palace made him to leave off his pleasant musings. It was midmorning, and the corridors should have been a hubbub of activity, full of priestesses and their guards walking to and fro while performing the god's work, *saffira* going about their daily tasks... but this portion of the palace was deserted.

Caol'nir launched himself into a run, his carefully gathered bouquet falling to the floor when he saw the Great Temple sealed shut.

Legend spoke of the Great Temple's creation, of how Olluhm had lovingly placed one stone atop another as Cydia looked on, lounging atop the flat rock that would become the altar. Once the temple had been completed Olluhm threw the doors wide, and proclaimed that from the moment he crested the horizon in the morning until he went to his evening rest, the doors were to remain open to allow sunlight, and therefore him, full access. It wasn't a widely known legend, and only one of Olluhm's priestesses, or a *con'dehr*, would realize that the temple doors being shut during the day meant that something was terribly wrong.

"Alluria!" Caol'nir bellowed as he threw his weight against the northern doors, solid slabs of granite meant to represent Parthalan's strength. The doors didn't so much as budge. He kicked it, pounded it with his fists, all the while knowing it was futile; brawn cannot override magic. A memory burst forth and he searched his jerkin, finding the stone Alluria had charmed to open the temple. Caol'nir stared at it for a moment, then he thrust it against the granite. The binding spell shattered, and Caol'nir pushed his way inside. What he saw made him wonder if he'd stepped into the pits of hell rather than the holiest of holy places.

Caol'nir saw why he needed to shove with all of his strength: directly inside the entry a *mordeth* lay atop of a priestess. He thrust his sword into the beast's back, and heard a sickening crack as the spine was severed. Caol'nir yanked his sword free and hauled the body from the priestess; the victim was Alyon, Alluria's sister priestess from the east. He lifted her from the bloody floor, relieved to find her breathing.

"It's Caol'nir," he said when she threw up her hands. "Where's Alluria?"

"I don't know," she replied with wide, terrified eyes.

"Can you walk?" he asked, and she nodded. He wrapped his cloak about her shoulders to cover the bloody remains of her robe. "Run. Find Rahlle, and bring him here," he said, squeezing her hand as he spoke. Alyon nodded and fled the temple, her bare feet soundless as she went in search of the sorcerer. Once she was gone Caol'nir shut the door, and faced the demons.

Caol'nir ran through the Great Temple, teeming with *mordeths* and their prey, the priestesses he as *con'dehr* sought to protect. His sword flashed in a silver arc as he killed first one, then another, hurriedly pulling the victimized priestesses to their feet and giving them the same instruction he had given Alyon. A girl screamed, but as Caol'nir went to her aid he tripped over a body.

"Fiornacht!" Caol'nir cried when he saw the familiar straw-colored braid. He was lying atop one of the novices; Serinha, Caol'nir thought was her name. Caol'nir assumed his brother was shielding the girl with his body. He grabbed Fiornacht's shoulder and yanked him about, revealing the gaping wound in his gut.

"Go in peace, brother," Caol'nir said as he shut the cold, lifeless eyes. He looked to Serinha and saw that she was also gone, her fingers tightly laced with his brother's. "As Father always said, we're more alike than not," Caol'nir said, then he bolted toward the altar calling his mate's name.

Caol'nir spied the recaptured girl too late, and sank his sword into the *mordeth's* back. He scanned the temple, not finding his mate. "Alluria!" he roared.

His reply was a wail that pierced the chaos of the temple; even in terror, Alluria's voice was beautiful. Caol'nir ran up the steps to the altar, finding the worst scene he could have imagined, far worse than stumbling across his dead brother. Mersgoth, the *mordeth* that had been briefly captured in Tingu, the beast that had scarred his neck, had Alluria on her back atop the altar stone, burning his handprint into her thigh.

A shaft of light shot down from the oculus and into Mersgoth's eyes, blinding him. As the demon stumbled backward Caol'nir flung himself forward, slamming into the beast and sending Mersgoth hurtling down the altar steps. In the next instant, Caol'nir snatched Alluria from the altar and into of his arms. He set her down against a statue of the doe and pushed back her hair.

"Alluria," he began, but she screamed and drew her dagger. Caol'nir turned as Mersgoth rose up behind them. He swung his blade and impaled the *mordeth* in the gut. As the demon fell to his knees Caol'nir saw that he was naked, his cock barbed and bloody and dripping...

Caol'nir screamed as his blade severed the demon's member, his booted foot connecting with the beast's chest and sending him once more tumbling down the steps. Caol'nir stood panting, then his gaze returned to the altar stone. Once pristine and shining, it was now covered in gore, defiled by the demon's foul seed. He couldn't bear that this of all places was ruined, and roared as his troll sword cleaved the stone in two. He kicked the pieces of the altar down the steps after the *mordeth*, hoping the slabs would crush him. Caol'nir's heart pounded as his blood shouted for further vengeance, but a whimper stilled him. Alluria cowered against the base of the statue, clutching her dagger in a white-knuckled grip.

"*Nalla*," he said, kneeling before her. "I'm here." Slowly, gently, he pried her fingers from the dagger, then took the weapon and shoved it into his belt. He tried to cover her with the shredded remains of her robe, but there was hardly anything left. Caol'nir unlaced his jerkin and pulled his shirt over his head, then he eased the bloody tatters from her body. Alluria sobbed, drawing her knees to her chest.

"I just want to cover you," he soothed. Caol'nir murmured quiet, calm words, until she relaxed her arms and let him put his shirt on her.

"*Nall?*" Alluria asked, touching his face. "You're really here?"

"I am," Caol'nir replied, then he tossed his jerkin across his shoulders and lifted his mate in his arms. He set his jaw as he surveyed the carnage that filled the temple and carefully picked his way down the steps. "Close your eyes, *nalla*," he whispered, and Alluria hid her face against his neck.

Caol'nir saw that Mersgoth's body wasn't at the foot of the altar, and didn't tell Alluria. He moved quickly to the northern door, reaching it as Rahlle entered with his three apprentices, as well as Atreynha and Alyon.

"Goddess above," Atreynha swore when she saw the interior of the temple, her hand shaking as it covered her mouth. She saw Alluria in Caol'nir's arms, and asked, "Is she alive?"

"Yes," Caol'nir replied, then he noted his mate's limp form; Alluria had fainted. "Are you unharmed, Mother Priestess?"

"Yes, I was with Rahlle," she replied, then looking over Caol'nir's shoulder. He turned, and saw Rahlle and his apprentices retrieving the surviving priestesses. When Caol'nir had left for the north, the temple had been home to over three score priestesses; now, only eight and Atreynha still lived.

"Did you kill them all?" Atreynha asked, her gaze skating across the temple. Seventeen *mordeths* were dead, and only Caol'nir held a weapon.

"I suppose I did," Caol'nir answered.

"Solon's son, greatest of our warriors," Rahlle said. The mad sorcerer's face was taken over by the same pensive gaze as Grelk's whenever he mentioned Solon.

Alluria stirred in Caol'nir's arms. "We need to leave," he snapped. "Atreynha, can you seal the door?"

"Of course," she murmured. As she recited the incantation, Caol'nir explained to Rahlle what he had learned in the north and the location of the *Ish h'ra hai* beyond the eastern foothills.

"First, we will go to my rooms and heal them as best we can," Rahlle said, indicating the priestesses with a sweep of his hand. "Then, we will join you under cloak of darkness." Caol'nir nodded, turning as he did so and revealing wounds on Alluria's legs and feet. "I will heal her, as well."

"What?" Caol'nir followed Rahlle's eyes to the burn above Alluria's knee, the *mordeth's* handprint." No," Caol'nir, tightened his hold, "I will care for my mate myself."

Rahlle bowed his head. Caol'nir left without another word as he brought Alluria to their chamber. *Good thing she charmed it,* he mused as the door opened and shut of its own accord. Once inside, he leaned against the heavy wood, worn smooth with winters of use, and held Alluria fast against his chest. He allowed himself a moment, then straightened and brought her to their bed. As Caol'nir nestled her among the furs he remembered the first time she had been in his chamber, and how surprised she had been by his soft, comfortable bed.

She thought I was a barbarian, Caol'nir thought as he stroked her perfect cheek, bruised and streaked with blood. He rose, halting when she grabbed his wrist.

"I'm only getting water," he murmured when he saw her terrified eyes. "*Nalla*, I won't leave you." Alluria nodded and withdrew her hand. Caol'nir retrieved a basin and sponges from the adjoining washroom. After he coaxed her into a sitting position, he set to washing the gore from her hair.

"Is there very much?" Alluria asked quietly.

"No," Caol'nir replied as he combed her hair, "not very much at all." Having finished with her hair, Caol'nir knelt and sponged the blood from her feet.

"Can you tell me what happened?" Caol'nir asked, trying to remain calm. He had hoped that Alluria had merely stepped in someone else's blood, but her cuts meant it was likely her own.

"Everyone was running, screaming," Alluria began. "I couldn't find Atreynha anywhere...I was so worried one of them took her." Alluria's voice caught, and she covered her face with her hands. Caol'nir rose up on his knees and kissed her forehead, murmuring that she did not have to continue if it was too much. "No, I'm fine," she said, wiping her eyes. He returned his attention to her battered feet. Alluria watched him spread salve across her abrasions before she continued.

"I didn't know what to do," she said softly. "The doors were sealed shut, and I was too far away to open them. Then the big one saw me...he pointed at me and said that I was for him, that I was special and set aside for him... He came at me and I didn't know what to do. I ran behind the statue of Cydia and used a glamour to hide... He was furious, roaring and bellowing that he would find me... Then he lunged forward and grabbed Keena. She struggled, but she couldn't get away. He... he ripped off her robe."

Alluria fell silent, and Caol'nir watched as rage and despair played across her face. "Beloved, who sealed the doors?"

"Sarelle," she answered, anger burning in her eyes. "She locked us in with them." His gentle mate had practically growled the words. They held each other's gaze for a moment, then Caol'nir bent his head, having cleaned the wounds up to the *mordeth's* handprint. He swabbed the edge with a damp cloth, mindful of her charred flesh.

"I will release you, if you like," Alluria said softly. "You deserve more than a mate that has been so defiled." Caol'nir dropped the cloth and grabbed her hands.

"You will never release me," he said fiercely. When she refused to look at him, he nudged her forehead with his. "Alluria, you are my mate, the only mate I will ever have. You are not defiled. You are injured, and I will care for you, until these wounds heal and for the rest of my life." Alluria nodded as a tear ran down her cheek. Caol'nir kissed it away, then resumed dabbing at her burn. Needing to distract her, he asked her what happened after the *mordeth* took Keena.

"I ran toward her—I know I should have stayed hidden, but I couldn't just watch while he hurt her—and the strangest thing happened. I had my arm outstretched, and as I yelled at him to let her go, I moved my arm. He staggered, as if I'd pushed him."

"Was it a spell?" Caol'nir asked.

"It was no spell that I know," she answered, "but when I did it again, he staggered. Then, like a fool I stood there staring at my hands, and he grabbed my neck."

Caol'nir abandoned his healer's tasks and took Alluria's hands in his.

"He told me that I was special," she continued, "that I was for him alone, and I would give him his heirs. I told him I was bound, so I could only bear my mate's child...he said it didn't matter, that he would have me anyway. Then I told him I already carried my mate's child, but he said he would rip the baby from my womb so his could grow there instead." Caol'nir sat next to her, and placed his hand on her belly.

"Alluria, are you..." His words trailed off, and she shook her head.

"No. I lied to the demon. Then I stabbed him, just like you taught me."

"That's my girl," Caol'nir said as he squeezed her hand. "Where did you stab him?"

"Here," she said, stroking the side of his neck. "How did this happen?" Alluria asked as she examined the unfamiliar scars.

"I used your firestarting spell against a demon," he replied. "The demon you met today."

"You should have made the fire hotter," she said. "I will teach you how." Alluria let her fingertips explore the new, slick skin upon his neck, then Caol'nir asked what happened after she stabbed Mersgoth.

"He dropped me, but all stabbing him really did was make him angrier. He had me again in an instant and grabbed Keena, and then he dragged us to the altar... He threw Keena on the stone and me on my face...he held me down with his foot as he took her, saying over and over that he would do worse to me. Then he was done with her, and he threw me on the stone, into what was left of Keena...he ripped open my robe and I saw him, bloody as if he'd ripped Keena apart from the inside... and then the pain as he burnt me..."

Alluria's voice trailed off and Caol'nir pushed up the edge of her garment, looking at the gouges on her inner thighs. He steeled himself against her possible response, and asked what the *mordeth* did after he marked her. To his great surprise, she smiled at him.

"Then I heard you," she replied, "you were there in time." Caol'nir pulled her into his arms, tears running down his face.

"I'll never leave you again," he promised. "You were right; I shouldn't have left you behind." He ran his fingers through the soft strands of her hair, knowing that he was holding her too tightly for her injuries but unable to let her go. Alluria wrapped her arms around him, all the while whispering that she had not been afraid, that she had known he would come for her. When Caol'nir opened his eyes, his gaze settled on something unusual nestled in the bed.

"What's this?" he asked, retrieving one of his shirts from the furs.

"It's the shirt you wore the day before you left, when you sparred with Caol'non. I've slept with it every night since you left."

"It must have smelled horrible," he observed.

"It smelled like you," she corrected. "I'd hold it and pretend you were here with me."

"You missed me so much?" he asked, stroking her cheek.

"Caol'nir, every night I ached for you," Alluria replied, pulling him into her arms. As she lay back against the furs, Caol'nir's hands moved across her hips and then to her back, and he felt fresh bruises beginning to swell. He murmured that she was hurt, that she should rest; he did not want to worsen her injuries.

"I'm fine," she breathed, "as long as you're here, I'm fine."

The shadows had grown long before Caol'nir acknowledged that time was slipping away. Alluria was asleep against him, her shining hair spread around her, and he was loathe to wake her. Then he felt Alluria's hands move across his arms, and she brought his wrist before her face.

"You still wear it," she said as she ran her fingers over the blue ribbon, now so battered it was more of a dusky gray than the sapphire hue of her eyes.

"Does that surprise you?"

"No," she replied, "not at all." Alluria kissed Caol'nir's wrist, then tugged his braid over his shoulder. She unwound the leather thong, and unwove his hair. When it was loose, she said, "I missed the way your hair fell around me, like a sun-colored curtain, I missed watching you sleep..." her voice trailed off while she ran her fingers through the long strands of his hair. Alluria moved to her side and regarded her mate. "Why did the demon say I was for him alone?"

Caol'nir stroked Alluria's hair, trying not to lose himself in her deep blue gaze. She was certainly beautiful enough to have divine blood in her veins. "*Rihka*, you told me you were born in the temple. What else do you know of your parents?"

"I know that my mother arrived at the temple shortly before I was born, begging sanctuary. I know nothing of my father."

"What became of your mother?"

"Before my first winter she was gone. Why are you asking me this?" Caol'nir did not answer readily. "Caol'nir, if you know something of them you must to tell me."

"There is a belief, one that was shared by the *mordethgall*, that you are Olluhm's daughter." Alluria stared at him, and Caol'nir explained what he had learned of Sahlgren's plot with Ehkron.

"Why would our king commit such terrible acts?" Alluria asked once the tale was finished.

"He desired power, and Ehkron was his means to get it," Caol'nir replied. "Rahlle believes Sahlgren has become bored as king of only Parthalan and will seek to conquer the nine realms with his abominable legion."

"And this... this is why the priestesses were brought to Teg'urnan, yet the priests left behind," she murmured.

"He brought the priestesses to the Great Temple as an offering for the *mordeths*, with you reserved for Ehkron," Caol'nir confirmed.

"This is why Sarelle didn't care if I left the temple," she said at length. "It didn't matter to her if I was chaste; I just needed to be there when they came." Alluria pulled away from Caol'nir and covered her face with her hands. "When she sealed the doors, she looked right at me. She even convinced me to be an herbalist, to single me out by dressing me in that bright green robe." Alluria laughed shortly. "My leaving the temple certainly helped her plan along."

"It also made me very happy," Caol'nir reminded her as he kissed her shoulder.

"I...cannot be Olluhm's child," she whispered. "I just can't. Atreynha never mentioned it, and she spoke of my mother often. She never mentioned my father."

"Atreynha probably wasn't present when they made you," Caol'nir said. "Was your mother a priestess?"

"No," Alluria replied. "I...I know nothing of her life before."

"Has Olluhm ever honored women who were not of the temple?"

"It has happened," she admitted, "and those children are revered, for they are even fewer than those born of the order." Alluria looked up at her mate, her eyes as wide as a child's. "If I was his daughter, wouldn't I know? How would the *mordeth-gall* know but not me?"

"I don't know, *mea nalla*," Caol'nir said as he stroked her hair. "It would make sense, you being his daughter; he never claimed you, and he released you to come to me. Remember when we were bound? He kept referring to you as his child."

"We're all his children," she said, but without conviction. She rolled flat on her back and stared at the ceiling. "Is this even possible?"

"Of course it is possible. You command magics elusive to all but the highest sorcerers; you understand plants as if they speak to you... Even the wind bends to your will. And," he added, raising himself up on one elbow, "I have always thought you more beautiful that any goddess." He drew a line from her cheek to the hollow of her throat, then kissed her neck. "My divine mate."

She grasped his hand and nestled herself against his chest. "So it was Ehkron that attacked me?"

"Ehkron is dead," Caol'nir said flatly. "The demon you encountered was Mersgoth, his right hand. It was he I used the fire spell against," he reminded her, then pressed her fingers to the newly healed scar.

"Did you kill Ehkron?"

"No, an elf girl did in the mortal realm." He kissed Alluria's forehead, then rolled her onto her belly to examine the wounds on her back. He could see where the demon's hoof had held her down. "Does it hurt badly?" he asked as he stroked her ribs.

"Yes, but I can manage," she replied. Caol'nir moved Alluria to her back and retrieved the salve, turning his attention to the scratches that raked across her torso.

"I meant what I said," he whispered as he traced the angry red welts; luckily, the gouges weren't deep. "I'll never leave you again."

"Caol'nir, don't blame yourself. You're the one who saved me, not the one who did me harm." He rubbed ointment into the scratches then he met her blue gaze. He smiled, then he examined the mark burned into her thigh.

"Can you walk?" he asked. She nodded as he salved the burn then wound a bandage around her leg. "I need to get you out of the palace." Caol'nir helped her to her feet, and after a few steps, she confirmed that she could walk under her own power.

"Where are we going?" she asked, and he told her of the *Ish h'ra hai* camped beyond the eastern foothills. He also told her that they would take the palace on the morrow and bring Sahlgren to justice. Caol'nir then mentioned that he needed to find his brother, and Alluria touched his elbow.

"Fiornacht..." she began, and he gathered her to him.

"I saw," was all he said.

"He was the only *con'dehr* in the temple when they came," she said, her voice cracking. "He tried defending us, but there were so many." Caol'nir stroked her hair; he had wanted to protect Alluria from the evils of the world, not leave her in the middle of them. "He was very brave," she said, wiping her cheeks.

"What of Caol'non?" he asked, kissing away the last of her tears.

"He's the head of the king's guard." Caol'nir regarded her for a moment and wondered if his brother could be as corrupt as the Sahlgren.

"Then we will leave him be. The safest place in Teg'urnan, for now, is with the king."

Alluria frowned but didn't argue, and dressed herself in one of the simple frocks she wore when not in the temple. Caol'nir pulled on a shirt and then his jerkin and felt a familiar weight in the inner pocket, so familiar he'd nearly forgotten what was there. He withdrew the silver disc offered it to his mate.

"Do you know what this is?" he asked. Alluria grasped the disc, fingering the edge as if it may transform at any moment.

"It's a portal," she murmured. "You found this in the temple?"

"No, Mersgoth used it to escape from the north," he replied. "Is this what Sarelle used?" Alluria nodded, then continued her examination of the object.

"The High Priestess, bearing a demonic portal," she murmured. "Have you used it?"

"I don't know how," he replied. "I threw it to the ground, like Mersgoth did, but it just laid there."

"You need to hold your destination in the forefront of your mind," Alluria explained. "So the spell knows where to take you."

"Can we use it to leave the palace now?" Caol'nir asked.

"That would not be wise," Alluria replied. "The way I understand them, whoever created the portal is aware of each use." Caol'nir took the disc from her and shoved it inside his jerkin, then knelt as he wrapped Alluria's feet in soft bandages and eased on her riding boots. Once he pulled Alluria upright, she moved to buckle the sword belt she was now accustomed to wearing, but Caol'nir stayed her hand.

"Take this instead," he said as he retrieved a different belt, complete with the blade she had always seen him carry.

"But this is your best sword," she protested.

"I had a new one made," he said, and drew his troll sword from its scabbard and laid it across the bed. Alluria traced the fine engraving that ran the length of the blade.

"Dame-of-the-wood, hart's tongue, lover's ease, flaedyne, toadflax, Cydia's brambles," she murmured, naming each of the herbs as her fingertips traced their outline. "These are the herbs we gathered the first morning you brought me to the meadow."

"They are," Caol'nir affirmed, drawing her attention to the sparkling blue stone. "I want you to know that you never left my thoughts, not even when I was half a world away. I also picked you some sunbonnets this morning, but I seem to have lost them along the way," he added with a sheepish grin.

"You can pick me more," she said, linking her arms behind his head. Caol'nir let himself relax into her embrace, then he pulled away and pinned a cloak about Alluria's shoulders.

"Come, *nalla*, we must make haste." He drew her toward the door.

"How are we to leave?" she asked.

"No one knows I've returned," he replied, "and only those who were in the temple know what's happened. We will simply walk out."

Alluria nodded. "That…that will work?"

Caol'nir wrapped his arms around her. "The demons are sealed in the temple. If anything else tries to harm you, they'll have to go through me."

Alluria smiled, then she darted out of his arms and retrieved a leather thong. "And if anyone tries to harm you, they must go through me," she said as she tied back his hair. The mates smiled at each other, and left their chamber.

That walk through Teg'urnan was the most nerve-wracking experience of Caol'nir's life; he was more nervous traversing the halls he had known since a child than when he entered a temple filled with demons. They avoided the well-travelled corridors, and the king's quarters, and both breathed a sigh of relief once they were in sight of the stable.

And then they saw Caol'non, speaking with the stable master about a horse that had turned up with distinctively elfin riding gear.

"Turn," Caol'nir hissed as he shoved Alluria toward the *sola*. She stumbled, so Caol'nir carried her behind the arena with one hand clamped across her mouth. Once he was certain they were alone, he set her on her feet. Alluria's eyes blazed as she waited for him to explain himself.

"I can't let him see me and leave unawares!"

"But he is your brother! Surely he would help you—" Caol'nir placed his fingers on her lips.

"Unless he has been compromised." She tried to continue, but Caol'nir spoke over her. "If Sarelle can set demons loose in the temple, if our king can make us slaves, anyone can be compromised." Once Allluria nodded, he led her to the northern edge of the palace complex.

"Where are we going?" she asked.

"The north watchtower." Once they had climbed to the platform, she looked down at the smooth outer wall of the palace.

"There are no steps on the other side," she observed.

"It wouldn't be a very good fortification if there were," he said, flashing her that grin of his. He tossed a length of rope over the side of the tower, then turned back to his mate. "Do you think you can climb down the rope?" Alluria peeked over the side, and Caol'nir noted her taut expression. "I can carry you, if you need me to."

"I can do it," she affirmed, forcing a smile. "Don't worry, *nall*. If I can survive a demon who thinks I'm his intended mate and a crazed High Priestess, I can make it over a simple wall." Caol'nir smiled, his heart swelling at her bravery.

Caol'nir went over the wall first, assuring Alluria he was right below. All went well until the very end, when her foot slipped and she fell onto Caol'nir. They landed in a heap, tumbled but unharmed.

"The most beautiful women are also the heaviest," Caol'nir observed.

"Hush, we didn't fall that far."

"No, you didn't fall that far; you landed on me almost immediately." Alluria swatted his shoulder as she sat up, then looked at the rope dangling from the tower.

"You don't think that rope is conspicuous?"

Again, he flashed her that grin, then he generated a small bit of fire in his hands. While Alluria watched Caol'nir threw it at the rope, burning it away from the stone column.

"Modifying my spells?" Alluria asked.

"Always," Caol'nir said. "A good warrior uses any means necessary."

"I never realized what a well-trained warrior you are," Alluria murmured as he retrieved the rope.

"I hoped you'd never need to know," he answered. Caol'nir looped the rope over one arm as he extended the other to his mate. "Come, *rihka*, they're waiting for us just beyond the hills."

Chapter 25

As the mates took the roundabout route around the eastern hills, Caol'nir nearly forgot about the terrible events within the Great Temple. Instead, his thoughts were of his many outings with Alluria to gather herbs, the thrill of spiriting a priestess from Teg'urnan's walls. Then Alluria stumbled, reminding him of her wounds.

"I'm fine," she insisted, leaning against Caol'nir's arm.

"We can rest," Caol'nir said, but Alluria waved away his concern.

"I'd rather just get there," she said. "We'll both be safer surrounded by your warriors." Caol'nir laced his fingers with hers as they walked in silence to the crest of the hill. Alluria sucked in her breath at the sight of a seemingly endless sea of tents.

"So many," she murmured. "Where are the slaves?"

"There." Caol'nir indicated an orderly encampment to the left, then swept his arm to a vast expanse of tents, "and those are the elves. Behind them are the dark fae." Alluria nodded, and then looked to a smaller group.

"And them?"

"That's what's left of the legion," Caol'nir replied bitterly. Caol'nir bent his head, again wondering how this could have happened before their very noses. *Fiornacht knew something was wrong,* he thought. *If only I'd tried talking to him...* Caol'nir shook his head. He hadn't made time to speak with his brother, and now he was lost to him.

"Fiornacht thought you were a good man," Alluria said quietly. Caol'nir had long ago stopped asking her if she could read his mind. "He was honored to have you as a brother."

"As was I," Caol'nir replied. They said nothing more until they approached the center of the camp, marked by a large green silk tent that proudly waved the banner of Tingu. Alluria murmured that it needed no standard, for it was obviously the king's residence. As they drew close to Lormac's tent the Prelate emerged.

"Daughter!" Tor rushed forward and took Alluria's hands. His happiness faded as she winced. He saw the dark bruises coiled around her wrists. "What has happened?"

"Horrible things," she replied, then retreated to her mate's arms.

"When I arrived, the Great Temple was sealed," Caol'nir began, forgoing the pleasantries of a greeting.

"During the day?" Tor asked, and Caol'nir nodded.

"Eighteen *mordeths* had gained access to the temple and were sealed inside with the priestesses," Caol'nir said, keeping his voice steady for Alluria's sake. "Most of the priestesses are now dead; Rahlle and his apprentices are tending to those who lived, and will bring them here when they have done all they can. Fiornacht..." Caol'nir dropped his eyes, his voice low when he continued, "Fiornacht fell before I arrived."

"A hero's death," Alluria added. "A valiant hero's death."

Tor swallowed hard, and nodded. "And Caol'non?"

"Alive and well, he now leads the king's guard," Caol'nir replied. "I thought it best to leave quickly and quietly, so I did not speak with him. He is safe, for now." Tor nodded again, then affected the stoic mask of the Prelate of Parthalan.

"Lormac," Tor called into the tent. "We cannot lay siege to Teg'urnan. The attack has already begun."

Caol'nir explained the events of the morning to Lormac and Balthus. As they plotted how they would take Teg'urnan, Caol'nir felt Alluria stiffen in his arms.

"What is it, *nalla*?" he murmured. Before she could reply, Tor announced that Rahlle was now within the camp, having materialized along with his three apprentices and the surviving priestesses. Caol'nir said that had he known the sorcerer could transport so many they could have saved their walk, but Alluria remained silent. Behind Rahlle was a familiar swath of orange silk, and Caol'nir understood his mate's alarm.

"Sarelle!" Alluria shouted, freeing herself of Caol'nir's arms. "Betrayer! Blasphemer! How dare you betray Olluhm and those sworn to him!" Alluria's arm was outstretched before her, and she shoved Sarelle without touching her.

"Foolish girl," Sarelle spat. "You could have wielded more power than any of us, yet you gave it all away to lie with that oaf!" Sarelle pointed at Caol'nir, lest there be any doubt of whom she was speaking. Alluria made a quick motion and knocked away Sarelle's arm.

"Since you're so convinced that I'm Olluhm's child, you'd do well not to anger me further," Alluria growled. Sarelle stepped back, but Alluria clenched her fist and rendered Sarelle immobile.

"*Nalla*," Caol'nir began, falling silent at the rage in Alluria's eyes.

"What is this about?" demanded Tor. "Alluria, release her!"

"No." Alluria said the word quietly, a simple word made more powerful by whom she was refusing. "Sarelle is the king's whore—a traitor's whore—and I will see her punished." Her musical voice was discordant as she levied her accusations against Sarelle. Tor stared at Alluria, stunned that she had refused his order, since as Prelate he was not refused often. He faced Caol'nir, who spoke loudly enough for all to hear.

"Sarelle cast the portal that admitted the *mordeths* to the Great Temple," Caol'nir said. "Then she sealed the doors. Fiornacht died defending them."

Tor looked from his son back to the High Priestess, his eyes cold as he drew his sword. "For the death of my son and the deaths of the priestesses, your life is forfeit," he declared.

"You cannot," Sarelle shrieked.

"I can," Tor bellowed. "I am Prelate, or have you forgotten?"

Sarelle's mouth worked, and Caol'nir thought she was reciting a spell, then he realized that she couldn't breathe. Incredibly, invisible fingers seemed to depress the flesh of Sarelle's neck. Alluria was choking her.

"You cannot kill her," Caol'nir said to Alluria. "Let my father handle her punishment." Caol'nir watched Alluria's fingers clench and unclench, allowing Sarelle enough air to keep her from fainting, no more. Alluria eyes were globes of sapphire flames fixed on Sarelle's helpless form.

"He marked me!" Alluria's shrieked. "I'm the property of a demon! Damned, because of you and your lust!" Alluria's fingers clenched again, and she raised Sarelle by her neck.

"*Nalla*," Caol'nir said quietly, "stop. You're not like her."

Alluria dropped her hand and Sarelle fell, struggling for breath like a fish plucked from the sea. Caol'nir turned Alluria away from the gasping woman and tucked her head against his neck. He murmured soft, soothing words to her, relieved when he felt Alluria's hands against his chest. Then her fingers were inside his jerkin, and she snatched the portal and flung it at Sarelle.

"No!" Sarelle cried, scrambling back from the disc. A white light blinded the onlookers, and then the High Priestess was gone.

"Where have you sent her?" Caol'nir asked.

"To the underworld," Alluria replied. "Now she will be the one suffering at the hands of demons."

"She truly is a god's daughter," Lormac observed. Alluria and the wounded priestesses had been relocated to the healers' tent, and Lormac ordered that they be treated with the same courtesy that would be extended to Nexa herself. He and Caol'nir watched the healers as they bustled about, preparing their poultices and salves. "Her justice was swift and cruel, yet also fair."

Caol'nir nodded, not wishing to give credence to Lormac's words. He watched yet another healer spread ointment across Alluria's thigh, only to shake his head when the mark remained unchanged.

"Why was she the only one marked?" Caol'nir mused. Rahlle had checked all the bodies within the temple and only Alluria bore a *mordeth's* print.

"Isn't it obvious?" Lormac countered. "Your mate is the embodiment of everything demons lack. She is a soft, fertile field where they are naught but charred earth. By marking her, Mersgoth sought to ruin her."

"He did not succeed," Caol'nir insisted, yet it tore at his heart that his mate would forever bear such an evil brand upon her flesh. Alluria, who had spent most of her life believing herself unwanted, would likely be shunned due to her injury. He looked sidelong at the elf king; while Caol'nir didn't believe that Asherah had been marked, the beasts had used her in far worse ways. Yet Lormac loved her regardless. "What would you do if Asherah was marked?"

"Our duty as warriors is to defend our mates, yet sometimes tragedies occur that are beyond our reach. How we respond to such events is what makes us men, and not just boys playing with wooden swords."

"Have you given that same speech to Leran?"

"Many times."

"So tell me, wise Lord of Tingu, what would a man like you do if a *mordeth* marked your lovely mate?"

To Caol'nir's surprise, Lormac grinned. "I'd continue bedding her every night, and if the stinking bastard dared to try and take her from me, I'd castrate him and choke him with his own member."

Caol'nir snorted. "I did castrate Mersgoth. When I found Alluria on her back before him…" Caol'nir didn't continue, since Lormac's mate had suffered what his narrowly avoided. Lormac clapped him on the shoulder.

"Just what I would have done."

Caol'nir nodded at Lormac, grateful for the elf's advice. He had meant what he said to Alluria in their chamber; he would not forsake her, not even if she bore the marks of a hundred *mordeths*. Lormac's steadfast nature made the situation somewhat easier for Caol'nir to bear. As he resolved to help his mate carry her burden, Alluria approached him with Atreynha beside her.

"Alluria has questions for me," Atreynha said. "You may as well come along, warrior, so I don't need to tell the same tale twice. Lormac, may we speak in your tent privately?"

Lormac acquiesced to her request, and Caol'nir laced his fingers with Alluria's as they followed the Mother Priestess into the palatial tent. Atreynha settled herself in one of Lormac's camp chairs and Alluria knelt before her, Caol'nir standing at her shoulder as if he was still naught but her guard.

"Do I look like her?" Alluria asked. Atreynha smiled, the corners of her eyes crinkling, and stroked Alluria's hair.

"You are lovely, child, but no; you don't look like your mother." Alluria gazed at Atreynha, so she continued, "Annalee had tawny-red hair, close in color to the moon, and pale brown eyes. She was also very small; even when she was heavy with you she was tiny."

"She was already with child when you met her?" Caol'nir asked.

"She arrived in the middle of a thunderstorm, soaked to the bone. At first, we thought she was a young boy, for her hair was cropped above her shoulders. Then we got her out of her sodden cloak and saw her belly. We knew that her child would soon come."

"Did she say where she was from?"

"When we asked, she said she came in from the storm and never any more. Eventually, we stopped asking and just accepted that she was our charge." Alluria pursed her lips, unsatisfied with Atreynha's explanation. "She couldn't have walked far in that storm. I'd assumed that she had come from the village, but we never did find anyone who would admit to knowing her."

Alluria looked at her hands. "Did she speak of my father?"

"She never uttered a single word about him." Atreynha leaned forward and with one long finger lifted Alluria's chin. "Child, I have told you all of this before."

"I know," Alluria said softly. "It's just... How could she have appeared and not my father? Would he leave my mother unprotected in the midst of a storm?"

"That I cannot answer," Atreynha replied. "What I will say is that when Annalee first came to us, her manner made us wonder if she was somehow addled."

"What changed your mind?" asked Caol'nir.

"Alluria's birth," Atreynha replied, now gazing at the former priestess with a mother's pride. "It was the darkest part of the night, the storm having whipped itself into a fury. Annalee was calmer than any woman in childbed I had ever seen, and Alluria will attest, I have helped many a babe into the world. She just kept telling us to wait, to stop rushing around..." Atreynha smiled, remembering that night so long ago. "She calmed us with her gentle voice, soothing like chimes on the wind... Alluria, you do have her voice."

Alluria's cheeks darkened as she ducked her head. "And then, Mother Priestess?" Caol'nir asked.

"I hope you're this eager when your own children are born," Atreynha said, thus darkening Caol'nir's cheeks as well. "Well, as I said the night was still as death, and Annalee lay in her bed patiently waiting for her child. Suddenly there was a blinding flash, and our Alluria was here."

"You mean Annalee bore her," Caol'nir said, but Atreynha shook her head.

"No, she was simply here. There was no blood, no pain, just a flash of light and then Annalee held a tiny, perfect girl to her breast."

"So that is why people thought I was Olluhm's child, because my mother bore me with no pain?" Alluria asked.

"Those who give birth to the god's children are spared the pain of childbirth. Annalee's odd manner made sense once we realized she had lain with Olluhm, for only priestesses are prepared for him. When he visits an untrained maiden, she can come away from the experienced dazzled by his glory." Atreynha touched Alluria's cheek, and caught up a length of her hair. "You are a rare and precious girl, my child."

"If I'm so rare and precious why did she leave?" Alluria asked bitterly. "You'd think she would have wanted me."

Atreynha sighed. "She wanted you more than anything. It tore at her heart that she couldn't remain with you, and she made me swear to care for you as if you were my own child." Alluria hung her head, and Caol'nir realized that she had never heard Annalee's story in its entirety.

"Why did she leave?" Caol'nir persisted.

"She never said she would," Atreynha replied. "I rose one morning and found Alluria alone in the blankets, and I've not seen Annalee since." Alluria whimpered, and Caol'nir squeezed her against him.

"I still don't understand," Caol'nir said. "Annalee arrived during a storm, bore Alluria with no pain, and left in the dark of night. That is all well and good, but what makes you think Alluria is Olluhm's child?"

Atreynha took up more of Alluria's hair in her hands, raking her fingers through the length of it. "Alluria, tell your mate about the birth of his ancestor."

Alluria blinked, and then recited a story that Caol'nir already knew well. "Olluhm would not leave Cydia's side as she swelled with his child, yet when the time came and Cydia felt the pains of birth Olluhm became despondent, for had he not gotten her with child she would not be in such discomfort. He railed against himself in the skies, whipping the elements into thunderclaps and lightning, then in a great flash of light equal to the sun's brilliance Solon was born."

Alluria fell silent, having told the story so many times she no longer heard the words, so Atreynha finished the tale. "And for every child born after Solon, and there were many for Olluhm loved his mate dearly, he took from her the pains of childbed and kept her in comfort."

"Don't you see?" Caol'nir said to Alluria. "You came into this world the same way as his other children."

"You should not have such faith in legends," Alluria admonished.

"Child, of all the questions you have asked me over and over, you have never once asked me who you resemble," Atreynha said.

"You claim I look nothing like my mother."

"You don't. You resemble your father."

Alluria gasped, looking from Caol'nir to Atreynha. *She always wondered why the other priestesses gawked at her, why she had no friends save Alyon and Atreynha,* Caol'nir thought. *They couldn't bear the sight of the one who looked like their god.*

"I do?" Alluria asked, her voice little more than a whisper.

"Yes, child, you do." With that, Atreynha rose and left the mates to ponder what they had learned.

"You never knew?" Caol'nir asked as he knelt beside her. He drew Alluria into his arms; she felt just the same, soft and warm and his, regardless of the *mordeth's* mark.

"I never asked." Alluria nestled herself against Caol'nir's chest. "How could others know?"

"They must have heard the story of your birth." Caol'nir held her for a time, rocking her as one would a child. "Or perhaps it's your appearance; Olluhm's blood must be strong within you." Alluria nodded. And then asked the question she dreaded.

"You said there were eighteen *mordeths* in the temple?"

"Yes."

"I counted seventeen bodies."

Caol'nir squeezed his eyes shut. He had entertained the notion of not telling Alluria of Mersgoth's escape, of letting her believe that she was safe. "Mersgoth was not there."

Alluria's hand went to her thigh. "He can find me."

"I know."

Chapter 26

The *Ish h'ra hai* debated how to take the palace long into the night; the attack within the Great Temple proved that the demons had a stronger foothold than suspected. As the elder sun rose, those involved left the now-stuffy confines of Lormac's tent, hoping the fresh air and breaking dawn would clear their muddled thoughts. Balthus sketched a map of Teg'urnan's walls in the dust, but Tor and Caol'nir maintained that an outright attack against Teg'urnan would fail.

"What we need to do is enter unawares, a few at a time," stated Caol'nir.

"That won't work," said Tor. "The gatekeepers will notice such a large influx of elves and notify—" Tor stopped abruptly. "Caol'non. They will notify Caol'non."

Balthus's lip curled, but a sharp glance from Lormac made him hold his tongue. While Lormac was always the first to defend an elf before a faerie, it was not the time or place for infighting; more, Lormac hoped to never share Tor's pain of losing a child. Lormac turned to Asherah, heretofore a silent observer of the debate.

"Asherah," he began, "what should we do?"

"But what can I do?" she asked. "I have never been to Teg'urnan, and I certainly don't know how to breach the walls."

"You are the deliverer," Lormac reminded her. "Deliver a solution."

Asherah muttered something about Lormac's faith in her becoming a hindrance rather than a help, gazed over the plain. Her black eyes contemplated the palace for a time, then her gaze swept over the foothills, eventually settling upon Rahlle.

"Master Sorcerer," Asherah began, "I know that you cannot act against the king, and I would never ask you to compromise your oath, but is there some way you could assist us in gaining entry to the palace?"

Rahlle turned his storm-cloud gray eyes to her, lightning cracking behind his pupils. "What do you need, child?"

"We must enter from below," Asherah said.

"Below?" Tor repeated. "There is no entry from below."

"Exactly. They'll expect us to come through the gate, or over the walls. Hells, they may be expecting us to drop from the sky, but they'll never expect an attack from beneath," she explained.

"That just may work," Tor murmured, the he asked Rahlle, "Can it be done?"

"It can, but I will require assistance from the daughter," replied the sorcerer.

"Me?" Alluria's voice squeaked as if she was a mouse.

"Our father built Teg'urnan as a love token for his mate," Rahlle explained. "I cannot displace it without his permission."

Alluria nodded, then the two of them walked to the highest of the foothills. They stood together with their hands joined as they gazed upon the first home of the fae. Alluria was silent while Rahlle murmured an incantation. Then the ground trembled—no, it *shook*—and the mighty stone palace shuddered where it sat on the plain. Only it was a plain no longer.

"You raised the palace," Caol'nir shouted, catching Alluria as she swooned. Indeed, they had raised the palace. Teg'urnan had rested in the exact center of the plain but was now perched at the crest of a hill half again as tall than the one they stood on.

"We still cannot gain access," Tor stated. "If anything, Teg'urnan being atop a hill makes it more easily defended."

"The hill is not merely a hill," Rahlle said, and with a sweep of his hand seven glowing orbs appeared across the plain. "These orbs mark the entrances to tunnels that now wind their way beneath the palace. With them, you may breach the walls without detection."

"Master Sorcerer, words cannot express my thanks," Asherah said. "Thanks to your help, we will bring Sahlgren to justice."

Rahlle bowed his head as Asherah turned to address the assembled *Ish h'ra hai*. Neither noticed Rahlle's youngest apprentice as he made a few furtive motions with his hands, nor the sparks leaping from his fingers as he made ready to hurl his spell at Asherah. Only one did.

"No!" Torim leapt in front of Asherah, shielding her with her body. Asherah spun about and saw Torim crumple to the ground, her tunic burnt away and her back blackened and charred. She caught Torim and they fell together, Asherah cradling the burned woman to her breast.

"What happened?" Asherah demanded.

"Sorcerer's flame," Lormac growled, grabbing the boy by the throat. "Isn't that so?"

"S-She would have harmed the king," the apprentice rasped, his eyes on Torim's scorched flesh. "I needed to stop her."

"You saved me," Asherah murmured, stroking Torim's damp cheek. "Torim...why?"

"Need you ask? You saved me many times," Torim whispered. Asherah noticed the burns curling up and over Torim's shoulder.

"Why is it spreading?" Asherah demanded of Rahlle. "Help her!"

"Sorcerer's flame consumes the whole of the body," Rahlle said. "I have taken her pain. That is all I can do." The sorcerer bowed his head and gathered his cloak about him, his form appearing wracked with pain.

"Don't leave me," Asherah begged. "Torim, I cannot live without you."

"It was I that couldn't live without you, and now I won't have to." Torim touched Asherah's hair, her fingers crumbling to ash as she made contact. "You are strong, where I was weak. I love you, Hillel, never forget that I do."

Torim glanced to the side, fixing Belenos in her gaze. "I loved you, as well."

Belenos fell to his knees, tears wetting his beard. "Must you go, sweet girl?"

"I must," Torim said. Her golden bracelet, a love token from Belenos, clattered to the ground by Asherah's knee. The ash had taken Torim's neck, and was creeping up her chin.

"I'll never love anyone as I love you," Asherah whispered as she kissed Torim for the last time. Then what was left of her dearest friend crumbled and blew away in the summer breeze. Asherah stared at the dust that coated her hands and stuck her fingers in her mouth; the ashes were sweet. *Sweet ashes mean that she had an honorable soul,* Asherah mused, then wondered how she even knew that.

Asherah crouched upon the crest of the hill while the remains of Torim were slowly dispersed by the wind. When the last of Torim was gone, she stood and strode to where Lormac held the apprentice immobile.

"Your name," she demanded.

"Elnic," he whispered, Lormac's crushing grip not allowing him a louder voice.

"Who holds your oath?" Asherah asked.

"The king," Elnic insisted. "I am beholden to remove threats to his safety. We are all sworn to the king!"

"You lie," Asherah hissed. "Rahlle does not seek to harm us! His other apprentices do no harm here! Yet you struck out the moment my back was turned." Asherah grabbed the apprentice's robe and wrenched him from Lormac's grasp, dragging him to his knees in the dirt. "I ask again, who holds your oath!"

"The king," Elnic insisted again. Asherah struck him, sending teeth and blood spattering. She was about to strike again when Lormac stayed her.

"Rahlle, you created the fae binding oaths, correct?" Lormac asked the sorcerer, who nodded. "Can one be sworn to more than one?"

"Yes," Rahlle answered, his voice heavy with sorrow. He placed a wizened hand atop Elnic's head. "My boy, tell me who else you are sworn to, and I will do for you what I can."

"Ehkron," Elnic admitted.

"Where?" asked Rahlle.

"In the king's chamber," Elnic replied, and tugged aside his robe to reveal the *mordeth-gall's* handprint upon his flesh. Again, lightning cracked in Rahlle's eyes as a soundless thunderclap reverberated across the landscape. Elnic writhed in agony at Asherah's feet, the sorcerer's flame burning him from his core outward.

"You said—" Elnic began, and then ash consumed his throat.

"I said I would do what I can," Rahlle replied. "All I can do for you, you who undertook dark congress with the *mordeth-gall* in my home, is offer a traitor's death." Elnic screamed without a sound, his throat blackened like coal, and Rahlle turned to his remaining apprentices. With a sharp movement, their robes were whisked open; one of the three bore a demon's mark above his heart. The untainted apprentices backed away as their brother crumbled, his ashes mingling with those of Elnic and Torim as the wind swept them away. Asherah watched as the dust of her friend comingled with that of her murderer, then she turned and walked away.

Asherah speaks...

She's gone!
 She's gone.
 She's gone she's gone she's gone...
 I reached the bottom of the hill and stumbled, but didn't slow. My feet kept moving, past the ranks of the Ish h'ra hai, past the cooking fires and tents and heaps of bedrolls and supplies...past everything, for none of it mattered. Torim needed no bedroll on which to lay her charred head, she needed no supper to fill her ashen belly.
 Torim... It had been my life's mission to keep her safe. I sought to escape the doja so she would no longer be tortured, I killed demons so she wouldn't be recaptured, I sought war with the faerie king to keep him from ensnaring her ever again. Now...it had all been for naught. Because she was gone.
 "Torim..."
 I spoke her name as both a shriek and a whisper as I tumbled to my knees, my legs unable to hold the weight of my grief. I stared at the dirt beneath me, so like the ashes that were now all that was left of Torim, and yet not like

her at all. Warm arms encircled my cold flesh, and Lormac was there like a living, breathing mountain. Had he been following me the entire time? I suppose he had.

Lormac said nothing as he drew me close, holding me fast against his chest while he tucked his face against the nape of my neck; his breath was warm, damp, alive. My Torim wasn't.

"I want to go home," I croaked.

"Then she will have died for nothing."

His words struck me to my core. If I abandoned this cause now, her sacrifice would be meaningless. That was wrong, I knew it was wrong, but it didn't make going on any easier.

"I... I don't know how to do this without her."

"Then let me help you."

I turned and flung my arms about Lormac, throwing myself at him with such force he landed flat on his back. He didn't complain, but then Lormac never complained, and we lay together in the dirt for who knows how long. My thoughts turned to the prior evening, when Torim had made up some sort of errand so she might leave us alone for a time; later, I leaned that she had gone to Belenos. I was safe and warm in Lormac's arms, while he made promises of what our life in Tingu would be like.

"I'll give you a hundred sons," he had proclaimed as we burrowed deep in the blankets, "who will all grow to strong men, true warriors to defend Tingu from the Sahlgrens of this land."

"What if I don't want to bear one hundred children?" I'd asked. I had propped myself up on one elbow, and a curl of my hair tumbled over my shoulder and onto his chest. He grasped it, loosely plaiting it together as he replied.

"Then we will have none." he said quickly; I wondered if he still worried I would run, as I had tried so many times. Fortunately, Lormac was as stubborn as I, and he held on tightly to those he loved. And those who loved him.

"What if I want one thousand?" I asked, tracing circles on his chest. "And maybe a few could be girls."

"Maybe they will all be girls," he continued, "and elfin women will be the warriors, and the men will keep the hearth." I laughed; of all things I could imagine, Lormac sweeping the threshold and mending worn clothing was not one of them.

"Then will you cook for me?" I teased. "Mighty Lord of Tingu, will you bake me bread every morning and offer me a hot bath before bed?"

"Baking? No. But bathing you," he uttered a contented sigh—perhaps it was more of a moan—as he abandoned my hair and rolled me underneath him, "that I will enjoy." I had expected him to kiss me then, but instead he stared so intensely I couldn't look away. "You will stay, won't you?"

For a moment, I was speechless—of course I would stay! I had accepted the Sala, what, three times by now, his lords had sworn fealty to me as their queen, his son called me Mama...

Hmm. He put the Sala on me three times before I managed to let myself wear it.

"I belong with you, my mate," I replied. "I... I am so—"

"Bind yourself to me," he said, cutting off my apology.

"I thought elves didn't believe in bindings."

"We don't. But then, Tingu has never had a queen who is not an elf."

I remembered what Harek had told me of my first day in the doja, that I'd screamed and railed of being promised to another, that they couldn't take from me the one gift only I could give my mate. That man had never come for me, or perhaps he died in the attempt; no, somehow I knew the truth. He had never come. He left me to the monsters.

Lormac would never leave me.

"Nothing would make me happier," I said, and then I showed him how happy he had made me. Afterward, I nestled in the crook of his arm as he made outlandish plans for our return to the Seat.

"There will be feasting," he proclaimed. "We will celebrate you as queen, and all my lords will toast your health and beauty. No, minstrels will compose songs about your beauty; Asherah, already a legend in the first year of her reign!" I laughed again—gods, had I ever been so happy?—and he went on, "Of course, the first order of business will be obtaining a larger bed."

"Why? Will we be holding our own private Madoc'na?" I teased. Lormac's bed was easily as large as a small cottage. I doubted a bigger bed existed and couldn't imagine why we would need one.

"Seductress," he accused, nuzzling my ear. "But there will be you and I, and Leran, and I imagine Torim will remain with us, so we will need a larger bed."

"You truly don't mind about Torim and me?" Lormac sighed, squeezing me against his chest as he replied.

"Do I mind? I do want you all to myself, to ravish as the need strikes me. To share one's mate with another is unnatural. Once, I did mind, and I wanted nothing more than for you to leave her be."

"And now?"

"And now I understand what she means to you, and you to her," he softly replied. "Besides, what man wouldn't want two lovely faeries in his bed? However," he added with a stern glare, "Belenos is not invited." I swatted his shoulder, but in truth his words had made me happier yet, that not only I but also Torim had found a home.

Now, I felt nothing but the cold, aching void in my chest that used to be Torim.

"We won't need a bigger bed," I murmured, and he tightened his arms around me.

"You still have Leran and me to contend with," he pointed out. "Leran does tend to steal the blankets." I made a noise that was meant to be a laugh, but ended up more of a snort. I moved so my face was over his, my hair falling about his shoulders.

"If we go back," I began, "if we fight, we need to win. I need to win, for Torim."

"For Torim," he affirmed. He put Torim's ash-covered bracelet on my wrist, and we got to our feet. Lormac laced his fingers with mine, so tightly it hurt, but it was a good sort of hurt. We walked in silence back to the hill. The rest were still there, looking at Lormac expectantly. No, they looked at me expectantly.

"For Torim," I repeated, and we moved to invade the palace.

Chapter 27

"*Nalla*, I cannot fight a battle and watch over you at the same time," Caol'nir said to Alluria for at least the hundredth time. "You'll distract me, and a moment's distraction could get us both killed."

"*Nall*," Alluria said in the same tone one uses with recalcitrant children, "I'm going with you."

Gods, she is the most stubborn woman in Parthalan. Caol'nir paced the length of their tent, gesturing wildly as he recited the many reasons why Alluria should just stay put. He was in the midst of explaining that while he loved her dearly she would only prove to be a liability to him and all the warriors around him, when he found that he could no longer move.

"Having trouble?"

Caol'nir looked from his feet, firmly planted upon the ground as if he had sprouted roots, to where Alluria reclined on their bedroll. She didn't hide her smile, or her arm extended in a halting gesture. "Would you like me to release you?" she purred.

"*Nalla*," he began, thoroughly exasperated, "must you continue practicing this talent on me?" Already that evening, Alluria had flung cushions at her mate, wrapped him tightly in a blanket, and made his boots walk across the tent without the benefit of his feet, all with her newfound power. When Caol'nir had asked her to cease, she responded by attempting to pull his tunic over his head, nearly strangling him in the process. He stared at her, trying very hard not to glare daggers at this woman he had missed so.

"As you wish," Alluria said, releasing her hold. "Don't you want someone with you who can keep a demon from advancing while you kill it?"

Caol'nir sighed. "Yes, but not if that someone is you." He wrapped his arms around Alluria and drew her against him. "What if the battle takes many days? What if you're hurt?"

"I'm hurt already. What if you are hurt?" she countered. "Do I not have the right to stay at my mate's side and keep him from harm?"

Caol'nir fell back onto the bedroll and covered his face with his hands. *She refuses to listen to reason.* Alluria climbed onto his chest, and he sensed heat and light through his closed lids.

"Can any of your warriors do this?" she asked, a tiny ball of fire in her palm. She made the puff of flame expand until the tent was nearly as bright as day, then snapped her hand shut and extinguished the flame. Caol'nir sighed and tucked her head against his neck. Clearly, this battle had been lost.

"Since you're coming no matter what I say, there are rules I need you to abide by." He glanced downward, ensuring she was paying attention. "You will stay behind me at all times. Your first thought will be finding shelter, and use your glamour as much as possible. You will not engage any foe unless I am beside you, otherwise you will hide." Caol'nir pulled her up so her shining chestnut hair framed her face in the soft waves he so loved. "And if the fighting proves to be too intense, I need you to leave with no argument," he said softly. "*Nalla*, if anything more happens to you, it will kill me."

"What if something happens to you?" she asked softly, tracing the scars on his neck. For the first time fear, crept into her voice, and Caol'nir wondered how he could have been so blind. *She is as worried for my safety as I am for hers.*

"I've been in many battles. I can take care of myself. I also know that you're going to follow me no matter what I say, so please just agree to my rules now. I know you won't abide by them, but I can pretend that you've listened to me."

Alluria had smiled sweetly, then agreed to each and every rule he put forth.

"Hells!"

Caol'nir curse was met by a sharp look from his father. "These tunnels are little more than holes in the ground," he explained.

"What did you expect from a tunnel?" Tor asked. Caol'nir ignored him; his father's relaxed attitude toward *the invasion of Teg'urnan* was more than annoying. His frustration was only magnified by Alluria, who was already breaking the first rule of staying behind him at all times.

"Alluria," Caol'nir snapped, "behind me, now!"

Alluria glared over her shoulder. "I am lighting our way." She turned and revealed the flames dancing upon her palm.

"Forgive me," Caol'nir muttered. His mood was hovering somewhere between fearing for her safety and wishing he had knocked her over the head and left her tied up at camp.

"This time," she said, then resumed leading them through the tunnel. Caol'nir hated the confines of the tunnel, the dank, rotting smell of the earth. Most of all he hated not knowing where the tunnel would emerge. Rahlle assured him that each led to a safe location within the palace where the king was not likely to be, and while Caol'nir did not doubt the sorcerer, the images of *mordeths* in the Great Temple were still fresh in his mind. Demons were not supposed to be in the temple, either.

At least I'll be able to get Alluria out of the palace safely. Tor and Lormac agreed that trying to move all of the *Ish h'ra hai* through the tunnels would take far too much time, not to mention that someone would notice all those elves appearing in the midst of Teg'urnan. Caol'nir suggested that he and Alluria be the first through the tunnels so they could open the gates and allow the *Ish h'ra hai* entry. Being that Caol'nir's twin was the head of the king's guard, the gatekeeper wasn't likely to question him.

The plan had been readily agreed upon, but Caol'nir had an ulterior motive: once the gates were open, he would secure a horse and get Alluria out of the palace, away from the battle. As he crept behind her in the tunnel he wished he had told her of his plan, but he couldn't say anything now with his father and ten elfin warriors at his back.

Alluria stopped before a door—an actual oak door, replete with hinges and a brass knob—at the end of the tunnel. She flattened herself against the dirt wall and let Caol'nir push it open and examine their location.

"We're underneath the grand steps," Caol'nir whispered, then he stepped out of the tunnel. He squinted, the daylight blinding compared to the damp darkness he had just emerged from, and motioned for the rest to follow.

"You'll see to the gate?" Tor asked.

"We will," Caol'nir affirmed. Tor nodded, then grabbed Caol'nir in an embrace that was as awkward as it was unexpected.

"Be safe," Tor said hoarsely. "I will not lose another son." Tor released him and ascended the palace steps, the elves trailing close behind.

"We're not staying together?" Alluria asked.

"He is going to retrieve Caol'non," Caol'nir explained.

"And we?"

"We," Caol'nir began, smiling at her with that grin he knew she loved so, "are going to invite our friends to join us."

"We've reached the end."

Lormac pushed open the door that was so out of place alongside the dirt walls, and surveyed their location. "It would appear that we are in the corridor outside the great hall," Lormac announced. "Balthus, please request an audience with Sahlgren."

"You're announcing our presence?" Asherah asked.

"A good king—a true king—always treats his opponents honorably, regardless of what they deserve," Lormac replied. They stepped aside as Balthus and his warriors filed past, then Asherah moved to follow.

"Wait," Lormac implored, his hand on her arm. Asherah began asking what they were waiting for when Lormac kissed her hard.

"Another elfin custom?" Asherah asked breathlessly.

"A Lormac custom," he replied, tracing her jaw with his thumb. "I refuse to enter a battle without first kissing my mate. No matter the outcome, you need to know that I love you."

"You think the outcome may be bad?" Asherah asked, and Lormac saw fear in her eyes.

"No matter what happens when we walk through that door, I will be right beside you," he murmured. "Every one of my warriors is sworn to defend you with their lives. You are the safest woman in Parthalan." Asherah nodded, and he crushed her against him. "When this is done, I will take you home—"

"And give me those sons?"

"We will start working on them, yes," Lormac finished with a wry grin. There was a soft noise from beyond the door; Balthus calling them, letting his king know that all was well. "My star, know that I love you."

"And I love you, my mountain," she said, kissing him again. They stood shoulder to shoulder, fingers laced, and walked out of the tunnel into the palace of Teg'urnan.

Neither saw Harek as he crept out of the tunnel behind them.

Tor strode through the palace, hardly acknowledging those he passed. While he had never been one to abuse his power or position, today he drew the authority of Prelate of Parthalan around him like a suit of the finest mail. He entered the king's chamber and made his way to the corridor that joined it to the great hall, knowing that the captain of the king's guard would be standing behind the king's throne.

"Caol'non," Tor said. His son turned, and Tor motioned for him to join him in the king's chamber; once inside, Caol'non stared at the elfin warriors.

"What is happening?" Caol'non demanded. "Why are you with elves dressed for battle?"

"Come," Tor said, his voice resonating throughout the chamber. "There are things you must see."

"Just open them, man," Caol'nir growled, trying very hard not to strike the gatekeeper. As a member of the *con'dehr*, Caol'nir far outranked the gatekeeper, and the man should have thrown open the gates immediately upon request. However, that hadn't happened, and Caol'nir's exasperation with the man's need for protocol was wearing thin his temper.

"My lord," the gatekeeper said patiently, "I have explained to you, they've been ordered shut. My hands are tied."

"I'll tie them, all right," Caol'nir muttered. Alluria whispered for Caol'nir to control himself, lest the gatekeeper raise the alarm, then she tried reasoning with the man.

"Who ordered them closed?" Alluria asked.

"The Prelate," the gatekeeper responded.

"Impossible," Caol'nir snapped. "My father has been in the north for many moons. He has issued no such directive."

"The new Prelate," the gatekeeper clarified.

"My brother? My brother Fiornacht?" Caol'nir asked, and the gatekeeper nodded. "He is dead, killed by *mordeths* sent by the king. Now open this gate!"

The gatekeeper stared, slack jawed. Caol'nir could not decide if the man would faint or call for guards, but he was done with this foolishness and struck the man unconscious.

"Should have done that in the first place," he grumbled. He propped the gatekeeper's limp form against the wall, then turned his attention to the various ropes and pulleys that controlled the gates.

"Can you open it?" Alluria asked.

Caol'nir pursed his lips; in all his years of training, first with the legion and then the *con'dehr*, Caol'nir had learned nothing of engineering.

"What about this?" Alluria asked as she depressed a lever that Caol'nir had not so much as noticed, and the massive iron gates swung open with nary a creak.

"*Nalla*, I truly would be lost without you," Caol'nir said, then grabbed her hand as they ran to the tower. Once they reached the top, Alluria looked out over the plain toward the eastern foothills, and created a puff of fire in her hands. That in itself was not so amazing, for her, but then she used her newfound power to throw the flames far above their heads.

"The fire is as beautiful as you," Caol'nir said as the sparks rained down on the plain. "As beautiful as you."

Upon the crest of the hill, Rahlle stood near where Torim had died. When Alluria's fire leapt over the great plain

Atreynha touched his shoulder, then the sorcerer raised his arms and the carefully constructed illusion dissolved away. The residents of Teg'urnan, who heretofore thought they had merely experienced a small tremor early in the morning, now saw that they were not only upon a hill that had not existed the night before, but they were surrounded by *Ish h'ra hai*.

"It is done," Rahlle murmured, his head bowed as his now sightless eyes saw the Teg'urnan that was.

"Great works of magic require a sacrifice," Atreynha said. "You did not need to use yourself."

"To stop the king, it is worth it." With that, Atreynha grasped Rahlle's elbow and led him down the hill.

"You did not wonder at the Great Temple being closed during the day?" Tor asked Caol'non.

"The king told us that Sarelle sealed the doors early yesterday," Caol'non replied. "I did not presume to question the High Priestess." Caol'non glanced over his shoulder at the ten elves that shadowed his father but didn't ask what their purpose was, not after Tor's reaction to his earlier queries. The man who never withheld information from his sons had told Caol'non that all would be revealed shortly and refused to say anything further.

"You did not think to question," Tor repeated. "It is Olluhm who decreed that the doors were to remain open from dawn until dusk."

"The king—" Caol'non began.

"Leave it, for now," Tor said as they approached the northern doors. "As you can see, they remain sealed."

"Sarelle must not have reopened them yet," observed Caol'non.

"You are correct," Tor stated. "What you don't know is that Caol'nir came to the temple yesterday, and I'm about to show you what he encountered." Tor produced a smooth white stone from within his tunic and unsealed the door.

"Olluhm's balls," Caol'non swore, then covered his mouth against the stench. The altar stone was shattered at the base of the altar, the steps dull with dried blood. He stared, aghast, counting the seventeen *mordeths* on the temple floor.

"Are they all dead?" Caol'non asked, bending to arrange a fallen priestess into a more dignified position. Tor jerked his head, and the elves set about collecting the priestesses to the rear of the temple.

"Nine priestesses still live," Tor replied. He did not know if Sarelle still lived and, truth be told, he cared not about her fate. "If Caol'nir had not been here, I imagine all would have perished."

"Alluria?"

"She is with Caol'nir." Tor walked around to the far side of the platform, following the path Caol'nir had described in horrid detail, and looked upon his eldest son.

"No," Caol'non said, sinking to his knees upon seeing his brother. Tor crouched beside him.

"Alluria said that when the demons attacked, Fiornacht was the only *con'dehr* here," Tor said, his eyes never leaving Fiornacht's face. "He fell before Caol'nir opened the doors."

"Caol'nir killed the rest?"

"Yes."

Caol'non grunted. "Caol'nir said he would cross the plains of hell for Alluria. I never thought that hell would be here." Tor squeezed Caol'non's shoulder, and they mourned Fiornacht together.

"My lord?" One of the elves roused Tor.

All of the priestesses had been arranged with as much grace and dignity as possible, save Fiornacht and Serinha. Tor rose to his feet, Caol'non following suit, and stepped aside for the elves to retrieve the bodies.

"Keep them together," Caol'non called after the elves, then explained to his father, "Fiornacht loved her, easily as much as Caol'nir loves Alluria."

"Do all my sons have a penchant for priestesses?" Tor asked. Caol'non's sheepish face was answer enough. The moment was all too brief, and they watched Fiornacht receive his place of honor among those he had given his life to defend.

"How do we stop him?" Caol'non demanded. "The king must die."

Lormac marveled at Asherah's calm demeanor; if he were about to confront the man who had ordered his enslavement, his skin would be crawling. As it were, he was fighting the urge to barge into the hall and strangle Sahlgren where he sat. Then those assembled before them shuffled about, and Asherah saw the king for the first time.

"So that's him," she murmured. "I don't know why, but I expected to recognize him."

"I wonder if he'll recognize you," Lormac said. Asherah pursed her lips, and Lormac silently berated himself for letting her accompany him. Torim had died only that morning, and now Asherah was to come face to face with the man responsible. He briefly considered sending her back to the camp with Balthus as an escort. Asherah need not endure a meeting with Sahlgren or the battle that would surely follow on this already terrible day.

Lormac turned to his mate, taking in her squared shoulders and the lift of her chin, and he knew that Asherah would not suffer being left behind. She truly was warrior born, and he loved her all the more for it.

"You know what I love?" Lormac asked her. "That you left your hair loose." He thrust his fingers into her hair, raking them through the pale strands. "I keep imagining it flowing wildly about you in battle. You are beautiful, my warrior queen." Asherah cocked an eyebrow at him—he loved it when she did that, too—but before she could respond, Balthus returned and advised that they would be announced directly.

"The Lord and Lady of Tingu!"

Lormac noted how Asherah's fingers dug into his forearm as they approached Sahlgren. The faerie king was seated upon a throne wrought of gold and gems, far larger and more ostentatious than Lormac's throne. The grandiose elements did not end there, for the dais itself was cloaked in plush crimson velvet, making the throne appear balanced upon a giant cushion. Drapes made of the same rich fabric, edged in gold, surrounded the whole of the dais, giving the effect that the king was a puppet upon a stage.

"Lormac," Sahlgren called, descending from the dais. His clothing was as pretentious as his throne, and the king was wrapped in velvets and silks with lace ruffs at his wrists and collar. A silver chain glinted amidst the heavy fabrics, shining silver orbs reflecting the light. "It has been too long."

"It has," Lormac replied, forgoing any elaboration. He had a reputation for arrogance among the fae, and meant to use it to his full advantage.

"I didn't know you'd taken a mate," Sahlgren continued, now gazing upon Asherah. If Sahlgren thought it odd that the Lady of Tingu chose to meet the King of Parthalan attired in leather armor rather than a gown, he made no indication. "My lady," Sahlgren greeted, extending his hand.

"My lord," Asherah replied. Her words were clipped, and she did not accept the proffered hand, preferring to clutch Lormac's arm ever tighter.

"You're fae, are you not?" Sahlgren continued, and Asherah nodded. "Lormac, you've deigned to dilute your fabled bloodline with one of my kind? Tell me, how did you come across such an example of loveliness in the cold north?"

"She found me," Lormac replied, pulling Asherah against him. "She escaped from a prison called a doja and came to Tingu, begging for aid." Sahlgren's mouth twitched, but he made no other sign of recognition.

"A doja?" Sahlgren asked. "I've never heard of such a thing."

"Oh, they've become quite common," Lormac assured. "They are scattered across Parthalan, and recently some have been erected in my land."

"Who runs these prisons?"

"*Mordeths.*" Lormac replied. "The demons are enslaving your kind, Sahlgren. Don't you want to stop them?" Lormac continued, raising his voice for the entire hall to hear.

"Yes!" Sahlgren agreed. "Call for the Prelate, we will deal with this at once."

"My lord!" Tor strode across the hall, Caol'non at his side and ten elves close behind. "I am here at your command."

"Where is Fiornacht?" Sahlgren asked, then more elfin warriors assembled behind Lormac.

"My son is dead on the temple floor," Tor replied, his calm tone belying his fury. "But you knew that, didn't you? You knew he would die when you ordered Sarelle to seal him inside with the *mordeths*!"

"I hold you accountable, Sahlgren," Lormac proclaimed, his voice cold. "For crimes against your kind and mine, I judge you guilty."

"You cannot judge me," Sahlgren shrieked.

"I can, and I have." Lormac then spoke to Balthus, his eyes never leaving Sahlgren. "Take him, and throw him in whatever passes for a dungeon in Teg'urnan." Balthus moved to apprehend the faerie king, but Sahlgren backed toward his dais. "Come along, Sahlgren, you won't know true suffering until I inter you at the Seat," Lormac taunted. Sahlgren continued backing away while he fingered the gaudy chain about his neck. Every time he moved, the heavy silver baubles glinted.

"Stop him! The necklace is hung with portals!" Asherah yelled as Sahlgren flung the chain to the floor. The portals melded together, the edges becoming a swirling, organic mass of magic and limbs as demons pulled themselves free of the arcane doorway and leapt into the hall. Lormac shouted for his warriors as Belenos stamped out the portals and Tor and Caol'non rallied the *con'dehr*. Amidst the confusion, Sahlgren fled the hall.

"We're leaving?" Alluria demanded, as Caol'nir rushed her toward the stables for the second time in as many days.

"Yes." Caol'nir didn't look at her as he replied, choosing instead to shield her from the crushing crowd. As the first company of the *Ish h'ra hai* descended into Teg'urnan, a wave of bodies flowed toward the palace, threating to sweep his slight mate away.

"We cannot," Alluria said.

"Alluria," Caol'nir began, tugging her toward the stables, but she stood firm. "If you won't walk, I'll throw you over my shoulder," he warned. When she still didn't move, he was forced to look at her. "What would you have me do?"

"Fight for our home!"

"You hate it here! I want to take you away from this place so you never have to look upon it again!"

"You do?" Alluria asked, shocked, then she murmured, "I thought we would always live here."

"It was to be my gift to you," he said softly. "I want to take you far from Teg'urnan, far from everything you hate about this life." Alluria stared at him, and Caol'nir added, "But if you want to stay, we can."

"What about your father, and your... Caol'non?" she asked.

"Rahlle severed my father's oath, so he need not remain. As for Caol'non, he will need to make up his own mind."

"So your great plan was to just leave? How would they find us, if they wished to?"

"They could. Alluria, we don't—"

She touched her fingers to his lips. "Why are you really doing this?" Caol'nir drew her against him, brushing his hand against her cheek; he needed to get her away from the palace and into hiding before the *mordeth* that marked her came looking, but he didn't know how without making her seem like a liability. She wasn't a burden; she was his life. Caol'nir resolved to tell her frankly, when King Sahlgren emerged from a hidden doorway.

"Stop him," Caol'nir shouted, and with a flick or her wrist Alluria had the king pinned against the stone wall. "Where are you off to, my king?" Caol'nir demanded, but Sahlgren ignored him as he stared at Alluria.

"You're her daughter, aren't you?" Sahlgren asked. Alluria looked to Caol'nir, who shook his head. "I knew I'd found you that day on the road when you called yourself Annalee. So tell me, is the whore's daughter truly Olluhm's as well?"

Alluria flinched as Caol'nir grabbed Sahlgren's throat. "Her mother was no whore," Caol'nir growled.

"Oh, but she was," Sahlgren sneered. "She plied her trade at The Swan. Ask your father if you don't believe me." Caol'nir drew back to strike him, but Alluria stayed him with her hand on his shoulder.

"Let him speak," Alluria said. Caol'nir halted, but didn't drop his hand. "What do you know of my mother?"

"She was everyone's favorite, all tawny hair and soft curves, falling out of her corset as she served ale." Alluria clenched her fist and Sahlgren choked on the last words;

once he had turned a sickly shade of blue Alluria loosened the pressure upon his neck.

"Continue," she demanded. Sahlgren slumped to the ground, wheezing.

"As I said, she was the favorite," Sahlgren rasped. "I'd heard of her charms from a few of my men, and I sent for her to be one of my *saffira*."

"You bedded my mother?" Alluria's tone was icy cold, and Sahlgren was again against the wall, this time with his feet dangling well above the ground. Then Alluria unclenched her hands and he fell in a heap of limbs, only to have his head thrust back.

"I did not," Sahlgren gasped. "She refused me, like she refused everyone once she came to Teg'urnan. Then her behavior became unpredictable, and we thought she'd gone mad."

"Unpredictable?" Caol'nir repeated. "How?"

"She'd stare at a wall for hours, forget to eat for days. Then we noticed her belly's swell, and no one would admit to fathering the babe. Rahlle claimed that she had been touched by Olluhm. Sarelle railed against him, saying it wasn't possible that Olluhm had gotten such a common wench with child but Rahlle, as ever, was in the right."

"And then?" Alluria prompted. "I was born far from Teg'urnan."

"By no choice of mine," Sahlgren snapped. "I offered to make her a queen, but she screamed and cried whenever I drew near. Finally, I had her locked in the southern tower. That night there was a terrible storm, and once it had passed she was gone. No one knew how, but she was gone. I had no idea of where she'd gotten to, until stories came from the east of a woman turning up at a temple in the midst of the storm, alone but heavy with child."

"So you brought the priestesses here to find the god's child," Caol'nir surmised. "To seal your plans with the demons, you offered Alluria to the *mordeth-gall*." When

Sahlgren remained silent, Caol'nir drew his sword, and said, "I should kill you for what you've done to my mate."

"Have you the strength to take your king's head, boy?" Sahlgren sneered. "What would Solon think of his heir, breaking his oath to snatch the throne?"

"My father holds my oath, not you," Caol'nir said as he rose to his feet, looming over the king. Sahlgren cowered against the wall, and Caol'nir was struck by his pathetic appearance. Sahlgren had always appeared noble, in every way the revered monarch of Parthalan. Not so now, his rich velvet pantaloons caked in dust and spilled wine, the lace about his neck tattered and dirty.

"And I don't want your throne," Caol'nir said, and then he struck Sahlgren with the hilt of his sword, rendering him unconscious. He hefted the king across his shoulder and grabbed Alluria's hand. "Come, *nalla*, it's time for this man to be judged."

The battle raged within the hall, and Lormac had one objective: to reach his mate. She had been swept away in the tide of battle, and he had only caught glimpses of her pale hair. Even through his concern, he saw that she fought as well as any of his warriors, as if she had been born to the blade. *My warrior queen*, he thought, smiling as he cut down another demon. Then Asherah was before him, panting as she leaned on his arm.

"He's not here," she said, craning her head to look about the room. Nearly all of the demons that had emerged from the portal had either fled or been killed. "Where would he have gone?"

"We'll find him," Lormac assured. "Sahlgren will not escape punishment." Lormac spun and sank his sword into a demon's gut. As he yanked the blade free, Tor yelled across the din.

"Follow," the Prelate bellowed, and fae and elf alike became a morass of limbs and weapons as they rushed behind the dais.

"They must have found him," Asherah cried. She took a step toward the crush of warriors, then turned and pressed her lips to Lormac's, lingering until they were alone in the hall.

"An Asherah custom?" Lormac murmured.

"Yes, an Asherah custom," she replied. Tor bellowed again, and Asherah smiled before she ran toward the Prelate's voice.

Lormac tried to follow, but couldn't move. He didn't feel the ripping, tearing pain in his belly until he looked down and saw the blade; he had been run through. Hot blood spilled from the wound, and Lormac dropped to his knees.

"I alone keep her safe," was growled into Lormac's ear. Harek withdrew his sword from Lormac's gut and shoved the elf king to the ground, his boot grinding Lormac's hand against the floor as Harek stepped over him.

"Asherah," Lormac cried, but she didn't hear him. The last sight Lormac's living eyes beheld was his beloved's back as she raced away.

"Where are we taking him?" Alluria asked. They had walked from the stable to the palace with the king's limp form draped over Caol'nir's shoulders.

"To my father," Caol'nir answered. Sahlgren could have only taken one route to emerge where he did, and Caol'nir knew that Tor and Caol'non would be tracking the king in the same way. He hoped to meet up with them, then leave the judging and inevitable execution of Sahlgren to Lormac, while he and Alluria slipped away.

"Harek!" Caol'nir called as they rounded a corner and nearly walked into him. Caol'nir noted that Harek arrived from the direction of the grand hall. "I thought you were leading the *Ish h'ra hai*."

"I left it to Drustan," Harek replied. Then Tor and Balthus emerged from the small corridor. Tor shot a glare at Harek, for the Prelate disliked when his orders were ignored, then he dragged Sahlgren from Caol'nir's shoulders.

"Awake, traitor," Tor demanded as he slapped Sahlgren hard enough to split his lip. The king's blood splattered across the dusty ground as Tor dragged him to his feet. "I'm taking you to the square to be judged."

As Tor said the words, Asherah emerged from the same corridor as the Prelate, her eyes wild and searching. "Balthus, I can't find Lormac!"

"I'll find him," Balthus assured. Asherah nodded as he left to locate her mate, then turned to Tor.

"Well, Prelate, what shall do we do with the king?"

Asherah speaks...

The legends of that day are great and many. They say I cleaved Sahlgren's head from his body in one stroke and then strode into Teg'urnan, my composure never faltering until I entered the Great Temple and saw the carnage wrought by the mordeths. In my grief, I shed two tears, then went on to rule Parthalan as I do to this day.

As tends to happen, the reality was quite different from the stories told 'round the hearth on cold nights. I did indeed take Sahlgren's head, however his death was anything but clean. Tor forced the king to his knees as he begged for his life; the great King Sahlgren's last act in the living world was to humiliate himself. The assembled crowd chanted, demanding his death for the atrocities he had perpetrated against his people, and I thought of Torim, my poor, sweet, dead Torim. I remembered all the times she had been returned to our cell bloody and broken, of how she had been used nearly to the point of death more times that I could count, how I swore to her than no demon would harm her again. And that the man responsible for her torment and eventual death now cowered before me.

Harek and Tor stood over him, shouting out his crimes to the throng, when Tor suddenly turned to me. He proclaimed that it was I who freed the slaves, I who had saved the fae from being enslaved by Ehkron and his followers, and with a great sweep of his arm he said that these were my people now, mine to lead into a golden age of Parthian history. I wanted to scream at him that I couldn't lead anyone, that my only strength was derived from Torim and Lormac's belief in me, and now that Torim was gone, all I had was Lormac.

I was about to answer Tor, to announce to all the Parthians (my Parthians?) that I would lead them with Lormac at my side, when I saw the litter. With the great amount of dead and wounded I couldn't imagine how one individual would warrant such treatment; then I noticed that Balthus and Sibeal carried it. I looked at the body, which I could tell was tall and lean despite that it was covered, and realized that the shroud was Lormac's cloak. That horrible, ugly brown cloak that he insisted upon wearing, that he had wrapped around me so many times...I hated that cloak, never more than that moment. My gaze returned to Balthus, and his pained expression confirmed my fears.

Lormac was dead.

Torim was dead.

The two I loved most were dead, and I was alone...

Rage and fear and a horrible sense of loneliness overtook me as I grabbed Sahlgren by the back of his head and bared his traitorous neck; his eyes were wide and pleading, as if he thought he somehow deserved mercy for what he had done. The blows were not clean, and it took me three hacks to sever his head. And then I stood there, I who was nothing more than a slave stood there, covered in the king's blood while a crowd shouted my name.

No, not my name. The only ones who knew my name were dead.

I cast the head aside and ran into the palace. I had no idea where I was going, having never been to Teg'urnan before that day, and eventually I pushed my way through a set of massive stone doors. I later learned that it was the northern door to the Great Temple, the stone symbolizing the strength of Parthalan, strength I so dearly needed.

I didn't recall having ever entered a temple, much less the Great Temple which was the heart of our land, and the awful scene shook me from my grief. I walked slowly past the bodies of mangled priestesses and the mordeths *who'd taken them, who had in turn been killed by Caol'nir. My mind could hardly process the information before me, that Sahlgren and Sarelle had engineered their alliance with Ehkron because of their lust for power. I wondered what sort of power was worth so high a price.*

I made my way to the sacred stairs and dropped to my knees before the shattered altar stone, exhausted in body and spirit. I stared upward, gazing at the oculus situated above where the altar rightfully belonged, and tried praying for guidance; instead, I collapsed into sobs that echoed through a temple filled with nothing but corpses.

"Asherah?"

I started, and saw Caol'nir's mate approaching me. I was amazed that she would deign to enter the temple after what had befallen her only the day before. Alluria knelt beside me and enfolded me in her arms as I cried.

The legend says that I shed two tears; in reality, it was closer to two thousand. Alluria held me as I wailed, kneeling amid her fallen sisters as she comforted someone she hardly knew.

"How can you bear to set foot here?" I asked when I found my voice. "So many lost..." My words trailed off as I again gazed around the temple. Rivers of congealed blood snaked across the floor, the statues of the gods toppled and shattered. Her eyes followed mine for a moment, only to rest upon the broken altar where the mordeth *had marked her, upon which her sister priestess had been torn to pieces.*

"Caol'nir claimed me upon that altar," she said, "and then he destroyed it, once he saved me from the fate Sarelle had set for me. I'll not enter this place again." Her gaze returned to me, and she smiled such a heartbreakingly sweet smile my tears flowed anew. "I only entered now to ensure that our new queen was well."

"I am no queen," I said bitterly. "I am nothing...no one."

"You're wrong. Many were oppressed, but you alone fought back. You are the one who revolted against Sahlgren. If not for you, the one slave with the strength to rise up against them, we'd all be slaves to demons."

"If your mate hadn't left the palace to join me, you wouldn't have been harmed," I said. Alluria had been marked, a torment even I had managed to escape. That such a gentle woman would have to bear such a burden was not right; add that to the long list of what wasn't right.

"Who's to say? If Caol'nir hadn't burst into the temple, he wouldn't have killed the mordeths, and I daresay all the priestesses would have died. Maybe it was right that he went to you." Alluria stood, and pulled me to my feet. "One thing I can tell you is that it does no good to wonder at what might have been. You need to worry about what is, and for you, it is that you have saved Parthalan. We owe you a debt that will likely never be repaid. You are the Asherah, and you have saved us all."

"Torim used to tell me that."

"I'm sorry she is gone. She was a wonderful, deserving companion." Alluria tucked a lock of my tear-soaked hair behind my ear. "As was your mate."

I murmured that they were, and Alluria took my hand and led me back toward the northern door. "Are you really Olluhm's daughter?" I asked. Alluria was thoughtful as she looked at his statue, the only one left standing. It depicted a man with unnaturally long and slender limbs, somber eyes, and flowing hair.

"I've always wondered if this is really what he looks like," she mused. "After all, the tales of him walking among us say that he takes the form of a stag. Do you think this is his form as he drives his fiery chariot across the sky?" She was silent for long moments, regarding the god who might be her father, before she turned to me with a glint in her eye. "You'd think if I were his child, I'd know these things."

Against my will I smiled, as much from her gentle nature as her jest. Alluria returned it with one of her own, and as we exited the temple together, I understood Caol'nir's devotion to his mate. I too believed that she had divine blood.

Once we reached the platform above the grand steps, Alluria placed her hand on my shoulder. "We can't present you to your people this way," she said, wiping my cheeks. Her gentle touch calmed me more than I had thought possible, then she smiled and opened her hand. Her palms, which should have been wet with my tears, held two pale blue jewels.

"Your sadness," she explained. "I've taken a measure of it, so you may go on as you must."

Then Rahlle appeared at Alluria's side, fumbling as he took the jewels from her hand. I later learned that great magic comes at a great price, and in cloaking the Ish h'ra hai from view he'd sacrificed his sight. But his sadness was tempered by joy, and the priestess Alyon remained with Rahlle to see to his care. It seemed that she had been born barren, but when Rahlle healed her, he restored her fecundity and thus ensured her undying devotion.

The rest of that day is a blur, and I only carry fleeting images in my mind's eye. Once the child sun went to rest, I was led before Lormac's funeral pyre, and with shaking hands I set the kindling alight. As I stood before the flames, I thanked him for everything: the aid he so selflessly gave, his willingness to believe a group of ragged slaves and assist them in overthrowing the king who'd reigned for *three thousand years, his unwavering conviction in me, his endlessly loving heart.*

Gods. I thought I would die without his touch.

The next morning, I said my final goodbye to the other love of my life. Caol'nir procured an oak seedling and I planted it at the crest of the hill, on the very spot where she died. Afterward, I knelt in the freshly turned dirt and stared at the tiny tree, wondering if it would even grow atop this windswept peak. I looked to the other foothills, all of which were bare at their crests. If anyone could thrive in such conditions, it is my Torim, *I thought as I rose and made my way back to Teg'urnan.*

Not surprisingly, Caol'nir had made the decision to take his mate far from the palace. I envied Alluria for having a mate who was so devoted to her and wanted nothing but her happiness. Caol'nir grinned as he described the home he would build for his mate and of the many children they would fill it with.

I was more disappointed than surprised when Tor and Caol'non informed me that they would leave the palace as well. Tor's oath had been sworn to Sahlgren, and when Rahlle severed the oath he had forfeited his position as Prelate. Caol'non could have remained, but claimed that Teg'urnan without his father and brothers was not for him. I understood their decisions, but it would be the first time that one of Solon's line had not served in Teg'urnan. Tor suggested that Harek be named the new Prelate, for he had remained true to Parthalan even when Sahlgren had been led astray. Indeed, without Harek and his brother's assistance we may never have escaped our slavery, and he was so named.

Thus they left, and the decision was made to list Tor as having perished that day, and his son's names were omitted from the records, the original scrolls having been given to Atreynha to secure in the vaults below Teg'urnan. Alluria bore the mark of a mordeth, *not just any* mordeth *but Mersgoth, and I knew better than anyone that the monster wouldn't rest* until he had extracted his revenge. Caol'nir hoped to evade the beast by taking her far, far from the palace. I hoped his plan would succeed... but we both knew that while there was breath in his foul body, Mersgoth would not stop searching for Alluria.

I traveled once more to Tingu, though it broke my heart to set foot upon the land of Lormac's birth. When the Seat came into view, I nearly fell from my mount under the weight of my despair, but I couldn't give myself the comfort of mourning my mate before his warriors. I was now their ruler, and I'd learned from Lormac that a ruler always needed to appear strong, even when being rent apart inside, if for no other reason than to give his (my?) people hope.

So I squared my shoulders and set my jaw as I opened the Gate. I rode to the palace staring straight ahead. I was met first by Aldo, who understood without asking; I and all my warriors wore yellow, the elfin color of mourning. The old saffira-nell merely bowed his head, unsuccessfully hiding the tears in his eyes. And then, the second worst moment of my life occurred, far worse than any day I had spent in a doja, when Lukka stepped aside and Leran ran toward me.

"Mama!" he cried, flinging his arms about my neck. I held him tightly, murmuring of how much I'd missed him, and how I never wanted to leave him again.

"But where's Da?" he asked. I knelt before him and held his hand, smoothing back his hair that was brown and soft like his father's.

"Leran," I began, "I'm so sorry, but Da will not be coming home." Understanding dawned in Leran's gray eyes, Lormac's eyes, as he looked from me to the sad faces of the yellow-clad warriors, and he wrenched free of my grasp. "Leran, please, let me explain."

"You lied!" he shouted back. "You promised he would come back! This is your fault!" He ran from me then, the little boy that had asked me to be his mother, who begged to sleep in my arms, all the while hurling curses at me that no child should know. Lukka moved to follow, claiming she would punish him for speaking that way, but I implored her to let it go.

"Leave him be," I told her. "He has lost his father and has every right to mourn. I'll not take that from him."

I didn't see Leran again that day or the next. That time was filled with me putting Tingu's affairs in order; while I was Lady of Tingu, I was also Queen of Parthalan and would reside at Teg'urnan. I placed Balthus as Leran's regent and signed a proclamation confirming Leran's right to rule when he came of age. While I had no suspicion's concerning Balthus, I also had no guarantee that he would live long enough to see Leran grown. I vowed to personally destroy anyone who tried to stand between Leran and his birthright.

What I did not do was return the Sala. It was mine, given to me by my mate, and I would be damned if I was going to give up the one part of Lormac that was left to me.

Lormac...

Two days had passed before I could bring myself to enter his chambers (I suppose they were my chambers, too), and half of the next before I made my way up the winding passageway to the Seat. While I would have denied it if anyone had thought to ask, I held a desperate hope in my heart that Lormac's spirit was somehow within the Seat, that even if I couldn't touch him I would be able to feel his presence, perhaps even talk to him again... But no. His stone was cold and dark, taking on that same opaque layer of the stones that represented his ancestors. Only Leran's remained bright and warm to the touch.

As I stood there staring at the lifeless stone, I felt as if my last shred of sanity had been taken from me. I turned away, only to have my gaze land upon the smooth indentation in the floor where I had once lain in Lormac's arms. I stumbled down the passageway, my vision blurred with hot tears, and climbed onto his bed, pausing only to draw the curtains shut before I willed sleep to claim me.

"Asherah?"

My lids protested, but at last I won and opened my eyes and was greeted by the bleary vision of Harek perched on the edge of the bed. Lormac's bed. "Yes?"

"You've been in here for three days," he said softly. "I worried you were trying to starve yourself."

I looked past him to the platters laden with food; I suppose the fruit did look a bit mushy. "I went to the Seat, and...and I have been sleeping since." I did not mention that in my dreams Lormac was alive and hale, that I could touch him and kiss him and talk to him, that every time my body tried to wake me I refused and dove deeper into my dreamstate.

"Where do dreams come from?" I asked. "Are they gifts from the gods? Are they our ancestors trying to guide us? Or are they the disjointed ramblings of a weary mind? More, can one reenter a dream?"

"I don't know," he said, "perhaps Sarfek would."

"Sarfek," I said slowly, "I will need to speak with him." My mind reeled with my upcoming conversation with the magic handler, imagining that he would give me some sort of spell or potion to reenter my dream of Lormac, and I would never truly be apart from him...

"I'm sorry."

"What?" I had forgotten Harek's presence. But there he was, a solid, real man, not the dream I was chasing.

"About Lormac. Asherah, I never wished for you to be in pain." He looked as if he genuinely mourned my fallen mate. I had always assumed that Harek disliked Lormac, for many reasons, but Harek must have also held a measure of respect for Lormac. After all, my mate was a warrior, like Harek.

"Thank you," I said softly, and then I grasped his hand. "But we will go on. You are now my strength, Harek. We will go on."

I left Tingu the next day, after a private meeting with a child I loved, who hated me with every fiber of his being. Leran glared at me as I showed him documents proclaiming that Balthus would be his regent until he came of age, others that certified his bloodline lest anyone raise doubts concerning his parentage. While Tingu would never want for wealth, I still established a stipend for Leran's personal use, and left instructions that Leran was to have no need unmet, that as long as I lived he had not only the legion of Tingu but also the Queen of Parthalan as his ally.

"I am regent only when you are in Parthalan, my lady?" Balthus clarified.

"Yes," I replied, "while I am in residence I will act as Lady of Tingu."

"I don't want you here," Leran spat. "If Da can't be here, neither can you."

Others moved to reprimand him, but I waved them away and knelt before Leran. "I won't come back unless you invite me," I said. I almost promised him, but I had broken my last. I did not think he would accept another.

"I won't."

"I know." I tried to take his hand, but he snatched it away. "I am going now, Leran. I will heed your wishes, and I will not return without your consent. But please know that I love you as if you truly were my son. I understand why you hate me, and I don't blame you. If you ever have need of anything, be it big or small, send for me and you will have it."

I stood and walked toward the door; now that Leran's care was established, my business in Tingu was ended. I walked quickly, for I didn't think I could bear another of Leran's outbursts, when I felt a tiny hand in mine.

"Da would see you to your horse," Leran said, staring straight ahead.

And so Leran, Lord of Tingu, escorted me to my horse with all of the respect and formality his father would have afforded the Queen of Parthalan. He went so far as to accept the reins from the handler, and guided my mount to its place at the front of the procession. Leran was nothing if not *brave as he stood before the assembled warriors of Tingu who granted us passage through the Gate. As the ancient structure creaked open, I again knelt before the boy.*

"I would bring him back, if I could," I said softly. "With Da gone, you are now the one I love most in this world." A single tear rolled down his brave little face, and as I moved to wipe his cheek he knocked my hand away. I assumed I'd angered him, but he caught me in a fierce embrace.

"Mama," he whispered, and that was all. Then he released me, and I rode away from the only home I had ever known to make a new one in a place far, far from Tingu.

I am Asherah the Ruthless, Queen of Parthalan, Lady of Tingu. I wield more power than Sahlgren ever did, more than any monarch in memory.

I would give it all away to be in Lormac's arms again.

Epilogue

Alluria smiled as she looked across the field; though he was naught but a dark speck on the horizon, she would know her mate anywhere. Of late, Caol'nir only spent mornings tending to the grain, returning to her side shortly after midday. He claimed that since their sons now helped in the fields there was less work what with three pairs of hands, but as Alluria stroked her large belly she knew the truth. The time drew near for their child to be born, and Caol'nir wanted to be by her side.

It would be their fifth child, and Alluria still didn't know if she carried a boy or a girl. With their first she had known from the quickening it was a boy, and lo and behold, Tor entered the world. She remembered Caol'nir's father's face when he first held his namesake, how his eyes were misty and his voice soft as he cooed over the baby, nothing like the stern manner of the Prelate.

Then she was heavy with the next, a boy named Fiornacht before he was born, and she was just as certain that the next two were to be girls. She knew that Caol'nir had assumed she guessed at the gender of the first two, but after Nessa was born he took her a little more seriously, and when she proclaimed that the fourth was also a girl he was not surprised when they welcomed little Brida.

Therefore, it was unsettling that Alluria could not see her fifth child. As with the first four, she could only see them in her dreams but she had seen them clearly, as if they were already in her arms, and had known everything about them. For instance, she had known that Tor would grow to be taller that his father, with Fiornacht's height only slightly less, and how Brida would crave sweets while Nessa liked sour and bitter foods. And that they all would look like their father, for Solon's blood was indeed strong.

Alluria looked toward the mill where her sons toiled away, and caught sight of them returning home for the midday meal. Except for that extra hand's breadth of height had by Tor, they could have been twins, both with thick, sandy hair and leaf green eyes. When they stood with Caol'nir, there was no question as to who had fathered them. It was the same with the girls, for while they had their mother's delicate limbs and features they also bore Caol'nir's blond hair and green eyes. Alluria would frequently lament that while she had done all the work of bearing the children, none looked like their mother.

This one will be different, she thought, feeling her child move. While the dreams had not been as vivid with this one, certainly not vivid enough to determine a gender, she saw shining chestnut hair and deep blue eyes that she had previously only seen in a mirror. She thought that meant she would bear her third daughter, but was reticent to declare as such.

Caol'nir at last reached his mate, streaked with sweat and dust from the field. He tried to keep his filthy hands from her, but she cared not for the dirt as she wrapped her arms around him. He kissed her temple as her encircled her shoulders with one arm, his other hand coming to rest on her belly.

"Beloved, this child will look like me, of that I'm certain," she declared. Caol'nir laughed; he knew that she wanted a child to take after her, and while it did amuse him that all of their children had taken after him, he didn't see how it made a difference.

"A girl as lovely as you?" he inquired. "We will have young men beating a path to our door from all directions."

"I did not say girl," Alluria pointed out. "But this child will have my eyes, and my coloring, and be talented with magic, and perhaps even work with herbs."

"A blessing," Caol'nir murmured. They reached the small open area before their cottage, their home that began as a simple one-roomed structure housing only Caol'nir and Alluria. Once Tor was born, it retained its cozy feel, but as he and Fiornacht grew it became cramped, so Caol'nir added extra rooms, and enlarged the hearth where Alluria baked her delicious bread. After the girls came along Caol'nir added a second story, and when Alluria pointed out that he added more sleeping chambers than they had children to sleep in them he caught her in his arms, murmuring that they already had four beautiful children, why not add a few more?

Alluria smiled as she remembered that day two winters past, and covered Caol'nir's hand with her own. Their time together had not dampened her love for him in the slightest, and, in truth, she would bear a hundred of his children and love them all with the same abandon as she loved her mate. But this one, the one she carried now, was different somehow; yes, this one was special, and would take after her.

"Beloved," Caol'nir murmured, rousing her from her thoughts, "look." She followed his gaze skyward and saw a hawk gently skimming overhead. The mates watched him for a moment, observing how its dark feathers shone in the sunlight. It hung, seemingly suspended over the field until it suddenly darted to the ground. It reappeared in a moment, sailing away with its quarry.

"Well?" Caol'nir asked. "What does a bird of prey on the wind bode for our child?" Alluria took both of his hands and kissed them, then placed them atop her belly.

"It means our child is destined for great things."

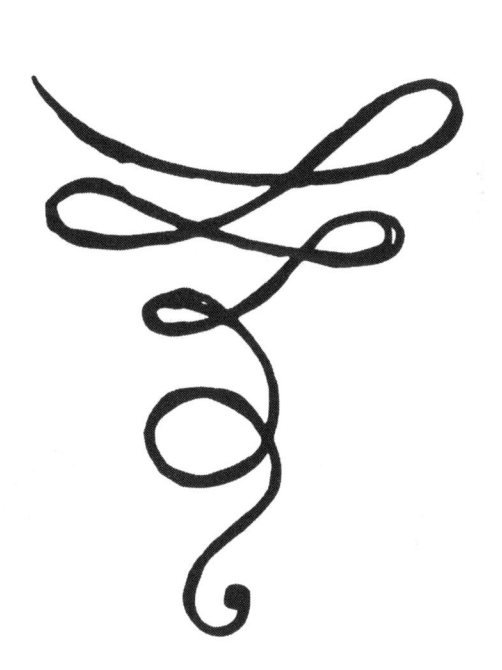

Acknowledgements

A wise person once said "it takes a village", and nowhere is that more true than in the production of this book. Truly, *Heir to the Sun* was our labor of love.

Where to begin, where to begin… How about with our senior editor, Trisha Wooldridge; without her, this book would be much quieter. All kidding aside, Trisha is one of those rare editors that will force you to kill your darlings, all for the greater good of the story. Add that to the innumerable other ways she's helped me over the years, and she is nigh on priceless.

Jenn Carson, who is responsible for the print edition's beautiful formatting (not the ebook; those errors are mine alone). She is an excellent editor, artist, and friend.

Veronica Jones, who created the amazing cover art. It's the most beautiful cover ever and I can't believe it's mine! Either I'm really good at describing characters or she can see into my brain. I'm betting on the latter.

I have a gaggle of friends who are always there for me, even though we're separated by distance, commitments, and the elusive yet deadly creature called the day job. Amy, for being the real life Amy Poehler (Yeah, I know Amy Poehler is a real person. Just go with it.) and getting my nerdy jokes. Ann, for pursuing your dreams and giving me the courage to pursue my own. April, for being a constant show of support. Eleanor, for always knowing just when to text me, and always making my day. Without you guys, I'd probably go nuts.

Then there's the Wonder Twins, Ember and Robby. I'm really doing all of this for you, so neither of you ever feel trapped in a meaningless corporate job. Follow your dreams! What the heck else is the point, really?

And Robb, always Robb. Love you, baby.

About the Author

Jennifer Allis Provost is a native New Englander who lives in a sprawling colonial along with her beautiful and precocious twins, a dog that thinks she's a kangaroo, a parrot, a junkyard cat, and a wonderful husband who never forgets to buy ice cream. As a child, she read anything and everything she could get her hands on, including a set of encyclopedias, but fantasy was always her favorite. She spends her days drinking vast amounts of coffee, arguing with her computer, and avoiding any and all domestic behavior.

Find her on the web here: http://authorjenniferallisprovost.com/
Friend her on Facebook: http://www.facebook.com/jennallis
Follow her on Twitter: @parthalan

Made in the USA
Charleston, SC
17 June 2015